Praise for *The Sweetest Getaway*

"A fun female caper filled with comedic mishaps and adventure...that is unexpectedly entertaining from start to finish. The strong friendship between Nari and Jennifer pulled me in, but the camaraderie among the crew kept me going until the very end."

—Natasha Jackson,
Readers' Favorite: 4 out of 5 stars

"It's a gripping, girl-powered caper that sees a community of women joyfully come together as they work to get their bag."

—*LoveReading*

"It will engage women readers looking for an escape—and for characters and causes to cheer for."

—*BlueInk Review*

"A lively, funny, action-filled scheme, spiced by romance and fueled by female solidarity... It's delightful to read."

—*IndieReader*

"Roommates deepen their friendship while blurring the lines between right and wrong in the electric heist novel *The Sweetest Getaway*."

—Lynne Jensen Lampe,
Foreword Reviews: 5 out of 5 stars

The Sweetest Getaway

The Sweetest Getaway

A NOVEL

SASHA PRESTON

Heart &
HORIZON PRESS

ISBN: 979-8-9924676-0-4
Cover design: Marina Drukman
Editors: Ema Barnes, Jason Letts, Hilari Cohen
Interior book formatting: Daniel Pyle
www.sashapreston.com

First edition
Printed in the United States of America

Heart & Horizon Press
hearthorizonpress.com

Mission Briefing (Before Things Get Wild)

If you love clever capers, chaotic brilliance, and fearless women doing the wildly unexpected, consider this your secret assignment: Leave a quick review when you're done. It helps more readers discover the crew, and supports this indie writer's next big scheme.

Amazon (especially helpful): https://bit.ly/AmazonTSG

Goodreads: bit.ly/GoodreadsTSG

Oh, and don't forget to flip to the end for a little something extra as a thanks: a free bonus chapter.

Thanks for hopping in the getaway car. Let's pull this off in style.

To my mom:
Thanks for teaching me how to love stories. You're the
original partner-in-crime (the legal kind). Love you.

To Anusha, my literary ride-or-die:
Thanks for cheering me on.
Love you, roomie.

Dear Reader,

This book is for you.

For the dreamers, the schemers, the ride-or-dies.

For anyone who's ever wanted to rewrite the rules, reclaim their story, or just disappear for a little while into a world where the adventures are thrilling, the girl-friendships run deep, and the hijinks are always available.

I wrote this story to celebrate clever women, found family, and the special joy of coming together to shake things up. If you laugh, cheer, or feel even a little bit seen—I've done my job.

Never stop dreaming. Never stop adventuring.

Thanks for coming along for the caper. Now let's have a blast.

With love and your own getaway crew,

Sasha Preston

CHAPTER 1

JENNIFER

"All we have to do is confidently walk to the door like we're supposed to be here," Nari said under her breath.

She and Jennifer argued in the parking lot of Omaha's largest mansion as glamorously dressed revelers approached the entrance, arm in arm.

"I'll enter five minutes before you. When they ask for our names, remember that I'm Doris and you're Béatrice. After that, everything will be easy. No big deal," Nari explained.

Right. It was no big deal to Nari because she was endlessly charming, constantly meeting new people, and making loads of cash from random schemes that took her all over the world. Jennifer, on the other hand, was great at petting her neighbors' dogs and getting lost mid-conversation in daydreams about faraway lands she'd never visited.

Doris Huang and Béatrice Boivin were wealthy business-women who were *actually* invited to the gala. Jennifer had helped Nari find an Asian and black woman on the guest list that they could impersonate. Doris and Béatrice looked enough like them, although Doris was in her fifties. Luckily, Doris wore glasses, so Nari could hide her youth behind a pair of round black frames that complemented her off-the-shoulder, gold metallic gown.

"Honestly, Nari, I don't think it's going to be that easy." Jennifer tapped her fingers nervously on her arm. "What if Doris and Béatrice are inside already? Why don't we look for a back entrance to sneak into instead?"

At least there would be fewer witnesses if they got caught at the back entrance. Maybe they could even pretend they were lost, ask for directions, and then decide to scrap the whole mission and return to their cozy apartment. "Oh well, that didn't work. At least we tried!" Jennifer would say peppily. Nari would shrug. They'd end the night bingeing on popcorn and singing nineties hits into their TV's karaoke app.

But Nari would never give up that easily. "Nah, we're early. We'll have at least an hour before these two fabulous women show up. They're always late for events like this. Besides, our target is already inside."

Jennifer groaned. "This is nuts. I've got to pretend to be French like Béatrice." She shook her head. "I can't even tell the difference between a good macaron and a bad one. They're *all* delicious to me. I don't know why I let you talk me into this."

"I know why you said yes, *mon amie*," Nari said, grinning. "Remember, you'll be getting twenty-five percent of whatever deal we pull off after today. If I can close this deal, it could be worth half a million dollars."

Jennifer had almost forgotten about the payout. Normally,

Nari compensated her for these wild rides with chili cheese fries. She sucked in air through her teeth. "I... I can't really say no to that," she said, goosebumps covering her arms.

With that kind of money, maybe she could travel far beyond Omaha's borders. She'd meet wonderful, surprising people. People who spoke five languages, painted in their spare time, and effortlessly rode their electric scooters through crowded street markets before arriving at home to make love to their beautiful spouses. Maybe she could even quit her job as a marketing analyst.

Nari swept her arm out in front of her, as if she were showing off her kingdom. "Welcome to the business world. There's tons of cash just waiting for you."

Money came easily to Nari, even though she had the attention span of a gnat. She could have her own massive condo if she wanted to, but she chose to live with Jennifer to feel a sense of home so far away from her family. Jennifer, however, was thirty-six years old and broke. If she didn't live with Nari, she would have to start a window washing side hustle to be able to afford her student loan payments.

"It's my favorite business world, the one where we have to sneak into galas to close deals," Jennifer snorted.

"It'll be worth it this time, I promise. Our target, Karissa Hirsch, is North America's largest diaper buyer," Nari said.

Jennifer laughed and adjusted her gown. "Diapers, Nari Park? Did I hear that right? I thought this was for another wig deal."

Nari's mouth curved into a half smile. "Hey, if the margin's good, I don't discriminate. Sumeet brought me the cheapest nappies I've ever seen."

"Ah, Sumeet..." Jennifer liked Sumeet, but she wasn't sure if Nari should be working with her ex again.

"What can I say? The man's got the most amazing connections," Nari said, her eyes sparkling. "Alright, so I've been tracking Karissa all weekend. She and her business partner Daniela are already inside."

Jennifer nodded, remembering Nari's brief. It was impossible to meet with Karissa alone at the office. This was a problem, because Daniela was conservative when it came to risk. No supplier was ever good enough for her. They needed to infiltrate the gala so Jennifer could distract Daniela while Nari built trust with Karissa.

"All we need to do is get Karissa alone so I can pitch my diaper deal to her. Remember, Daniela is obsessed with foreign cultures and ancient history, like you. You'll just need to be yourself," Nari said.

"No problem," Jennifer joked. "I have lots of experience bonding with multi-millionaires."

While Nari exuded confidence around the wealthy, Jennifer stumbled around them, literally and figuratively. She imagined introducing herself to Daniela. She'd make Daniela laugh and she would feel a sense of satisfaction at how well things were going. Then, inevitably, she'd trip over her ball gown and crash headfirst into a stack of plates. It was bound to happen. She was in way over her head.

"I'm really not sure we can get past that bouncer," Jennifer said, trying to hide the tone of hope in her voice. If they got turned away, she wouldn't have to pretend to be charming or French.

"You'll easily fool whoever is working the door." Nari

winked. "You look as classy as Béatrice Boivin. Maybe even better."

Jennifer caught her reflection in the car's window. Her coral ruffled dress hugged her long, lean frame and popped against her golden-brown skin. Her red fingernails, glimmering eyeshadow, and shoulder-length twists pulled the whole ensemble together. The dress was Nari's, so it was a little short on her—almost floor-length. She was wearing her most prized shoes—gold, strappy designer stilettos that she kept in their original box and wore once every few years on special occasions. Jennifer beamed. At least she got to impersonate someone with good style.

"Thanks, Nari." It was the boost of confidence she needed to make it to the front door. But Jennifer would need at least fifty compliments, all in quick succession, to work up the courage to talk to people. "What should I do if someone at this party knows Béatrice?"

"Good question," Nari said. "Once we're inside, you don't have to be Béatrice anymore. Introduce yourself as Ava from Omaha."

"Oh, thank God." Jennifer exhaled loudly.

"Follow my lead," Nari added, adjusting a twist on Jennifer's forehead. "People are going to love you."

Jennifer wiped her sweaty palms on her flowing skirt. After a year of living together, this was probably the third time she had plunged forward into one of Nari's wild schemes. They weren't getting any easier.

Before meeting her roommate, the most daring thing Jennifer had done during her mild suburban Detroit upbringing was sneak into her friends' living rooms while they were playing hide-and-seek so that she could talk to their parents for a few minutes about their cultural traditions. No one ever caught her, and it was thrilling. Her friends thought she was terrible at seeking.

But Jennifer really wanted to own a business one day. She'd quit her low-paying, decade-long job at Essentrix Labs and taste financial freedom for the first time in her life. Maybe learning to be bold was just the training she needed to leave Omaha behind and go explore the world. She would just ignore Nari's other lessons about crashing events and impersonating people.

"Shall we, m'lady?" Nari asked.

"Here goes," Jennifer said, taking Nari's arm. Their high heels clicked in sync on the pavement as they walked toward the entrance. A dark-haired woman with a floor-length black tufted ball gown and cream-colored skin walked beside them, holding the arm of a tall man in a suit. The woman's gold, bejeweled clutch bag shimmered, and she tilted her head forward approvingly as she walked past.

Nari and Jennifer approached a set of stairs leading up to a vibrant garden, complete with perfectly manicured bushes. Guests congregated at a row of tall round tables, each one adorned with a vase of white roses at its center. Men and women in black suits stood behind a large rectangular counter serving appetizers and drinks.

"Here we go, roomie," Nari whispered. "Find someone to chat with for five minutes while I enter. You and I don't know each other."

Jennifer felt heat rise to her face. She bit her lip and tapped her thigh to keep herself from running as fast as she could in the opposite direction.

"Can't I wait in the car?" she pleaded.

"Wait here so you can start to blend in," Nari murmured, squeezing Jennifer's hand. "Don't worry. You'll do great."

Of course, Jennifer was worried.

Nari took the steps up to the garden and walked confidently toward the door on a red-carpeted pathway. Jennifer glanced at a group of three young men standing near an outdoor heater. They looked American enough. Maybe they wouldn't question her accent or her fading French vocabulary.

Jennifer waited a beat before climbing the stairs and approaching the heater. Her heels sunk slightly into the grassy lawn with each step. "Well, *'allo* there, *les mecs*," she said in her best French accent as she reached the group. They all smiled at her.

She peeked over her shoulder. Nari was giggling as the host waved her through. The knot in her stomach began to loosen, but she still had an uneasy feeling that the host was going to quiz her on French provinces before declaring her a fraud.

Jennifer glanced at her watch. 6:03 PM. Five more minutes of small talk in a French accent before she could relax and be Ava from Omaha.

"What brings you to the gala?" a man with mahogany-brown skin and a close-cut mohawk asked. He backed up, motioning for Jennifer to join the group.

She opened a can of seltzer from the table and took a sip as she approached.

"I can't wait to bid on some cats and dogs," she blurted out, before feeling her cheeks burn.

Well, that was awkward.

The Omaha Animal Shelter was probably not going to

auction off any animals. But that would make for an incredible game show. Two glamorous women in ball gowns would be engaged in a bidding war over a Shih Tzu.

A blond-haired man with fair skin in a shiny black suit laughed. "Hey, fair enough. I'm the male version of a crazy cat lady myself."

Jennifer chuckled, grateful for the joke. She looked down at her watch. Only three minutes had passed.

"Are you based in Omaha or just visiting for the gala?" a freckle-faced man with dark-brown hair asked.

She cleared her throat, reaching deep within herself to channel wealth and intrigue. "I'm here for the *moment,*" she said, silencing the end of the word. "I'm visiting from Martinique to work in..." She racked her brain for the technical phrase from Béatrice's bio. *Chimeric something.* The men looked at her expectantly. "Stem cell technology." *Close enough.*

The man with the short mohawk beamed. "What are the odds?" He lifted his hands up in excitement. "It's so great to meet you. I'm working on bioprinting for organ regeneration!"

She laughed nervously. "*Quelle coïncidence!* How fascinating. I get so excited thinking about all the things you can do with...kidneys!" She backed away into a plate of meatballs.

The man cocked his head to the side. "What's your focus?" he asked. "I'm working on pluripotent stem cells, and I'd love to get your take."

She coughed and downed some seltzer water, her throat burning as she swallowed. "It's been so lovely chatting, but nature calls! Please, *excusez-moi.*"

The men waved cheerfully at her. She hurried away, twisting around to assess the meatball damage to her dress.

Amazing, she thought with relief. There was only one small red stain. She grabbed a stray napkin and dabbed her skirt before tossing the cloth square onto a nearby table.

She slowed down and tried to look natural as she walked the soft red carpet to the front door. A muscular man with a bun and glasses met her gaze.

"Welcome to the Paws and Promises Gala," he said warmly. "Who do I have the pleasure of checking in today?"

"Uh...Béatrice," Jennifer said. She cleared her throat and summoned her French accent again. "Boivin."

"Ah, Béatrice. Welcome. Your husband's inside already. Table seventy-two," the man responded warmly.

Jennifer wanted to throw her head back and cackle. Now she had at least four people to avoid. "*Merci beaucoup,*" she said, stiffening her body as she walked inside.

"Wait!" The man handed her a paddle. "Don't miss the auction, Ms. Boivin."

Jennifer grasped the paddle in her shaky hand. It had *Béatrice Boivin* printed on the handle.

The main gala ballroom was huge and covered with lush red Persian-style carpet. She gasped as she eyed glimmering clutch bags and diamond necklaces, beaded gowns, and elaborate hairstyles. Large tables with white tablecloths filled the room, each one meticulously set with eight gold chairs, fluted champagne glasses, and a fixed menu tied with a purple ribbon. A smooth saxophone played in the background. There had to be at least seventy-five people inside already.

Jennifer let out a tense breath and adjusted her dress. She could finally relax into her role as Ava from Omaha and focus on more important things, like finding the appetizers. She hadn't eaten out in at least two weeks, and it was driving her crazy. Her financial spreadsheet had politely suggested that she skip going to restaurants, singing at karaoke bars, and rolling a bowling ball for the rest of the month. She was going to crack soon, and maybe some fancy appetizers would tide her over.

As she scanned the room, she spotted a waiter carrying a platter covered with small bites. Her eyes lit up and she approached him, passing by the sounds of clinking champagne glasses and party-goers chatting.

"Would you like an appetizer, madam?" he asked, lowering his tray. "We have vegan foie gras mousse on toasted brioche, mini crab cakes with lemon aioli, caprese skewers, and avocado cream sushi."

"Thank you!" she gushed. "I don't mind if I do." She took a plate of crab cakes and loaded it with two each of the remaining appetizers, stacking items on top of each other so they would all fit. The man's eyes widened, and he chuckled.

She bit into the toasted brioche, and her taste buds flooded with pleasure. Off to her right, she saw a couple daintily taking one caprese skewer each from another server. Her cheeks flushed, and she tried to hide her crowded plate behind her auction paddle.

She glanced up to see a gawky, tall, and pale man with glasses grinning at her. He looked like he was in his fifties. "I had a hard time choosing as well," he said in a light German accent, motioning toward his plate of three appetizers. Not bad.

"You have good taste. I'm always happy to meet someone who appreciates a good small bite. I'm Ava." Jennifer extended her hand.

"Johannes. Pleased to meet you," he said, his handshake

surprisingly firm. "What brings you to this gala? Is it your love for cats or your adoration of dogs?"

She chuckled. "That is a loaded question. I absolutely love dogs, but cats are so smart and independent. And they don't need you, which makes you more desperate for their love."

"Spoken like a true dog lover," he joked.

Her face flashed with mock outrage. "Hey! That's not fair! I have loved and been ignored by plenty of cats in my day. How about you?"

His gaze flickered across the room at a glamorous couple that was making an entrance. "Much more of a cat person. They're cold and powerful leaders. Like me, I like to think."

"You don't seem too cold." She glanced at his high-end black suit and gold watch. "But powerful, sure."

His half-grin remained permanently glued to his face. "Ah, you'd be surprised. But I'm glad I've got you fooled for at least half of my goals. No one back in Austria thinks I'm powerful though. I have to leave the country every now and then to find people who believe that. Thanks for making this trip worth it."

"Oh, Austria," she said, her eyes widening. "That's so far away. I hope you didn't have to leave a cat behind."

He crossed his arms. "A dog, actually."

She snorted. "A dog? No wonder your coldness isn't where you want it to be."

Her phone buzzed in her pocket. *"Come join us near table seven,"* Nari texted. Perfect. That seemed far away enough from Béatrice's husband at table seventy-two.

Jennifer looked up at Johannes. "So sorry, I've got to get going. But it was great talking to you. Maybe I'll see you later for more appetizers."

His eyes crinkled with amusement. "Nice meeting you, Ava. Is Béatrice a friend of yours?" He pointed toward her auction paddle.

Her breath caught in her throat. She wrapped her palm around the handle. "Yes! Going to see her right now. She's such an avid bidder."

Her heart pounded in her ears. Perfect time to get away. She scanned the room and spotted Nari standing at table seven with two women wearing stunning floral strapless ball gowns and diamond jewelry. They looked like they were in their mid-forties.

She glanced down at her appetizer plate and back to the group. Now was her time to shine. She laid her auction paddle down on a table, turned her back to the group, and savored five incredible appetizers before walking over. She felt powerful, like the entire world and all the food she could ever want were at her fingertips.

Nari's face flickered with recognition as Jennifer approached. "Ladies, meet my associate, Ava." The women waved. Jennifer couldn't read their expressions, but they seemed friendly enough. The smell of rose and sandalwood perfume wafted to her nose.

"I'm Karissa, and this is my business partner, Daniela," the taller woman in a black and white floral gown said. "We work for Diapers Unlimited. We're the largest e-commerce diaper seller in North America."

"I bet you guys really *clean up,*" Jennifer said, giggling. "Get it?" She wanted to laugh harder but suppressed the urge.

Karissa and Daniela chuckled. "The jokes write themselves, but that's a new one," Karissa said. "What do you do, Ava?"

"A little bit of everything," Jennifer riffed. "But my favorite project is writing comic books." That part was true.

"Really?" Daniela asked, her eyes wide. "Tell me more."

Jennifer could overhear Nari continuing a separate conversation with Karissa about diaper margins.

"I'm currently writing about ancient Mayan heroes who travel to the present-day Yucatan beaches of Tulum," Jennifer said dreamily. "They team up with their modern descendants to battle evil." She had never been to a real beach outside of the Great Lakes, but at least she could transport herself there in writing.

"I am obsessed with the Mayans." Daniela beamed. "I'd love to read your comics when they're all done. I've always wanted to be a guest at one of the Mayan ceremonies."

Jennifer raised an eyebrow.

"An invisible guest," Daniela corrected herself, chuckling.

Jennifer smiled. Her gaze met Nari's, who tilted her head toward the other side of the room, indicating that Jennifer should guide Daniela away. Jennifer winked back.

"My characters are pretty wholesome when they're not battling. They're bartering with chocolate, dancing in rain ceremonies..." Jennifer murmured.

"Now those are some ceremonies I could show my face at," Daniela quipped.

"More my speed too," Jennifer replied. "Daniela, I'd love to get your take on..." She glanced around the room, now getting even more packed with guests. There was no dance floor yet, which would have been her first choice. There was no karaoke booth, her second choice. There weren't even any actual pets for them to play with. Her eyes landed on a sign for the silent auction wing. There we go. "On the silent auction," she said, feeling relieved. "There are some interesting things on offer."

Daniela leaned in slightly, the silk fabric of her dress making a swishing sound. "I'm always a fan of bidding. Shall we?"

"We'll be back in a minute!" Jennifer called out to Nari and Karissa, who were lost in conversation. Karissa nodded back as Jennifer and Daniela took off.

"How's business going? I know absolutely nothing about diapers," Jennifer said as they passed under a glittering chandelier casting golden light onto Daniela's face.

"You know, it's been going well," Daniela said. "We're expanding all over the United States. In fact, there's some sort of random baby boom going on in Hawaii. We've seen lots of growth there recently."

"Fascinating!" Jennifer replied. At the mention of Hawaii, she completely lost her focus.

Starting around ten years ago, Jennifer dreamed of one day moving to the Aloha State. It was perfectly multicultural, with all the ancient history she could want. She would open a surf shop, serving frozen fruit slushies out of coconut shells. She would get to know the locals, flirt with the tourists from distant lands like Spain and Mozambique, and have a fling or two.

She had read mythic stories of ancient Polynesians and wanted to experience their brand of surfing—spiritual and celebratory—under the beautiful Hawaiian sky. It didn't matter that she didn't know how to surf. It was only a matter of time.

Within her imagination, a tall, shirtless stranger from Brazil, Rodrigo, would speak Portuguese to her breathlessly in between kisses. She wouldn't understand him, but they could always speak with their hands. In more ways than one.

She just needed a little self-control to save up the money to make the move. It wasn't her fault that there was no better way to celebrate the end of a work week with friends than by eating sashimi salads and belting into a microphone at the newest karaoke bar.

"Ava?" Daniela looked at Jennifer's face in confusion.

Jennifer looked up and refocused her eyes. "Sorry! Lost in thought." She straightened her body and glanced off to her side, her eyes falling on Béatrice walking into the silent auction room. She was unmistakable from the photo Jennifer had viewed online: thin and glamorously dressed in a red floor-length taffeta gown, with a long, thin nose and full cheeks. Jennifer coughed to keep herself from choking.

Daniela stepped into the silent auction room. Inside, wooden tables lined the walls with prize displays and clipboards with bids written on them. There were about twenty people inside.

Jennifer hesitated. Béatrice didn't know she had been impersonated, right? She took a deep breath and was about to suggest to Daniela that they go somewhere else when a man's voice called out, "Hey!"

Out of the corner of her eye, Jennifer could see the blond man from the heater conversation outside approaching. *Oh snap,* she thought, her pulse quickening.

"Hey again!" he said, waving.

Jennifer could feel her face growing hot and tapped Daniela on the shoulder. "If you'd excuse me for a moment, I've got to go use the restroom." She started to walk away quickly.

"Sounds good," Daniela responded distractedly.

With her head down, Jennifer hurried toward the

restroom. At least the man couldn't follow her inside. Suddenly, the blond man reached her side and tapped her on the shoulder. "Hey there! There's someone I want you to meet."

Jennifer curtsied halfway. "*Desolée, mon cheri.*" She took off walking again. "I'd love to chat with you later, but I've got to go."

There was a hallway with a sign for the restroom at its opening. She could hide out for five minutes, wait for the man to leave, and then find Daniela.

The blond man grinned and tilted his head forward as Jennifer resumed walking.

As she approached the hallway, she saw a security guard off to her right pointing at her frantically. "There you are!" he shouted.

Oh my God, Jennifer thought. Her breath caught in her throat. She paused for a beat, ran back into the dining room, and grabbed a menu from a table to cover her face before dashing toward the door.

"Hey! Stop right there!" the security guard yelled.

She broke into a run, hobbling in her high heels before colliding with a white-coated chef carrying a platter of tiramisu cups. The cups went flying and clattered onto the floor loudly behind her, sending a cloud of cocoa powder into the air. "Sorry!" she cried, stumbling.

The security guard was close behind her. "Someone stop that woman! She's trespassing!"

Jennifer ran on the balls of her feet and took short, quick strides. She weaved in and out of shocked partygoers, bumping into tables and knocking over glasses of champagne in unsteady hands.

"Pardon me!" she called out. *Perfect. Black woman running in heels. This is going to go over well.* Her cheeks grew warm.

Her heel tilted underneath her. She lost her balance and crashed right into a suited man's back. As he turned around slowly, she realized it was Johannes. "So sorry!" she shouted as she kept running.

She sprinted out the front door and across the lawn, where a few remaining staff members turned to face her in bewilderment. She leapt toward the stairs and jumped down, taking them two at a time. Mid-stride, her heel pierced the skirt of her dress. Before she could get it free, she could feel herself tumbling in slow motion. A strip of her skirt ripped off as she fell down the stairs and onto her face on the grass below.

"Someone stop her!" the security guard bellowed as he emerged from the building.

She scrambled up off the grass, ripped off the dangling fabric from her skirt, and sprinted as fast as she could into the parking lot ahead of her. Her legs were shaky, and her ankles were getting sore. She looked across the lot at Nari's car as she ran, desperately wishing for the key.

The security guard's feet pounded the pavement a few meters behind her. She glanced back and saw the man's face reddening as he shouted something. Her chest filled with panic. The cops could be on their way at any time. Digging deep within herself to her high school track days, she pictured herself accelerating. She took short, quick breaths, relaxed her shoulders, and focused her eyes ahead. Then she surged forward with a newfound energy and adrenaline across the parking lot and onto the sidewalk.

As she picked up speed, the ankle straps on her shoes began to loosen. She landed on the balls of her feet, her heels sliding from side to side as the straps flicked her ankles. *Keep going, Jennifer,* she chanted internally.

Within seconds, she stumbled as her shoe flapped, and her left ankle popped out onto the ground below. She would have to take her shoes off soon or she would fall. Quickly, she squatted to the ground and struggled to open the buckle on her left ankle strap. It didn't move. She yanked on the shoe and barely squeezed her foot outside of the loop. Sweat poured down her forehead.

Jennifer could hear the security guard getting closer. She yelped in exasperation and forced her right foot free. She sprung up on one hand, favorite stilettos in the other, and sprinted barefoot across the sidewalk.

Sprinklers sprayed streams of water onto lawns across the hilly residential neighborhood. The cement was wet on her toes. She dodged a car that was backing out of a driveway as her high heels slapped against her arm.

The security guard was bent over and panting on a hill a few blocks back. Jennifer pushed her foot hard into the soft grass and pivoted around a corner, almost running into a group of teenagers chatting on the sidewalk. A discarded scooter was beside them. *Perfect!* she thought in jubilation.

"Sorry, guys! Going to borrow this for a second!" she announced, glancing at the mailbox. 702 Chestnut Street. She vaulted onto the scooter and pumped her bare foot on the ground.

"Hey!" a lanky teenage boy in a striped shirt protested.

"Thank you!" she called out behind her. "I'll bring it back!"

Good. This area was starting to look familiar. Jennifer went running here sometimes. She had about a mile left to go before she'd reach their apartment in the Dahlman neighborhood of Omaha. She doubled down and flew across the sidewalk, feeling each bump beneath her feet. She looked behind her again. There was no sign of the security guard. She might have lost him, for now at least.

When she turned her head back to face forward, she noticed she was headed straight for a couple holding hands on the sidewalk, their eyes widening with panic. They scattered to either side as she swerved to miss them, running up onto the lawn and nearly losing her balance as the handlebars jerked upward.

"Sorry!" she yelled back at the couple as the scooter slowed and thumped across the uneven grass. She pushed her foot onto the soft lawn and maneuvered herself with a bump back onto the concrete.

She breathed a sigh of relief. She might avoid going to jail today. The security guard would have no idea where she lived. And no one else would notice a woman flying by on a scooter at full speed in a ripped, muddy ball gown, right?

A light breeze blew through her hair. She coasted and laughed to herself under her breath.

•   •   •

The front door opened. Nari entered, her arms wide and her ball gown stained. "Jen! I'm so glad to see you! Are you alright?" she asked in a concerned tone.

Jennifer lay on the couch with her feet up, still wearing her torn dress. She was too exhausted to move. "Oh my gosh, I outran a security guard in stilettos and stole some kid's scooter. I think my shoes are destroyed."

Nari's eyes widened, and she threw her arms around Jennifer. "You poor thing! But did you really outrun that guard while wearing *heels*? That guy was pretty fit! I knew you were a track star, but *dang*."

Jennifer nodded back weakly. "I'm going to have to sign up for Omaha's formalwear track and field competition," she quipped. "Did you make it out okay?"

"Somehow, I escaped," Nari explained. "Once I saw the guard going after you, I snuck out the back. I was going to grab the car and come pick you up, but another guard came looking for me with a flashlight. Luckily, I dove into the bushes in time. I hid until he stopped searching."

"Oh, thank goodness!" Jennifer whooped, sitting up in excitement.

"I think I held my breath for five minutes," Nari joked. "Sadly, I don't think I'm going to be able to close the deal. Karissa saw you running and saw me sneaking out the back. She turned the palest white I've ever seen. I guess it wasn't meant to be." She shrugged. "But I'm so sorry you had to run, roomie. I've totally failed you. We were supposed to sneak out before either of us got caught. I guess I underestimated how much Béatrice wanted to be at that party."

Jennifer shrugged. "At least now I have a good story—one I will never tell a soul." This was by far the most daring thing she had ever done. In spite of herself, she could feel a smile forming on her face as her cheeks flushed with pride.

"I owe you big time," Nari said. "For starters, can I treat you to some Thai food and some new heels?"

Jennifer sighed in relief. "Thai food sounds amazing, as long as we can get takeout. I don't think I can move."

CHAPTER 2

NARI

Nari walked alongside her ex-boyfriend and business partner, Sumeet, toward the aquarium. Summer was just taking off, and the evenings were getting warmer as the daylight stretched on. Their strides were in sync as she took in the lush landscaping and modern, marine-toned building. Its white roof was covered with undulating waves and coral designs.

"I failed completely at closing the deal with Diapers Unlimited," she said, glancing at Sumeet. He raised an eyebrow. "I got some face time with the founders at the gala, and Karissa loved my ideas for partnering together, but the whole thing crashed and burned when Jennifer and I got caught. You know, for sneaking in and impersonating people."

Sumeet stifled a laugh. "Wow, I would never expect anything less from you. Wish I could've been there to see it all. Did you escape, or did the cops walk you away in cuffs?"

They walked around a multi-colored fish statue in front of the building and entered through the front door. A reserved teenage boy was working behind the booth. Sumeet flashed his visitors' passes, and the boy waved them through nervously.

Nari smirked. "I've still never been cuffed. I hid in the bushes. Meanwhile, Jennifer ran from a security guard in bare feet and a ballgown. She's my hero." They entered a chilly, darkened room filled with glowing floor to ceiling fish tanks. A wide array of colorful creatures swam by.

Sumeet's eyes widened. "That is incredible. I need to join *her* boot camp."

She glanced at his athletic body, taking in his muscular arms and chest. Her gaze ran over his closely-trimmed black beard and his glimmering honey-colored eyes. For a split-second, she wanted to touch his golden-brown skin, kiss him, and melt into his side and stay there for hours.

Stop it, Nari, she told herself, frowning. She had jeopardized her business prospects one too many times with feelings. Enough times that maybe she should join a nunnery for entrepreneurs.

Almost a year ago, Nari met Sumeet at a party for high-net-worth singles. She'd snuck into it, of course. They hit it off immediately, joking about how to sell wigs to Rapunzel. The next day, they went into business together selling luxury hair-pieces. In one venture after another, Sumeet sourced incredible deals and Nari sold them. Together, they'd built an empire.

At the same time, their chemistry was undeniable. Within a couple of months, they were making out in his car between deals. They cuddled and talked about profit margins. They flirted and commented on prospects. But soon she couldn't think clearly anymore. She was too distracted and less calculating while making deals. She had to end it. Getting attached would slow her down. It always did.

"She's the fastest runner I know," Nari said, willing herself to bring her eyes back to Sumeet's face.

He nodded. "Don't worry about this deal. Diapergate's already been a huge success." They sat down on a bench in front of a tiger shark exhibit.

She grinned, remembering the string of humor-filled presentations she'd done for sad corporate types in windowless offices, each of them hungry for some entertainment. "It's too easy to sell diapers, especially since we're working with Ashwin Uncle."

Sumeet's uncle Ashwin sold stolen goods across the world for less than half their list price. He had built an impressive black market network, including a manufacturer in China that sold him diapers for almost nothing. He probably got that deal because he was supplying the company with something even sketchier. But none of that made the diapers *illegal*, since Sumeet paid for them fairly.

"Actually, that's what I wanted to talk to you about. I've got some bad news." Sumeet glanced at Nari.

She raised an eyebrow. She knew the diaper deal wouldn't last forever. "Did Ashwin Uncle get arrested?"

"Not quite, but I'm sure he will be soon," Sumeet chuckled. "He got into a gun fight in Chongqing. Our diaper supply has dried up."

"Almost as dry as the diapers themselves!" Nari replied. "You set these jokes up for me."

He sighed. "Diapergate is over. It's the end of an era."

She had been ready to move on for a while. "We had a good run. We built our own diaper dynasty." She reached out for a high-five and enjoyed the sensation as he returned it.

The pair stood and started walking around the exhibit. They paused to look up at the jellyfish tank, a glowing pack of apricot and yellow-colored sea creatures swimming upward in a graceful, pulsating motion.

His eyes met hers, and they smiled at each other. He paused and reached out to put his hand on her shoulder. She drew back, feeling an electric charge through his fingertips. She didn't want him to be within touching distance, for her sake and his.

"Sorry," he said, looking away quickly. "We've got maybe ten pallets left, one hundred grand profit. I know you're going to have no problem selling the rest. You can have the profit on these. I've already taken enough commission on these deals."

"Thanks, but I'll still give you twenty-five percent. Cash flow's never been a problem for us." She paused and glanced at a plaque about clownfish. "Now that Diapergate's over, I'm ready for my next gig."

They walked ahead into a tunneled exhibit. Sea turtles, sharks, and a colorful array of fish swam overhead. Nari opened her mouth in awe as her eyes ran over the animals. Sumeet watched her, smiling.

"I don't have much in the pipeline right now, but I'll keep an eye out," he replied.

"Not even one little lead?" she asked playfully.

"Nope. No one worth telling you about." He looked like he was lost in thought. "I do have an Austrian contact who brought me a deal worth millions. Johannes. But I said no immediately. I've never worked with him and never will. Give me a couple of months. I can find a better partner for you."

Strange. He had never said anything like that before.

She hesitated, unsure why Sumeet—a man who was comfortable with just about anything—wouldn't want to work with Johannes. But if anyone was ready for a new challenge, it was her. Plus, if she could crack a deal worth millions, maybe she could finally impress one of her biggest entrepreneurial influences—her mom.

She cleared her throat. "I'm down. Put us in touch."

He shook his head and sucked in his breath. "I don't think it's wise. I'm not sure you can believe what he says. He did a deal with a friend of a friend a while back. I heard he gave her false instructions, and she took the fall. Now she's in jail, and he got away."

She stopped walking and turned toward him. "People talk a lot when things go sideways. It doesn't mean what they say is true. I can work with anyone." She had worked on tons of back alley deals—literally—and was great at building relationships with questionable types she'd never met through a series of burner phones.

"I know you can handle your own," he began, looking at her eyes. "But there are some people you don't want to get involved with."

She leaned her hand onto the wooden bannister lining the exhibit. "Listen, Vora. If I need to back out, I'll make that call. But I at least need to see what this man has to offer. My mom didn't teach me to turn down millions."

He smirked. "I guess there's no harm in making the introduction, but be careful. And there's one detail you should know. Johannes is old school. He'll need to meet you in person before he can trust you."

Her eyes brightened. No sweat. She could charm anyone, anywhere. Even when she missed the mark—rarely—she could always redeem herself.

"Here's what I'd recommend," Sumeet continued. "Johannes is actually in town for the next few weeks. You could reel him into your circle by throwing a party filled with powerful and well-connected people. He's drawn to those types."

This was a really easy ask for Nari. This basically described her friend group.

"That's an enticing proposal," she said, a mischievous tone to her voice. "All I have to do is get the Midwest's top talent all in one room, and I'll reel in Austria's finest."

He smirked. "I wouldn't exactly call Johannes Austria's finest. Don't let your guard down."

That evening, Nari sat at her antique wooden desk in her bedroom, cleared her throat, and plunged into her contact book. She was on a mission. In two weeks, she'd need to get the wealthiest people she knew into one room. She scrolled through her phone, mass texting every affluent woman and man she knew in the greater Omaha area. Then she expanded to her mover and shaker friends in Iowa, Wisconsin, and beyond. Her Midwestern hustle network was vast.

"I'd love to celebrate my recent wins by getting some of the sharpest Midwestern entrepreneurs together," she typed.

Other than their money, her invite list shared very little in common. She loved the excitement of bringing an unusual group of people together and seeing them interact. It could go surprisingly well, with people of disparate backgrounds enjoying each other's company, happy to get to know each other. Or it could be an explosive powder keg. You'd never know until you tried it out.

Either way, she was ready for it.

She still felt a little unsettled that Sumeet didn't want to work with Johannes personally. Sumeet was in fact no stranger to the seedy. He'd basically gotten into the drug trade when he'd sold underground diet pills sourced from Uzbekistan to desperate suburban moms across the Midwest who were trying to lose their baby weight. Not that it *seemed* illegal. The pills worked like a charm. Sales exploded. Women bought bottle after bottle, and the product seemed to have no side effects. Other than strange facial hair growth.

Why would Sumeet suddenly draw the line at working with Johannes? It was puzzling. But then again, with Sumeet out of the picture, there would be a bigger share of the pie for her.

After decades of trying, Nari could finally join her mom's elite world. She'd no longer be stuck making hundreds of thousands on each deal while her mom steadily closed eight-figure transactions. Her mom had never said it explicitly, but the message was always there. "You can close bigger. You can be better." The million-dollar mark had always felt out of reach, but not anymore.

And if she needed help, this party was going to be full of talented people who she could cut into the deal.

Of course, Jennifer would help with anything. When they met on a roommate posting board online, Nari had been looking for someone sweet, a down-to-earth Midwesterner who could soothe the pain of her homesickness. Jennifer had fit the bill. She had opened up to Nari almost immediately, sharing stories about the ancient kingdoms of Mali, and the early scientific innovations of the Persians. Nari had found her passion endearing, her nerdiness adorable. This wholesomeness made Jennifer endlessly dependable.

But the rest of her network was incredible. Their diverse skill sets were so vast that Nari could tap into them for anything.

Some of the people were relative strangers, and she couldn't be sure how much she trusted all of them. But she knew they would all make a good impression on Johannes.

CHAPTER 3

JENNIFER

One Saturday afternoon, Nari walked in the front door of their apartment, buzzing with energy.

"You're not going to believe this." Nari twirled on her cherry-patterned socks on the bright, yellow-tiled kitchen floor that smelled of lemons.

The living room's blond wood floors were gleaming after their roommate cleaning night last week, filled with pumping ballads and singalong breaks between broom and mop swipes. Sunlight streamed in through the large windows which overlooked a lush, green courtyard.

Jennifer looked up from her comic book draft. She knew Nari was cooking something up and couldn't wait to hear all about it. "Lay it on me, Park!"

"I sold the last pallet of diapers that Sumeet was holding for me to an e-commerce business in South Dakota. A ten-thousand-dollar profit on that order alone. Cash is coming *in,* m'lady! We're having a party with Korean barbecue tonight!" Nari exclaimed.

"That's so amazing! Congrats!" Jennifer jumped up and danced alongside Nari in the open-concept kitchen, her oversized plaid pajama shorts swaying back and forth. She put her hands on the black breakfast bar that separated the kitchen from the large living area.

Jennifer was still disappointed that Nari had ended her wig business. She knew Sumeet fell into surplus products from time to time, and he needed Nari's hustle to sell them. But how he found these deals was a mystery—one Jennifer preferred not to know too much about.

Today, she could get excited to enjoy some thinly sliced, succulent beef bulgogi with scallion pancakes. And that was enough to keep her going. She kept her questions to herself and danced enough to keep getting invited to Nari's celebrations.

"I knew you'd be as excited as I am!" Nari said. "I kept one diaper as a keepsake."

"As long as you save it for your firstborn, I'm happy," Jennifer joked.

"Very funny," Nari replied. "I might have to make a baby mobile out of it for my friend's daughter. You know, use some glittery string and beads. Maybe create an under the sea disco theme."

That would be the perfect theme for an event Jennifer could throw in Hawaii. Rodrigo could come with his surfboard, wearing a mesh shirt with his pecs showing through.

"Jennifer!" Nari laughed. "Your head's cocked to the side again, so I know I sparked some sort of daydream. I can only hope it's not PG this time."

Jennifer felt her face flush. She lifted a couch pillow and lightly tapped it to Nari's butt. "It's always PG! Mind out of the gutter."

Jennifer glanced at Nari's face. With her barely concealed smirk, it was clear she wasn't buying it.

"Whether you were showering with your fantasy man again or not, we've got to get ready! I invited some friends to dinner." Nari moved her arms rhythmically, dancing like Jennifer imagined a little chipmunk would, before plopping down on their antique magenta brocade couch. It was the most unique thing in the house. Jennifer sat next to her.

Jennifer raised an eyebrow, wondering which people would show up this evening.

With Nari, you never knew whether an oil magnate, magazine publisher, or nightclub bouncer would show up. Or truth be told, all three. Jennifer pretended to find this parade of people frustrating. But really she loved the excitement of never knowing who Nari would introduce her to next. It gave her more fuel for her fantasies, for starters.

As long as they weren't *too* wealthy. She needed more advanced notice to emotionally prepare.

"Are these people so rich that their throw pillows are worth more than my car? Or are they medium rich, like they don't check food prices at the airport?" Jennifer quipped.

Nari chuckled. "Don't worry. They're wealthy, but they're all entrepreneurially minded. Like you. You'll have plenty to talk about."

"Like me?" Jennifer asked, embarrassed. "I work in a windowless office as a marketing analyst all day. The closest I've come to being a business owner is selling cookies to people at church when I was a kid. And I'm pretty sure they bought my desserts because I was cute."

"Hey, that'll still make you sales today. You're going to open the best surf shop Hawaii has ever seen," Nari responded. "And you should tell everyone about it. Anyway, you'll love these people. They're the best and brightest of Omaha and beyond. Some of them know me as Gwen, heads up."

Jennifer ran her fingers over her plaid pajama shorts. "Well, Gwen, I hope they don't mind me showing up in these," she joked.

"I've got you, girly," Nari replied. "I've got a yellow satin number that would look perfect on you. God, I *wish* I had your body."

Jennifer was five-foot-ten, lean, and addicted to thirteen-mile runs. Nari was at least half a foot shorter, solidly muscular, and obsessed with strength training.

Both women tried to convince the other one to join them when they worked out. And sometimes their attempts were successful. The longest stretch was last year. Jennifer joined Nari at the gym for two straight weeks when she wanted to experiment with cross-training and building up different muscle groups.

But each weightlifting session felt like a sacrifice, caging Jennifer into four walls, surrounded by sweaty gym goers, when she was made to be free, running in the open air by the Missouri River.

Jennifer blushed again. Nari was too kind. "Your body is amazing! Your guns would intimidate any intruder," Jennifer told Nari, who managed to look stunning no matter what she was wearing. Her dark-brown eyes sparkled against her glowing skin, often bare except for the bold eyeliner she drew on every morning.

"You do have a point," Nari giggled, disappearing into her bedroom. She emerged holding a yellow satin dress on one hanger and a ruffled, flowery pink dress on another.

Jennifer's eyes widened as she took in the flowery dress. It would look so good on her! And it was so summery! But she knew what Nari was trying to do, break years of tradition and get Jennifer to wear something different for once. Turn down the girly, fun, and flirty number for something more... *sophisticated.*

"You know which one I want, but I can fight the urge," said Jennifer.

"That's right! I knew you could do it," Nari squealed. "Plus, I wanted to be the flirty one this time. I've got a prospect I've been eyeing."

"You'll look amazing in that dress," Jennifer remarked. "Those colors will look great against your olive skin tone."

Nari smiled. "Thanks, girl. Now let's get to it! I want to get there early so I can hug each person as they saunter into the restaurant."

•　•　•

Seoul Kitchen was a new restaurant located in downtown Omaha's historic Old Market district, Jennifer and Nari's favorite part of the city by far. On a main cobblestone thoroughfare, the restaurant was nestled between an art gallery and an eighties dance bar that both roommates loved.

Nari's vibrant guests filled the room, taking up two rows of twelve seats each. There was no way Seoul Kitchen had seen so many people at once before.

The crowd was well-off and dressed in high-end designer wear. Even the more casual guests still wore perfectly tailored outfits that looked like they'd never been wrinkled. Nari had done well for herself, as usual. Jennifer could see Nari making the rounds from one table to the next.

"You should really meet Parisa," Nari said to a woman with zigzag braids twisted into a high bun as she motioned to her neighbor in a red dress across the table. "She summers in the Azores too." The woman's face glowed.

Nari immediately noticed when someone needed a chair, joked around with people who seemed lost, and handed menus to people who seemed hungry. She was an incredible host. Jennifer, on the other hand, had no idea how she was going to talk to these wealthy people.

Her heart sank as she noticed that the sleek, black table tops were empty. She'd even be willing to brave some spicy food to keep her *hangriness* away. For the sake of her evening and everyone around her, she planned to order a few stacks of scallion pancakes soon.

Seoul Kitchen was elegantly styled, not the sparse, newly opened place that Nari had described. A small fountain trickled beside a miniature tree that adorned the front desk. She noted the sound when she walked in, an ASMR tingle running up her spine as she focused in on it. Not that you could hear it anymore.

Colorful silk scarves lined the walls. Paintings of Korean women covered the place, each of them unique and beautiful. Jennifer felt a strange camaraderie with the faces on the wall. Each one was portrayed so sensitively and with so much depth.

She stood and glanced around the restaurant. A woman who looked like Nari's description of the owner walked toward her from across the room. Perfect. She'd be a good, down-to-earth place to start.

"You must be Jennifer. I'm Haeyeon. Nari has told me all about you. I'm so excited to meet you." Haeyeon threw her arms wide for a hug.

Nari and Haeyeon had bonded a few months ago when Haeyeon had welcomed her in with tofu soup and nurturing words that made her feel homesick and yearn for her mom's company.

Jennifer immediately felt the warmth radiating from Haeyeon that Nari had described so beautifully. "It's great to meet you too," she gushed.

With her family all in the Detroit suburbs, Jennifer longed for a sense of comfort and support from an older mentor figure who could reassure her that everything would be okay. Maybe Haeyeon would pat her shoulder and tell her that she'd travel one day, become a successful entrepreneur, and meet a nice guy who would be perfectly attuned to her emotional needs.

"Your restaurant is lovely. It's so nice to be here, finally. I'm impressed by what you've built from scratch." Jennifer swept her arm around the room for effect. "You know, Omaha really needed a good Korean barbecue spot."

Haeyeon's face brightened. "You're too kind! I hope you like your meal. I've been experimenting with my cooking. I want to get each recipe just right for the Midwestern palate." She waved to Jennifer and started to walk toward the kitchen. "I'll see you soon. You look wonderful, dear."

Oh no, Jennifer thought as Haeyeon walked away. She

would have to talk to these rich people now. She racked her brain for stories. She could tell them her favorite party story about how she learned to skateboard at her cousin's house and crashed into a leaf pile while trying to impress her neighbor. *No! Not relatable enough! Too pedestrian!*

Would she casually drop how she went to the exclusive Chez Jacques in Detroit and enjoyed a four-course meal? No, too obvious! She would need to keep practicing with these crowds if she wanted to be rich one day.

Come on, Jenny, she thought, choosing the moniker her grandma used for her. She reserved it for serious occasions only. *Get it together.* She pinched her leg. These people would love her normally quirky, dreamy personality. *You rock, Jenny. You're funny. You're fun to be around,* she told herself, digging up some of her favorite motivational affirmations.

Jennifer took her seat again. She glanced around the table, taking in all the new faces around her. Her eyes fell on a woman with luscious, shiny red hair, green eyes, and a paisley long-sleeved dress who was sitting diagonally from her. The woman smiled at her when they made eye contact.

"I mean, stocks, right?" Jennifer laughed nervously, before feeling her face go hot. *Why did I say that?*

The red-haired woman raised an eyebrow and looked at her in confusion.

Jennifer held her breath and searched for an excuse to escape the conversation.

"Personally, I'm more of a bonds woman myself." The red-haired woman winked.

Jennifer looked up in surprise and smiled. "I could tell you were a stable kind of woman." The woman tapped her index finger forward in agreement, and Jennifer felt her tension loosen.

As she scanned the restaurant, her eyes fell on a tall, awkward man entering. She immediately recognized his stride. It was Johannes, the middle-aged Austrian man from the gala. He was dressed less formally this time, wearing beige slacks and a black polo shirt. The last time she had seen him was when she crashed into his back while running in heels to escape a security guard. She slumped down sheepishly into her seat. Maybe he hadn't seen her yet.

But soon she could feel Johannes's gaze fixed on her. "Hey, Ava," he said, waving.

Here goes. Jennifer stood and walked over. "Hey, Johannes!" She paused to clear her throat and gain her bearings. "I had no idea you knew Nari."

"I will soon." Johannes adjusted his thin-rimmed glasses. "We have a mutual friend, Sumeet Vora."

Who doesn't Sumeet know? she wondered. "Wow, that's so random. Sumeet's a great guy. It's so funny seeing you again."

"Likewise, Jennifer," Johannes said, grinning.

Her chest tightened. It was too late to pretend there was some mistake and she was actually Ava. The jig was up.

"How... How do you know my name?" Her heart pounded. She wondered if Johannes was like a comic book villain, carrying a face scanner in his beige pants pocket that he could use to access everyone's tax records.

"Don't worry. Sumeet told me," he remarked. "I've used fake names many times before. In fact, I'm not even sure my real name is Johannes."

She felt her body go slack. "Phew!" she said, laughing. "I

was scared for a second there. I hope you can forgive me. Now that you know my real name, I'm Jennifer from Michigan."

"Well, Jennifer from Michigan, you're a good runner. I was impressed by how quickly you made it out of that gala," he said. "In high heels no less."

Her throat went dry. "I guess all those years of high school track kept me on my toes."

He crossed his arms, looking around the crowd. "You're quite the athlete. I like your earrings, by the way. Very convincing stones."

"Thanks," she said, bringing her hand to her ears to remind herself which earrings she was wearing. "I've never met a man who noticed my jewelry."

"Gemstones are my true passion," he remarked. "I got into the business with my wife Mercy, the most incredible woman I've ever known. I'm glad to eat Korean food today in her honor. She loved *bibimbap*."

Loved. Past-tense. That didn't sound so good.

"Tell me about Mercy," she replied. "Any fan of *bibimbap* is a friend of mine."

He beamed. "We were married for twelve years. The night we met, Mercy was wearing a lacy red dress with a flower in her hair. Out of everyone at the bar, she smiled at *me*." He paused and had a faraway look in his eyes. He lowered his voice. "I wasn't used to having such a beautiful woman's attention. We were inseparable. She died in a car crash three years ago."

Jennifer felt a pain in her chest for Johannes. "I'm so sorry to hear that. Mercy sounds amazing. I'm sure you miss her."

"Every day." He sighed deeply and fumbled with his collar.

"I cook *ugali* once a week to remember what it felt like to be around her. It's a porridge from Kenya, where my Mercy was from."

Jennifer's eyes lit up. She had at least ten anecdotes about Kenya she could share. She bit her lip, trying to keep everything from tumbling out all at once. "I love that you have a way to remember Mercy. Kenyan culture is so lovely. I've never been, but I've read all about it.

"When I was a kid, my dad and I used to sell cookies at church to raise money for the Kenyan democracy and women's movements. Usually white chocolate macadamia nut, because those cookies taste like freedom."

"I can't believe you know about those movements." His eyes widened. "Those causes were very important to her." He inhaled slowly and looked like he was holding back tears. "She fought for the rights of women who were arrested for protesting the government."

Jennifer felt her heart swell with emotion. She glanced around the room. It seemed like everyone was lost in conversation, and no one would notice if she went missing. "There's a store down the street, Zamani Treasures. They specialize in African handicrafts, and they even have a whole Kenyan section. I'd love to take you there."

He smiled. "I'll grab my coat."

CHAPTER 4

NARI

Nari's face glowed with satisfaction as she looked over her glamorous group of guests. She'd worked with most of them on deals at some point. She listened distractedly to two friends talking about their new hair salon empire, her eyes on the door. The table shook lightly as she jiggled her leg with impatience. Every time she glanced at the clock, only a couple of minutes had passed.

She downed three cups of barley tea to calm her nerves, its familiar nutty flavor from childhood flooding her taste buds with nostalgia. Finally, Johannes arrived at the party. She recognized him immediately, but not because he was the only person she didn't know. That helped. But his calculating demeanor gave him away as someone who wanted to transact. Bespeckled and tall, he walked awkwardly. He looked like someone who was perpetually out of place. It made Nari feel more empathetic toward him. She felt the urge to make sure he was taken care of.

She tried not to focus on him too much. Instead, she wanted to appear calm and detached as she spoke with other guests and waited for him to approach.

"You're so smart to invest in commodities," Nari said to her friend across the table. "Corn never goes out of style."

Before she knew it, Nari turned to see Johannes approaching. She stood up and grinned, preparing herself for a handshake and a friendly hello. But he walked past her and straight toward Jennifer. They greeted each other like they'd met already. Nari arched an eyebrow and felt her cheeks flush.

Better to play it cool. Let him come to her. She had a party full of incredible guests to talk to.

She sat down and turned back to her companions. "Eleanor, I've been dying to ask you about your trip to Casablanca."

Eleanor's face glowed. "The old city was stunning." She leaned in closer. "But I hate to admit it, the best part of the trip was supporting my sweetener addiction. I found an incredible supply of Sweet N Yum packets in Morocco."

Eleanor's neighbor Gertrude chimed in, "I've been looking for those *everywhere*. You've got to share some with me."

Nari smirked. "Sweet N Yum? The artificial sweetener? My roommate puts that into her drinks all the time."

"Not anymore, she doesn't," Gertrude said, narrowing her eyes. "There's a shortage right now. Eleanor, I will pay you however much you want for a few packets."

Eleanor leaned back in her chair. "Let's say I can spare a few. I might have stopped by every convenience store before I left Morocco so I could stock up."

Gertrude nodded. "I would have done the same. Smart

woman. I'll be getting your number. And then maybe we can start a sweetener tour group in Morocco."

Nari giggled before glancing to her right to see if Jennifer and Johannes were getting any closer to her. But they were gone. She felt her chest tighten as she looked around the restaurant. No signs of her lovable roommate and her prospective business partner.

"If you'd excuse me for a moment, ladies," Nari said. Eleanor tilted her head in acknowledgement.

Nari stood and looked around the room again, her jaw clenching as she crossed her arms around her chest. She spotted Haeyeon and approached her.

"Hey, have you seen Jennifer?" Nari asked.

"I did. She left with a tall pale man. They turned right when they left the restaurant," Haeyeon said, pointing.

Puzzled, Nari strode out the front door holding her small golden clutch. The door's bell jingled as she made a right onto the sidewalk. Her red satin heels immediately started to pinch her toes. The street was alive with restaurant patrons and revelers. It was primetime for Old Market.

Jennifer and Johannes hadn't been gone for that long. They couldn't be far by now, unless they'd gotten into a car. Nari sent a text message to Jennifer, *"Roomie, where are you?"*

She scanned both sides of the street, although she couldn't see much through the throngs of people. She bumped into a man who was animatedly telling a story to a large group. "Sorry," he said, reaching out in apology.

She pulled out her cell phone and called Jennifer. No answer.

What if she didn't get face time with Johannes? She'd have

to throw another party, and maybe he'd be back in Austria by then. Millions of dollars would be flushed down the drain. She didn't know when she'd get another opportunity this perfect to close an incredible deal and show her mom how capable she was. Nari groaned. She paused and tried to think of where Jennifer would take a random person she had just met. There was a comic book store nearby, but even Jennifer wasn't that obsessed.

What about an art show? Nari remembered the gallery next to Seoul Kitchen, which made a lot more sense.

She turned around and started to walk back toward the restaurant, her heels clicking rapidly on the sidewalk as her heartbeat quickened.

What could Jennifer possibly be talking to Johannes about? She loved her roommate, but what if she was boring him to tears with detailed analysis of ancient philosophy? What if Johannes had decided that this party wasn't for him and left already?

The fate of this meeting was in Jennifer's hands. Nari's breath quickened as she neared the gallery.

Soon, her phone started to buzz. It was Jennifer.

"Hey, Jen, where are you?" Nari asked, trying to keep her voice even.

"Zamani Treasures. I'm here with Johannes," Jennifer said brightly. "I had to show him these handmade baskets."

Ah. African handicrafts. Jennifer had taken Nari to the shop during their first week as roommates. But this was random, even for Jennifer.

"How festive. Are you guys planning on coming back to the party anytime soon?" Nari asked, an edge to her voice. "I wanted to talk to Johannes alone."

She could hear Jennifer inhale. "Oh my gosh, of course!" Jennifer replied. "We'll just buy a couple of things and come back to the party."

Nari hung up and shook her head. She felt herself giggling. *Oh, Jennifer.* Maybe her dreamy, goofy roommate hadn't trashed the deal after all. She slowed her pace, her heels pinching as she walked back to the restaurant.

CHAPTER 5

JENNIFER

Jennifer entered Seoul Kitchen first with Johannes behind her.

It turned out that Johannes was as passionate about ancient African kingdoms as she was. His wife Mercy had taught him a lot and awakened a passion in him. After Mercy died, Johannes bought every book on African history he could find. He and Jennifer had read many of the same ones.

Since Jennifer's dad died, she longed to have someone to talk to about ancient history. Most people would simply smile and nod while she excitedly told them about ancient Somali trade routes. But her dad had always been a great audience. He loved ancient history and was passionate about all things African. He connected historical threads to modern struggles and often added anecdotes that she had never heard before.

Her mom tried to engage with her on the topic, but it wasn't the same. "I'm sorry," her mom would say with regret. "I know you and your dad had a special bond."

When Johannes started to talk about the powerful Swahili city states of ancient Kenya, it was like reading a captivating book that she couldn't put down. She found herself gesturing passionately when he asked for her opinions on ancient globalization, like she did with her father. She could have stayed at Zamani Treasures with him for hours.

As she stepped into the restaurant, Jennifer met eyes with Nari, whose face was strained. "Sorry," Jennifer mouthed apologetically. She turned to face Johannes.

"Thanks for taking me to Zamani Treasures," Johannes said. "That was a wonderful experience. I felt the spirit of my Mercy in there. She loved supporting African artisans, especially women."

"I'm so happy to hear that. Now, I'd love to introduce you to Nari." Jennifer motioned to her roommate, who approached the pair. "She is amazing."

"That sounds great." Johannes beamed.

"The famous Johannes. It's so great to finally meet you," Nari said. "I see you're already friends with my roommate, Jennifer."

"It's great to meet you too, Nari," Johannes remarked. "You're lucky to know Jennifer. She's incredible."

Jennifer's face lit up. "Aw, Johannes. You're pretty amazing too. Well, it was so great chatting with you. I've got to check out some..." She glanced around the room, looking for an excuse to leave Nari and Johannes alone. "Some tea. I'll leave you to it."

Nari smiled at her gratefully.

Jennifer scanned the party for an open seat. Maybe she'd sit somewhere else this time to keep things fresh.

She took her seat across from a woman in a form-fitting black sheath dress who was mid-conversation. The woman had a luxurious snakeskin pink bag, probably soft and textured to the touch.

"I love her bag too," the woman sitting next to Jennifer said, interrupting her thoughts. Startled at the mind reading, Jennifer giggled nervously and looked up.

A stunningly beautiful woman with curly, dark-brown hair bouncing past her shoulders was smiling at her. Maybe even staring at her. "I'm Martha," she said, extending her hand for a shake. She had a lovely singsong accent. "I don't really know anyone here. Normally I'd be at my home in Mexico City at this time of day, catching up on crime dramas, eating greasy takeout on my couch, and painting my toenails. You know, typical Friday night."

Jennifer was taken aback. With her perfectly fitting green suit, patent pumps, and expertly made-up face, Martha looked like she made at least seven hundred and fifty thousand dollars a year. Minimum. And here she was talking about how she got takeout and painted her own toenails while binge watching TV like a regular person?

This party was turning out to be a great time.

"I'm Jennifer," she replied. "To be honest, that sounds like my ideal Friday. I'd be writing a comic book, putting my hair into curlers, and snacking on deluxe mixed nuts. Lap of luxury."

"My kind of woman!" Martha swirled her spoon in her tea. "Maybe we should get together for a Friday night in while I'm still in town. I'll bring the romcoms and the nineties jams."

Nothing sounded better. Nari was out often, and Jennifer's other close work friend Karlie had a kid. She needed a night-in buddy to fill in the gaps. Maybe she could get around to finally using that movie night popcorn maker she had received a few Christmas gift exchanges ago.

"Oh yeah, count me in!" Jennifer pointed to Martha in agreement.

Martha's voice shifted to a whisper. "Maybe you should invite that guy too, every now and then. He's kind of cute." She pointed surreptitiously, covering her finger with her other hand, at a clean-cut, preppy-looking man with blue eyes and blond hair.

Jennifer drew in a breath. "Wow, Nari sure does know some good-looking guys. He can definitely join us. Maybe bring his brother along."

Jennifer's mind could have gone to a dark place, picturing a battle with her newfound friend over which of them got to date which brother. But instead she imagined a wholesome, harmonious, four-way pillow fight. She'd get the biggest, softest pillow from her room so she could pummel the others hard, guilt-free. The perfect double date.

Her eyes refocused into the present. *Right. Conversation with Martha.*

"Sounds like a plan. Although I'm married, so you can date them both if you'd like," Martha said playfully.

Jennifer giggled. "So what brings you to Omaha? Don't tell me you came all this way for Nari's party."

"I love Nari, but I was in Chicago for business. Much closer than Mexico City." Martha raised an eyebrow. "I've known her for years. We met back in my twenties when we were both based in Montevideo for a month. She would join my friend and me for lunch every day, always bringing her perfectly packed bento box filled with vegan treats. I could never eat as healthily as she does."

"Ah, she kept up that phase for a while. We had tons of chickpeas and almond milk in the apartment," Jennifer explained. "She binges on onion rings every now and then too. I've been her roommate for the past year. She's the most fun person I've ever lived with."

She thought back to the pajama-clad karaoke session they'd enjoyed last week. Dancing around and singing to nineties boy bands. It was exactly what she needed after a long week battling it out with her coworker Lorinda for opportunities at work. She felt so lucky to have Nari.

"That's amazing. I can totally see that. Nari is fun to be around. But sometimes, I'll admit she can be a bit strange..." Martha took a sip of her tea.

Nari was unconventional, sure. But strange? Jennifer would not choose that adjective to describe her freewheeling and scheming friend, so full of love and great ideas. "Strange?" She furrowed her brow. "What makes you say that?"

"Oh, you know. She's highly driven, she generates deals out of thin air, but she never follows through on anything long enough to grow it to its full potential. It's got to be exhausting to keep finding new deals. As her roommate, I'm sure you're tired just watching her," Martha said.

Ah. That type of strange. Jennifer could agree.

"But it goes deeper than that." Martha leaned in closer. "Have you thought truly, deeply about *why* Nari doesn't stick with any of her business deals for very long?"

Jennifer shook her head. She always assumed Nari liked the thrill of the chase.

Martha lowered her voice. "I think she's running from something. Never sticking with anything for too long so she can avoid detection. It seems like something is on her heels. Why does she go by the name Gwen sometimes? It's not even her middle name." She cupped her hand around her mouth and whispered into Jennifer's ear, "She might have a dark past we all know nothing about."

•   •   •

Nari stood to make a speech. She tapped her knife against a glass, and the crowd quieted.

"Thank you so much everyone for coming here tonight. I really wanted to celebrate my recent success with you all. As you know, business has been booming."

Jennifer surveyed the room. People were watching Nari expectantly. It was great to see her in her element—holding the attention of a room, commanding respect.

Jennifer felt a little uneasy after what Martha said about Nari's hidden past. Admittedly, Jennifer had only known Nari for a year. And sure, it took time to get to know someone. But it felt like Nari was an open book.

They'd spent a lot of time together, talking about their pasts and their dreams and aspirations. Jennifer knew all about how Nari had moved around a lot as a child and how that made her love to travel but want to keep her home base steady. It made her reluctant to leave Omaha, even when she felt like she had outgrown the city. Jennifer had learned all about Nari's exes and flings and childhood summers spent kayaking and dancing in parades. She felt like there was nothing left to learn about Nari, only new memories to be made with her.

"I couldn't be where I am today without all your support," Nari continued.

Jennifer looked down at her teacup, swirling the liquid around absentmindedly. At this point, she wanted the night to end. She wanted to go back home with Nari, order a pizza, and bond about the amazing evening. They'd dish about all the hot guys who had shown up and enjoy a normal, chill night. Each roommate would know all they needed to know about the other, with no surprises.

"To Nari!" a Latino man with a beachy California vibe exclaimed. The group applauded. Jennifer put down her teacup to clap too.

Nari half bowed, half curtsied. It was cute. Jennifer whistled.

Finally, Haeyeon and two waiters emerged with steaming hot trays of food and started to serve the group. Jennifer's mouth started to water when her plate arrived. Somehow, she had forgotten how hungry she was. She dug into her steaming bowl of veggie bibimbap. At the last minute, she had opted for something healthier: thinly sliced tofu, a hard-boiled egg, and crispy rice stuck to the bottom of the bowl.

Martha broke open her chopsticks. "Please forgive me. I look like a fool when I use these."

As Jennifer surveyed the room, she met the gaze of a stunning man sitting two seats to her right.

Oh. My. God. She hadn't gotten a good enough look at this guy on his way in. He was *hot*. He had curly black hair a little on the longer side and a deep-olive skin tone. He wore a cool leather jacket with the right amount of hardware and had a perfectly manicured, close-cut beard.

She took him in for a moment. She realized she was holding her breath.

"I'm Amir." He smiled to reveal deep-set dimples.

Wait a minute, did his brown eyes twinkle?

She cleared her throat nervously.

"It's, uh, nice to meet you. I'm...Jennifer," she managed to choke out.

"Your dish looks amazing," Amir said, his voice low. "You've got to tell me what it's called. I haven't had Korean food in ages."

She couldn't form the words to tell him the name of her dish. She couldn't remember what her home address was, let alone anything on the menu.

She glanced over at Martha, wondering if she was seeing how gorgeous this guy was. A knowing glimmer crept onto Martha's face. "Here," Martha said to Amir. "Let's trade spots. I want to be closer to my friend, uh, Geraldine." She pointed vaguely and winked at Jennifer.

Amir switched spots dutifully. Jennifer drew in a sharp breath as he sat next to her, imagining the two of them walking hand in hand on a tropical beach in Thailand, eating freshly cut mango from a seashell. The smell of coconut intermingled with the sea breeze would fill the air.

"I've known Nari for so long, but I can't believe I've never met you before," Amir added.

She started to feel dizzy. *He wishes he'd met me before?*

"I live in Michigan, but I'm down here often enough to visit suppliers. Glad we're finally connecting," he continued.

She felt a jolt in her body. He was from Michigan! What were the odds? Of all the people at this party, she *knew* Michigan! Amir could have talked to anyone in the room, but he chose her. She would charm him with insider cultural knowledge and jokes about the high-five state.

Well, maybe. She only knew her corner of the state, barely. She'd spent so much time researching other parts of the world that Michigan didn't make it into her daydreams. Maybe that was a problem. It definitely seemed like it now that she needed to impress a hot stranger with stories from the motherland.

"I'm from Michigan too!" She reached into her memory for an anecdote. He probably wasn't interested in her stories about racing hot dogs down her snowy backyard hill with her cousins. She pulled out her palm to show Amir her hometown on Michigan's mitten-shaped surface. Definitely more relatable.

"This is me," she said, pointing. "Where are you from?"

He took her hand in his. His hands were smooth, warm, and soft. He lightly traced her palm. She felt goosebumps go up her arms.

"Right here in Dearborn." He stopped on the eastern side of the state, right near where she had pointed. "We're neighbors." He winked. "My family's been there for a few generations. We came from Lebanon to work in the auto industry and never left."

"Come for the cars, stay for the Detroit-style pizza," she snorted.

"It's crispy enough to keep us rooted there, scraping our windshields off every winter," he remarked.

"You need all the motivation in the world to get you out of your warm bed to scrape," she said knowingly. "What brings you to Omaha? Did you come for Nari's party?"

"Funny you should ask." He leaned in. "I've got some new business opportunities that brought me here. I was going to come see Nari anyway. The timing worked out perfectly. And as it turns out, I wanted to pitch some ideas to her and hear her perspective. Maybe partner with her on some things. She's always been a sharp thinker when it comes to commerce. I'm looking forward to getting some time with her later."

Maybe this meant Amir would be here for a while. Jennifer pictured the three of them binge watching a reality show together on their magenta couch. They'd laugh and make fun of the contestants. Then Nari would yawn and apologize. She would claim to have had too much wine and would need to nod off early. She'd leave Jennifer and Amir in the living room, alone.

•   •   •

Jennifer and Amir had been talking for what seemed like ten minutes, but when she glanced at her watch, she realized an hour had passed. Every now and then, Martha and the good-looking preppy blond man would interject, sharing stories about golf courses, VIP travel lounges, and purebred dogs. Of course, the implied wealth was staggering but mentioned in such a casual, offhanded way that Jennifer felt like they were talking about visits to the local Shop N Save.

As the night wore on, Amir had revealed more and more endearing things about himself that only made Jennifer want to spend more time with him, staring into his eyes and wondering where dimples came from.

He was allergic to gluten, so he lived above Dearborn's best

Lebanese restaurant specifically to indulge his cravings with the smell of fresh-baked pita every night.

"I also have an unhealthy obsession with peaches. It's gotten to the point where I have to limit myself to one per day in the summer," he said.

"Relatable," Jennifer joked. "I'm the same way with peas during the spring."

He cocked his head. "I thought no one actually liked peas, except me."

"Oh, me and peas go way back," she said. "We've been in the same pod since day one."

He chuckled. "This is an amazing discovery. I feel so bonded to you now. All those years of helping my sister eat her *bazela* pea stew when my parents weren't looking have finally paid off."

"You were training for this moment." She winked. "Are you and your sister close?"

"Absolutely." He met her gaze. "She understands me better than anyone else. She's going through a lot right now, and through it all she's still stronger than almost anyone I know."

Jennifer leaned forward. "She's your ride or die, *and* she's your family. Amazing combination."

"I completely agree. Who are you closest with in your family?" he asked, his voice softening.

"My cousin Sheila. I'm an only child, but she's always been like my sister," Jennifer replied breathlessly. "She's got her own wealth management business, and she can persuade anyone to do anything. I want to follow in her footsteps one day."

"You want to start your own business?" He lifted his eyebrows.

Whoops. She glanced away and her face flushed. "Well, yes," she responded quickly. "To be honest, my dream is to open my own surf shop one day. You know, when I figure out how to pay for it." There. It was out in the open now.

"That's incredible. Do you love to surf?"

She laughed uncomfortably and wished she were better at lying. "You know, I've never actually been. But I think I'm going to love it. So many diverse ancient cultures came up with their own form of surfing because it's so universal to connect with the ocean that way. I know it sounds crazy." She expected Amir to smirk, but instead he had a knowing look on his face.

"That's beautiful, and it makes sense to me. Sometimes you know when something feels right. You don't have to experience it to know that. I felt the same way about running, but I was too intimidated to get started," he explained.

She nodded. Relatable.

"Ten years ago, my sister signed me up for a race without asking me. She knew I would never say yes." He rolled his eyes. "In the beginning, I had no idea what I was doing, but I loved it even when I was struggling. Within a few months, I could run five miles at a time, and now I even run in the winter."

Jennifer's eyes lit up. "Me too! Nari thinks I'm crazy, but it's amazing to go for a run right after a light snow. You just need the right gear—like screws in the bottoms of your shoes to keep from sliding."

"Yes! Those screws are game changers! But I must admit, I'm a twenty-five degrees and above kind of guy." Amir beamed, his dimples showing through.

She felt herself melt. She scanned the room for Nari. She needed to make sure Nari was seeing how much she was excelling at this flirting thing. But Nari was nowhere to be seen.

"What I'm saying is, I really think you should go for it," he continued. "Tell me more about what makes you so excited to open a surf shop."

She took a deep breath. "I think surfing is meant to be a spiritual experience. Once my customers see what they're capable of, they'll feel liberated. They'll start to believe in themselves."

"That's incredible. That's the kind of thing that can change people's lives. You know, there's no reason to let capital stop you from pursuing your dream. I started off with nothing but a small business loan," he explained.

Jennifer froze. She felt exposed. She would have to actually create a business plan to qualify for a loan, which was way too scary. It was probably not the best time to admit that to Amir after he opened up about overcoming his fear of running.

"Thank you," she said, searching for a change of subject. "Now, I've got an important question for you. Do you like dogs?" This was a critical topic. It could seal the deal for her, making Amir the perfect man.

"Oh, do I." Amir's face lit up. He pulled out his phone and scrolled to a picture of a corgi in a banana Halloween costume. She leaned in to get a closer look, her bare arm touching his. She felt a shiver of pleasure.

"This is Gus," he explained. "We're thick as thieves. I take him with me almost everywhere. He helps me close all kinds of deals. Last year, I spent every night for a month teaching him to bring my business card to prospects and shake their hands. It still pays off to this day."

"Gus is adorable and clearly your best employee," she said in awe. "I absolutely love dogs. My grandma had two, and I swear to you, one of them knew how to dance."

"Breakdance, I hope," he said.

"Always," she replied. "Well, I see Gus likes Halloween. Is that your favorite holiday too?"

"I used to love Easter, but I'm a little bit scared of bunnies," he replied. "So now it's Thanksgiving for me."

"Wait, back up! Bunnies? I have to hear the story behind this!"

His smartwatch buzzed. "Aw, shoot. Jennifer, this has been a lot of fun. I've got to head back to my hotel for a call, unfortunately. I'm going to have to leave the bunny mystery hanging until next time. I didn't even get the chance to talk to Nari." He pulled out a business card before handing it to her. "I'd love to see you again. And next time you're in Michigan, let me know."

Jennifer felt thirty different emotions welling up inside of her that she couldn't quite identify. But she knew she wasn't ready for Amir to leave. She felt herself pull toward him and longed for the night to continue.

He made his way to the door and disappeared into the night.

Jennifer wanted to hug Nari and thank her for the amazing evening, wherever that wild child was. She pulled out her phone. *"All good, Nar?"* she typed. Her phone buzzed. Nari sent her a thumbs-up emoji.

Now was as good a time as any to wrap up. Jennifer got

Martha's phone number, gave her a hug, and waved to Haeyeon. She walked out the door.

It was a beautiful night, and she wasn't wearing heels. *At least I can walk home,* she thought as she laughed to herself.

CHAPTER 6

NARI

Finally, Nari had some time to talk to Johannes.

"Omaha has been brilliant so far. I even got to enjoy a lovely gala for the Omaha Animal Shelter." He raised an eyebrow.

Oh God. If he had seen Jennifer getting chased out of the event, that would be enough to derail this deal.

"You made some pretty serious mistakes," he started, "but I admire your style. You're bold, not afraid to take risks."

"I appreciate that. Thanks for being so forgiving," Nari replied.

Johannes chuckled. "I know potential when I see it. Tell me, how's business going lately?"

"Business has been booming," she said. "Omaha is a great place to invest. We've got so many brilliant entrepreneurs in this room from all over the Midwest. I hope you'll get the chance to speak with many of them."

He glanced across the room. "I hope so too. I'm eager to talk further. Let's go somewhere more private."

"Absolutely," she replied, shifting her weight from one foot to the other. She had slipped out of the party undetected the first time. Maybe no one would notice that she was gone this time either.

Her chest caught with excitement. Now was the time. Maybe Johannes would finally reveal his opportunities to her. Would he be selling sharks to wildlife collectors off the coast of Bali? Maybe renting yachts to wealthy convicts so they could trade their stolen minerals? She had trouble imagining what capers he might be up to that would be both lucrative and dastardly enough to turn Sumeet away.

The two of them exited the restaurant and started to walk down the Old Market cobblestone streets. Nari's high heels started to pinch again, and she immediately regretted wearing them.

"This place is charming," Johannes said.

She beamed. The evening was beautiful. The setting sun shone on the historic district, and the skies were turning to a mix of amber and pink. It felt like the air was full of possibility. And not only because of the business that was about to go down.

Omaha was the perfect setting for launching dreams. A big, flat, blank, beautiful Midwestern canvas. That was why Nari had stayed for so long. Okay, so she had only been there for a year and a half. But considering her last longest stay anywhere since she had turned seventeen was five months in Jupiter, Florida, her time in Omaha felt like an eternity.

"I've heard you're one of the best hustlers in the Midwest.

You can turn any opportunity into gold. I believe it after seeing the group you assembled in that room. It speaks for itself," he started.

"Thank you. I'm lucky to know so many talented people," she agreed.

"Sumeet assures me I can trust you. I may know hundreds of powerful people who can move mountains if they want to, but I can only depend on a few of them. That's why it's so valuable to meet someone like you." Johannes paused to clear his throat and walked forward with an awkward stride.

Even if Johannes didn't really trust her, Nari still felt his loneliness and wondered if he had many friends or family.

At least she could trust most of her business associates. She had sold large wig orders to contacts she had known for minutes, needing to front the money from her own savings for inventory. She had purchased a shipping container full of ink tags after testing just one of them during a back alley deal. She was no stranger to risk. But everything always turned out fine. Sometimes, you had to take a leap and stay open to keep the money circulating.

"I've built many relationships on trust. I may switch gigs quickly, but I always follow through on my end of the deal. I never leave something undone," she started. "In fact, I will stay up all night if I need to finish something on time. I am a woman of my word. Of course, I don't expect you to take me at face value. You might need to work with me first before we can build that foundation. And I understand that."

And she meant it. You couldn't lay it on too thick if you were being sincere, Nari's mom had taught her.

Johannes smiled and adjusted his glasses. He really seemed

more human than she had expected. "I've got an opportunity you won't want to pass up. I can't guarantee how long it will last, but apparently that doesn't bother you anyways."

"Lucrative and unpredictable? That's my niche," said Nari. Johannes chuckled.

They passed Zamani Treasures. "I believe you know this store already." She glanced at the front window display featuring hand-carved wooden bowls, colorful beaded jewelry, and painted outdoor scenery full of blue and yellow birds.

"Lovely little place," he remarked. "I'm so lucky Jennifer gave me a tour. She was so thoughtful to take me there."

Jennifer's wholesomeness might be opening doors for Nari on this deal. She had to remember to thank her later. And maybe get her in front of more partners. "I'm so glad you enjoyed it," she said.

"I've got a contact here in Omaha who can help us pull this deal off. Let's call him a distributor. We're going to pay him for the product, far below market rate." Johannes looked Nari in the eye. "Below cost, even. This product is so in demand that it's one of the best opportunities I've seen in years.

"I've also heard you don't mind being a little...flexible with the law. That's important to me. I'm only telling you about this opportunity because I want to work with you."

Ah. One of those opportunities. It was true. Because her mom had shown her what a little legal ambiguity could do for their family, Nari saw the law as a set of suggestions you could ignore if you needed to. Especially if the deal was good enough, you figured out a way to avoid getting caught, and no one was getting hurt. Or at least no one was getting hurt who didn't deserve it.

"Sorbelate is an ingredient used in artificial sweeteners to keep them from caking," Johannes began. "There's currently a global shortage, and demand is exploding."

Her eyes widened. The opportunity sounded like a goldmine.

He took in her expression and beamed. "Essentrix Labs in Omaha is importing a European formulation that hasn't been approved in the US yet. Even better, this is a concentrated formulation of Sorbelate. Its potency is at least one hundred times higher than a normal formulation, so one kilo does the work of one hundred."

Nari's throat tightened. Essentrix Labs was Jennifer's employer. This should be interesting.

"I'd love to get you involved in selling it for me," he explained. "And the longer we can make it last, the larger the empire we'll build. I've got a contact here at Essentrix Labs that can facilitate it all for us. His team will sneak off a bit from each shipment and sell it to us below cost. It'll be months before Essentrix Labs figures out what the team is up to. The margins will be incredible. I promise it'll be worth your while.

"It's not exactly legal, but I know the business owners in Omaha. They're not good people. They use their profits to fund all sorts of bad things, like cobalt mining in the Congo. They're hurting the very families of Bantu artisans who make those traditional handicrafts." He motioned in the direction of Zamani Treasures.

"Cobalt is toxic. Essentrix Labs primarily employs young women, who mine the cobalt with pickaxes, sometimes bringing their children with them. The women breathe cobalt in and touch it constantly. They have no other way to make a living.

Essentrix Labs pays them less than fifty dollars per month, and the company profits substantially," Johannes continued. "Then they use the cobalt in their animal feed division. By hurting Essentrix Labs, we take power away from the mines."

And there it was. All the confirmation Nari needed to go through with this job.

"Sounds like they need to be taken down," she said.

He nodded. "But the irony is, as we hurt the company, we interrupt our own supply chain. We won't be able to steal from Essentrix Labs if they can't afford to buy Sorbelate anymore. We've got to figure out a way to manufacture the formula ourselves. That will make this project more sustainable. As long as we don't get caught before then."

Nari knew more than a few food manufacturers in Europe. "That shouldn't be a problem."

"I hope you keep late hours. You'll have to work at night. And you'll have to be nimble and strong." He paused to take in her reaction.

"Totally within my wheelhouse. My bench press is on point. And I can make the hours work. I'll pretend I'm in Austria," she replied.

Johannes laughed. "That always works for me. Like I said, the opportunities to profit are huge. I need your hard work and hustle to sell it here. The Midwest is a growing market. I've got over one hundred boxes for you. I'll put up all the capital and give you a fifty percent cut. Fifty thousand dollars per box will be yours.

"Now, I'm putting a lot of trust in you. I don't have a network here, so you'll need to find a partner we both can trust. And quickly. The first handoff is tonight. I just finalized the plans with my associate. Let's go to a cafe where we can sit and I'll share them with you."

Oh snap. Tonight? There was only one person who could be her ride or die on such short notice. One person who had shown up for her again and again. She was a kind, nerdy woman from Michigan who had probably never even broken a traffic law in her life. And she happened to work for Essentrix Labs.

•   •   •

Nari took Johannes to her favorite twenty-four hour diner, Silver Spoon. They sat in a red padded booth, its vinyl seats worn from decades of use. Within minutes after ordering two black coffees, he began, "You're going to need to move quickly and follow these instructions exactly."

They sat for about an hour. He drew maps of the routes Nari would need. He explained the ins and outs of the process, where the commercial park was situated, and how to avoid the cameras. She watched carefully.

They finished planning around midnight. Johannes called a taxi to take Nari back to Seoul Kitchen. Her red satin heels were killing her, and she was grateful to avoid the walk. She'd return to the party for enough time to avoid raising suspicions.

Nari had to execute this mission perfectly. She didn't want to be responsible for giving her roommate a rap sheet.

In the back of the cab, her finger hovered over her cell phone. She had the urge to call Sumeet. But calling him would feel like she was admitting she couldn't pull off this deal herself.

CHAPTER 7

JENNIFER

Jennifer fell asleep almost immediately. She had one incredible dream after another, all from distinct times in her life. She was back in second grade, racing Melissa Carter. Breathing heavily but miraculously running much faster than Melissa. Winning races, getting lifted up on her classmates' shoulders.

Next, she was in college, pitching an idea for a business over a breakfast buffet as the audience got increasingly excited.

Suddenly, Nari appeared in her dream, shaking her as she was about to get to her profit margins. "I've got to tell you something!" Jennifer's eyes burst open. Real world Nari was on top of her, shaking her shoulders.

"Wake up, Jennifer. We've got an amazing opportunity, but we've got to go now," Nari blurted out.

Stunned, dazed, and suddenly craving pancakes, Jennifer realized both of her feet were numb and tingling.

"What are you talking about? Go away. I'm sleeping," Jennifer mumbled groggily.

"I need your help. I'll explain later!" Nari grabbed her hand and guided her out of bed. Jennifer glanced at the clock. It was 2 AM. Maybe the kitchen was on fire. Or maybe Nari had a sudden drunken craving for tacos and needed a ride to the drive-thru. Nari was going to owe her big time if it was the latter.

Out of habit, she put on her robe and took her cap off. She stumbled behind Nari to the front door, struggling to find her shoes as she tried to figure out whether or not she was still asleep.

She followed Nari into the crisp, cool black of the night sky. A car was waiting for them. Jennifer assumed it was a rideshare as she and Nari got inside.

"We're going to Papillon?" the driver asked. Something about him seemed oddly familiar.

"Yes," Nari replied as the car sped off into sleeping Omaha.

"I know you're wondering what the hell is going on," Nari started. Gross understatement, although Jennifer was too dazed to come up with questions. "I can explain. First off, thank you for joining me. You're going to be grateful you did."

Jennifer watched Nari's face expectantly. Her beauty was still visible in the dark night air as the car sped past one street lamp after the next, illuminating Nari's face in half-second intervals. It almost looked like a stop-motion animation movie was playing on her face.

"I've got an opportunity of a lifetime for us. It involves artificial sweeteners," Nari said, growing serious.

Jennifer couldn't help but giggle. "You woke me up in the middle of the night and dragged me into a car for artificial sweeteners?" She was happy she could laugh about it.

"I know it sounds funny, but there's an ingredient in many of them. Sorbelate. It keeps them from caking. There's been a shortage lately, and the price has skyrocketed."

Jennifer remembered her last trip to the grocery store. She didn't buy her usual Sweet N Yum, as the price had tripled. She had switched to agave this week in her tea. Ginger, turmeric, and agave. Not a bad combination. "I know what you're talking about..."

Nari continued, "Your new friend Johannes can sell us an alternative. *Below cost*. It hasn't been approved for use in the US yet, but it's all over Europe. It's safe. We can sell it here and fly under the radar. They've formulated it to look like Sorbelate from a chemical perspective."

"What? How do you even know enough about this to know whether it's legit?" Jennifer shook her head. Nari didn't know anything about chemistry. Or food. Or health and safety.

"I've done some serious internet searches. It's safe. And I know we've got a gold mine on our hands," Nari explained.

"That leaves the biggest question." Jennifer rubbed her eyes. "Why did you need my help in the middle of the night?"

Nari paused. "I'm intercepting a shipment. Borrowing it, actually! I've got someone on the inside who's selling it to us. I need your help to load and unload. You may not have my arm strength. But I know you're fast and a good packer."

Great. Now Jennifer's childhood knack for Tetris was coming back to haunt her. She bit her lip and held back tears. This sounded more than a little illegal. This sounded like stealing.

She knew Nari was a little wild, but there was a huge difference between sneaking into a party and *theft*.

She started to feel sick. She thought about how best to escape the moving car. Maybe she could open the door a bit and roll out onto the pavement below.

"I know it sounds crazy," Nari continued, "but think of the riches that will be *ours*. I'll cut you in, fifty-fifty. And we're not talking, 'getting groceries at a health food store' money. We're talking about buying a surf shop in Hawaii a few times over."

Nari knew Jennifer all too well. This was her financial kryptonite. No more cramped office work with soft lighting and few windows. No more polite battles with her coworker Lorinda that she stewed on for days. Just witty banter with world traveling magnates. She'd take lunch breaks in the ocean, put wild jasmine in her hair, and spend time lovingly polishing surfboards and paddleboards until they shone in the sun. Maybe she would even have enough money to hire a business consultant who would help her begin.

Jennifer breathed in deeply. That kind of money would change her life. But what kind of deal involved *intercepting* a shipment in the middle of the night? "What are you talking about? I want to be rich, but this sounds like *stealing*! What is wrong with you? Are you a criminal? I thought you liked roller skating and karaoke as much as me!" Her words trembled.

Nari nodded in the darkness. Her voice was even and calm. "I know it sounds like stealing. Technically, it is. We'll be going against your employer, Essentrix Labs. They run dangerous cobalt mines in the Democratic Republic of Congo. They pay their workers—mostly women—a few dollars a day to breathe in toxic dust and risk their lives. Then they use that same cobalt in their animal feed products. You've been working for them for years, being underpaid and supporting evil without knowing it. If we take down Essentrix Labs, we destroy the mines."

She scrolled on her phone and handed it to Jennifer. "These are screenshots of a conversation Johannes has been having with one of the mine workers."

Jennifer paged through the screenshots. She felt her stomach churn as she read about women working without safety equipment, dying in landslides, and becoming gravely ill with lung disease.

She had learned about the DRC's cobalt mining industry before. It destroyed communities. She had been helping Essentrix Labs market to new customers for over ten years and had worked on projects for the animal feed division many times. She was good at it. And that money went straight to the cobalt mines. Had she helped exploit people? Were there women with lung disease because she had delivered great insights on the farmers who raised cows and sheep?

Her eyes welled up and started to sting. "I'm shocked. I've gone to so many Christmas parties, researched tons of competitors, and sat in countless meetings drawing doodles. I can't believe I didn't know what I was supporting."

Nari grabbed Jennifer's hand. "That's exactly why we've got to take this opportunity. Essentrix Labs has been exploiting you too. They've been forcing you to promote evil without even knowing it."

Jennifer nodded. She looked out the window, as tears started to fall. "Maybe we could even give some of our profits back to the women in the Congo..."

"I completely agree," Nari said firmly.

Jennifer thought about it. If she went through with this plot and succeeded, she could be a wealthy woman who fought modern-day slavery *and* gave money back to the people who deserved it. Her dad had taught her to fight injustice by selling cookies and cutting grass to raise money for people in need. This sounded like it would change a lot more lives.

But this was still stealing.

"I'm not a criminal. Can't I fight back in some other way? Maybe I can quit my job and convince Karlie to do it too," Jennifer said, regretting it immediately. There was no part of her that wanted to quit her job with no savings. She'd have to move back in with her mom and get a few part-time jobs to pay her student loans. No more restaurant hopping with Nari.

Nari shook her head. "If you quit your job, the evil continues. The only way to stop Essentrix Labs is to dismantle their power. But I don't want to put you in danger to do the right thing. That's why we've got this planned out so well."

Jennifer drew in a shaky breath. "*If* I were to do this with you—and that's a big if—how would we avoid getting caught?"

"We've got to move quickly. Johannes has mapped everything out for us to avoid the cameras." Nari pulled what looked like a hand-drawn map out of her bag. She grabbed her cell phone and turned on its flashlight. Yup, totally hand-drawn but impressively meticulous.

"We'll have exactly eight minutes while the security system is down for maintenance to find the shipment and load it into the van." Nari traced the route with her finger. "As long as we're on time, we'll avoid getting locked in."

Great. Jennifer's future—and criminal record—would be

in Nari's hands. She had to trust Nari completely to navigate them through a narrow passageway to avoid detection. She wouldn't be able to validate the set up on her own. She didn't have someone on the inside to test it out and see if they appeared on camera.

Jennifer realized she still hadn't said yes to Nari. She could stay in this car, let Nari do her thing, and pretend none of this ever happened.

"This plot is crazy. I've got so many things I still want to do in my life, like buy a Chihuahua and train it to roll over. I've never been to Ethiopia. I can't meet my future husband in a women's prison. I don't want to risk my freedom," Jennifer remarked.

Suddenly, she became conscious of the driver who had been here this whole time. Was he listening? Probably. Did he get a look at her? Also likely.

Nari turned to Jennifer calmly and put her hand on her arm. "I agree. I don't want to risk my freedom either. That's why this is planned out so perfectly. But even if we do get caught, I'll take the fall. I promise, you won't be risking anything. I'll tell the cops I forced you to do it. I even woke you up in the middle of the night, so that story seems legit."

It seemed so straightforward, the way Nari put it.

Jennifer felt a twisting sensation in the pit of her stomach. Was her intuition telling her to run? Or should she push through like a comic book hero, earn a massive payout, and help the women in the Congolese mines?

Jennifer was a caring person. She helped her friends move, she helped Nari with her schemes, and she volunteered at senior living centers every now and then. But she had never helped anyone break free from bondage—let alone an entire village full of people.

She also had been broke for as long as she could remember, and her old ways of thinking would result in more of the same. Maybe this was the opportunity she needed. Maybe she could finally travel and see the world. She could open her own business and answer to no one except her worldly customers.

Besides, they were still *buying* Sorbelate, probably directly from someone who was underpaid like her. She and Nari could make off with millions, share their fortunes with the mine workers, and even help one of her coworkers too. It could be a win-win for everyone. Well, almost everyone.

Jennifer shook her head and closed her eyes, willing her doubts to go away. "I'm in."

As if on cue, the car slowed down in front of a park across from a dimly-lit facility. Her heart started pounding erratically.

Nari threw open the car door. "Run!" she called out, grabbing Jennifer's hand.

Jennifer stumbled out of the car, tripping over her bathrobe. She fumbled with the sash and untied it, throwing it off to the side as they ran.

The air was strangely cool and refreshing as they bounded across the field toward the facility. Although she was an amazing long-distance runner, she was not used to running in the middle of the night, thank you.

She wanted to stop and catch her breath, to pause and lounge in the grass. She forced one last sprint out of her system until they reached a stack of white boxes hidden among the shrubs. It was as if they were glowing in the street lights. There were also a handful of recycling bins filled with boxes.

"Grab as many as you can carry, but don't overload your-self," Nari said hurriedly. "If we run around these trees, we can avoid the cameras."

The boxes were heavy. She grabbed one in each arm and fol-lowed Nari again. Nari, ever the overachieving weightlifter, had two in each arm.

They started running again, Jennifer willing herself not to trip. She pushed herself to reach the fence, chanting her grandma's pet name for her, Jenny, in her mind as she ran.

Like clockwork, Nari had guided them to the gap in the fence she had described. Jennifer felt a mixture of awe and re-lief. She knew Nari wouldn't let her down.

"We've got to shimmy through here," Nari whispered. "No cameras will catch us if we stay against the wall. Follow me closely." First, she slipped the boxes through the gap one at a time. Then she turned her body sideways and squeezed through the opening between the fence and a brick building. Jennifer followed, sliding the boxes and then her body through the gap.

She watched as Nari inched along, back against the brick wall, toward a white van.

Jennifer didn't know where the camera was. She had never even been to this facility before. She tried her best to hold the boxes close to her body so they wouldn't show up on video. She looked down at her plaid pajama bottoms and wanted to laugh. She was starting her career as a high-powered business thief while wearing pajamas. Of all the things she could have been wearing, Jennifer knew she wouldn't have it any other way. Might as well be comfortable as you rob, right?

Nari bent over and ran the short length between the brick wall and the white van. She slid open the side door and started throwing the boxes inside. "Come on. Let's do this!" she said in an exaggerated whisper. "Half the boxes are already inside the van. We've got seven minutes left to load the rest."

Surprisingly nimble given the time of night, Jennifer's muscles had warmed up. She sprinted to the van and threw her items inside too. The next few trips would be easier after this first round of practice.

Jennifer followed Nari back the way they came—inching along the brick wall, squeezing sideways through the fence, and running to the tree to grab more boxes. Sure enough, her feet seemed to skim across the wet morning grass. She almost didn't feel any resistance. Maybe she was high on adrenaline at this point.

She and Nari kept pace with each other. She couldn't believe how fast they were moving.

"We've got two minutes left. Let's get out of here!" Nari cried.

Jennifer saw that four boxes remained. She desperately wanted to go back and get them but hesitated instead.

"Jennifer! Leave them! We've got to go!" Nari hissed.

Jennifer turned around and chased after Nari. As she tried to rush through the fence, her pajama shorts caught on a wire. She pushed herself free, ripping the leg of her shorts.

She raced forward, scooting sideways against the brick wall, before running to the van and diving into the passenger's side. Nari reached across to open the glove box, digging through its contents. Jennifer heard a jingling as Nari unearthed the keys and pulled them out.

Jennifer prayed for a quick departure. She hoped she hadn't slowed them down.

After what seemed like forever, the van's engine fired into action. Nari backed up the vehicle and spun it around to leave the facility. They reached a locked gate.

"Shit," Nari said. "They didn't tell me about this. Check for a key card!"

"Uhh..." Jennifer froze. Oh right, the glove box. She opened it up and rooted around. A plastic cup. Something soft and fabric-y. Why was there so much stuff in here?

She felt a small plastic rectangle attached to a lanyard. Ah, this must be it. She pulled it out and glanced down to see if she could make out a face. It was too dark. She tossed the lanyard to Nari.

No power windows. Nari tried to quickly roll down the window, one jerky motion after another. She threw the badge against the entry box. No dice. Jennifer felt a sense of panic. Maybe this was the wrong badge? She started to root around in the glove compartment again. She opened the center console and searched.

What time was it? Were they going to get caught after all this hard work? Because they couldn't find the right badge? Who was behind this anyway, and why didn't they clean out their glove box?

"This is bad," Nari said, panicking. "Maybe this is why Sumeet didn't want to work with Johannes. We've got one minute left!" She pressed and held the badge against the entry box. "Keep looking!"

Jennifer raised an eyebrow and started to check the door pocket. The gate started to open creakily, sliding along an invisible track at the bottom.

"Yes!" Nari cheered.

As soon as the gate opened, Nari maneuvered the van through and sped out.

Jennifer realized she didn't know where they were going. But now was probably not the time to ask. The moon shone brightly in the night sky. Jennifer glanced down at the clock. It was only 3:03 AM. Somehow, they had escaped detection. At least so far. Jennifer's face flushed as she considered the fact that this was a stolen vehicle. Another offense for her rap sheet.

"We did it." Nari beamed, looking over at Jennifer. "Thank you. We've got at least one hundred boxes back there. We are set for a while! Each one's got a margin of, like, fifty thousand dollars!"

Jennifer did some quick math. That would be at least five million dollars. After paying the mine workers, at least some of that would be all hers...

"Oh my God," Jennifer breathed, thinking of what she could do with all that cash. "But how are we going to sell the Sorbelate?"

"Don't worry, my love. I've got that covered," Nari replied. "But first things first. We're going to a parking garage in Papillion to switch to the getaway van. It's parked on the roof, which is the one level with a camera blind spot. We've got to move these boxes over as quickly as we can."

Oh right, cameras. Jennifer had almost forgotten about those again. She reached down and touched her pajama shorts leg. It was ripped and barely hanging on, thanks to her stretchy waistband. Hopefully she hadn't left any fibers behind.

So this is what being a criminal felt like. Her heart raced. She looked the same, but her body was filled with an electric charge.

"Did we do the right thing?" Jennifer asked.

Nari held out her hand for a high five. "Think of how much impact we're going to make on these women's lives. We're giving them *freedom*."

Jennifer nodded. Was going to prison worth doing the right thing? There were scores of African women activists before her who had gone to jail for protesting corporate abuses like land destruction and low pay. Her dad had passionately taught her about their causes and their impact. Maybe he would be proud of her for being brave and taking a stand. And hopefully he'd be excited about her payoff too.

But she wasn't exactly protesting peacefully. She shivered as she remembered the stolen boxes in the back of the van.

Slowly, the van's gentle movements quieted her mind, and her eyes grew heavy. She was defenseless against nighttime car rides ever since her mom used the technique to help her sleep as a baby. This seat was shockingly comfortable.

Jennifer awoke to Nari shaking her shoulder. "Get up! We've got to transfer these boxes!"

They were on a parking garage roof with faint lighting. In her sleepy stupor, Jennifer had forgotten what they were doing.

This was more than a little like what she imagined bootcamp to be.

As she came to, Jennifer remembered the riches that would be hers to share, if she could only move quickly enough and avoid getting caught. She snapped into action and jumped up, digging deep to find that one last ounce of energy that could get them past the finish line.

Nari was already ten steps ahead of her. Jennifer followed

her to the back of the van and sloppily grabbed three boxes. She dropped two of them on her five-foot journey to the black getaway vehicle.

Great. This sure was off to a good start.

Picking up two of the three boxes and feeling as haggard as a woman three times her age, Jennifer made it to the getaway van to load up.

Looking over at Nari, who seemed to be well-rested, sharp, and moving smoothly, Jennifer couldn't help but feel like she had done this before.

They unloaded the rest of the boxes into the second van. Nari took off, and the tires squealed as they left the parking garage.

Jennifer had held a summer internship in Papillon, so she knew the drive back to central Omaha well. They drove past the shuttered water park where she had gone for her junior year summer trip. The park reminded her of home, suburban Detroit summers with friends. It had been bittersweet leaving them behind.

But that was a far cry from her current reality. None of her college friends would ask her to steal lucrative ingredients and sell them. Or at least, not that she imagined. Only her trusty internet-sourced bestie would do that.

CHAPTER 8

NARI

Jennifer's pureness of spirit lent itself to theft, it turned out. It seemed like she was harboring a secret, adventurous streak.

Before long, the surreal process was over. Nari pulled the van into the car park behind their apartment building. Luckily, their assigned spot jutted right up to their apartment.

Now, they needed to unload the boxes. Nari didn't have a good place to store them on such short notice.

"I don't want to store these boxes in our apartment," Jennifer said as they parked. "Then we can't deny anything. I really don't want to go to jail, Nari."

"I don't want to go to jail either." Nari touched Jennifer's arm. "But listen. This is temporary. No one will suspect us. No one is going to find anything."

Jennifer closed her eyes. "As long as we're not on camera."

"It'll be like we were never even there," Nari reassured her. Jennifer sighed and relaxed her shoulders.

They both exited the van, less rushed this time. It was nearly 3:30 AM. Both women took their boxes and filed into the apartment. They passed Jennifer's framed, brightly-colored print of a comic book scene, her hero Amina Keita fighting a band of thieves in ancient Sudanese markets lining the Nile. Nari had already cleared out the hallway closet.

One trip after another left the closet packed and nearly overflowing. Jennifer meticulously arranged the boxes as they went. As Nari creaked on a floorboard on their final trip, Jennifer jumped and dropped her boxes.

"You were amazing." Nari felt a swell of gratitude as she hugged her roommate. "I couldn't have asked for a better partner. Thank you. I can't wait to celebrate with you tomorrow over some blueberry pancakes. We made it."

Jennifer sighed. "This is crazy. If we can pull this off, we're going to be so rich and help so many people. Goodbye, Omaha." She lowered her eyes. Nari could sense a sadness about Jennifer as she bade the town farewell. Nari felt it too.

As she drifted off to sleep that morning, Nari envisioned money raining down on her—gently, peacefully. She opened her arms wide and welcomed the stream of cash.

All that was left to do was sell the Sorbelate.

Like a walk in the park.

CHAPTER 9

JENNIFER

Jennifer woke up with a hazy, contented feeling, cozy under her fuzzy lavender blanket. As her brain fog lifted, she started to remember what had happened the night before. A vague sense of shock settled in. Had she really helped her roommate technically steal millions of dollars' worth of merchandise? From her employer?

She rubbed her eyes and contemplated what it all meant. What if they had been filmed and the manhunt was already on? Goosebumps started to form on her arms and a cold sweat trickled down her back. What if there were cops on their way right now?

She pictured a news story. "Two women are on the loose in greater Omaha after robbing Essentrix Labs," the newscaster said as Jennifer and Nari's faces flashed on the screen. In her imagination, Jennifer chose a super flattering photo of herself.

She strained to listen for sirens. Nothing. Their quiet

neighborhood was characteristically silent. Not even the crashing sounds of Nari getting arrested—and resisting, knocking over pots and pans—in the kitchen.

Maybe this calm was a sign of things to come. Had it really been that easy?

Or was it, like she had seen in so many cop dramas, the quiet before the storm?

Her breath caught in her throat. She knew she still had to go into work on Monday, but what if someone knew about the heist? How would she be able to lie all day? It seemed so risky to go into the office. Maybe she could call in sick and take a home-based seminar—led by Nari—on lying.

Jennifer covered her face with her blanket and contemplated staying in bed all day.

Slowly, the corners of her mouth turned upward. She had broken the law. Why did she feel a strange tingle of excitement? It was like when her friend Cara suggested they try stealing butterfly hair clips at the mall in seventh grade. Jennifer pretended to do it—when in Rome, right?—slipping a clip into her pocket, before replacing it back into the bin when no one was looking. But the feeling of what could have been—breaking the rules, getting a prize—had stuck with her for decades, along with a sense of guilt for feeling a thrill at the idea of stealing.

As she stretched, Jennifer could smell the scent of Nari's delectable pancakes wafting into the room. Nari was so tricky. She must have been the reason Jennifer woke up. Her pancakes were like an alarm clock that could only be quieted with mounds of butter and second helpings.

She reached for her bathrobe and remembered with a

shiver that she had tossed it aside the night before. She put on a sweatshirt instead.

She made her way to the kitchen and could hear the faint sounds of dance pop. Typical Nari.

Bright morning light streamed through the windows. Nari had outdone herself this time. She had cooked a fantastic spread of blueberry pancakes and hash browns, laying them out on the white countertop. Both were perfectly crispy on the outside and, Jennifer knew, pillowy and chewy on the inside. There was even a bowl of fresh cut fruit that Jennifer normally only saw in movies, where a wealthy family has a pool party in the summer heat, and somehow they constantly have a tray of perfectly arranged fruit. It would always come in a stunning variety that you'd never find pre-cut at Shop N Save. Way beyond your standard cantaloupe, grape, and watermelon combo. More like passion fruit, mango, and kiwi.

"Where did you find that fruit?" she murmured. Her hunger had broken the barrier between thoughts and speaking.

Nari giggled. "I've been waiting for you, girlfriend. Come in and celebrate. I've made your faves."

Jennifer would let herself go today. Two glasses of orange juice, minimum. Extra pulp.

"It's kind of a blur, but it feels like we stole from my employer yesterday?" Jennifer leaned against the counter.

"Technically, yes. But more in a Robin Hood sort of way. We're giving the wealth back to the people who created it," Nari explained. "And taking a commission, like a nonprofit."

"I guess that's not so far from the truth." Jennifer furrowed her brow. "Except taking a salary from the Omaha Animal Shelter doesn't usually land you in jail."

"You have a point there," Nari admitted. "But we're not going to jail either. We left nothing behind but good vibes."

Jennifer's thoughts drifted back to her missing dressing gown, and her muscles tensed. "That's not *quite* true. This morning, I realized I dropped my robe last night when we got to the facility. It must be in the park somewhere." She wiped her sweaty palms on her shorts.

Nari nodded. "Is there anything on your robe that could tie it back to you?"

Jennifer paused. "I don't think so. I love it, but I think it's pretty generic."

"No worries then." Nari patted Jennifer's head. "You should be fine."

This seemed pretty logical. After all, how could the cops trace a random sage-green bathrobe back to her? Jennifer exhaled slowly and tapped her fingers on her leg.

"You were amazing last night. I was so impressed by your speed and your confidence. I feel like you're a new woman," said Nari playfully.

Jennifer couldn't help but feel a sense of contentment. She had performed quite well, hadn't she? And if the queen of scheming had noticed, maybe she had some hidden talents.

"I went to get groceries this morning. Nothing has changed. No one looked at me strangely. Ms. Martin waved. I think we're in the clear," Nari said.

Jennifer felt both relieved and shocked. How did Nari already get groceries and cook breakfast without looking like a zombie?

"I'm excited to go for a walk together, sharing our secret that we're both about to be millionaires," Jennifer said dreamily. She pictured them out to brunch underneath a banner that read, "Millionaire or bust." No. Too flashy. They could get matching tattoos instead. Maybe they'd say "7 figures" with some extra flourishes. Classy. Understated.

She didn't actually know whether Nari already had a million dollars. But she was okay with that.

"We're going to be swimming in dough," Nari shared before rapping a few lines, *"Making those sales, no paper trail."*

Oh right. Sales. "I forgot we have to sell these boxes." Jennifer motioned to the closet. "I had hoped we could drop them behind a dumpster somewhere, and the money would get wired to us."

Jennifer didn't have the slightest idea how to sell the Sorbelate, but she felt a sense of relief knowing that Nari did. "I won't be any good at pitching, but I can help research our customers. What they like, and what they care about."

"Don't worry. Selling's my forte," Nari replied. "I've got contacts in food manufacturing that I can charm into buying from us. We'll have straight profit coming in after we pay off Johannes. And don't worry about the paper trail. We can wash the money through a few of my shell businesses."

Of course she did. Jennifer pointed her fingers and danced happily. "We're gonna be millionaires, millionaires."

If only her friends from seventh grade could see her now. She had forgone the butterfly clips for something bigger. Much bigger.

· · ·

The next morning, Jennifer couldn't believe she still had to set foot into Essentrix Labs while they waited for the cash to come rolling in. Would people know that the Sorbelate was missing? She would have to evade any conversations by hiding in the bathroom. There was no way she'd be able to lie about it.

But soon, she'd be free. She'd never have to work for Essentrix Labs again. She couldn't wait to casually tell Lorinda it was her last day.

That was a little while off though. Maybe a week at least. She didn't know how long these things took. She'd have to avoid getting caught until then. She shuddered.

She browsed through her closet for something to wear. Something that said, "I'm wealthy but humble about it." She settled on a black pencil skirt, a ruffled red chiffon blouse, and some black ballet flats with deceptively good tread. She didn't need any additional height. Plus, she never missed the opportunity to walk to work on a beautiful day, and ballet flats always did the trick.

Nari had already left the apartment when Jennifer came to the kitchen looking for cereal. She had probably gone to the gym like she did every Monday to kick the week off right.

Well, no worries. All the better for Jennifer to watch old episodes of trash TV while she ate her breakfast, which was going to be bowl after miniature bowl of Fruity Crunch, eaten in small quantities so it would stay crispy.

She couldn't believe it had been two nights and no cops had knocked at their door. She hadn't seen any news stories about the missing Sorbelate. No one from work had called her up to confront her. Goosebumps covered her arms. She glanced into the mirror on the opposite wall to see if she looked any different. Nothing.

After a few mini bowls, her alarm went off. It was her ten-minute reminder to cut herself off from her reality cooking show and grab her lunch.

Her lunch was extra special today. Nari had made falafels, and Jennifer had treated herself to honey-roasted cashews. Maybe a dollar more than she'd normally spend, but she would have the budget for it soon.

The sun was shining brightly that morning. A colorful array of birds chirped in the trees. Jennifer waved to her neighbor, who was walking his dachshund. As she rounded the corner, she put in her earbuds and turned on her favorite podcast. Another trash piece, except no one knew about this obsession. This show focused on the secret love affairs of ancient, influential leaders from around the world. The host intoned about Marc Antony and Cleopatra's controversial love affair. Some believed it led to Marc Antony's downfall, the host explained, but Jennifer couldn't help but feel loyal to Team Cleopatra.

"Hey," a familiar male voice said. Shocked, Jennifer looked up.

It was Amir. He looked incredible. Form-fitting sweatpants, a nice zip-up running jacket. It looked like he was coming from the gym. She drew in her breath, unable to hide her excitement.

"Amir!" she exclaimed. "You're still in town?"

"I'm flying out today. I was finishing up on some deals. It's so good to see you." He sounded genuine.

She felt her cheeks flush. "You too. So what are you up to today?"

"Actually, I've got a bit of time. I've got to head to the airport this afternoon, but if you're free now, I'd love to get coffee with you," he said.

She glanced at her watch. No one would notice if she walked into work a few minutes late. She was normally late to the office anyway. "There's a great coffee shop nearby that draws animal shapes in your milk foam," she replied. "They always draw a bunny for me, but I'll get a different animal in your honor. I'd love to show it to you."

"I can't wait to see it," he said. "I'll let you lead the way."

Chills went up and down her body. They took off walking together, passing by trendy, minimalist shops that were still closed and brick apartment buildings. "I'm going to get a drink with foam so I can see one of these bunnies," he said. "I've got to face my fears."

Jennifer looked at Amir's perfectly smooth, olive skin tone and his luscious curly hair. She breathed in slowly and willed herself to focus. "I could tell you were a brave man. But now the anticipation is real! Why are you afraid of bunnies?"

He looked at her and smiled. A light breeze rippled through his hair. "It all started with the Easter bunny. I took a photo with him at the mall when I was about six. When I sat on his lap, I noticed some of the fur was coming off his face. I could see the plastic grid underneath. And he smelled like old rice. Something about him seemed deranged. I couldn't get the image out of my head, and I started to feel like bunnies had bad intentions."

Jennifer began to snort uncontrollably. "That's too good, Amir!" she said between gasps, pausing on a manhole cover to catch her breath. "It all makes sense. I mean, rice is so delicious.

How could you let it go bad? But now I'm concerned about something else. Does that mean you stopped hunting for Easter eggs? Tell me it's not so!"

"I had to stop right then to avoid getting caught by the Easter bunny. But to be honest, I hated looking for those eggs. My neighbors were too good at hiding them. I mean, who thinks to look inside a mailbox?" he explained.

A professionally-dressed couple walked by them, flirting and playfully touching each other.

"I know exactly what you mean!" Jennifer shielded her eyes from the morning sun. "My dad was the worst. My cousin and I would search for hours. Then when I finally found the eggs, they'd only be filled with jelly beans. And so many green ones! Can I at least get a chocolate coin for all my hard work?"

"You are speaking the truth right now," he replied. "The green jelly beans were the worst! Yellow all day in my camp."

"I can respect a yellow jelly bean, but I would still trade fifty of them for one chocolate coin." She grinned.

He chuckled. She couldn't help but feel like this conversation was going well. She would throw caution to the wind and celebrate her wins by spending two dollars more on a medium coffee.

They approached the coffee shop, Harvest & Hearth. Its floor-to-ceiling windows revealed a cozy scene of students sipping coffee thoughtfully at tables, commuters stopping in for a cup, and older men and women taking a pause to sample muffins. The cream-colored cushy chairs and dark wood table tops made even the most stressed, coffee-deprived person relax and settle in.

"Here we are," Jennifer said. "I can't wait to be impressed

by your bravery." She crossed her fingers behind her back, secretly hoping for an empty table and more free flowing conversation. It was a good luck habit she had held onto since kindergarten.

"I can't back out now. I've already committed my bunny order to you. Thanks for being my accountability partner." Amir opened the door and motioned for her to step inside.

She smiled and crossed the threshold with Amir close behind. The decadent smell of freshly ground coffee beans filled her nostrils immediately. She closed her eyes and inhaled happily.

They strode up to the cash register. He ordered a caramel latte, and she got a pistachio iced coffee, to mix things up.

"Amazing choice," he said. "My mom brings back the best pistachios when she visits our family in Lebanon. You've got to try them sometime. You wouldn't believe how buttery they are."

She felt her face grow hot. Was he saying he wanted to see her again? Her heart pounded quickly. "Wow, I would love to try them," she managed to breathe out.

He pulled out his wallet. "It's on me. How often do I get to have rabbit aversion therapy with one of Omaha's most beautiful tour guides?"

The blond, middle-aged cashier took his credit card. "This guy's a keeper," she said to Jennifer, who couldn't stop grinning. Her cheeks started to ache. It seemed like her red chiffon blouse was really pulling its weight today. Maybe she looked like a glamorous millionaire already.

"Thank you," Jennifer said shyly. "I really appreciate it."

"Anytime," Amir replied, his dimples deepening.

As they stepped down toward the end of the counter to wait for their drinks, Jennifer looked up and locked eyes with her coworker, Lorinda. *Oh God. Why is Lorinda here?*

Lorinda beamed. "Jennifer! It's so good to see you. You have great taste in coffee. I love Harvest & Hearth," she said in her rhythmic accent.

Lorinda was a driven woman from Nigeria who was always getting promoted—it seemed like weekly—for putting in one twelve-hour day after another. She and Jennifer were two of only three black women at the company, which was a tough adjustment after growing up in the diverse Detroit suburbs. Jennifer's childhood friends were black, Iraqi, Laotian, Salvadorian, and Senegalese Americans. She never felt like she stood out.

Jennifer was jealous of Lorinda's meteoric rise in the operations department and more often than not felt like she was in direct competition with her for accolades. Coworkers often talked about how Lorinda had helped them get a project through the finish line, just in time. They marveled over how insightful she was and how lucky they were to have someone with her level of experience.

It made the hairs on Jennifer's neck stand up straight and prickle her skin when she heard her team talk about Lorinda. It was even worse that Lorinda was so nice to her. Jennifer wanted to hate her for stealing all the limelight. But it was so *hard* to hold a grudge against her.

"Hey, Lorinda." Jennifer tried hard to mask the frustration in her voice. "So good to see you here. This is my friend, Amir." She hadn't even known Amir for a full day, and she already had to introduce him to Lorinda.

"It's so nice to meet you," Lorinda said, shaking Amir's hand. "I'm Lorinda, Jennifer's coworker. We've known each other for years. Jennifer is so smart. And she's also a great singer at karaoke, I hear." She tilted her head toward Jennifer, who forced herself to smile.

Jennifer's jealousy didn't make sense, and she knew it. Lorinda liked her. She was positive and good-natured, full of interesting stories about life back in Nigeria. And she didn't seem to notice that Jennifer's fists clenched during meetings when managers thanked Lorinda again for her innovative solutions.

"It's great to meet you too," Amir responded. "I had no idea you were a karaoke queen, Jennifer. I love to throw down on a mic with the best of them."

Jennifer imagined Amir on stage crooning classic easy listening music, and she felt weak.

Lorinda laughed. "You both would make a great duet, I'm sure. I miss singing. I used to do it every week back in Nigeria."

Jennifer looked at Lorinda, reluctantly admitting to herself that she was quite beautiful. Lorinda had a heart-shaped face and perfectly manicured eyebrows. Jennifer could never handle the pain required to get those. Her clear, dark-brown skin gleamed, and she had high cheekbones.

"One medium raspberry white-chocolate latte," a lanky man with reddish skin announced at the end of the counter.

"That's me!" Lorinda took her drink. "I'll see you back at the office, partner. You two enjoy your coffees. Hope to see you again, Amir."

Amir waved as Lorinda walked toward the door.

"I wish I had more time here with you," Amir said as he

turned toward Jennifer. "It seems like you really know the best of Omaha. I'd love to explore it with you."

Jennifer felt her pulse quicken. She crossed her fingers behind her back and hoped Amir would be back soon.

The man at the counter called out their drinks. "It's finally time!" Amir exclaimed. He removed his lid and looked at the design on top. "I think you might have cured me. This is so cute. I might even be able to partake in Easter again."

Jennifer glanced into his cup. There was an adorable outline of a bunny's face, its ears sticking straight up, with decorative ferns along each side. "That even exceeded my expectations. Well, that settles it. You've got to come back to Harvest & Hearth sometime for more fine art."

He laughed. "This place is like a museum. Shall we?" He gestured toward an empty table in the corner. "Unless you need to get back to work. I totally understand if you do."

"Well, I don't have to leave *yet*," she said. "Who knows when you'll be in Omaha again. I'm sure my work won't notice if I take an extra five minutes."

She wanted to stay through the afternoon. Maybe she'd skip work. Tell Amir all about the heist and the millions of dollars that was about to come raining in. Something about him made her want to share her life story. He was so warm and made her feel as if she could confide in him. Even more, she wanted to celebrate with him. She imagined telling him her news. Instead of being blinded by the money, he would be impressed and happy for her.

Except she knew that was a bad idea. He would be gone in an instant if she told him about the heist.

"I would love to stay longer and talk with you," Amir said.

They made their way through the morning crowd to sit down. "It's great to be back in Omaha. I love the charm of this city, and I've got amazing business contacts here that I can always come back to."

Jennifer realized she had no idea what he did for a living. She took a sip from her iced coffee. "What kind of contacts do you work with? I'm curious about what you do."

"I'm kind of all over the place like Nari," Amir admitted. "I've got a few different businesses. But my favorite is the e-commerce business I run with my sister and my mom. We sell technical aids for seniors, like large-button keyboards and smart home systems. Things to help keep them safe and better navigate this modern world. I come to Omaha to meet with suppliers and negotiate better deals. My sister and I work on the product side.

"My mom travels to customers' homes to help them implement the systems. She loves it. And our customers like having someone from their generation to help, someone who's more tech savvy than them. My mom used to teach computer science at our local community college before she retired, so it's perfect for her. I've also got an online course business, some real estate holdings... A little bit of everything."

He worked with his family and helped seniors? Jennifer felt herself falling even harder for him. "That's incredible," she said.

He thanked her as he blew on his coffee and asked about her line of work.

"Oh you know. Marketing analyst for a food manufacturing company." She paused and felt her stomach turn as she thought about Essentrix Labs again.

"Oh yes. You work for Essentrix Labs, right?" He froze and looked like he regretted saying it.

She looked at him, puzzled. It didn't seem like something Nari would have told him. "How do you know that?"

He paused and cleared his throat. "I have a confession to make. Nari asked me for a ride a few nights ago. I had no idea what I was getting myself into. I came to pick you up in the middle of the night, and I drove you guys to the Essentrix Labs facility."

Jennifer's mouth fell open. She felt her arms prickle and sweat form on her hands. She glanced around them to see if anyone was listening. There were people lost in conversation, and rushed commuters glanced at their cell phones. No one seemed to be paying attention or even be in earshot.

She leaned in closer to him and whispered, "You were there the whole time? You heard our conversation? How much do you know?"

"I know it's a lot to take in," Amir responded. "Please know you can trust me. After the party, Nari called me up and asked me for a ride. I was up late at the hotel watching stand-up comedy and eating red licorice. My biggest vice. Nari's always been there for me, so of course I said yes."

Jennifer gulped.

"I didn't know you were going to be there," he continued, his voice hushed. "I was so excited to see you again, but you were wearing your bathrobe and seemed so dazed. I could tell you didn't know what you were getting into either. I wanted to give you some privacy."

"I was worried the driver knew what I looked like. I had no idea the driver might know me already." She wrung her hands, fighting the urge to down her entire drink all at once.

"We're in the same boat on this. I can't even jaywalk without getting chills. I never would have driven if I knew what Nari was asking me to do." He paused, bringing his hand toward his chin thoughtfully. "But I understand why you agreed to the mission. Essentrix Labs is the definition of evil. You must feel so betrayed after working for them for so many years."

Jennifer shivered. The hottest guy she'd seen in years already knew about her foray into the black market.

"I... I don't know what to say," she started. "I promise I'm not a criminal. It's not something I would normally do. I can't even lie to my mom when she asks what I'm eating for lunch and the answer is junk food. I couldn't sit by and watch while my employer profits off of people's suffering. I had to do something."

"I understand." Amir glanced around the room. He ran his fingers through his hair, and she glanced at his pec muscles as they shifted. "I might have even done the same thing myself. You can trust me. I'll never tell anyone. I like you a lot. And technically, I only dropped you off and drove back to the hotel. I have no proof of anything. For all I know, you wanted to go for a nighttime picnic in pajamas."

Jennifer laughed. "That would be pretty fun. Let's start a new evening trend where you have to guess what you're eating based on taste alone."

"I'm totally down for that." He shifted in his seat before taking a sip of his coffee. "If it's alright to ask, how did the mission go?"

She cleared her throat and whispered, "I think it went pretty well, as far as I can tell. I'm pretty sure we're going to be able to sell the...product. Nari's so good at sales."

A man sitting a few tables away coughed and looked at Jennifer, who froze. His gaze flickered back to his laptop. "And once that's done, we'll be able to do so much with the money. These women are going to be free. I might even be able to open my own surf shop in Hawaii," she continued.

Amir grinned. "That's incredible news. I'm so happy to hear you're planning to follow your passion. I'd love to be your first customer."

Jennifer's head was spinning. It seemed like he had forgiven her already. At least she wasn't entering into this new world of crime and riches alone. She had Nari and Amir by her side.

She glanced at her watch and frowned. "I should probably head to work before anyone gets suspicious. It was so good to see you. I appreciate the support and the open mind. And the coffee."

"Thanks for taking me out. I had a blast. And your secret's safe with me." He held her gaze and smiled.

The pair stood up, pushing in their chairs. She desperately wanted to stay. Maybe she could call into work, claiming fast-acting food poisoning from the pistachios. She and Amir would sit for a while, and she would playfully graze her fingers across his arm. He'd look at her hungrily, and within a minute they'd be making out. Time would stand still.

She felt an intense physical pull toward Amir. She wanted him but wasn't ready to make the first move. What if he didn't want anything serious?

"You're so welcome." She hesitated before barreling forward, unable to stop herself. "I really would love to see you again... Let me know the next time you're in Omaha." Her heart was pounding so hard in her chest that she could practically hear it.

The pair walked to the sidewalk in front of the coffee shop. "I absolutely will. And hit me up the next time you're in Detroit," he added.

She felt herself melt. A huge grin covered her face. *Stay cool, Jennifer,* she told herself.

Amir hugged Jennifer. It was warm with the perfect level of tightness and closeness. It seemed genuine. She felt herself relaxing into his embrace, wanting to stay there longer than was socially acceptable.

He pulled away slowly, his eyes shining.

"Goodbye." Jennifer waved him off.

He seemed like he wanted to see her again, but he hadn't asked for her number. Was he trying to be nice? Was he actually interested? Maybe she had misread his signals. As she walked to work, she bit her lip and replayed their conversation in her mind.

• • •

Jennifer breathed in deeply and tried to put on her most trustworthy face before walking through the entryway of her office building. *No one suspects us,* she thought as she stepped through the lobby and smoothed out her pencil skirt.

She said hello to her favorite security guard on duty, pulling out her badge to scan herself through the turnstiles.

The guard waved back, his face serious. "Hey, we've had a security incident. I'm going to need to check your bag."

Oh my gosh. She felt goosebumps form on her arms. Did she accidentally slip something incriminating into her purse? Maybe a random Sorbelate label?

"Sure thing," she said louder than intended. "Let me make sure that...my phone is in there!"

The security guard tilted his head toward her, looking impatient.

She opened her bag and squinted as she quickly rifled through, cursing her inability to keep her bag clean. "My phone always hides at the bottom, I know it's in here!" She giggled nervously.

The guard stared at her incredulously. She coughed and searched frenetically. She needed one more minute.

"Please, Jen. You're making it look like you're hiding something in there," he said with an edge to his voice.

She gulped and pulled out her phone. "There it is!" she exclaimed, passing her bag over in shaky hands.

If the guard found anything, she would pretend she had let someone else borrow her purse for the weekend. Someone she barely knew who also happened to have really bad judgment.

The security guard called a colleague over and whispered something to her. Jennifer bit her lip and closed her eyes. *I am a beautiful, mostly law-abiding marketing analyst, and I am not getting arrested today.*

He opened her bag and looked through, pulling out her hand sanitizer and a pack of tissues as he went.

"All good." He tipped his head toward her. "Thanks for your patience. We found some contraband on-site, so we've got to check everyone's bags."

Contraband. That didn't sound like stolen Sorbelate. Her throat went dry. "Have a great day," she replied as she walked over to the elevator. As soon as the doors closed, she bent over and leaned on the handlebar to steady her nerves.

Jennifer exited into her office lobby, glancing from one side to the other. She listened closely. It was quiet, except for the pounding in her ears. Some of her coworkers were chatting normally. She tried her best to walk casually past rows of desks on her way to the break room. Her colleagues smiled at her and milled around, settling in for the day. No one looked at her suspiciously.

Her fists loosened as she entered the cramped break room, stepping on the floor's large white and brown zigzag pattern and passing by two large high tables with padded stools. She slipped her lunch into the fridge, excited to eat Nari's home-made falafels. Lorinda was standing next to the counter.

"Hey, partner," Lorinda said. "Your boyfriend is cute."

Jennifer felt a knee-jerk sense of embarrassment, which gave way to something like pride. Lorinda had mistaken Amir for her boyfriend. Maybe one day he would be. And eventually their adorable kids would draw *oohs* and *ahs* everywhere. Their son would take after Amir, and their daughter after Jennifer.

"He's not my boyfriend," Jennifer replied, "but I agree. He is totally cute."

"Sure, he's not," Lorinda said playfully. "By the way, I'm having a New Yam Festival party this Saturday. Have you ever heard of that?" She handed Jennifer a colorful flyer with bold lettering.

It was like asking Michelangelo if he knew what paint was. "The Igbo festival of *Iri Ji*? Where the whole community comes together to offer up yams to their ancestors and the gods? I've been reading about this tradition since I was a kid," Jennifer said breathlessly.

Lorinda chuckled. "I had a feeling you'd know about it. I'd

love for you to join us. You can bring your roommate if you want."

Jennifer's chest tightened. She felt conflicted. She'd always wanted to celebrate *Iri Ji*. But why did it have to be with Lorinda?

"Thanks for the invitation." Jennifer willed her cheek muscles to mask her grimace. "I'll have to check my schedule."

Jennifer's work bestie, Karlie, walked into the break room. Her bright-blue eyes lit up when she saw Jennifer. "Happy Monday! It's great to see you!" She touched Jennifer's shoulder.

"It's great to see you too." Jennifer wanted to tell Karlie everything. How Essentrix Labs was evil. How she'd take them down but make sure Karlie landed on her feet. How she had run into an amazing guy this morning. But she willed herself to stay calm and act like everything was normal.

"Wasn't that contraband check crazy this morning? I've got to get to a meeting, but I can't wait to hear all about your weekend later." Karlie waved.

Great. Jennifer would have some extra time to devise a completely unconcerning story about how she stayed at home and looked at curtains online. She walked to her desk and turned her computer on. She sat at a big brown desk in a private office with three taupe walls and one glass one. There were no windows to the outside.

The welcome screen featured a picture of Jennifer, Karlie, and Nari belting into a karaoke microphone. Jennifer stood in the middle, an impassioned look on her face as she sang what looked like a drawn-out "O." Looking at the picture steadied her. Maybe they were singing an old-school R&B tune. She pictured Amir in the audience cheering them on. What a supportive, fun-loving partner he'd be.

Time to get to work. Jennifer opened her to-do list and stared at it blankly. Nothing looked interesting enough to start.

Her mind flitted back to the boxes of Sorbelate in their hallway closet. If the landlord knocked on the door and needed to look in the closet, she would panic.

Maybe it was best for Nari to hold down the fort for a while. Or she could leave scripted messages behind for Jennifer to follow if they had any unexpected visitors. Of course, Jennifer could always blast Motown music if anyone came over, pretending not to hear a thing.

"Hey, happy Monday." Her manager Mandy appeared in the doorway. "I've got a new project for you to work on. I think you're going to like it."

Jennifer blinked to clear her Motown fantasies from her mind.

"I'm here for it, boss." Jennifer winked. She tried to appear enthusiastic, even though Mandy sometimes oversold how enjoyable a new project would be.

Mandy was a pale, brunette woman with full cheeks and freckles who was down-to-earth and always treated Jennifer with respect. She was part of the reason Jennifer had stayed in the role of marketing analyst for so long, despite never getting a promotion. Her salary hadn't increased in seven years, although Mandy had fought for it.

"Your pay is actually *decreasing* with inflation," Nari had told her. "You need to find something better."

Jennifer knew Nari was right. She could have left the

company many times. She interviewed for jobs that paid more and even turned down a few job offers. Her reasons to stay made no sense. The air-conditioning was too strong. She'd have to sit next to a man who nervously shook his leg. She wouldn't be able to walk to Henry's to get fries on her lunch break anymore.

With a higher income, Jennifer could have saved up the money she needed to move to Hawaii and open her surf business. She only needed the capital to rent her surf shack, buy some boards, hire a team, and make smoothies.

But the truth was, she was terrified. If she made enough money, she'd have no excuse not to start her own business. And what if she had no idea what she was doing? So year after year, she shrunk back and kept accepting her small paycheck. But that was all going to change.

"I knew you would be," Mandy said. "You'll get the chance to do a lot of research for our new line of chunky peanut butter products. Your fave."

Jennifer cheered internally. No connection to cobalt, at least directly.

"You'll get to help the department advance in our market," said Mandy.

She nodded. At least Jennifer could make her coworkers' lives easier. None of them had done anything wrong, that she knew about.

"And you'll get to work with Lorinda," Mandy finished.

Jennifer felt herself wince but tried to cover up her anguish before it registered on her face. She smiled aggressively, probably a little too hard. Mandy drew back.

"Awesome." Jennifer gritted her teeth and swallowed hard.

Just what she needed. More competition with Lorinda to send her off. Although maybe this was a good parting gift, a welcome reminder of all the things she'd be excited to leave behind.

Mandy described a high-level overview of the project. Jennifer's mind drifted off. She was barely listening.

"Let me know if you have any questions." Mandy pivoted on her feet before turning back to face Jennifer. "Also, I forgot to ask. What were you doing on Saturday night? Say, around 3 AM?" Her face hardened.

Jennifer's throat went dry, and she suddenly couldn't speak. She didn't have an alibi prepared.

"Y-you know, uh... Mandy..." Her voice strangled as she grasped for a response. "I... I can't be so sure." *Great*. That was one of the worst things she could say, short of admitting to the theft. She eyed the exit and wondered how quickly she could make her way to the stairs without knocking over any desks. Mandy wasn't a runner. Jennifer could easily get ahead, putting a few flights of stairs between them. She tensed her muscles in case she needed to sprint.

Mandy raised an eyebrow. "Well, it sounds like you missed out on the blood moon! I should have told you about it sooner. I'm sorry about that. Let me show you some pictures." She pulled out her cell phone.

Jennifer's head was swimming. She tried to focus as her boss enthusiastically paged through one moonlit photo after another. "So stunning. I'll see you soon," Mandy said, tilting her head forward as she stepped out.

Today was going to be an amazing day. Jennifer just needed to stop shaking and visualize it. Everything would be perfectly normal. No one would suspect her of anything. She'd do only enough work to avoid getting fired. She'd stay away from all projects related to cobalt.

And then, one day, she would disappear, move to Hawaii, buy a beach condo, and open her surf business. Maybe some of the Essentrix team could join her. Then, instead of working with Lorinda in a windowless conference room, her biggest problems would be eating pineapple without the juice dripping down her chin and keeping sand out of her bikini bottoms.

She'd bring Amir along for the ride. Nari would develop elaborate systems for detecting the cops. It felt like a pretty good plan.

Oh right. Amir. A few days ago, Jennifer would have waited nervously for him to text her. But she had millions of dollars' worth of Sorbelate sitting in her hallway closet. She felt a boldness surge through her. She wasn't going to enter year thirty-seven merely imagining a relationship. Even if she had no idea what she would say, she needed to contact him.

She pulled out her phone and texted Nari, *"Hey, roomie. I met this guy at your party. Amir. Can you text me his phone number?"*

Within a minute, Nari wrote back, *"Oh my gosh! Of COURSE."*

CHAPTER 10

JENNIFER

That Tuesday, Jennifer stood next to Nari in a musty lobby.

A friendly man named Jimmy had buzzed them in. Jimmy was lanky and had an oily face. His khaki pants were too short, and his yellow button-down was too big for his frame. Was it also kind of see-through? Jennifer wondered.

The ceilings were low, and the lighting was yellow. Faded kitten posters adorned the walls. Come to think of it, the walls were faded too. There was something about this place that made it seem like it hadn't been updated—or even used—since the 1980s. At least there was a cold-water dispenser, which Jennifer took advantage of, downing three refills of the icy liquid that burned her throat from cone-shaped paper cups.

There was a lot at stake here. If they couldn't sell the Sorbelate, she wouldn't even be able to bail herself out of jail, let alone help anyone. This was the third pitch Nari had gone on this week to a prospect she had found through her network. What if they weren't interested either?

Nari asked Jennifer to come this time for extra support. Lorinda had teased her when she asked for the extra lunch time. "*Ohh*, going to see our boyfriend, are we?"

You had to *have* a boyfriend to sneak off and see one. But Lorinda's comment made Jennifer feel a quiet thrill. Maybe a relationship with Amir wasn't far off. She wanted to trace his juicy lips with her finger and stroke his curly dark hair.

Nari cleared her throat. She was looking at Jennifer knowingly.

Right. This Sorbelate needed to be sold so Jennifer could buy flight tickets for her and Amir to visit the beaches of Maui. It would be great to get the boxes out of the house too.

Even if she didn't know how to sell, she could always jump in with entertaining stories about how she and her dad had developed *the best* catapult to scare away squirrels in her backyard in suburban Detroit, modeled on Viking designs from their local library, of course.

Jennifer looked at her watch. They'd been waiting for nearly an hour past their appointment time. She was going to need more ice water to steady her nerves and a bathroom.

She wiped her clammy hands on her tweed skirt. Where was all this sweat coming from?

"Ms. Wales is ready to see you now," Jimmy called out from behind his too-large desk, pointing.

The first door opened into Ms. Wales's sparsely decorated office. There was one small, framed print with a pair of crossed flags. The US and Wales, was it? *Great sense of humor.*

The walls were probably white at some point, but now they

were faded yellow with years of built-up grime. The lighting was soft. There was one small window in the corner, but it was mostly covered up from the outside world by a noisy air-conditioning unit.

"Please, have a seat," Ms. Wales said in an upbeat, nasal voice. Jennifer and Nari obliged. Jennifer noticed with a smile that the floor was carpeted.

"Welcome to Flatland Industries. We're happy you're here." Ms. Wales handed them thick booklets with the company name printed on the front. Her tanned skin stood out against her pink skirt suit and white button-down.

Jennifer looked at Nari's calm and collected face. It steadied her.

"Our family business has been passed down across generations, each one sharper than the last. My great-grandpa was an immigrant from Ireland, and he started this company back in 1924 when he was only making a dollar a week as a farmhand. He wanted a piece of that American dream. Ten years ago, my mom retired and passed the business down to me. We're now the largest producer of white label diet soda pop syrup in the Midwest. We supply all the major and generic brands." Ms. Wales tucked her shoulder-length auburn hair behind her ears. "Jimmy tells me that you've come to sell me Sorbelate. We're in dire need."

"That's right," Nari said in a charming tone. "We are your connection to all things Sorbelate, sourced straight from Europe."

Ms. Wales grinned eagerly. "Great. Tell me about your company."

Jennifer's stomach dropped. They didn't even have a

company name, let alone a story to tell. What was a good, foreign-sounding name that inspired confidence?

"Uhh..." Jennifer started. "We've been at it for years. We've got, uh...chemists."

"That's right," Nari stepped in. "Here at Cambray Foods, we've got a team of chemists in Europe that have helped us formulate a healthier, more affordable version of Sorbelate. You can consume as much as you want with no side effects.

"Jennifer and I have been working side-by-side to improve the formulation for the past five years. Our blend is one hundred times more potent than our competitors, so you can use far less and save on every part of the logistics chain. Now it's been so dialed in that we're selling like hotcakes across Europe. We're the number one brand in Estonia and Ireland, for example."

"That's incredible," Ms. Wales replied, her green eyes sparkling. "I think my great-grandpa would be honored to use an ingredient that's popular in his homeland."

Jennifer watched in awe. She had no idea how Nari came up with these last-minute anecdotes.

"We're getting ready to launch in the US, since we've seen how high demand is here," Nari continued.

"You're not kidding." Ms. Wales tapped her khaki-colored fingernails on the desk. "We've been low on Sorbelate for months now. Our soda pop prices have skyrocketed, and we're losing out on sales. How much have you got?"

Wow. This might be an easier sell than Jennifer had thought.

"We've got so much that we're the most in-demand women in the Midwest." Nari winked. This was definitely not true, Jennifer thought. They only had one hundred boxes.

"I'd love to see some samples," Ms. Wales replied.

Jennifer hadn't thought of bringing samples. She started to panic. This whole sales pitch was going to go down the tubes.

"Sure thing, Ms. Wales. I'm happy to share some with you." Nari reached into her purse. She pulled out a manila folder containing a small Ziploc bag that reminded Jennifer of the drug bags she saw on her favorite crime shows.

Ms. Wales looked at the bag and turned it over in her palm. "I'll have our team test this. If everything looks good, we'll take four hundred and seventy-five kilos to start."

Four hundred and seventy-five kilos? Jennifer couldn't believe her ears. She did some quick math on her phone. That would be ninety-five boxes. Fifty thousand dollars a box. *Oh my gosh...that's almost five million dollars.*

"We'd love to fulfill your order," Nari said. "We require payment on delivery. As you know, we are the most in-demand ingredient in the soda pop supply chain right now. It'll be worth your while."

"On delivery?" Ms. Wales paused. She furrowed her brow and stood up from her desk.

Jennifer's heart sank. This was quite the roller coaster. Was that a normal request? Had Nari said something totally unprofessional? She readied herself for Ms. Wales to ask them to leave.

"That works for us," said Ms. Wales. "I'll have Jimmy look into it for me. We'll be in touch with you soon after testing is complete."

CHAPTER 11

JENNIFER

Lorinda lived in a tree-lined, quiet part of Omaha that Jennifer had never been to before. It was easy to tell which house was hers. Dozens of cars were parked outside, and a handful of balloons were tied to the mailbox. The sounds of rhythmic Afrobeat music emerged into the street.

"Oh my gosh," Jennifer said, her mouth open. "I'm so excited for this party!" Nari had convinced her to go, but deep down she had wanted to be persuaded.

Something about being there in the moment, ready to celebrate *Iri Ji*, made Jennifer forget her desire to unseat Lorinda from her workplace throne. She smoothed out her bright-green and orange *Ankara* printed blouse, gifted by Nari as a heist advance. It was form-fitting at the top and fluted out at the waist in a wavy pattern. Nari looked great in her matching coral and brown number.

The pair danced together as they walked up the path, the

music growing louder. The door flew open before Jennifer had the chance to knock.

A woman in a colorful traditional shirt with a button nose and shoulder-length cornrows opened the door. "*Nnọọ!*" she exclaimed, hugging Jennifer and then Nari. "That means 'welcome' in Igbo! I'm Lorinda's cousin and roommate, Uchenna. Come on in!" She had a strong Omaha accent.

Jennifer felt a sense of validation that Essentrix Labs's star employee was also in her mid-thirties and living with a roommate.

The room was filled with people wearing brightly patterned clothing, holding drinks and chatting pleasantly.

The walls were covered in palm leaf decorations. A table stood in the middle of the room, covered in *Ankara* fabric with multi-colored geometric sunbursts and decoratively piled yams in woven baskets. There were vases of flowers and bowls of fragrant fresh fruit. The smell of spicy fried yams floated up to Jennifer's nostrils.

No one was dancing yet, but she knew it was coming. She could talk to Uchenna for a bit then slip into a casual dance-off with someone who could teach her some Igbo phrases and dance moves.

"I was just talking to my friend Roberta," Uchenna said. "I'd love to introduce you." Roberta turned and smiled and shook Nari and Jennifer's hands.

Roberta had dark hair and light-brown skin. She wore a yellow, red, and blue *Ankara* blouse with piping down the front and large, ruffled sleeves.

"Hi, Roberta. I'm Jennifer, and this is Nari. First New Yam Festival, I'm guessing?

Roberta grinned. "Nice to meet you. I haven't had the privilege of joining one before. Luckily, Uchenna saved me the cost of a plane ticket to Lagos. She even let me borrow her blouse."

"The full experience of the Igbo villages without the time change. That's the worst part. Please, make yourselves at home. You have to try some Zobo. Let me get you each a glass." Uchenna walked up to a side table and filled three plastic cups with a dark-purple liquid from an ice-filled glass dispenser. "This is a traditional hibiscus drink with ginger and cloves. It's my grandma's recipe, but I'm sworn to secrecy!" She snorted as she passed the cups out.

"I'm impressed! My grandma would never share her recipes with me. You must be a master of persuasion." Nari tasted her juice. "Wow, this is amazing."

"I'm so glad you like it. Enjoy the top secret recipe, ladies. I'll be back soon!" Uchenna waved and disappeared back into the crowd.

Jennifer sipped her Zobo, and a sweet and spicy flavor touched her tongue. The drink was so cold that she flinched.

"Tell me, are you two from Omaha originally?" Roberta asked.

"Sadly, we can't claim these cornfields as our own," Nari said. "I've been here for about a year. My roommate, on the other hand..." She motioned to Jennifer.

"Fifteen years." Jennnifer beamed. "I'm still a Michigan woman at heart, but I guess now I have dual citizenship." She laughed at her own joke.

"For now, at least," Nari added.

"Two out-of-towners. I love it," Roberta replied. "I'm an Omaha local myself, born and raised."

Karlie emerged from the crowd and tapped Nari on the shoulder. "Hey, friends!" she called out. Jennifer waved as Karlie and Nari greeted each other.

"Love that," Jennifer said to Roberta. "Native Omahans are the best. It's such a friendly city. I never thought I would be here this long, but something always convinces me to stay." Her bank account was what always convinced her to stay, but that was all going to change soon.

"I hear you. I left for a few months in college, but Omaha's like a magnet," Roberta said thoughtfully. "It drew me back in. I'll put up with the winters to be near my amazing friends and family."

Jennifer nodded. "So how do you know Uchenna?"

"Oh, we go way back." Roberta waved dismissively. "Uchenna and I played on the basketball team together in junior high. We've been competitive ever since then. She thinks she'll play better than me someday, but she never will. Don't tell her I said that. She'll tell you the opposite."

Jennifer giggled. "Basketball, huh? It sounds like you two still play together."

"Oh yeah," Roberta said. "We play in a women's league at Walnut Park every Tuesday night. You should join sometime if you're into that kind of thing."

"I love basketball, but I'm more of a runner. Hand-eye coordination is not really my thing," Jennifer remarked.

Roberta grinned. "Fair enough. How do you know Uchenna?"

"You know, I met her today. I work with her cousin Lorinda. She's...my coworker," Jennifer stammered, trying to keep herself from launching into a tirade about Lorinda's excessive perfection and professionalism. She gulped down some Zobo and flinched again as the cold stung her teeth.

Roberta tilted her head to the side. "Lorinda's a sweet person. She's always trying to cook for me."

Jennifer couldn't bring herself to imagine Lorinda being a good cook. She had to be bad at something. "What line of work are you in, Roberta?"

"I'm a police officer with the Omaha State PD. You could say it keeps me busy," Roberta said, taking a sip of her Zobo. "How about you?"

Jennifer felt her face get hot and had the sudden urge to run. If she stayed in this conversation much longer, she would accidentally say the word "Sorbelate" and end up in a high-speed foot chase across town. At least she was wearing ballet flats this time.

Roberta looked at her expectantly.

"I... I'm a marketing analyst," Jennifer managed.

Roberta seemed to be picking up on Jennifer's panic. She cocked her head to one side and narrowed her eyes. "Interesting. You know, in my typical workday, I deal with a lot of people who are hiding something."

Jennifer gulped. It was as if she had a flashing sign above her head, reading "thief." She paused. Now would be the worst time to turn and run. She'd only look more suspicious. She crossed her fingers behind her back for good luck and tested out some breathing techniques from yoga class. In through the nose, out through the mouth.

"Really? That's so fascinating, Roberta," Jennifer said, trying to steady her voice.

"Yeah, I might even venture to say that you're hiding something from me." Roberta's face was serious.

Jennifer felt her hands shaking. She smoothed the edges of her *Ankara* blouse and glanced at Nari. She wondered what would happen if she tossed her lipstick at Nari to get her attention. Nonchalantly, of course.

"Oh, you know. I hide all sorts of things," Jennifer said. "Like my distaste for boy bands. Even the ones from the sixties."

Roberta laughed, but with an ironic edge. "I think you're hiding something more serious."

Jennifer gritted her teeth. She wondered if she could cut a deal with Roberta. They would give back the Sorbelate calmly, and Roberta would reward them with no jail time. Maybe just roadside community service, picking up trash on the highway. "Really, Roberta?"

"Yeah, I think you don't actually like that juice." Roberta raised an eyebrow.

"What?" Jennifer coughed, suppressing the dazed urge to laugh.

"Every time you drink it, you make a sour face. Like you've eaten a lemon. It's an acquired taste. I don't blame you. I'm heading to the bathroom, I can dump it for you," Roberta said. "No one will know."

Jennifer grinned sheepishly and handed her cup to Roberta. She'd get another cup of Zobo when Roberta wasn't looking. "Thanks for the support. It was great meeting you."

"Likewise. I'll see you soon." Roberta turned and walked toward the hallway.

Jennifer approached Nari and Karlie.

"You came!" Karlie danced excitedly. "I never thought I'd see you at Lorinda's house," she added under her breath.

"You've got to check out the spread here," Nari said. Jennifer wanted to warn her that a perfectly normal-seeming woman lurking in the bathroom and clad in an *Ankara* blouse was actually a police officer.

Lorinda approached the group, enveloping each woman in a tight hug. "It's so good to see you all!" She motioned toward a side table covered in food and drink. "Please, help yourselves. We're going to start the ceremony soon!" She rushed back into the crowd and continued hugging and greeting people.

"Nari," Jennifer hissed, motioning for her roommate to join her in the kitchen.

Nari looked at her with a mixture of confusion and amusement. They stepped into the kitchen, which was unoccupied but packed with cutting boards, plates of appetizers, and stacks of dishes and napkins.

"There's a cop here," Jennifer whispered.

Nari stared blankly. "And..."

"And we need to leave now," Jennifer said, her voice hushed. "I could accidentally reveal anything at any time."

"Play it cool," Nari responded smoothly. "It doesn't look good if we leave right after you met the cop. We should stay a little bit longer. Is she the black-haired woman you were talking to with the ruffled sleeves?"

"Yeah, that's her," Jennifer said.

"We need to act natural, like we have nothing to hide," Nari explained, her voice low. "No one even knows the product is missing."

Jennifer was grateful for Nari's clarity. She only needed to forget that she and her roommate were thieves for a little while.

The sound of a microphone's feedback reverberated into

the room, and the music lowered. Jennifer looked up at Nari, who nodded encouragingly. They walked back into the living room, where Lorinda's cousin Uchenna stood next to the yam table.

"Welcome, everyone!" Uchenna exclaimed into the microphone in her charming Omaha accent. "We're excited to celebrate the New Yam Festival with all of you today."

The crowd murmured. "Go, Uchenna!" a full-figured woman dressed in a pink *Ankara* top cheered.

"I'd love to get some help from my good friend, Roberta, as we kick off the ceremony." Uchenna gestured to an array of yam preparations on the table, including fried yam balls, which Jennifer recognized hungrily as *ojojo*.

Jennifer watched as Roberta walked through the crowd toward the microphone. Her shoulders tensed. She blinked and tried to imagine that Roberta was a random delivery driver who stumbled into the party to drop off some soda. She only wanted to get a good tip and didn't care about anyone's backstories.

Nari was already deep in conversation with Karlie, who had rejoined them. "You know, I've never been to Nigeria, but it's on my bucket list," Nari said.

Jennifer peered into the backyard. Lorinda was outside pacing, and her voice was growing tense.

"First, we are going to thank our ancestors and our Earth goddess who brought us this bountiful harvest," Uchenna said excitedly into the microphone.

"This is like Jennifer's Super Bowl," Nari joked.

"Oh, you know it." Jennifer's eyes flitted across the room. Above the murmur of the crowd, she could hear Lorinda's voice rising in the backyard. She was speaking animatedly. At least she seemed happier now.

Jennifer couldn't fight the urge to investigate. "I'll be right back," she murmured.

"Make sure you get some yams," Nari said.

Jennifer tried to look confident by taking measured steps toward the backyard where Lorinda was standing. The crowd was so focused on the yam table that no one seemed to notice her. She leaned against the door frame and strained to listen.

Lorinda's back was facing Jennifer. "Is your contact at the Ministry of Finance still cooperating?"

Jennifer inched forward slowly.

"Great. If we can make it happen, this deal could be worth at least one hundred thousand euros." Lorinda turned to pace the yard. "We'll split the commission."

Jennifer froze and backed up behind the door frame. What kind of lucrative government mission was Lorinda on? She imagined Lorinda walking the island streets of Nicosia, Cyprus, flanked by four other women in sunglasses and formal office wear. They'd surround the stubborn official from the Ministry of Finance in an alleyway and push him into the back of a vehicle with blacked-out windows.

"Perfect. Seems like we can smooth this out at our meeting on Thursday." Lorinda turned her gaze toward Jennifer and their eyes met. "Talk soon." She hung up quickly.

Jennifer willed herself to smile and tried to glance around casually. "This party is great," she said, her voice shaking.

"Hey, I'm happy you could make it," Lorinda said cautiously. "How long have you been standing there?"

"Oh, a minute or two," Jennifer replied, as laid back as she could.

"Let's go inside. You've got to try a few types of yams, and it's going to be time to dance soon." Lorinda grinned.

Inside, Roberta and Uchenna were passing out plates of yam balls and shiny roasted yams with a delectable-looking red sauce to each guest in a long line that coiled around the living room.

"Don't forget to grab a glass of tamarind juice!" Uchenna exclaimed to a slight pale woman with short brown hair and glasses.

Lorinda motioned toward the line. "Please, try some yams, Jennifer," she said. "I think you'll love the *asaro*, yam porridge, with plantains on the side."

Jennifer's mind was racing. Lorinda was the most beloved employee Essentrix Labs had ever seen. What was this Omaha queen of operations doing with some Ministry of Finance in Europe? What covert side hustle was she working on? Lorinda must be up to something sketchy. What if she was successfully evading the cops in multiple countries?

Suddenly, Jennifer didn't want to avoid Lorinda anymore. In fact, when this mission was all over and the Sorbelate was sold, Jennifer would have loads of money and plenty of free time. Maybe Lorinda needed her help.

Rhythmic Afrobeat music started to play over the speakers, a man and a woman singing together melodically. Uchenna motioned for the guests to join her on the dance floor.

"Now, it's time to celebrate our harvest!" she announced. "Lorinda and I will teach you some traditional dance moves!"

Nari and Karlie came over and each grabbed one of Jennifer's hands.

"Come on, Jen," Karlie said.

The three women joyfully followed Uchenna's lead, copying her graceful shoulder rolls and waist twists. Roberta danced alongside her.

"You're a natural at this!" Nari exclaimed.

"I'd like to thank all of our kitchen dance parties for preparing me for this moment," Jennifer said.

Lorinda started to step rhythmically. "Now it's time to move your feet!"

The entire crowd swayed and danced, singing along with the high-energy music.

Maybe Lorinda wasn't so bad after all.

•   •   •

That night, Jennifer couldn't stop thinking about Amir while she pinned up her twists and got ready for bed. She wanted to see him again, even if that meant she had to go to Michigan.

Her breath caught in her throat. It was time. She was ready to text Amir. Maybe with her new heist woman energy, she'd come up with a message. She pulled out her phone, typed in Amir's name, and wrote, *"Hey, Amir. It's Jennifer."*

She paused. She wasn't ready to tell him how she felt yet. A joke would be much safer. *"It was so great to see you. Hopefully you've made it back safely—no bunny encounters."*

Within a minute, her phone buzzed. *"Jennifer! It's so great to hear from you. I've been thinking about you. Luckily, I've been bunny-free. But thanks to you, I'll be ready if I see one."* Amir ended the message with a winking emoji and a bunny emoji. Another message came in a second later. *"Want to chat sometime?"*

Jennifer couldn't stop smiling. *He wants to talk to me sometime?* She re-read the message to be sure. *"I would love that,"* she replied. She would prepare for their conversation later.

CHAPTER 12

NARI

The gym was packed that morning with men and women of all ages. Nari was synced up with two other women in the circuit training section in front of floor to ceiling mirrors. She sat at the leg extension machine, grasping the handles and straining to move a higher weight than normal.

Her phone started to buzz. It was Ms. Wales.

Nari gasped and fumbled to answer. She paused her leg extensions.

"Thanks for calling Cambray Foods. This is Nari. How can I help you?" Nari stood and nodded at the woman next to her, who was waiting for the leg extension machine.

"This is Ms. Wales. I'm so happy to call you. Our lab sent the results back, and your Sorbelate performed perfectly in every test. I spoke with the team, and we'd like to order more," she said.

Nari raised a hand to her mouth. "That's fantastic news.

Cambray Foods is thrilled that you love the product. We'll go the extra mile to deliver for you. How many kilos would you like?"

"I'd like to double our order. Your product is incredible and shelf stable. Let's go with one thousand kilos total," Ms. Wales said. "We can pay on delivery, like you requested."

They only had five hundred kilos total. Small detail. Nari bit her lower lip. She would have to figure out how to get the extra Sorbelate, but she was ready for any challenge.

"Wonderful. We're thrilled to do business with you," Nari replied. "We can have the order ready for you in two months." That seemed like enough time.

Ms. Wales paused. "I'm sorry, but we can't wait that long. We need the Sorbelate delivered by the end of the month. If you can't fulfill the order by then, we're going to have to move forward with another supplier."

Nari gulped and wiped her hands on her shorts. The end of the month was a little over three weeks away. "That'll be no problem. We want to work with you here at Cambray Foods. We'll shift a few things around so we can fulfill your order by month's end."

"Great," Ms. Wales responded cheerfully. "I really wanted to work together. I'll have my team send over the purchase order today. Thanks for bringing us this opportunity."

"You're so welcome. Looking forward to it. Talk to you soon." Nari's pulse quickened in excitement, and she lightly pumped her fist in the air. She exited the gym and waved to the woman working the front desk.

Feverishly, she started to do the math in her head. One thousand kilos was two hundred boxes. At a profit of fifty thousand dollars per box, she and Jennifer would make ten million dollars total. A massive grin overtook Nari's face. Eight figures. That would really make her mom proud. She couldn't wait to make it happen.

As she walked to the parking lot, she dialed Johannes's number on her encrypted calling app and immediately shared the news.

"Excellent," Johannes replied. "Let me make some calls and see how we can make this happen."

•   •   •

Once Nari arrived back at the apartment, Jennifer greeted her excitedly. Nari forgot she was working from home today, although it looked like she was barely working. "Guess what? I've been texting Amir all morning. He's so hilarious!" Jennifer jumped up and down and danced goofily in her home office black jeggings.

"That's amazing news! You two are so perfect together!" Nari cheered.

Nari's phone started to buzz. It was Johannes. "Excuse me, roomie." She stepped into her room so that Jennifer wouldn't overhear the conversation.

"Hi, Nari. My contact can get you three hundred more boxes, even more than you need," Johannes started. "But you'll have to retrieve them all in one night. They can't split them up for you. You're going to need a bigger team. You'll be able to get them before the end of the month on the twenty-ninth. Come by the same location at 1:00 AM. Bye."

Nari couldn't believe their luck. She was excited to tell

Jennifer how much money they were about to make. But first, she had to ask Jennifer for her help to pull off another, bigger mission. That might not go over so well.

Slowly, she walked back into the living room. Jennifer was flipping through a comic book on the couch. "Hey, you have to see this spy scene in ancient Ethiopia. The artistry here is incredible."

Nari bit her lip to hold in her guilt and sat next to Jennifer. "Wow," she said, glancing over the page. "That's really well done. Listen, I've got some news to share."

Jennifer's eyes lit up. "Tell me, roomie."

"We passed the inspection at Flatland Industries," Nari started. "And Ms. Wales wants even more Sorbelate."

Jennifer bounced in her seat. "Yay! *We're going to be so rich*," she sang. She looked up at Nari's serious facial expression. "Wait. This is good news, right?"

Nari paused. "Johannes can get us the product that we need, but we're going to have to run another heist to get it."

"No, Nari..." Jennifer's voice rose. "I am not going anywhere near that facility again! Why don't you tell Ms. Wales we can only sell her the amount we already have?"

Nari stood and faced Jennifer. "We could stop there. But why would we when we can make so much more money?"

"You know why burglars get caught? Because they're never satisfied. They stay in the same towns and go back to the same banks. The cops catch on." Jennifer was speaking quickly now. "I can't wear my GPS watch in jail. How would I track my runs? If you want to do another mission, you need to find someone else."

Nari felt a heavy, sinking feeling in her chest. She ran her fingers through her hair and walked back and forth across the living room. She would need to regroup. "Alright, fair enough," she sighed. "You don't have to join. I'll split the first-round profits with you, and I'll bring in another team for the second job. I can't ask you to do something you're not comfortable with."

"Good," Jennifer responded, her facial expression softening.

Nari would need to find at least two more people to scale up for the next job, hopefully three. It wouldn't be nearly as fun without Jennifer, but luckily she would have a few days to build her team this time around.

She wondered who she could call for help. Maybe Martha, the beautiful food services magnate from Mexico City. She was creative, powerful, and used unconventional techniques to get what she wanted. She was also fit and could probably hold her own in an urban obstacle course. Although the money wouldn't be that big of a draw—Nari was pretty sure she was worth many millions—she might be drawn in by the opportunity to take down a bad company.

They would need at least one more person. Who could she invite? Then it hit her. She knew which shrewd businesswoman would have no trouble bending the law and would keep absolute discretion. Someone with a commanding presence and incredible track record that she desperately wanted to impress.

Nari hesitated, knowing she might lose some control over the heist if she brought on such a towering figure. It had been so long since they had worked together. She might get turned down if she asked for help. Worse, she might even look weak.

She swallowed hard. She had no choice if she wanted to build a powerful team. She stepped into her bedroom, typed *"Mom"* into her phone, and called.

CHAPTER 13

JENNIFER

Twenty-four days until heist day

Jennifer walked into the break room at Essentrix Labs. She had gotten into work early for a change.

The room was empty, except for Lorinda, who was standing at the counter pouring a glass of orange juice.

"Jennifer!" Lorinda embraced her tightly. "Uchenna and I had so many leftover oranges from the party that I had to make some fresh juice for the team. Here, have some." She poured some juice into another glass and handed it over.

"Thank you." Jennifer took a sip. The juice was cool and the perfect balance between tart and sweet.

She glanced at Lorinda, who was humming and cleaning off the counter.

Her mind flitted to Lorinda's secretive phone conversation at the Iri Ji event. She bit her lip and tried to organize her thoughts. "At the party, I overheard you talking about a Ministry of Finance," she began slowly. "I totally understand if it's private, but I would love to learn more if you're open to sharing." There. That could have been much worse.

Lorinda froze and stood silently. She took a sip of orange juice from her glass and placed the pitcher back into the refrigerator. After a moment, her expression lightened, and Jennifer felt her tension loosen.

"I'm happy to tell you more," Lorinda said slowly. "I like you, Jennifer. Just don't tell anyone at Essentrix Labs what I'm about to say."

"Your secret's safe with me," Jennifer responded.

Lorinda drummed her fingers on her arm. She glanced around the break room, seeming to check whether it was still empty. "I'm working on some projects in Africa..." She paused for a beat. "With European government officials. It's kind of a side gig."

Jennifer's eyes widened. "How did you get involved in that? That's so cool," she gushed, taking a napkin from the counter to dab orange juice from her upper lip.

"You know, I always wanted to do this type of work. To be honest, there's so much corruption back home. But a lot of it is supported by foreign governments in ways that no one ever talks about," Lorinda said.

"I know that is absolutely true," Jennifer agreed.

"I help European politicians invest in West African businesses." Lorinda lowered her voice and leaned in closer to Jennifer. "We work with local nonprofits to train and fund women entrepreneurs."

Jennifer couldn't believe her ears. "I'm so impressed. How do you find politicians to work with you?"

Lorinda cleared her throat. "That's the fun part. They've all profited from shady businesses across the African continent. Their wallets got fat while people suffered. So, I...put some pressure on them." She took in Jennifer's expression and her face lit up. "All they have to do is invest in women-owned businesses every now and then. In return, I promise not to tell the media about their crooked pasts."

Jennifer pressed a palm to her chest. Lorinda was blackmailing bad guys. She was quickly turning into Jennifer's new idol.

"It works. Public attention is high, and people are demanding accountability from their politicians. I know you care about small African communities. I'm doing what I can to raise them back up," Lorinda finished.

"You're amazing. But I've got to ask. Why are you still working here at Essentrix Labs?" Jennifer asked.

"I'm still getting my projects off the ground. Plus, Essentrix Labs just submitted my green card application, so I'm loyal," Lorinda explained.

"I can't believe you have the time to be our top employee and also fight global corruption," Jennifer said in awe. "What countries will you invest in?"

"Someday, I want to support every country on the continent." Lorinda looked off to the end of the break room. "But for now, I've got projects in Nigeria, Angola, and the DRC. I've got partners who can speak Portuguese and French, as well as other local languages."

The DRC. *The mines.* Jennifer felt a warmth rising in her chest. Everything was falling into place. Together with Lorinda's team, the heist crew could transform the mine workers' lives. Jennifer would just need a convenient story to explain to Lorinda why she suddenly had millions of dollars to invest. One step at a time.

"If you ever need help, I'd love to volunteer for you," Jennifer said. She could stick it to some bad guys and maybe meet some powerful people in foreign governments along the way.

"I might need an extra set of hands sometime," Lorinda replied warmly. "I think you'd be perfect."

Jennifer beamed. "Thank you." She lowered her voice. "I've always wanted to step outside of Essentrix Labs and move on. Maybe do something on my own, like you. You inspire me."

Lorinda's eyes sparkled. "You always have such great insights. I think you could start a business anytime. What would you launch?"

Jennifer tilted her head to the side and savored Lorinda's words. "That's amazing of you to say. I'm not sure I could ever pull it off, but I'd love to open a surf shop in Hawaii someday. I want to help people step away from their regular lives and learn to *ride the wave*," she snorted then lowered her eyes. "I wouldn't be helping people in the same way that you do though."

Lorinda laughed. "That explains those beachy pictures taped to your monitor. I think that's such an exciting idea. If it brings joy to you and others, it's worth doing. If you had all the capital you needed today, would you do it?"

Jennifer exhaled jaggedly and wrung her hands. "There's so much to learn. You're so knowledgeable. I wouldn't know where to begin. I've got to find and understand my customers. I've got to choose a good location. Somehow, I need to hire and motivate a team to work hard, instead of drawing hearts in the sand. I don't even know how to do my *own* taxes..."

Lorinda reached out and touched Jennifer's shoulder. "You don't have to figure it all out right now, partner. You just need to recognize how to take the next step. I've learned everything I've needed at exactly the right time to grow my business. You've got to trust in yourself, and you'll find all the answers that you need."

Jennifer relaxed her shoulders.

CHAPTER 14

JENNIFER

Twenty-two days until heist day

As Jennifer watched Nari pace the apartment explaining the second heist to her new recruits, she felt a pang of regret. The feelings confused her. Why did she feel left out? She had a stable job, a great apartment, and most importantly her freedom. She could write comic books anytime she wanted, run on the Missouri River, and once the payout from the first job came in, she and Amir could swim with dolphins on a glittering beach in Lebanon, taking breaks to dip radishes in lemony hummus.

She would be rich and free.

Two days after their conversation, Nari was putting on mascara in the kitchen mirror as Jennifer read the paper and got ready for her run.

"Great news." Nari buzzed with energy as she focused on

her eyelashes. "My mom is joining the team. She knows exactly what to do to evade the cops. And Martha is onboard too. She says she talked to you at Seoul Kitchen. She's a hacker who can get inside anyone's head and into any database."

Jennifer smiled, trying to hide her growing desire to join them. She took a sip of her electrolyte mix. "The team sounds really impressive. I'm really happy for you. Also, I had no idea your mom would be into this sort of thing."

Nari walked to a set of hooks on the wall and removed her keys. "Oh, my mom is the original mastermind. We've already had a couple of encrypted video chats, but the planning gets real this weekend when they arrive!" She clapped and squealed. "It's all coming together. I'm heading to Shop N Save. Do you need anything?"

Jennifer shook her head. "All good, roomie."

Nari grabbed her bag and waved as she left the apartment.

That day at the office, Jennifer tried to distract herself with long chats with coworkers and extra trips to the break room. She drank double her usual ice water quota and focused more than usual on her boss Mandy's presentations.

But she couldn't stop herself from researching the Essentrix Labs mines. In a private browsing window, of course. She read stories of once-vibrant communities struggling with lung disease, injuries, and even early death. Her hands tightened into fists, and she felt sick. When she went to the bathroom, she couldn't stomach seeing animal-feed pamphlets on the hallway shelves. She told Mandy she wasn't feeling well and needed to leave early. It was true.

That night, Jennifer couldn't sleep. She spent hours imagining herself joining a group of women bandits in the ancient city of Timbuktu. They scaled walls to steal gold coins and blocks of salt from tyrannical rulers and delivered the riches to the townspeople. Of course, the bandits would keep some wealth for themselves. They had camels to buy too.

Jennifer felt restless, a fire in her skin. She opened her eyes.

I can do the same, she thought. Her dad had taught her to stand up for what was right, even when it was hard. If she and the team could pull off a second heist, the women in the mines would be set for life. They could get entrepreneur training, launch thriving businesses, and transform their communities. They would be free. They would throw boat parties on the Congo River, get matching pedicures, and feel as powerful as she did. They would all get rich together.

And Essentrix Labs would crumble.

Jennifer sat up. She couldn't deny her impulses anymore. She wanted to be in on the action, learning from everyone involved and making a difference in the miners' lives.

More importantly, she was thirty-six, and her life was probably almost half over, give or take a few years. Was she going to keep getting her adventures from comic books and daydreams alone?

The next evening, Nari and Jennifer glided across the smooth roller rink floor in their matching glittery pink roller skates as seventies disco tunes blared through the sound system. Nari had gifted them a roommate set last Christmas. She bounced and shook her arms to the rhythm.

"You know, I've been thinking," Jennifer began as they passed by a crew of teenagers joking around and chewing bubble gum.

"Mhmm?" Nari replied cheerfully.

"Do you have room for one more on the heist team?" Jennifer whispered. "I think I'd like to join."

Nari whooped and covered her mouth to dampen the sound. "There is no one I would rather have on my team than you!" She embraced Jennifer tightly.

CHAPTER 15

NARI

Twenty-one days until heist day

The Sorbelate heist team had just doubled in size.

Now that everyone had arrived at Jennifer and Nari's apartment, the four women could get to know each other and plan their mission over the perfect Midwestern meal: breakfast for dinner, complete with pancakes, hash browns, and sausages. Jennifer had suggested it, of course.

Out of the corner of her eye, Nari could see Jennifer glancing around their dark-wood dining table to see if anyone was watching. When the coast was clear, Jennifer doused her entire plate with maple syrup from a sticky takeaway container.

"What do you do, Martha?" Jennifer asked. "We never got to talk about it. It's great to have you join the team."

Martha beamed. Her sleek white pants and ruffled red shirt looked great against her light beige skin. "Thanks for having me," she said in her lovely, melodic accent. "You know, I grew up on a mango farm in Jalisco. I thought I was going to be a farmer one day too."

Jennifer nodded, a look of fascination on her face.

"But instead I moved to Mexico City when I was in my twenties and started selling my parents' mangoes to high-end restaurants. Things kind of snowballed from there..." Martha said.

"Now she has an empire of food and beverage businesses across Latin America," Nari added.

"You could say that." Martha grinned. "I've gained a lot of experience with hacking over the years to enter my business into new markets."

"Okay, you can't leave it at that." Jennifer cut her pancake with a knife and fork. "You have to tell us more."

"There are so many ways to get what you need, *amiga*." Martha's eyes glinted playfully. "Like last month, a competitor tried to get the Panamanian government to deny my permits. So I leaked their communications to the media. Then I slipped into the government database to move my documents along."

"Your skills will be an asset to the team," Hana said, her familiar accent muddling a touch of Seoul with the American East Coast. At sixty-five, she hadn't aged at all since the last time Nari saw her. Her skin was radiant, her shoulder-length black hair perfectly coiffed.

"Thank you," Martha replied warmly. "But I have a confession to make. I have a history with Essentrix Labs."

Nari's eyes grew wide, and she brought her hand up to her chin. "Unbelievable, Ramírez."

"A couple years ago, Essentrix Labs approached me for a

partnership. They wanted to use our mango extract for their tropical cereal line. It was going to be a huge contract. We sent over some samples and waited for the good news. Instead, they turned down our deal, and a few months later they stole our formula," Martha explained.

"No way!" Jennifer gasped. "That's one of our bestsellers!"

"They've made millions off of our blend," Martha agreed. "But that's nothing compared to what Essentrix Labs has done to others. I can't wait to fight back against them, and I'm even more thrilled to work with a group of smart women."

"You've come to the right place," Nari said, her voice swelling. "Perfect segue. This mission is going to pay off, big time. If all goes well, we're each going to make one million dollars, and we'll be able to give the women in the Congo six million dollars. Everyone will win. But we can't make mistakes. We need to work like a well-oiled machine."

Nari explained the plan of attack. They would do many of the same things as last time: grab the boxes from the park, slide through the fence, follow the perfect route to avoid detection from the camera, and load the truck.

They didn't have much time to prepare. The job was in three weeks. All of them would need to train with both weight lifting and running.

"I can lead the team in sprint training," Jennifer said. "It'll speed up our pace faster than long-distance running. We'll run for three hundred meters then walk for one hundred meters. On and off."

Nari agreed to guide them in weight training for their arms, legs, and core. "The boxes weigh five kilos each, and we'll each need to be able to run while carrying at least four at a time."

"I'm in," Martha said. "I work out every day. Pilates and strength training. I have no problem kicking it up a notch."

The group turned to look at Hana.

"I took Pilates once," Hana joked. "But don't worry. I can get back into the game. I eat healthy too. I've even cut out red meat." Nari gave her a surprised look as she bit into her sausage. "Well, most of the time," she added.

The group pushed in their chairs and began migrating to the living room.

"Come here, *nae jasik,* my child," Hana said, embracing Nari and stroking her hair. "I'm so proud of you. You're really blossoming as an entrepreneur. You're discovering opportunities everywhere."

Nari beamed. Her mom's approval meant everything to her, and she didn't always get it. She had the urge to luxuriate in the moment with a pot of her mom's warm and spicy *sundubu-jjigae* tofu soup that she would excitedly share with the team. Through all her childhood moves, the soup was a constant.

She glanced around the room and felt excited to be working with a team of such talented women.

Martha had a peaceful expression on her face. She had already shared great intel on how to stay one step ahead of the cops, and Nari was lucky to have recruited her.

Jennifer hummed and cleaned off the dining room table. Her wholesomeness would really be an asset to the mission.

She looked up at her mom, whose face relaxed as she adjusted her black nautical sweater. Hana's years of experience would take the team to the next level.

For so long, Nari had fought the urge to pitch her mom on

new opportunities. She wanted to seem capable and independent. But this deal was different. It was so much bigger and worth risking her reputation to invite her mom onboard. And to Nari's surprise, her mom had said yes immediately. She would finally get the chance to work by her mother's side again. As a team.

Hana had retired a few years ago, joining a traveling artists troupe that held exhibits and live painting sessions across the Caribbean for tourists. She was happy, but Nari could tell she was getting more and more restless. She was an entrepreneur at heart. Like Nari, Hana needed to set her own hours and live a life of adventure.

The group settled in. Hana started pouring diet lemonade for everyone. Nari laid out floral paper napkins.

"Tell me about your life as an entrepreneur," Jennifer said, looking at Hana excitedly. "You know, before you retired. Nari says you're perfect for our mission. I want to know more."

Hana laughed. "I admire your enthusiasm. I've been an entrepreneur almost all my life. I sold my parents' dumplings to schoolmates as a child in Seoul. I was so much better at it than all of my siblings. Once I was hooked, I moved on to sell luxury goods from China to classmates through college. I smuggled them in my luggage to avoid paying import fees."

"Then she met my dad, and they both became doctors," Nari added.

"Is that when your entrepreneurial career ended?" Jennifer asked.

"Not quite," Hana explained. "We moved to New Jersey, where Nari was born. We couldn't get certified to practice in the US. I went back into business, but I got even sketchier this time. I sold smuggled pacemakers and pharmaceuticals from Sweden to doctors in the US." She paused for effect. Jennifer and Martha stared at her, unblinking.

"Oh my gosh." Jennifer's eyes widened. "Were they safe?"

"Absolutely," Hana replied. "They were approved for use in Sweden but hadn't passed testing yet in America."

Nari had raised the same concerns to her mom when she was a kid. She'd struggled with the question for months. But when Jennifer had the same safety questions about Sorbelate, Nari dismissed them. She swallowed, and her cheeks burned at the realization.

"There's so much opportunity and demand in that space," Martha remarked. "You need to get in at the right time with those regulatory lags and work with the right customers. Kind of like our Sorbelate formulation."

Nari could see Jennifer processing something. "Did you ever get caught?"

Nari tossed a mandarin orange from one hand to the other. "My mom never got caught, but she came close a few times. She took all kinds of precautions. At first, she was moving every few months to avoid getting tracked, while my dad and I stayed in New Jersey." Her voice rose with admiration. "My dad helped my mom launder money through some laundromats. We were millionaires."

"I was always really careful. I've learned a lot about how to 'work with' law enforcement over the years." Hana made air quotes as she spoke. "Even when our family reunited, my associates and I figured out a way for us to keep a low profile. We continued to move every few months when Nari was a kid."

"But then a deal in Kansas went bad," Nari interjected. "One of my mom's customers was working undercover for the FBI."

"*Dios mío*," Martha gasped. "Oh my goodness. What happened next?"

"We fled to a safe house in Turks and Caicos, where Nari spent most of her childhood. We started off fresh. Nari got to choose her own name. She went by Gwen there. Within months, I started up another black market business." Hana rested her hand on the table. "I could have gone the legal route, but the margins are so much smaller. And besides, it's so much spicier to bend the law. I love the thrill of the chase."

"But now you're not chasing anything, Mom. Totally different vibe with your artists' troupe," Nari said.

Hana nodded. "The truth is, I wanted to retire and enjoy some time off from always looking over my shoulder. It's great to be able to trust people again. I'm relaxed, living in New York City in the summers and Turks and Caicos in the winters. But I've been bored. My life has been missing excitement..." she sighed. "When you called me, Nari, I couldn't wait to get back in the game."

Martha took a sip of lemonade. "I bow to you. I feel the same way."

"You've grown your business so much that you don't touch the day-to-day strategy anymore. I know how that feels. Welcome back to the party," Hana said, a small smile creeping up on her face. "Don't you worry, team. I've brought all my training, honed over decades on the job. And Martha brings an excellent background too."

"We're going to work very well as a team," Martha added.

"I'm very experienced in bribery too. But I fight back more with technology and hacking."

Jennifer tilted her head forward in approval. "You're all so impressive. I hope you'll let me stay on the team for a little while." She giggled. "I'm curious. Nari, how often do you and your mom work on deals together?"

"For years, I was like my mom's cofounder," Nari replied, growing quiet. "I met with suppliers. I helped her negotiate deals. We studied profit and loss statements together, and mapped out our next steps. But once I graduated college, my mom stopped working with me. I miss those days."

"I had to do it. You needed to learn how to make money on your own, *nae jasik*," Hana explained. "And you've come so far. You're finally becoming a real entrepreneur on this deal. I'm so happy to partner with you now."

Nari bristled. *Finally?* Sure, her mom's high standards made her better. Getting pushed off onto her own *was* a good thing, even if it stung at the time. But her mom was talking like her six-figure deals didn't mean anything.

Hana wheeled over a large black suitcase from the doorway and placed it on the table. She unzipped it and pulled out a thick, white binder. "I'm old school." She shrugged. "I stepped onto the plane with study packs for each one of you."

An electric energy overtook the room as Hana handed out a stapled pack of papers to each team member. The women began flipping through the documents.

"Let's go over again how we avoid getting arrested." Jennifer leaned in. "I think that's my favorite part of the plan."

Hana chuckled. "Well, no guarantees there. But for starters, we're going to need people on the inside. Who has Johannes connected us with?"

"He's never introduced us. We don't have their names either," Nari replied.

"Let's build our own inside team. We need leverage so that Johannes doesn't call all the shots. If we have the network, he can never lock us out of intel," Hana said.

What a great idea. Nari felt a flash of pride, followed by an aching to show her mom how many creative solutions she had.

"Jennifer, who do you know at Essentrix Labs who could help us with security and logistics?" Hana asked.

A pensive look took over Jennifer's face. She paused for an instant before lighting up. "Lorinda! She's perfect. She works in operations and is already fighting corrupt business investments in West Africa!"

"Perfect. Nari, you can prep Jennifer on how to approach Lorinda to join us. The next thing we'll need is a cop on the inside. They'll help us manipulate police intelligence, keep tabs on the force, and always stay one step ahead," Hana explained.

"I can't believe I didn't think of that," Nari murmured, her eyebrows lifting.

"I can't believe it either," Hana replied playfully. "But it's your first major mission. You'll learn, *nae jasik.*"

Nari swallowed hard. "I've had plenty of major jobs since college." She glanced at Jennifer and Martha's concerned faces and stopped herself before going further. She had nothing to be insecure about. Her deals were big enough to impress even the most hardened entrepreneur, even if they didn't mean as much to her mom.

Hana nodded in agreement and continued addressing the

group. "After setting up our team, we've got to think about our defense plan. One thing that's really going to help us out is some of this technology I've brought."

She pulled out a large black case and unlocked it to reveal slick and shiny equipment. One by one, Hana presented each of the items in the case. She had smoke bombs, noise machines, radio frequency jammers, tablets, and night vision binoculars. The team could communicate with encrypted smartwatch walkie-talkies that would scramble their voices to the outside world.

"These tools work like a charm," Hana said.

"Incredible," Martha began. "We'll also want to track the cops. Normally, I'd hack into their patrol car GPS systems. But the Omaha State Police recently invested in some intense cyber-security for their fleet, and I can't crack in without triggering alarms. I'm going to investigate a better way."

"You are probably the coolest people I know," Jennifer said buoyantly. "Maybe I can be almost as amazing with a little of your training."

Hana beamed.

Nari's phone buzzed on her encrypted app. Johannes wrote, *"Now that you've got the team assembled, I want to know who joined you. Did Jen lure them in with her macadamia nut cookies?"*

She hesitated and touched her hand to her chin before writing back. *"We still have some moving parts. I'll let you know soon."* She forced a grin and looked back up at her mom.

"We're off to an amazing start," Hana said as she hugged Nari and Jennifer.

Martha agreed. "I can't wait to see you both soon."

"Are you sure you don't want to stay with us? We have a pullout bed on the couch," Jennifer said.

"Nah," Martha replied. "I like having my own bed. Hana found a luxury hotel downtown. More my speed."

"But you still wanted to share a room," Hana chuckled.

"How else would it feel like summer camp?" Martha joked. The women waved as they exited the apartment.

Nari's chest fluttered with nervousness and excitement that night. She could barely sleep.

CHAPTER 16

JENNIFER

That night, Jennifer was brushing her teeth when she got a video call from Amir. She panicked and looked in the mirror. Her hair was up in a wrap, and she'd already put on a face mask. Gently, she lifted the edges of the face mask and peeled it off before placing it on the counter. She straightened her head wrap.

"Amir!" she answered. She had been so busy with heist prep lately that she hadn't called him yet. "It's so good to see you."

"Gus says hi," Amir said warmly, bringing his dog into the frame. Gus was wearing a little party hat.

"Oh my gosh, he's even more adorable on video!" she gushed. "Loving the hat. Gus seems ready to party."

"Oh yeah, it's my dad's birthday today," he added. "The fam had a feast to celebrate. I'm so stuffed. What are you up to in Omaha?"

Well, you know. Jennifer was busy getting ready to conduct a second heist. Right after telling Amir that she didn't normally do things like that. Right after he believed her.

"That's amazing." She reached for a story to tell him. "I ate pancakes for dinner today with Nari, her mom, and her friend Martha. Not sure if that trend has reached Dearborn yet, but you've gotta try it sometime." She exhaled slowly through a small hole in her mouth.

He laughed. "Oh, any time! That is my specialty! I go crazy on some scrambled eggs and hash browns at 7 PM."

She smiled. "How's everything going in your business? Is Gus still helping you close deals?"

"You know, sales have been increasing steadily. We're doing great, thanks to Gus." He waved Gus's paw, then paused thoughtfully and put his dog down. "My sister's been going through some struggles though."

"What happened?" Jennifer asked.

Amir glanced down and ran his fingers through his hair. "Before we went into business together, she worked for a big accounting firm. She noticed they were recording revenue for a few clients that was much higher than it should have been. So she started to document things. One of their clients was Essentrix Labs."

Jennifer's eyes widened. "No way."

He nodded. "She tried to report the problem to the CFO, thinking she was going to stop the fraud and help the company save its reputation. Instead, the CFO denied the accounting errors, forced her to resign, and started to spread rumors about her to competitors. He shut her out of the industry."

"Oh my gosh," she said. "She got blacklisted for doing the

right thing. That's awful. I'm so sorry to hear about that. Is there any way she can get justice?"

"Thanks," he replied. "I've been trying to help her fight back. I've made calls and gone with her to government offices. Her case keeps getting buried. No one takes her seriously. Now the company's trying to get her to sign a nondisclosure agreement and settle out of court."

"What a nightmare." She shook her head. "What does she want to do?"

"She's ready to settle peacefully. I want her to fight," he started. "We've been going by the book our whole lives. But now I'm starting to wonder if the system only works for people who break the rules."

Jennifer brought her finger to her chin as she thought. "I'm sure your sister's so grateful that you've never walked away. I hope she gets the justice she's looking for. And until then, thriving is pretty amazing revenge. The CFO tried to bury her, and now she's crushing it as an entrepreneur."

"Our business is exploding," he agreed. "She's so inspiring. She's grown the business so much since she's joined and completely transformed herself professionally."

"She didn't just bounce back. She bounced higher," she added.

Amir beamed, and his dimples deepened. Jennifer felt her insides grow warm. "Thanks for listening. It's so good to talk to you. I'd love to see you in person again sometime soon."

Her pulse fluttered. "I'd love that too."

•   •   •

Twenty days until heist day

The next afternoon at the office, Jennifer ate lunch at her desk so that she could go for a walk with Lorinda and catch up on the latest European political scandals. It was their new weekday routine.

The two women switched to their sneakers and set off into the neighborhood. It was a warm day, and the sun felt hot on Jennifer's back.

"I'm starting to invest in a new business in Angola," Lorinda said. "I've got funding from an embarrassed politician in Porto, Portugal." She pulled up a picture on her phone. The man was attractive and looked a bit like Amir.

Chills went up and down Jennifer's body as she imagined her wealthy future with Amir.

"Hey, Jennifer," Lorinda said playfully, bringing her back into the present. "I think you were lost in thought."

"Oh, sorry. Tell me about your new venture." Jennifer needed to break the ice first before launching into the heist pitch. Her palms were sweaty. She crossed her fingers behind her back. Maybe Lorinda would panic and tell everything to her boss Mandy. Jennifer would be arrested immediately. And she had no lies prepared. She gulped and looked at Lorinda.

"I'm so glad you asked. The Angolan business is run by a group of incredible women who provide legal advice to foreign companies investing in the country. They're doing great work, and they're going to use the capital to expand." Lorinda beamed.

"That sounds incredible. How exciting," Jennifer replied.

The two of them walked in silence as birds chirped

throughout the neighborhood. Jennifer inhaled and almost started. Her throat tightened, and she couldn't find her words.

"Were you going to say something?" Lorinda glanced at her.

One step at a time, Jenny. She cleared her throat and remembered what she had practiced with Nari. *Start off with the corruption hook.* "Did you know that Essentrix Labs has terrible investments in the Democratic Republic of Congo?"

A look of surprise came over Lorinda's face. She nodded. "I'm aware of what they're doing in the Congo. I'm surprised you know too." She paused and looked like she had more to add. "Essentrix Labs is one of the worst offenders I've seen."

"Are you planning to do something about it?" Jennifer asked.

"I've been thinking about it for a while. I can't go after them directly, because they're sponsoring my green card. But I can destroy them from the inside." Lorinda balled her hands into fists. "I've been gathering evidence about their labor abuses here in Omaha, and in the DRC. One day, I'll anonymously leak my notes to the media."

Jennifer lifted her eyebrows in approval. "I love that you're doing that. I've got another idea you might like. We can do more than destroy Essentrix Labs. We can take their wealth and give it back to the women in the mines."

Lorinda stopped walking and turned to face Jennifer. They stood in front of an historic blue home with a wide, intricate porch. "You have my attention."

It was now or never. Jennifer had to have faith and push through.

"How would you feel about taking some Sorbelate from

Essentrix Labs?" Jennifer exhaled slowly and watched as Lorinda's face changed. "It's in really high demand right now. The formulation is like nothing else on the market, and I may know someone who can help us sell it."

Lorinda glanced at the green lawn in front of them. "I would love to be involved." She looked back up at Jennifer's face. "But I can't steal from them. If I got caught, I would lose everything."

Jennifer nodded. She thought back to her talk track. "You wouldn't have to personally steal anything. I have a team that can handle that. You'd just help us with the logistics, behind the scenes." She took a deep breath. "Our team would plan through every detail, including how to keep you safe afterward."

Lorinda's jaw set. "How experienced is your team? I can't throw away my life for this."

"I totally understand. We've got some serious professionals with decades of experience. We'd only ever refer to you by a code name. We use encrypted communications, and I have burner phones for you," Jennifer explained. "We'd destroy any physical evidence that can link you to the heist."

"I like the sound of that." The corners of Lorinda's mouth turned upward slightly. "Who else is involved, and can you guarantee their discretion?"

"Excellent question," Jennifer said, feeling uneasy. What would Nari say in this situation? "It's a solid team of four... who know and trust each other. There's even a mother-daughter pair."

"That's great, but what if they're more concerned about protecting each other than the mission?" Lorinda asked.

Jennifer bit her lip. "Sure, they've got each other's backs." She hesitated. Lorinda watched her closely. "But that doesn't mean they won't have yours too. We're all in this together. If one of us goes down, we all go down. That's why we're all so motivated to protect each other."

Lorinda tapped a finger to her chin. "What support would you need from me?"

"We need you to help us build an inside team to get the Sorbelate and move it. They'd have burner phones too. And you have connections in security, right?" Jennifer asked.

Lorinda nodded.

"With your help, the heist team would be untouchable." Jennifer grew more impassioned. "I can't tell you there'd be no risk, but it's all worth it. Together, we can destroy the mines, we can free the women working for them, and we can ruin Essentrix Labs."

A fire flickered in Lorinda's eyes. "I've never seen this side of you before. You're bold, and you're doing the right thing. Thank you for approaching me with this opportunity. I'm in. But I have one requirement."

Jennifer watched Lorinda's face with anticipation.

"I'll help the team with logistics, but that's it. You have to keep me out of the rest of the planning," Lorinda said. "We'll do verbal briefings only."

"It's a deal," Jennifer agreed.

Lorinda glanced at her watch. "Let's get back to the office. And then let's take these criminals down."

CHAPTER 17

JENNIFER

Nineteen days until heist day

Lorinda arrived at Nari and Jennifer's apartment. Hana had offered to treat the team to all-day passes at Elysian Spa to kick off team bonding.

"You're a game changer for us," Martha said, enveloping Lorinda in a warm hug.

"There's no place I'd rather be than fighting to take down Essentrix Labs with you all," Lorinda proclaimed.

"We're a new team, but we're mighty. We all bring our own unique skills to the job. I couldn't be prouder," Nari added.

Martha pulled out a clear plastic bag of wigs. "Okay, ladies. Choose which alter ego you want today." She removed a clear, flattened bag containing a red-haired bob. "Lorinda, I think you should be Ursula."

Lorinda laughed and took the wig bag from Martha. "You've got it."

The women giggled and passed out wigs before filing out of the apartment and into Hana's SUV.

The luxury spa was hidden down a cobblestone side street. It had crisp, clean white walls with gleaming, blue stone floors. Gold accents were everywhere, and the aroma of jasmine and sandalwood filled the rooms. Jennifer had never seen anything like it before. She already felt a rush of excitement being able to catch a glimpse of so much wealth.

After an hour or so of hot stone treatments and cryotherapy facials, the women headed across the spa for foot massages. Jennifer had pushed for it. "Powerful ancient rulers used to get foot massages, in diverse kingdoms of Egypt, India, and Greece. If we want to be rich, we've got to follow in their *footsteps*! Get it?"

The team sat side by side in their plush robes and chatted lazily as women kneaded their feet. Jennifer felt her body loosening, and she relaxed into a haze as Martha shared insights into selecting the ripest mangoes.

Their next step was the sauna. Once they were alone, the women removed their wigs, and the planning began. Soothing music played over the sauna's speakers.

"Lorinda, tell us about the inside team." Nari wiped sweat from her brow.

Lorinda nodded and adjusted the straps on her blue floral one-piece bathing suit. Jennifer could barely make out her face through a cloud of steam. "I've identified a team of five people we can trust. I've known them for years, and they respect me. When I approached them, a few of them shared that they were part of the first inside team. They work in shipping and receiving, and they manage the Sorbelate inventory." She cleared her throat. "They're sharp and sick of being underpaid."

"Yes!" Jennifer pumped her fist. Martha and Hana turned to smile at her.

Lorinda chuckled. "And I've got Keisha in security who can work with us too."

"Incredible work," Hana replied.

"The team is onboard now," Lorinda continued. She pulled out a folded piece of paper from a mesh beach bag at her side. Jennifer squinted to get a better look at the diagrams on the page. "During the first heist, the inside team changed the shipping records every day for a week. Essentrix Labs was selling so much Sorbelate that they could easily redirect a dozen boxes here, eight boxes there. They stored them on pallets throughout the warehouse and marked them with decoy labels only they knew about." She pointed to boxes on the diagram where Sorbelate was hidden. "No one noticed."

Nari tightened her ponytail. "This is fantastic intel, Lorinda."

Lorinda grinned and shifted on the wooden bench. "When it was time to launch the first mission, a team of three loaded the boxes into vans for local delivery. They had to work during the day, in front of their unsuspecting team, since the product gets locked away each night and none of them have access.

"The team put a total of fifty boxes into each van, which is the limit for local deliveries. They entered fake suppliers into the system and got the paperwork ready to account for their activity. During peak delivery time, they drove one of the delivery vans filled with product to a corner of the lot that

Keisha in security had promised would never get patrolled. It's the perfect size for one van, and no one noticed it was gone for one day."

"Why not pack the van and leave it outside of the fence?" Jennifer wondered aloud, the heat of the sauna catching in her throat.

"Good question," Lorinda replied. "The vans have geofencing systems that alert an offsite security team every time they're parked outside of the facility. Our insiders had to work within normal hours and return the second van back to the facility. On the early morning shift, we don't typically have many people working. That's when they transported the remaining boxes to the park and hid them in shrubs and recycling bins."

"This time around, we'll be picking up more Sorbelate," Martha added. "So we'll need more delivery trucks."

"The team's got it covered. They're also building more elaborate systems for diverting and hiding inventory," Lorinda explained. "Security is also an issue. The good news is there normally aren't many people working on-site security overnight. During the first mission, Keisha managed to schedule herself to work solo. But she'll have to plan more carefully this time."

"It sounds like you've planned for everything," Jennifer said. "Unless we get attacked by zombies. Then we're doomed."

The group laughed.

Hana reached out and patted Lorinda's bare shoulder. The steam had cleared, and Jennifer could see Hana's approving face. "Let us know if you need anything, Lorinda. Excellent work."

Lorinda's face glowed. "Thank you. I can't wait to bring down Essentrix Labs and get the money to the women who need it."

"Fantastic. Up next, starting tomorrow, we've got to spend some time at the police station planting GPS trackers on patrol cars," Martha began. "Since I can't hack into their systems, we've got to go old school."

Lorinda held up a finger. "This has been amazing, ladies. Thank you so much for treating us, Hana. As long as we're all done with my part, I've got to get going."

"Wise woman," Hana said, hugging Lorinda.

"We're adding another expert to our quest, like in *The Odyssey*," Martha added as she embraced Lorinda. She looked at each member of the team. "We could never succeed without each one of you."

Jennifer grinned. The rest of the women stood to hug Lorinda. She waved and stepped out of the sauna.

"Alright, so what's next?" Nari continued. "Right, Martha's going to research which cop on the inside we can make inroads with."

"How do we get the cop on our side?" Jennifer asked.

"Ah, that's the easy part," Hana replied. "We find someone motivated by that mean, mean green."

Nari cocked her head to the side. "Even better if they're desperate. We find someone who's got a financial problem we can exploit."

Jennifer nodded.

"Now we're going to need someone who can win over the cop and build a relationship with them," Hana explained.

Nari turned to look at Jennifer.

"Don't tell me you want me to do it." Jennifer giggled as the sounds of melodic chants played behind her.

Martha, Hana, and Nari looked at her expectantly.

"You guys don't want me to do it, right?" Jennifer wrung her hands.

"I know you can pull it off," Nari started, a serious look on her face. She touched Jennifer's shoulder. "We'll train you. You're the best fit for the job. Your wholesome vibe would make the cop trust you and open up to you."

Martha leaned in slightly. "I completely agree. And I know you can do it too."

Jennifer slumped down a bit on the wooden bench. She looked over at the sauna's stone-filled heater. She'd been able to bond with Johannes, and he was a seasoned criminal. Maybe it wouldn't be so hard to get close to a desperate cop.

"I don't know," Jennifer said. "How would I even know what to say?"

"We'll guide you through the entire conversation in an earpiece," Hana replied.

Jennifer exhaled. "Well, that sounds much better. But what if the cop doesn't want to work with us? Can they arrest me?"

"They absolutely can," Martha said. "But you'll build a relationship with them and exploit their weaknesses. We'll get them on our side and only make the heist pitch once we feel good about it."

"Make sure that you listen closely and look cute." Nari winked. "I can help in the wardrobe department."

"And if they're not showing interest, we back out before we even make the pitch," Hana added.

Jennifer's team was looking at her, unblinking. She sighed. "Criminal master's degree, year two. I'm in."

The team cheered.

"Even though we'll be with you the whole time, we'll prep you so you'll be able to handle this conversation," Nari said.

Jennifer nodded solemnly. This was serious business. But she believed you could accomplish any goal with the right training. And besides, she was going to be led by the masters.

She could inhabit the spirit of a female spy during the ancient Egyptian era, gaining intel from rival trade caravans that would want her dead if they knew what she was really doing.

Only Jennifer would be bonding with someone who didn't want to kill her. Much better. All she needed was a little direction from her team and she could make a new cop bestie.

"The more you can get the cop to relax, the more they'll open up. We'll teach you all about cop pain points so you can speak their language," Martha said.

"That sounds like my day job!" Jennifer exclaimed. "Except instead of learning about how much crunch parents want in their peanut butter, I'll need to understand what makes a good set of handcuffs. Totally different audience."

Martha grinned. "Before we head home, Nari, we've got to take you to an empty parking lot to show you how to slide under a car and place GPS trackers."

"I'm all yours," Nari said eagerly.

Hana turned to her. "Make sure you pay attention to Martha and practice. I know you might not have as much experience working with cars. This part is critical to the mission, and I want to make sure you do it right."

Nari looked down and swallowed hard.

Jennifer winced a little. "Nari can do anything well." She tilted her head toward her roommate. Nari smiled softly at her.

• • •

Eighteen days until heist day

The next morning, Jennifer and Nari arrived at the hotel lobby. Jennifer was excited to join the team for their morning strength training session but nervous to find out more about her assignment with the Omaha State Police. She looked down at her hot-pink workout gear. Maybe not the subtle look Nari had suggested. At least she was wearing a wig, sunglasses, and a wide-brimmed hat.

Nari and Jennifer walked around the reservation desk to get to the hotel gym. Soothing jazz music pumped through the speakers. Jennifer started to sway to the light rhythm. "It's called easy listening because it's so *easy* to love," she murmured. Nari giggled.

Hana and Martha were waiting for them in the cold, empty gym. They were chatting and looking amazing in their form-fitting performance wear and curly wigs. Hana looked twenty years younger, as always. Jennifer smiled, noticing that Martha's flower-print outfit was as loud as her own.

The gym was filled with every type of equipment Nari could want. It was early enough that no one else was at the gym. If anyone came in, the team would pretend not to know each other and leave at staggered times.

"Hey, team!" Nari waved. The women gathered around the dumbbell rack. "Two each," she instructed. Each woman dutifully chose dumbbells. "What have you got for us, Ramírez?"

"It's been a very fruitful morning so far." Martha tightened her thick ponytail of dark-brown curls. "I've found our guy. Freddy Anderson. Forty-three. He's a lieutenant with a bankruptcy and mountains of debt, and he's in danger of losing his two-bedroom house. On top of that, the force has taken disciplinary action against him for botching a few cases due to sloppy paperwork."

Martha pulled his picture up on her phone and showed it to the group. He looked like a normal white guy in a police uniform. He had dark hair, a closely-manicured crew cut, and an oval-shaped face. A bushy mustache covered his face. There was nothing too noteworthy about him.

"Perfect!" Hana remarked. "This guy sounds like a great target. Alright, you're on deck, Jennifer!"

Jennifer stood alongside Hana and Martha, facing Nari and copying her movements. Each woman dutifully swung a dumbbell down between her legs in a squat motion, and back up over her head.

"This feels really unnatural," Hana said.

"Forgive me if my dumbbell goes flying," Martha agreed.

"How do I meet this guy?" Jennifer asked, bringing the conversation back on track. She had so many questions but figured it was best to start there.

"I've got his schedule here." Martha set down her dumbbell and pulled the calendar up on her phone. "Looks like Freddy works four ten-hour shifts each week. Luckily, today is one of them. He should be getting off tonight around 6 PM. You'll take one of our getaway cars and tail him. Find out what he's up to each night after work. Identify a way that you can get to know him and exploit his weaknesses."

"Perfect. I'll make sure I look casual but cute. Like a modern-day car racing spy," Jennifer quipped.

"Exactly." Martha grinned. "I could only find basic background on Freddy. In fact, there's so little available that I think he might have taken steps to bury his history. Who knows what this guy is up to? At least I can tell you he is originally from Omaha and went to college here."

Jennifer chewed on her fingernail. Martha's databases probably weren't going to give her step-by-step instructions, but she could only dream. *"Challenge Freddy to a dance-off, and he'll be putty in your hands,"* the database would say.

"That's better than nothing, right?" Jennifer asked.

"Absolutely, we'll use that to our advantage. You'll do amazingly, *patrona*. Boss babe. You're going to be Ava Robertson," Martha explained.

Jennifer nodded toward Nari. "I'm glad I get to be Ava again!" Except this time, maybe she wouldn't end up escaping from a security guard barefoot on a scooter.

Nari beamed. "You make the best Ava character. I could never."

Jennifer could feel a cramp in her left leg.

"You're going to be new to Omaha, Jennifer," Martha continued. "Give Freddy the opportunity to help you by teaching you all about the city."

"Ah, great call," Nari said as she shifted from swinging her dumbbell to keeping it still for squats. The rest of the team followed suit. "If Freddy gets the chance to help you, he'll get attached. He'll like you even more."

"I can do that," Jennifer replied as she squatted. "I'll pretend I'm myself from fifteen years ago. Anything else for my backstory?"

"We need to give you a charming job that's unassuming, doesn't always pay well but has access to cash. That'll get Freddy thinking about money," Martha said.

"Fundraising coordinator for a nonprofit," Nari said. "You've got a heart of gold and you're broke."

"That's perfect," Hana added. A smile appeared on Nari's face.

"I know the broke lifestyle well," Jennifer murmured.

"The rest of us will head over this morning to place the GPS trackers," Hana remarked.

Nari put down her dumbbell. "Speaking of which, I'm wondering if we need Jen on-site to create a diversion. You know, in case someone catches me on the lot."

Hana shook her head. "Not necessary. Smaller footprint, smoother mission." Jennifer felt her shoulders loosen in relief.

As the women came together in the hotel gym, Jennifer could feel their team spirit and sisterhood growing.

CHAPTER 18

NARI

Nari had pushed the team, and it seemed to have paid off. Her body buzzed with post-workout endorphins as they piled into their forgettable brown getaway car wearing perfectly planned disguises. As Hana drove over to the police station with Martha in the front seat, they rehearsed their morning.

"Timing is critical," Hana said. "I'll need to get straight to distracting the cops so that you two can get to work. The morning is their slow time, so we'll be likely to avoid detection if we get started a few minutes after 9 AM. We've got to move quickly, because the auto mechanic is due on the lot at 9:30 AM. Until then, they'll think Nari is the real professional."

Martha looked at Hana and beamed. "Don't worry. No delays on my end. I've been messing with their servers all week to give us an in."

Hana cleared her throat. "Nari, do you feel confident about placing the GPSs?"

Nari winced and drew in a breath. "Mom, I practiced for an hour with Martha last night. It was overkill, but I don't do anything halfway. If you give me an assignment, I'll perform."

Martha seemed to notice the edge in Nari's voice. She turned to Hana. "Nari knows what she's doing. World-class *patrona*."

Hana nodded and adjusted her curly black wig as she maneuvered the car over one lane. "You are a Park, after all," she said, her voice rising. "Well, I'm ready to roll out my government-auditor routine. Works like a charm."

"I know you'll be amazing, Mom," Nari replied. Of course, they should put the most experienced person in the auditor role. But anyone could do the grunt work of placing GPS devices. All Nari wanted to do was put on her own skirt suit and show her mom how well she could distract the cops. Since college, she'd developed the finesse and the people skills needed to pull it off. Her mom didn't seem to understand that.

Hana parked the car three blocks away from the station so they could walk over separately and not be caught on camera together. She took the lead, carrying her auditor briefcase. She was heavily made up with contouring to cover her facial features. Of course, her oversized glasses helped with that too. She wore a black skirt suit with a white button-down. Simple, no-nonsense. Nari couldn't recognize her.

Martha would enter the lobby shortly after Hana began to distract the team. She was dressed as an IT maintenance contractor and would slip into the surveillance room to dismantle the cameras.

Nari split off from the group and walked toward the parking lot's emergency exit. She'd be ready to sneak in when the time was right. She carried a toolbox and wore a low-slung, striped hat to cover up her face along with a maintenance worker uniform.

This was one of Nari's least favorite disguises. She looked like her mechanic uncle.

She sat casually behind a tree so she wouldn't be easily spotted by the early-morning arrivals.

Her phone buzzed three times in the encrypted app. It was Johannes. *"I want to get clear on which team member will handle each part of the heist preparations."* It was a strange request.

Nari paused. Something didn't seem right. It was best not to tell him the truth yet. *"Absolutely. We are still ironing everything out, but I'll keep you in the loop,"* she wrote. She set the toolbox by her feet and pulled out a green apple to snack on.

•   •   •

Nari's smartwatch vibrated. *"Cameras are off. Go, Nari."*

She hopped to her feet and stood outside the fence, surveying the lot. There were no cops in sight. She slipped through the emergency exit and into the parking lot. She had eleven minutes to complete the mission until Martha's loop of surveillance footage from the same day and time last week would end and the live footage would return.

Nari took a deep breath and prepared herself to walk across the lot to reach the patrol cars on the opposite side. She looked down at her coveralls, box of tools, and work badge. Maybe she seemed like she actually knew what she was doing. Maybe her uncle's look was working for her.

She passed by a group of cops. *Act natural.* She averted her eyes and walked forward like she had cars to fix. She would run this mission flawlessly, and her mom would beam in approval.

"There was glass everywhere," one officer said animatedly. "I think they busted the window in with a crowbar."

None of the officers even glanced at her as they strode into the station. She smiled to herself gratefully and checked the time. She had about six minutes left to place as many GPS trackers as she could.

She went straight for the patrol cars, which would be the first ones on the frontlines of any investigation. She got down immediately and pulled out the first GPS from her toolkit before shimmying underneath the car. Quickly and methodically, she clicked the GPS's magnet into place underneath the car near the rear bumper where it would be least likely to be detected.

After a beat, the GPS fell off the car and onto her face, clanging as it fell. She froze and inhaled sharply as a burning sensation shot up her nose. Her eyes watered. She looked around and listened for cops nearby. No one. Swiftly, she opened her tool box and pulled out a spare magnet, peeling off its adhesive and sticking it to the back of the GPS. She clicked the tracker into place and tapped it twice. It didn't move. Perfect.

She jumped up and moved to the next car, humming quietly to herself as she worked. She was a natural, fluidly securing one GPS tracker after another. Within seven minutes, she had already placed twelve trackers. There were four left to go.

"Yes!" Nari whispered as she stood up, pumped her fist lightly, and walked quickly to the unmarked SUVs. These would be most likely to survey the area before the heist. She ducked down and slid her head under the first car.

As she pulled out her GPS, she heard footsteps approaching. Her heart raced. Quickly, she shimmied the rest of her body and her toolbox under the car and between its wheels.

"She broke up with me over a text message," a man said emphatically.

Nari held her breath and looked for another pair of feet. Thankfully, it seemed he was alone.

The man came closer to the car and stopped. She bit her lip and willed him to get inside as quickly as possible. Hopefully the lot would be empty when he drove away and exposed her.

Her foot tingled with pins and needles. She exhaled slowly and tried to focus on the man's conversation. She glanced at her watch. Three minutes left.

"Yeah, her text came in while I was arresting someone! Unbelievable. So that's why I'm free on Saturday. She's crazy if she thinks I'm going to her birthday party," he continued.

Nari couldn't hold still anymore. Her foot was on fire. As she shifted her leg and shook it lightly, the metal button on her coveralls clinked noisily against the car's undercarriage.

Her eyes widened. She froze and gritted her teeth.

The officer's feet shifted slightly. "Is someone there?" he asked.

In a split-second decision, she slipped out from underneath the car and took her toolbox with her.

"I'm so sorry to startle you," she said. "I'm from Mighty Motors, doing some routine maintenance on the lot today. I've been checking the undercarriages for damage. You guys are pretty rough on these cars."

"Ah, thanks," the officer said slowly, his eyes narrowing. "I'll call you back," he said into his cell phone.

She couldn't believe her luck. On the opposite side of the lot, she saw what looked like another auto mechanic. He was early. Her breath caught in her chest.

The officer followed her line of sight and turned to glance over his shoulder.

"You really should check out your back left tire!" she exclaimed, pointing emphatically. "It looks like it's low."

The officer turned back to the car, grumbling. "I'm always having issues with my car! I've been telling Chief Hudson that he needs to invest a little bit more in our fleet. But *nooo*, we've got *'other priorities.'*" He bent down to inspect the tire.

Nari pulled her phone out of her pocket. "If you'll excuse me, I'm getting a call," she said.

"Go for it," the officer said, shaking his head.

She estimated that she had about thirty seconds before the cop realized she was a fraud and would start to raise a scene. She walked quickly across the lot and texted the team, *"Time to go."*

Her heart was pounding as she entered the lobby from the parking lot. She flashed her badge and waved to the secretary. Hana was holding a clipboard and talking to at least five officers, looking like she was drunk on power.

Nari smirked and slipped out the front door. She walked quickly toward the getaway car, where Martha was waiting for her.

"How'd it go, my little hustler?" Martha asked excitedly.

"We're golden!" Nari said. "I placed all but three GPS trackers."

Martha extended a hand for a high five. "*Vamos, chica!* The cameras should be coming back online in a few seconds. You made it!"

The front door opened, and Hana got inside, a lightness to her step. Nari sped away.

Hana exhaled loudly. "I feel incredible! It's been way too long since I've held the cops in the palm of my hand like that."

Martha and Nari laughed.

"All good on my end too," Nari added. "You know, other than getting caught."

Hana's expression hardened, and she turned toward Nari. "What happened?" she demanded.

Nari chafed and began slowly, "An officer heard me underneath his car, but I talked my way out of it."

"She placed almost all of the trackers." Martha clapped her hand on Nari's back. "I think she did an amazing job. You charmed your way out of it on your own. No diversions needed."

"Not bad, *nae jasik,*" Hana said.

Nari felt her body go slack and sped the car forward even faster.

Martha clenched the armrest. "Don't go too fast. We don't want to summon our new friends."

$$\bullet \quad \bullet \quad \bullet$$

The GPS signals were coming in clearly on Martha's laptop. The operation had been a success.

Hana, Martha, and Nari had gathered at the hotel room to debrief before Jennifer's mission began. Martha was fiddling around with the tracking settings when Nari's phone buzzed three times, signaling that it was her encrypted texting app. It was Johannes.

"The boss rings again," Nari giggled.

"Tell him to give us a bigger cut," Hana quipped.

"You know, we do have a lot of leverage," Martha added.

Nari grinned and pulled up the app on her phone. *"When is your next practice session at Essentrix Labs?"* he asked. It was a strange request, one of many recently. Her smile slowly faded.

Martha glanced at her. "What does the boss want?"

"He's been getting really demanding lately." Nari shook her head. "Something's fishy. He's asking when we're going to be at Essentrix Labs to practice."

Hana frowned. "Something's strange for sure. Don't tell him the truth. I'm not sure why he wants or needs to know that information."

Nari nodded and cleared her throat. *"Great to hear from you boss. We'll be there next Thursday at 8 PM,"* she typed. "I told him next week—it's realistic, and it gives us enough time to strategize before he catches us in a lie."

Martha held her fist out toward Nari. "Pound it," she said.

CHAPTER 19

JENNIFER

Jennifer arrived at the police station about twenty minutes ahead of schedule, in case Freddy cut out early for the day.

She glanced in the mirror and adjusted her wig of long, tightly coiled black curls. She was heavily made up so that her face appeared longer and her cheekbones higher. Even though it was strange looking nothing like herself, she couldn't help but feel like she looked like an international pop star. "Ava," she mouthed to herself in the mirror.

She looked ahead toward the police station and tried to distract herself by people watching as officers came and went. She even got to see an officer enter with someone in handcuffs.

This was going to be a walk in the park, Jennifer reminded herself. She'd gotten some great tips from the heist masters. Plus, they'd be with her the whole time in her earpiece. Ah, the beauty of modern technology. She reached up to adjust the device.

Uh-oh. She froze. Both of her ears were bare. Had she taken the earpiece out and put it somewhere? She started to search the car. The pockets of her purse, the center console, the glove compartment, even the cup holders.

It was gone. She started to panic. She pulled out her phone to text the heist chat group on her encrypted app. *"Help, team,"* she typed quickly. *"Earpiece missing."*

Her phone buzzed. *"Oh Jennifer..."* Nari wrote back. *"There's no time to replace it. You can do it. Stay strong. Be empathetic and be yourself."*

Jennifer gulped. A chill went down her neck. She could feel her arm hairs standing up straight. She texted Nari back, *"I've got this."* More to fortify herself than to reassure Nari, she added a muscle flexing emoji.

Her phone buzzed again. It was a picture of her comic book hero, Amina Keita. Another message came through from Nari, *"Found your selfie on my phone."*

Jennifer couldn't stop herself from grinning. She could see movement out of the corner of her eye. Looking up, she suddenly noticed Freddy emerging and walking toward his plain silver sedan.

Well, there he is, folks. She turned on her car and readied herself to follow him. If comic book hero Amina Keita could rise the ranks in ancient African kingdoms as a woman, Jennifer could easily tap into her gaming days and tail an officer.

Jennifer chuckled to herself. She had never followed anyone in her car, let alone a police officer. She kept an actual bucket list, and this was definitely not on it. *Could I get arrested for this?* Her pulse quickened.

She tapped a rhythm on the steering wheel as she waited for

Freddy to exit the parking lot. He was hesitating, but it wasn't clear why. Maybe he was messing with his cell phone.

She tightened her seatbelt. She would give anything to be relaxing in a Nordic hot spring with Amir and the team right now. They'd all be toasting a job well done and snacking on a bowl of juicy berries. It would be so festive and well-deserved.

Amir. Jennifer pulled out her phone and texted him. *"I'm about to do something daring,"* she typed. *"I'm trying to summon your bunny bravery."*

Within a few seconds, her phone buzzed. Amir sent her a dragon emoji. *"You're like a dragon facing off with a bunny."*

She beamed and put her phone back down. Finally, after what seemed like forever but was probably about five minutes, Freddy started his silver sedan and pulled it out of the lot. Her eyes refocused on the present. She breathed in deeply, counted for a few seconds, then followed him.

He could be driving anywhere. She might even have to get out and follow him on foot.

He drove quickly and erratically, passing cars and weaving in and out of lanes. It was hard to keep a good distance and still see where he was going. She dug her fingernails into the steering wheel and squinted hard to focus. She knew she could do this. They stopped at a traffic light with another car in between them.

Alright, this is going well so far, Jennifer thought, sighing deeply. Freddy was probably lost in thought, especially driving the way he was. He couldn't possibly have noticed her.

Finally, he turned into a Shop N Save parking lot. *He gets this wild for groceries?* She pulled in behind him. This would be perfect. She chatted with other shoppers at the grocery store all the time. This was totally within her wheelhouse.

The grocery store had blinding white lights and played easy listening music from the early 2000s. Jennifer felt at ease immediately. She couldn't help but start to sing along under her breath. No prohibition against that, right? She tried not to dance. That would be too flashy.

Dressed up in his police uniform, Freddy was wheeling his cart toward the produce section. Jennifer chose a handheld basket for convenience, threading her arm through the metal handles. She followed him. He was examining bananas.

She approached him. "You know, I really like the organic bananas here," she said in a friendly tone. "They're only five cents more, and I swear you can taste the difference."

He looked up in surprise, softening as his eyes met hers. "I've never tried organic bananas before." He set down his regular bananas and picked up a bunch of organic ones. "I'll have to give them a shot."

"You won't be disappointed." And because she couldn't help herself, she added, "You know, bananas originated in Southeast Asia thousands of years ago. People couldn't get enough of them. They spread through ancient trade routes to India and Africa, where they grew like weeds and became *complete* staples."

He chuckled, a charmed look on his face. "Thank you for that. I'll be sure to remember that the next time I eat a banana. Do you come here often?"

"Always. I should get a Shop N Save punch card for all the butter lettuce I buy here," she said naturally. It was the truth.

"I'm here all the time too," he replied, his eyes shining. "You've got great energy. I can't believe I didn't notice you before."

"You're too kind," she said. "I'm surprised we haven't crossed paths before. What's your name?"

"I'm Freddy," he said. "What's yours?"

"Je—" Heat rushed to her face. She cleared her throat nervously. "Ava."

"That's a beautiful name," he said.

"Thank you." She straightened her posture. "Have you been in Omaha for a while?"

"All my life," he explained. "I always thought I'd be gone by now, but that Midwestern charm draws you back in."

"I know the feeling. The place becomes a part of you. Sometimes, a city puts roots into you. Life wouldn't make sense somewhere else." Although she was riffing, Jennifer couldn't help but feel there was some truth to it for herself.

Freddy fixed his gaze on her. He seemed fully entranced. She decided to shift gears and dive into her rehearsed backstory.

"I love Omaha. I just moved here. You must know all the best places for a newcomer to explore," she said fluidly. It was easier to lie than she was expecting.

"I'm so glad to hear that you're enjoying Omaha," he replied. "If you're free, I would love to take you to one of the city's hidden gems, the Green Room. It's a dive bar in walking distance. I always meet my friends there. You'd love it. I was planning to go there for a quick drink after buying my groceries."

Jennifer swallowed hard. She couldn't believe he already wanted to make plans with her. It was so easy. Plus, he had invited her to a public place they could walk to. He'd have no idea what her car looked like, and there would be witnesses in case he suddenly wanted to kidnap her.

She laughed, trying to sound as natural as possible. "That'd be wonderful. You know, there's no time like the present to rub shoulders with Omaha's best and brightest. Once I get some bananas for breakfast tomorrow morning, I'd love to join you."

Freddy's voice quickened. "It's a date." His face reddened. "I mean, it's a deal. I can get groceries anytime, but how often do I get to grab a drink with a beautiful woman?"

They walked toward the registers and waited in line. "I came in for bananas and I'm leaving with a candy bar," he chuckled. He seemed much more normal than she had expected.

She put her bananas into a reusable mesh bag she kept in her purse.

The pair walked out the front door of the Shop N Save. "The Green Room is down the street," Freddy said. "I can't wait to show it to you."

"I'm excited to see it," she replied. *Be charming,* she reminded herself.

He was very talkative. During the ten-minute walk to the bar, she had already learned about his family's farm business, its acreage, and his fear of pigs—so unassuming yet so smart.

"I got into the force straight out of high school. I didn't want to be a farmer and didn't really know what else to do. Being a cop seemed like a good choice, with benefits," he explained.

"It's a steady job, and it seems like you're good with people. Plus, you don't have to get up early to milk cows," she quipped.

They entered the bar. Dimly lit, the walls were adorned with stylized posters and artwork from 1960s concerts and fairs. All of them had hints of green in their design. *Clever,*

Jennifer thought. Freddy pulled out two padded black chairs from the bar and motioned for her to have a seat.

"Welcome to the Green Room." He smiled nervously.

"Thank you," she responded.

He continued, "But to be honest, being a cop is not paying like I thought it would." He turned to the bartender. "One whiskey on the rocks, please. Anything for you, Ava?"

"I'll take a seltzer water with lime," she told the bartender then turned to Freddy. "They really don't pay you guys enough for what you do. I always say, police officers should get the highest salaries. I'm in awe of how you put your lives on the line."

Freddy's face glowed. "Thank you for saying that. What do you do?"

The bartender placed their drinks on the bar.

Jennifer breathed in and squirted her lime into her glass. "I work for a nonprofit as a fundraising coordinator." And to add an extra flourish, she blurted out, "I work in the major gifts department. I'm in sales, in a way."

Freddy's interest seemed piqued. "Interesting." He looked down at the bar. "You know, I really respect that you work for a nonprofit. I always wanted to start one to help farmers rehab their land."

"That's really sweet of you. I'm sure you'd be great at that," she said.

Freddy looked lost in thought. "Thanks. Tell me. What's your favorite thing that you've done in Omaha so far?"

Now this would be easy for Jennifer to answer. Even as a fictional version of herself. "I love the Lauritzen Gardens, especially this time of year."

His face lit up, and he sipped his whiskey. "Excellent choice. They're so lush and secluded from the city. You really feel like you're in another world."

She paused, realizing she needed to stop herself before listing off another dozen attractions that she had already been to. "So what do you like to do for fun when you're not out catching bad guys?"

"I love going to museums and spending time with my family. My sister has the most adorable three kids." He paused and laughed nervously. "I wish I could say I didn't love trying to beat random strangers at blackjack."

She nodded knowingly. There's the debt Martha was talking about. "Do you like to go to the casino?" she asked, keeping her voice even.

"I'm more of an online player. It's a little *too* easy to play." He inhaled sharply. "But I've got it under control. Most days."

Freddy's phone buzzed on the wooden bar top. He looked at it for a moment. "Dang it. I've got to get going. Official police stuff." He drained his glass and put a ten-dollar bill on the bar.

"Thanks, Tommy," Freddy said to the bartender. He turned toward Jennifer. "It's been amazing talking to you, Ava. Can I get your phone number?"

"Of course." Jennifer had gotten a burner phone for this purpose and gave the number to him carefully, having memorized it earlier. He typed it into his phone, digit by digit. She got his number too.

"Can I walk you to your car?" he asked.

"Thanks." Her voice wavered. She fidgeted with her fingers in her lap. "I think I'm going to stick around here for a bit. I like this neighborhood and want to explore."

"Good call. You're going to like it here in Omaha. I look forward to seeing you again," he said.

He walked out the front door. She pretended to fumble for something in her purse. A small grin formed on her lips. It seemed like Freddy liked her, even without her team's help.

She counted to *ten Mississippi*. That felt like enough time. She nodded to the bartender and exited the bar into the cool evening air. Freddy was walking quickly ahead toward the grocery store. She trotted to get closer to him.

Jennifer could hear him on his phone. "I know I'm behind," he said forcefully. She held her breath. It was a completely different tone than he had used with her. She wondered who he was dealing with. "Look, I'm not trying to run away. You'll have your money soon."

As they rounded the corner to the grocery store, he glanced back in her direction. She darted behind the store's dumpster, the smell of wet cardboard rising to her nostrils. As she slowly peeked around the dumpster lid, she could tell that he hadn't noticed her. He was still walking toward his car. She raced out and continued to follow him.

"If you send someone to my place, this gets messy for everyone." Freddy paused, his voice shaking. "Twenty percent interest wasn't part of the deal. Give me a little more time."

CHAPTER 20

JENNIFER

Seventeen days until heist day

"Welcome to Henry's!" a woman in her twenties said as she scooped a bowl into a barrel full of peanuts and handed it to Jennifer.

The restaurant was a bit of a dive, but it had a cult following. The ceilings were low, and the lighting was bright. Faded blue and white checkered tiles adorned the walls. A sign read, "*Since 1962.*" Jennifer's favorite part? The staff gave you a bowl of free peanuts in the shell when you entered.

She felt at home immediately. There were a few tables filled with rowdy teenagers, a middle-aged couple, and what looked like an elderly women's book club. She picked a seat in the back corner, a bit removed from the other tables.

It had been so easy to set the date. Freddy had agreed to

meet immediately. She secured her earpiece and smoothed her curly black wig before exhaling and closing her eyes.

A waitress wearing a blue and white checkered blouse and blue apron walked by. "We've got a special this week. Get a free soda when you buy a burger and fries." She winked at Jennifer.

"Sounds like an amazing deal. Thanks for telling me about it," Jennifer replied.

"You'd better get that deal," Martha said into Jennifer's earpiece. "Can you hear me?"

"Fries," Jennifer said, their code for yes. She held in a chuckle.

She glanced down at her watch. 12:11 PM. She hoped Freddy was still showing up. As she pulled out her phone to text him, he strode up to the table.

"So good to see you again, Ava."

Jennifer gave him a hug. They walked up to the counter, eyed the menu, and each decided on the free soda special.

Back at the table, Freddy continued, "I had such a great time meeting you yesterday. I wasn't sure if I'd get the chance to see you again. After my night last night, I thought, life's too short."

"Whoa boy," Martha said into Jennifer's earpiece. Jennifer jumped. She had forgotten Martha was there. "I bow to you, Jennifer. It only took one meeting..."

Jennifer refocused back on Freddy. "That's so sweet of you to say," she said genuinely. She didn't expect to have made such an impression.

The waitress walked over to deliver their meals. "Here you go," she said brightly. "I added a third soda for fun."

"Thanks so much," Jennifer responded greedily, mentally

claiming the extra cup. Sure, Henry's had free refills, but how else could she alternate between sips of cherry cola and grape soda?

She turned back to Freddy as the waitress walked away.

"Start off calm. Neutral topics," Martha reminded her through the earpiece.

"I've always wanted to learn how to surf," Jennifer said honestly. It was easier for her to talk about herself than to invent a new character. Much less work to remember what she'd said too. "I grew up near the Great Lakes, but you can't really surf there."

"That sounds incredible," Freddy agreed. "I'm an Omaha boy. We have rivers and smaller lakes, which I've always loved too. Do you ever do any water sports?"

"I'm a huge paddleboarder," Jennifer said. "I can spend hours out there."

"Now that sounds amazing. I'm a jet ski guy myself." Freddy looked like he was contemplating something.

Jennifer took in a slow breath. This conversation was going well so far. "Jet skiing. That sounds incredible. When did you get into that? Have you been doing it since you were a kid?"

Freddy beamed. "Yeah, since I was eight. That's when I tried it for the first time with my Uncle Steve. My dad's brother. He was always the daring sibling. My dad didn't want me to go, but eventually he gave in after he saw how much I loved it." He took a bite of his burger.

"I love that," Jennifer said. "It sounds like your Uncle Steve is important to you."

"Oh, huge. I wouldn't be the man I am today without him." Freddy took a sip of his soda. "I love how you caught onto that. Thank you."

"Alright, he's feeling relaxed and supported," Martha intoned through the earpiece. "We're going to shift over to your financial struggles. Make it easy to support you."

Jennifer focused on Freddy's face. He looked vulnerable. *Remember, you're offering him a solution. A way out.*

"It's been so great to be here in Omaha," she said. "But the truth is, I can't really afford to be here. I maxed out my credit cards to move. I'm living paycheck to paycheck. Right now it feels worth it, but I don't know how I'll repay my debt. I feel like money problems have been...sneaking up on me."

She was pleased with herself for coming up with this story. It wasn't that far from the truth.

"I know exactly what you mean," he replied. "The force doesn't pay too well. And I've got some...expensive habits. I'm working on cutting back too."

"Perfect," Martha said. "Let's dig deeper here. Show that you're sorry for him then ask him if he's in a bind."

"I'm sorry to hear that," Jennifer said. "I know how expenses can really creep up on you. I wish the police paid you better. Are you in a tough spot right now?"

Freddy paused. "Yeah, you could say that. My finances are in rough shape."

"I can imagine!" *Whoops.* Not the most graceful response.

He looked uncomfortable. "What's that supposed to mean?"

Jennifer cleared her throat nervously.

Martha's voice came through the earpiece. "Don't worry. Just get back on the empathy train."

"What I mean is, you'd be surprised how many people I know who are barely keeping their heads above water."

Jennifer gently placed her hand on the table. "There's no shame in that. It doesn't make you weak. We're all trying to get by. Are you struggling to pay rent?"

"It's touch-and-go." Freddy ran his fingers through his hair and took a sip of his soda. "You know, I've gotten involved with some of the wrong people. I owe them money. I'm trying to figure out how to make ends meet and pay them back."

"Ahí está!" Martha added. "Tell him about a friend you know who had huge, uncontrollable gambling debts. You're doing great, by the way."

"That sounds really tough, especially when you owe money to some unsavory characters," Jennifer remarked. "A friend of mine started playing online poker and got in with some bad loan sharks."

Freddy stopped chewing and looked at Jennifer.

She continued, "He ended up owing them tens of thousands of dollars. More than he had ever made in a year. They would come to his house and make threats. He was always looking over his shoulder in fear."

"What happened to your friend? Was he able to pay them off?" Freddy's eyes flickered with concern.

Jennifer looked down, unsure of what direction to take the story. What would he respond the best to?

Luckily, Martha's response came quickly. "He's been on the run ever since," Jennifer replied. "No one in our friend group has heard from him in years. Everyone misses him and wonders where he is."

Freddy swallowed a sip of his soda, slowly. Jennifer took a bite of her burger.

"Great. Now let it lie here, for a second," Martha said.

Jennifer looked at Freddy. He had made it through his burger and had a smattering of fries left. She really wanted to fill the awkward silence but stopped herself. Martha was right. It was like what Jennifer had learned in her one sales training, five years ago. It had stuck with her all these years because it was so effective—sometimes, silence did the work for you.

"You know, I've got gambling debt too," Freddy admitted after what seemed like a few minutes. "A lot of it. I'm worried I'm going to end up like your friend. I don't want to be on the run. I love it here. I've got to figure out a way to pay these people back."

"That sounds so scary," Jennifer said. "I'm so sorry you're going through that." For extra effect, she touched his hand.

He looked at her helplessly.

"Now you're going to transition it back to the opportunity," Martha said. "Start broadly. Don't tell him what it is."

"You know, it's important to me to be able to help my friends when they're in a bind. And I think of you as a friend," Jennifer began. Freddy watched her expectantly. "There's no shame in your situation. Everyone has struggles every now and then. What you need is an opportunity. And I know a few ways to make things happen. These chances don't come along often, if you know what I mean." She felt powerful, inhabiting this role of an underworld negotiator.

"Please, tell me more," Freddy said. "I really need help. I want to hear about your ideas."

"Introduce the project, but no specifics yet," Martha reminded Jennifer. "Emphasize how easy it is."

"My associate and I have a project coming up that could

really use someone on the inside in law enforcement. Nothing big, just a little protection. In return, everyone gets a reward. The risk is low. No one gets hurt. There's nothing messy," Jennifer explained.

Freddy put his fry back on the plate. "Is this a set up? Did Chief Hudson or someone else put you up to this?"

Jennifer clenched her jaw and felt goosebumps form on her arms.

"Stay confident," Martha noted. "Stick with empathy. You're offering him a solution."

"Not at all," Jennifer replied. "I wouldn't do that to you. This is a way out for both of us."

Freddy exhaled deeply. "I want to trust you, Ava. I'm looking for a way out. What are you pitching to me?"

"Alright, now's your time," Martha said. "Start to introduce the heist, little by little. Stay vague but be clear about his involvement."

"We've got a little something planned to earn a big payoff. Nothing dangerous. Just selling some stolen goods. We need someone to help us keep the cops away while we execute the plan. In return for some protection, our helper will be generously rewarded," Jennifer said.

"How much are we talking?" Freddy asked.

"Forty thousand dollars," Jennifer replied.

His shoulders relaxed. The corners of his mouth turned upward slowly.

Martha said, "Bring it on home. Talk about how easy his life will be afterward."

"Imagine how good it would feel to have all your debts paid off and your troubles behind you. You'd get to stay here in

Omaha. Your life would be back to normal. No more stress. No more debt hanging over your head. Just trips to the lake to ride your jet ski," Jennifer said, holding Freddy's gaze.

"Nice touch!" Martha added.

"Interesting." Freddy paused and seemed like he was considering something. "If this goes south, my career would be over."

"Nothing—" Martha began.

"No one will ever know you were involved," Jennifer ventured forward confidently. "It'll seem like you're doing your job. After you help us out, you're free. We take care of our own. Everything stays calm and quiet.

"Look, I know how hard it is on the force. You put in ten hour days and still have to buy your own holster. We're a powerful team and can offer you protection at work too. You deserve that." She could hear Martha cheering in her earpiece. She wanted to dance in her seat in celebration.

Freddy nodded knowingly. "You totally get it. I've been stuck in this home burglary case for weeks. My team dropped a few balls during the investigation, and we're struggling to get all the evidence we need. It looks bad that this happened on my watch. How could you help me with that?"

Martha's voice crackled. "With the identifying information, I can get to work on getting him the evidence, wherever it lies. And we can make the digital trail look good too."

"Your team is trying to do the work of twice as many people on half the budget. But you don't have to take the hit for this." Jennifer felt her excitement grow. "My team can fix it. Give us the case info, and we'll go to town. My colleague will get you all the evidence you need to get back on your game and impress your team. She can even create a digital trail that shows you logged the evidence properly."

"That sounds perfect. Thank you," Freddy paused. "I would do anything to get out of my financial situation. But how do I know you won't blackmail me later?"

Jennifer considered Martha's feedback, then began, "It's simple. We pay you half upfront and half when the job's complete. Then we all walk away clean. More importantly, we're all at risk. That keeps you safe. You could turn on us at any time, and we don't want that either."

Freddy raised an eyebrow. "What do you need from me?"

"Divert the cops away from our operation. Give them evidence that guides them away from us. They'll never know the difference. You can work with anonymous sources," Jennifer finished with Martha's help. "I bet you're senior enough that you won't be questioned."

"I am pretty senior," Freddy admitted. "And how do you know you can trust me?"

"A gamble, I guess," Jennifer said. "I'm a pretty good judge of character. You seem trustworthy and smarter than the other cops. I hope I'm right."

She knew it was time to get quiet again.

Freddy hesitated and dipped a fry in ketchup. "You're right," he said. "I'm a good guy who got mixed up in some crazy stuff. You can absolutely trust me. And I trust you, Ava. You seem to understand what I'm going through, and you've shown you're on my side. You've got yourself a deal. I'll do whatever you need. I'm glad you came to me with this offer."

"Woohoo!" Martha cheered into the earpiece. "You did it! Now, shake on it."

"The best deals are made over burgers. Shall we shake on it?" Jennifer extended her hand.

Freddy shook her hand firmly. "It's a deal. Let's make some money."

CHAPTER 21

JENNIFER

Sixteen days until heist day

It was 7 PM. Darkness had just fallen. The women filed out one-by-one from a tan getaway SUV, through the local Papillon neighborhood, and into the lush, green park before them. One family remained at the park, but they were packing up their picnic supplies.

It wouldn't be easy to map out their route at night, but the group needed to avoid being seen here together. Jennifer's hands were trembling. *We're not going to get caught,* she reassured herself.

Nari led the way, following the same route she and Jennifer had taken last time. She took the group around the fence perimeter to the facility and pointed out the locations of the security cameras. Jennifer didn't even have this knowledge last time.

"I tried to hack into the surveillance system, but it's not connected to the internet," Martha shared. "It's too risky to go into the office to disconnect the cameras. As long as we follow our route closely, we should be able to stay within the blind spots."

The group made their way through the gap in the fence. Nari motioned for the team to stay back against the brick wall as they entered, behind the line of sight of the security cameras. She pointed out where the truck would be. She briefly swept her flashlight across the lot to highlight each exit and entrance. All were fortified by an access gate.

There was one pedestrian entrance, also locked.

"These gates would slow down any cops," Martha said in a positive tone. "But they'd also slow us down as we exit. Are there any other places we can slip through on foot if we're being pursued?"

"You bet," Nari said. "Follow me, and I'll show you the other gaps in the fence." The group walked behind her, hugging the fence closely.

"There's a gap over there, underneath the streetlight." She motioned with her hand. "But it's very important you don't use that exit unless you're already being pursued. It's got a camera directly above."

"Got it. Thanks, Nari," Martha said, sketching on her notepad.

"There are no badge-less vehicle entry points," Nari explained. "As soon as we start loading the car, Jennifer, you can work on locating the badge. Once you find it, stash it in the glove compartment on top of everything."

"You've got it, chief," Jennifer said playfully, trying to push down her fears. She imagined them getting caught and cuffed mid-job and let out a shaky breath.

"Since we have a team of four, we should have someone on the lookout as we load the truck. I know, it's not ideal to lose a set of hands, but we're too vulnerable if no one's on watch duty," Hana said. "That can be me. I'm less fit than you three." Her face glowed in the moonlight.

"Perfect," Nari said. "I think there's a perch in that corner, if you take the ladder up a level. We'll still be able to hear you from the truck loading zone."

"If a worker or a cop shows up on-site, we'll rush for the van and drive away," Martha explained. "If that doesn't make sense, we'll leave any boxes behind in the van, slip out the fence gap, and run back in the direction we came from."

"That's the perfect time to use the smoke bombs and noise machines. The bombs reduce visibility to a few feet, and the noise machines make it sound like a real explosion is happening. If we use these correctly, the cops won't be able to see or hear us," Hana shared.

"And we might even divert the cops to investigate the explosions," Martha added.

A light breeze came through the trees. It felt refreshing on Jennifer's face.

"We could have a real explosion," Nari said.

Jennifer laughed then drew it back. The look on Nari's face implied she was serious.

"No," Jennifer said firmly. "I love you, Nari. But that's taking this too far. I'd rather go to jail than hurt someone. We can't put anyone in danger. No amount of money is worth that."

"You're right…" Nari murmured.

"I agree," Martha added. "No deaths or injuries. Strictly theft from a company that deserves it."

Hana nodded. "And if we really want to have an advantage against the cops, I can cut off the electricity, shutting down all the lights. We'll need to learn this yard exceptionally well in the dark. This will serve us well on heist day. We'll need to come back, probably every night for the next week. Then we can return every other day to keep it all fresh in our minds. We'll have to vary our arrival time, and take different getaway cars each time."

"On heist night, I'll hack in and extend the security maintenance downtime so the gates will remain unlocked until we're done. It'll look like a technical error the next morning," Martha remarked.

With Hana and Martha at the helm, Jennifer felt a little bit more confident. It seemed like they knew how to reduce the risk of getting caught. Nari had done none of this the first time around.

At least Jennifer had technically done a heist before, a thought that made her shiver. But the stakes felt so much higher this time. There was so much more product and more people depending on her. If she made one mistake, it could all be over. What if she tripped at the wrong moment and got caught on camera? She gulped and tried to reassure herself again. *You're brave and powerful. You're on this team for a reason.*

"We've got this. And no matter what happens, whether we end up running from the cops or not, let's promise to stick together. Heist girlfriends for life!" Martha cheered.

"It's a deal!" Hana replied.

"There's nothing that makes me feel more at home than you three ladies." Nari touched each woman's back.

Jennifer felt a tug in her chest. "Heist girlfriends for life!" she exclaimed.

As they walked back through the darkened neighborhood to their SUV, Nari grinned mischievously. "Jen and I are going to take a walk for a bit. We'll take a cab back home. See you all tomorrow."

Martha and Hana waved before getting into their car. Jennifer cocked her head. "What are you talking about, roomie?"

"I've got a surprise for you," Nari said. Jennifer loved surprises. As long as they didn't involve extra work that she didn't know about, like when her dad surprised her with a train table that she had to help him assemble.

"Amazing." Jennifer clapped her hands. "I'm so excited to see what it is!"

"You're going to love this one," Nari replied, guiding Jennifer across the sidewalk through a dark, quiet residential neighborhood. "It involves laser tag."

Jennifer gasped. "Oh my gosh, I am so good at laser tag! I even beat out Karlie's little five-year-old son. And let's be honest, *no one* can beat him."

Nari laughed. "There's even a surprise guest who will be joining us."

"Is it Karlie?" Jennifer asked. "Did I figure out my surprise already?"

"Almost," Nari said, rounding a corner onto the main street. They walked past a liquor store and into an empty plaza. "Your team awaits." She motioned toward the door of a shop called Laser Castle.

Jennifer couldn't wait to see who she was going to battle. The door opened before she could grab the handle.

"Surprise!" Amir cried.

"Amir!" Jennifer threw her arms around him. Electricity moved through her. As she looked into his eyes, Amir brushed a twist of hair from her forehead.

"Hey, Jen," he replied, "care to shoot?"

•   •   •

The black-lit laser tag course was filled with multi-colored glow in the dark walls that came up to Jennifer's shoulders. Electronic dance music blasted over the speakers, and air-conditioning pumped through the empty space. Each person suited up in a plastic vest attached to a laser gun, and they ran through the course shooting each other. Jennifer stopped to hide behind plastic rocks and building silhouettes. She stifled her laughter and hid to avoid getting shot.

After she had gotten in at least ten hits, Amir approached her with his hands up. "You're amazing at this," he said. "Is it weird that I like it when you shoot at me?" He looked incredible, even under the black lights.

"So you're into laser beams and a little danger. I can respect that," she teased, trying to control the urge to touch him.

"Only when it comes to you." He stepped closer and touched her arm. "You look beautiful."

Her bottom lip quivered, and she felt her heartbeat quicken. "Thank you." She paused for a moment but couldn't stop herself. "I really like you, Amir." He held her gaze, and she felt her knees go weak.

"I really like you too." He laced his fingers through hers, tilted his head to the side, and slowly leaned in to kiss her.

Her world stopped, and she couldn't hear the music anymore. He grazed his fingers along her back, drawing her closer. Chills went through her body.

As he pulled away, Nari sped around a corner and shot them both. "Gotcha, suckers!" she shouted.

•   •   •

"So what were you two up to earlier today?" Amir sipped from his strawberry milkshake at the empty diner next door. They sat in a burgundy padded booth in the back.

Jennifer felt her stomach tighten. She was *not* sneaking around a food service facility at dusk.

"Oh, the usual heist prep," Nari said casually.

Amir stiffened, and his eyes widened. Jennifer could feel herself starting to panic.

Nari froze. "Oops. I assumed Jennifer told you about that already," she said apologetically.

"I... I'm surprised." Amir frowned. "I thought the mission was over. You're not involved, are you Jen?"

Jennifer laced her fingers together and looked up at Amir. Her heart was pounding. "Well, you see, Nari needed some support for the second round, and I...couldn't say no."

She looked up at Nari, who had a sympathetic look on her face. "Sorry," Nari mouthed to her.

Amir was silent. He moved his arm away from Jennifer and fiddled with his straw.

"Is everything okay?" Jennifer asked.

"I'm surprised," Amir said. "I don't really know what to say. I didn't know you two were running a second mission. Why do you need to do it again?"

"We had more demand," Nari explained. "And we'll get to send more money to the women in the mines."

Amir tightened his jaw. "I support your cause, but this doesn't seem wise. It's dangerous." He glanced at Jennifer then Nari. "You know, I should get going. I've got an early morning tomorrow. It was so great to see you both."

Amir waved and left the restaurant. A heavy weight settled in Jennifer's chest. She watched the door, hoping he would turn back around and apologize for reacting so intensely. But nothing happened.

Nari's brows were furrowed in concern. "I'm so sorry, roomie. I had no idea."

Jennifer shook her head. "I... I don't want to lose Amir, but I can't step away from the mission. It's not an option."

CHAPTER 22

NARI

Fifteen days until heist day

One morning, Nari was writing on the sofa, her journal on a golden fuzzy pillow in her lap. Jennifer had left early. She had been gone for ten minutes before she came back in, tripping and flustered, looking for her work laptop. "See you soon!" she'd called out to Nari as she stumbled back out of the apartment, tripping over her floppy ballet flats that were at least half a size too big.

Nari chuckled and looked back at her journal. She had been brainstorming about what her trip to Vancouver would look like. It would take place in the summertime, of course.

Suddenly, her phone buzzed three times, signaling it was coming from the encrypted app. She jumped and looked at the screen. It was Freddy. What a pleasant surprise.

"Hi, Nari," Freddy said in a hushed voice, "I have an update for you."

"Amazing, thanks so much for calling," she exclaimed.

"Listen, someone called in an anonymous tip on the heist," he replied.

She froze. Her head started to swim, and her ears made a rushing sound. "When did that happen?" she asked breathlessly.

"This morning. Our team knows there's a heist being planned against Essentrix Labs. We don't have any leads on who's involved. I'm trying to divert resources away as much as possible," He paused. "When the time comes, I'll try to get rookies on the case so they'll be easier to control. Gotta go. Bye."

Nari went to the kitchen to fill her cup with ice and water. Her mouth had suddenly gone dry. The cops were onto them. Who would call in a tip? Was it someone on their team?

She paced the kitchen and opened up her phone's encrypted app to call her mom. She didn't know who else she could trust.

"Good morning," her mom replied happily. "I'm painting with my new friends. What are you up to, *nae jasik*?"

"I think we have a mole," Nari said, her tone serious.

There was a pause on the other line. Nari could hear shuffling noises. After a minute, Hana broke the silence. "Tell me more," she said.

"Freddy let me know the cops got an anonymous tip about the heist. They're onto us but don't have any leads yet. We need to figure out who did this." Nari ran her fingers through her hair.

"We don't know who we can trust. Don't tell anyone about this yet until we can figure out where the leak came from," Hana replied. "Now let's think about motive."

"We don't know Lorinda yet, and Jennifer mentioned she's trying to keep her green card. She seems driven to take down Essentrix Labs, but maybe that's an act," Nari began. "She has a lot to lose."

"Yes, definitely a possibility," Hana said thoughtfully. "I'm also not sure about the team on the inside. They haven't been fully vetted yet."

"I don't know what they would stand to gain by turning us in." Nari fiddled with her ring. "Unless someone did it by accident."

"If they're afraid of getting caught, they might want to tip off law enforcement first. Maybe they were never loyal," Hana said. "We've got five people on the inside team, so we're exposed."

Nari drew in a breath. "We gave Lorinda full control in recruiting them. Maybe we were too trusting." She paused. "Could it be Freddy? What if the department's on to him and they cut him a deal?"

Hana was silent. "Maybe he thinks he can double-dip," she added. "He'll take our reward and theirs. Then he'll qualify for a promotion."

"But I doubt the force can match our bonus. I'm also not sure if Freddy cares about their respect or his career. I feel pretty safe with him." Nari tapped her fingers to the coffee table. Her mouth fell open. "What if it's Johannes?"

"You've got a point, my child. He's been asking you strange questions. He's starting to get overbearing," Hana replied.

"And think about it. Why would he ask me and Jennifer to head this mission after he saw what happened at the gala?" Nari asked. "Maybe he wants us to fail."

"But why? That's the biggest piece of the puzzle," Hana replied.

Nari hesitated. "What if Johannes is trying to draw the cops away from himself? What if he's got a bigger scheme he's trying to pull off? If we take the fall, maybe he can get away with it."

"You could be right, *nae jasik*. We've got to consider stepping away from this job," Hana replied. "If it's Johannes, he's a powerful man. He could even tell the cops who we are. Some risks aren't worth taking."

Nari wanted to seem understanding. She knew on some level that her mom was right. But there was no part of her that was ready to back away. It was the first time she had been able to work with her mom—and lead her—on such a lucrative opportunity. If they stepped away now, her mom would fly back to New York, continue painting, and would never see how much Nari could accomplish.

She loved sharing this secret world with her mom. Even better, after all the time she'd spent learning from her mother's black market insights and poring over her profit and loss statements, *she* was the one leading the charge now. This time, she had brought a lucrative opportunity to her mom. She was finally giving back, and together they could take down an evil company.

She had to fight to see this through. "I agree. Whoever this mole is, they could do anything. But we've got a mighty team. You and Martha have both outsmarted the cops before. We can always remain one step ahead. Plus, we've got Freddy on our side."

Hana sighed audibly. "Nari..." she started. The corner of

Nari's mouth turned up into a half smile. She could tell by her mom's tone that she could be convinced.

"Think about it, Mom," Nari said.

"I will. Let's regroup, but we'll prepare to tell the team," Hana added. "We can talk to our inner circle about the mole, but don't talk to anyone else about it."

"Sounds like a plan," Nari said. She hung up the phone and tapped her finger to her bare arm. She needed to motivate the team to continue and convince her mom that it was a good idea. Maybe her mom would finally notice how driven and dependable she was.

A friendly, patterned knock at the door broke into Nari's thoughts. She let out a playful groan, thinking it was Jennifer coming back for her key.

"What did you forget this time—" she said lightly as she opened the door.

Except it wasn't Jennifer standing there. It was Sumeet.

"Hey, Nari," he said.

"Oh, you're not Jennifer." She felt her face grow hot, embarrassed that she hadn't put up her guard to tease Sumeet. She hadn't even been conscious of how she was acting in front of him.

"It's great to see you," he said with a familiarity that melted her defenses. He was wearing a form-fitting baby-blue tee that showed off his muscles. His skin was glowing, and his hair was loosely styled. Her eyes were drawn across his body, from his muscular arms to his warm expression.

She wanted to make an excuse to send him packing but knew she had nothing better to do. Instead, she bit her lip and felt the urge to let him inside.

"Come on in. I've got pretzels and cashew butter," she replied.

His face lit up. "It's like you knew I was coming over."

He came in and sat down on the brocade sofa, bringing a scent of salted ocean breeze in with him. Strange, as they were land-locked in the middle of the country.

He was carrying a red, reusable cloth grocery bag with him. From inside, he pulled out a single pink rose. "Don't get any crazy ideas. I cut this from my garden and wanted to share it with you."

She grinned. She wouldn't take the rose as a come-on. It was too tiring for her to think that way. Instead, she was touched that he had thought of her.

"I hear from Johannes that your project is coming along nicely. Congrats on the big order," Sumeet said. "I knew this would be easy for you. You've got the entrepreneurial instincts of a billionaire. You could sell mangoes to a mango farmer."

Apt description. She wondered if she could sell mangoes to Martha. She bet she could.

"You're too kind," she replied. "It's been an awesome experience. I've brought my mom, Jennifer, and my friend Martha into it. You know, the former mango farmer."

"I knew there was a reason that example was on my mind. That's amazing. I bet all three of them are great to work with," he remarked.

Nari felt a warmth with him as they talked. She felt herself moving closer to him.

He dipped a pretzel stick into the bowl of cashew butter, swirling it around.

Don't talk to anyone else about the mole. But she needed to ask him about Johannes. He had introduced them, after all. And of course she could trust him. She cleared her throat. "The cops have been tipped off about our heist," she began.

His face fell. "What, Nari?"

"Yup. There's a chance it's Johannes. He's been acting strangely lately. My mom and I are trying to figure out his motive. I haven't told the rest of the team yet, but I know you had your hesitations about him, so I wanted to tell you first," Nari explained.

"I'm so sorry I set you up with him." He sighed and ran his hands through his hair. "I always felt weird about Johannes. He gave me a bad vibe. Despite my doubts, I still introduced you, because I know you can navigate your way through any situation and come out on top. Probably better than me."

She enjoyed the praise but raised an eyebrow.

"But maybe I made a mistake," he finished. "Maybe my instincts were right about him."

She waved dismissively. "It's alright. I pushed you to do it. You were upfront about your hesitations. I went into it knowing there was risk."

"I have contacts that can get you and the team out of the country until things die down. I can help you get fake identities and passports. I'll do everything I can to cover your tracks," he replied with concern. Haltingly, he reached out and stroked her shoulder. "It's the least I can do."

She felt chills go through her body at Sumeet's touch. "Thanks. I'll talk to the team about it, but I want to figure out if there's a way to keep going with the deal and cut Johannes out of it. We'll keep him ignorant on the details. My heart's in this now. We've already built trust with an inside team at Essentrix to pull off the job without him."

"That seems a little bit reckless. Maybe over-confident. I don't think you should try to outsmart the police. I mean, think about it. You've made so much money doing other things. Why not walk away and start something else again? Maybe this wasn't meant to be," he finished.

Nari didn't know how to respond. He would find out eventually if they moved forward, so any lie now would be delaying the inevitable. She watched him silently.

"Again, I'm so sorry I introduced you to Johannes. It was totally a bad call," Sumeet said. She felt his gaze move from the wall in front of them, to her face. Something stirred inside her.

"It's okay. You had no idea something like this would happen," she replied softly. Nari looked up at Sumeet's face and took in his athletic body and broad shoulders again. She could see his pecs through his shirt. "Besides, I've loved this experience. I haven't felt this close with my mom in years, after she stopped bringing me deals in college."

"Ah, tough love," he said. "But now you're quite the magnate. What happened in college?"

She glanced at the coffee table. "Oh, you know. It's not interesting. We had some conflict. Could you pass the pretzels?"

"You can tell me anything, Nari." His voice was kind. "If you want to. I always love learning more about you." He tilted his head toward her. Something about him felt safe and welcoming.

Nari exhaled slowly. "I don't normally talk about this much..." She paused. "I was twenty-two. We had just closed a luxury handbag deal worth millions with an underground re-seller. Sure, it wasn't my deal, but I negotiated hard and helped win them over. My mom gave me a decent cut of the profit. Four hundred thousand.

"We washed the money through her shell companies. Once my payout hit my account, she cut me off. She told me it was our last deal together. I was lost. I begged her to take me back. I could easily close deals by myself, but I came alive with her by my side at the negotiating table. But she didn't care. She told me I'd understand someday.

"I'll admit, it was hard. But now I'm a much better woman for it. I'm sourcing and closing my own six-figure deals. I'm in the driver's seat. I want to show her what I can do. This Sorbelate mission may not be the biggest deal she's worked on, but I can still lead my mom to more money and power."

Sumeet's face softened. "That's really sweet. I love that you are getting the chance to work with your mom on this and finally lead." He reached out and touched her hand. She felt an electric charge running from her hand through her body. "It seems like your mom is comfortable with things that are... legally murky."

"You're absolutely right," Nari replied. "But that saved her. My first memories are of my parents yelling at each other about money. They were broke when they moved to the US."

"Sounds a lot like my parents," he murmured knowingly. "My dad bought a convenience store when he moved from India. My parents had to sleep on the floor until they could afford a place of their own."

Her eyes widened. "Wow, that's even more intense than I could have imagined."

"It's that immigrant lifestyle." He shrugged. "What happened next?"

"As the years went by, my mom seemed to break free from a trance. She'd get up early, be out all day, and come back late at night," she said. Sumeet was watching her intently. "Around that time, we started to move every few months for my mom's business. My parents seemed happier together, which was great. I saw my family change, and I knew it was because of my mom's business—her drive, resilience, and motivation."

"You are speaking my language right now. You take after her completely. You're one of the most brilliant entrepreneurs I've worked with," he observed.

Nari beamed. "Thank you. My mom told me that I could accomplish whatever I wanted in business. I could be free. But over the years, things got strange. She never met the same person in the same location twice. She got shifty when cops drove by. My mom told me never to speak of her work to anyone. She'd stop at new locations to make calls from different pay phones. She received mysterious packages, always hand delivered."

Sumeet touched Nari's shoulder tenderly. "How did that impact you? I can't believe you went through that at such a young age."

"You'd think I would be angry or even resentful. First, I was embarrassed," she explained.

"Naturally," he said emphatically.

"I had to hide my mom's work from my friends at school. I got really creative with my lies. But as I got older, I learned more about my mom's underground deals. Little by little, I started to accept her work. And then, before long, I was proud of her. So what if my mom had to bend the law to make a living?" she continued.

"If anything, your mom did you a favor, teaching you that lesson so young," he joked.

Nari pushed his shoulder playfully. "I learned from a young age that being rich was infinitely better than being not poor. None of my friends could live the lifestyle that we did. None of them could invite their friends on winter trips to Florida. None of them could pick out anything they wanted at the toy store."

"One hundred percent," he said emphatically.

"I saw what a little hustle could do for you. I've always been obsessed with that freedom from worries, that freedom of choice. And most of all, freedom to pursue joy in whatever form you want." Nari felt buoyant. She had never recounted these stories to anyone.

Sumeet's eyes softened. "I completely agree. But you're forgetting one thing, Ms. Park."

She knew what was coming next.

"You can't enjoy that freedom from inside a jail cell," he added.

She smirked. "Right, Mr. Vora. I know some risks aren't worth taking. I'll admit that sometimes you need to let missions go. But I'm so confident in my team. I know we can remain one step ahead."

He leaned in to touch her thigh lightly. "If there's anyone who can do it, it's you."

She felt a pulse running through her body. "There's something about you," she said slowly. To her own surprise, she leaned in and started to kiss him. She shivered with pleasure.

He kissed her back and ran his fingers through her hair. His hands made their way to her back, and he pulled her closer.

"I want you, Nari," Sumeet said, his voice breathy.

She trembled with each trace of his fingertips. His touch was smooth and familiar. She sighed and felt her body pull closer to him. It felt so right. She couldn't fight it anymore. Sumeet was *hot*. Nari stood up and led him to the bedroom.

CHAPTER 23

NARI

Fourteen days until heist day

Sumeet and Nari were in bed with their fingers entwined, each of them wearing a loose t-shirt. It had been an incredible evening. She had given in to her urges, against her better judgment. It felt so delicious.

"What are you working on now, after Diapergate?" She grinned as she looked over at him.

"I could tell you, but I have to wrestle you first!" He turned to face her.

"Oh, it's on!" She giggled. She popped up and threw her body on top of him, starting to tickle his ribs. He wriggled his body and laughed uncontrollably. "Not fair," he said between gasps. He flipped Nari onto her back and looked into her eyes.

"I'm selling black market bamboo to construction companies." He kissed her bare arm. "I have a team of misfits smuggling it in from Vietnam, labeling it as bamboo flutes to get through customs. I'm paying almost nothing in import taxes."

She chuckled. "You never fail to disappoint. Profit margin?" Sumeet smoothed his fingertips over Nari's arm and she felt chills.

"Eighty percent, baby," he extended his hand for a high-five. "Right here."

She slapped his hand. "Amazing, Vora." She got up and put on a flouncy black skater skirt and blue floral crop top. "Headed to the bathroom. See you out there?"

He saluted and reached over to squeeze her butt before she left.

When Nari entered the living room, Jennifer was sitting at the counter in a purple running outfit while drinking her homemade electrolyte mix and sketching. Her morning routine was comfortingly predictable.

Jennifer seemed to have no idea that Sumeet was there. She slept through anything, and it was a quality that many roommates appreciated in her. She also often went to bed early, giving Nari privacy when she brought a man home every once in a while.

"I was feeling nervous about the mission and Amir so I started working on my comic book again. Best distraction ever. Come check out this scene. The ancient and modern Mayan heroes are building a spear thrower with a laser guidance system," Jennifer explained.

Nari glanced at the elaborate drawing. The ancient hero wore a feathered celestial cape and intricately drawn jewelry. She stood next to the modern hero, whose casual shorts and crop top contrasted with the powerful weaponry they were creating. "Wow. This is incredible, roomie. Kind of terrifying, but genius."

Sumeet emerged into the living room, his hair tousled. He was wearing his t-shirt and shorts from the night before. His facial hair was irregularly matted and unkempt.

"Hey there, Sumeet. I didn't expect to see you this morning." Jennifer winked.

He grinned, taking in Jennifer's outfit. "Nari told me if I got here early we could all go workout together."

Normally, Nari would find an excuse to leave. She had already spent the whole night with Sumeet. But it felt so good being a part of his world again.

Maybe she could convince Jennifer to get breakfast at the diner with them. It would be so fun to joke around and finally have someone outside of the heist crew who they could discuss their plans with.

But Jennifer would not change her running schedule for anything. Not even a tornado warning, which she had shrugged off and ran right through last fall. "I'll come back if I see anything," she had said.

Jennifer giggled. "You should come jogging with our heist group sometime."

Sumeet glanced at Nari. "I would love to. I'm training for a 10k with my brother, so that fits right into my plans."

Nari felt a buzz as she imagined running alongside Sumeet. She caught herself and redirected her thoughts. *Relax, Nari.*

"It was great to see you, Sumeet. See you soon, Nari!" Jennifer put in her earbuds. Nari could hear nineties dance music blasting. Jennifer waved and walked out the front door.

Sumeet turned to Nari. "Want to get breakfast? And then maybe play some arcade games?"

It sounded like the perfect day. Nari agreed, and the pair took off.

•   •   •

As Nari battled Sumeet in wizard pinball in an empty pizza parlor, she knew she had to tell the rest of the group about the threat from the mole. But she needed to get some more intel first.

She won another round, spun in place, and took a sip of victory soda. "I need to step away for a second. I'm going to see what Martha can find on Johannes."

Sumeet smiled. "Do what you need to do."

Nari stepped into the parking lot and called Martha on her encrypted calling app.

"Hey, Martha," she said cheerfully.

"*Buenas tardes, amiga,*" Martha replied.

"You know how Johannes has been acting strange recently?" Nari started, choosing her words carefully.

"Totally," Martha responded, "do you want me to do some research on him?"

"Yes, please," Nari said. "Hack into his accounts. Find out what he's up to. I'm not sure we can trust him. And for now we're going to hold off on communicating with him until we can figure out what's going on."

"I can have something for you in a couple of hours. Let's meet in person to discuss," Martha replied.

Nari hung up and her phone buzzed again. It was her mom.

"I met Lorinda at a coffee shop, saying I wanted to talk about inventory security measures," Hana began. "Turns out, she's taken extra steps to divert anyone outside of the heist from getting too close to our operation. She's rescheduling inspections and working with the inside team to change training related to Sorbelate inventory."

"She's doing the right thing." Nari inhaled, feeling her shoulders relax. "On her own."

"We can trust her," Hana agreed.

• • •

That afternoon, Martha and Nari donned their wigs and met at a crowded bowling alley.

Martha gave Nari a warm hug. She could smell her floral perfume.

"Johannes is running a black market gemstone business." Martha rolled her bowling ball down the lane. "No surprises there."

Nari nodded. "Par for the course." She picked up her eight-pound bowling ball with its blue swirl pattern and rolled it toward the pins. She hit a strike. The pair high-fived.

"But there's a twist. I've intercepted some of their communications. Johannes is planning a heist himself in Omaha. He's got another team that wants to lift gemstones from a distributor across town, around the same time as our mission." Martha leaned in closer. "The shipment includes some incredibly rare blue diamonds, so the stakes are high. I don't know if we can trust this man."

"That makes so much sense," Nari replied, her anger swelling. "You're right. We can't trust him. Thanks for the intel."

"*De nada,*" Martha said. "We shouldn't reveal any heist details to Johannes until we can see how this plays out a little bit more."

Nari stood taller and raised an eyebrow. The team was up to the challenge. They could outsmart both the mole and the cops.

They bowled their last few frames, ate a plate of nachos, and went home.

• • •

That evening, Nari called the whole team together for a meeting at the apartment. She described the situation with the cops and the mole. Their faces became more serious the further she got into her explanation.

"I *knew* we couldn't trust Johannes. It was too easy. He just hands us this heist plot and steps away." Martha paced the room with her hands balled into fists.

"What a rat," Jennifer said forcefully. "I thought he sounded like such a nice person."

"You can't trust international criminals these days," Hana joked. "But it could be anyone. Lorinda, we'll need to explore if anyone on the inside team could be the source of the leak."

Lorinda nodded slowly, her eyes unblinking.

"This mission isn't worth it anymore," Martha spat out. "The danger outweighs the payout. I'm not putting my freedom on the line. I'm going to go back to Mexico City today, and I would recommend you all head to Mexico too. We need to act quickly."

"I'll head to Tulum," Jennifer added. "Maybe I'll get a job as a tour guide. I can't take this risk either. Not for any amount of money."

"I can't lose my green card," Lorinda said quietly. Jennifer looked at her sympathetically and touched her hand.

Hana was reading something on her phone. "Ladies, I was suspicious earlier, so I did some research. I'm afraid I have some bad news." She cleared her throat as she looked up. "In Nebraska, you can serve up to fifty years in jail for conspiracy to commit a crime. It's almost as bad as actually performing the crime."

Jennifer froze. Lorinda's eyes widened and she looked like she was going to be sick.

"I'm glad I'm just learning about this now." Martha shook her head.

"We could face serious jail time even if we stepped away now." Hana stood and folded her arms. "But then we'd have nothing, and the Essentrix Labs executives would walk away free while they continue to exploit people."

Jennifer brought her hands to her face. "Oh my gosh."

Hana continued, "I've evaded the cops many times before and learned a few things. I know how they think and how to be a few steps ahead of them."

"Hana, this isn't some negotiation in Turks and Caicos where you can pay off the cops to look the other way while you smuggle luxury bags into the country." Martha slammed her fist down on the coffee table. "This is large-scale theft, and we're going up against a powerful police force."

"You're right, Martha. But these cops are not as smart and adaptable as we are. There are so many things we can do to throw them off our trail," Hana replied calmly. "I feel confident we can pull this off. It's not time to end our mission yet."

Hana had the group's attention, Nari noticed with pride.

"I don't need the money, but the women miners in the Congo do. I want to give them my cut of the proceeds. If we stay with this mission, they can finally stand up to Essentrix Labs," Hana said in a commanding voice. "And besides, how empowering would it be to finally pull off this job? Don't you want to prove to yourself how much you can accomplish?"

Jennifer looked at Hana. Her expression seemed to soften.

"My mom's right," Nari said, her voice even. "We can pull off the mission by staying one step ahead of the cops. If anything, this makes our team stronger."

Hana paused. "Plus, I'm having a good time strategizing with you wonderful people." She grinned deviously.

Jennifer's eyes glimmered. "We can't change these women's lives without money. With millions of dollars, they'll be free. They can open businesses that elevate entire communities. Everyone can get back to being healthy, breathing fresh air, and dancing at festivals. I want that for them," she said passionately. "And to be honest, I would love some of that freedom for myself. I have so many things I want to do with the money. Like travel and go out to eat whenever I want..."

"Amen to all of that," Hana said.

"I'm not saying I'm going to go through with this. But what would you suggest we do to throw off the cops?" Martha crossed her arms across her chest.

"First, we'll plant an informant at Essentrix Labs who will

mislead the cops. Of course, Freddy will have our backs and will work on derailing the investigation. We'll feed Johannes false information. And finally we'll secure another backup getaway truck and conduct a decoy heist," Nari explained.

"A decoy heist?" Jennifer asked, a look of confusion on her face.

"We'll get a group together to run a copycat job at the Mill Creek Lane facility in South Omaha at the same time as ours. We'll have evidence that will lead the cops to the fake heist. The cops will monitor the wrong location, and we'll get away undetected," Nari explained, glancing at each team member.

"This sounds promising enough so far," Martha said.

"We'll need to plan out as many escape routes for heist day as we can. Mom, we'll need a different getaway truck waiting for us in the same parking garage as last time. If we have enough time, we'll transfer the loot to the getaway truck and leave the Essentrix truck in the garage," Nari continued.

"Copy," Hana replied.

"The good news is, if we go on with this mission, we don't have to pay Johannes anything. But we're going to need more money to attract the people who are willing to be the focus of the cops' attention," Nari said.

"You're right," Hana replied. "We'll need at least a few million more to attract a group of four. Lorinda, we would need your help to get us more product."

Lorinda tilted her head slightly forward in acknowledgment.

"We're going to have to get tighter to be able to move this product more quickly," Nari said.

She thought back to their recent workout sessions.

Everyone was getting noticeably stronger. More fit and more agile. Even her mom was able to lift more than usual. "Which shouldn't be a problem," she added.

"But with all this new product, you're going to need to learn how to drive a delivery truck," Hana said to Nari, who sucked in air. Of course she knew that.

"You're right, Mom." Nari tried to hide the tension in her voice.

"Lorinda, if you can get matching delivery trucks for each team, that will help us throw off the cops," Hana added.

"I know you mentioned working with Johannes, Nari. But what if he's the mole?" Jennifer asked. "I'm not sure we should even involve him at all."

Nari loved the way Jennifer was talking, as if the plans were still on.

"We can apologize to Johannes for being absent recently. We'll bring him back into the planning process gradually with small pieces of misinformation and fake plan documents. We'll only transmit decoy heist information to him." Nari leaned forward with her hands on the coffee table.

Nari's mom was beaming.

"But who would operate this distraction mission for us? Especially since the police would be after them?" Jennifer asked.

"I've got a few people I can count on," Hana said. "I've rewarded them well over the years."

"That's great." Martha brought her hand to her face. "But this is so risky. I have plenty of experience with paying off the cops, but I've always held all the cards. I've never escaped from them before."

"The danger is real," Hana admitted. "I can't deny that. But we've got state-of-the-art tools and the best team around. I know we can outplay the police."

Nari nodded. If she needed to, she could at least pull off a smaller-scale, two-person job with her mom. Maybe with fewer people, her mom would give her more of a say.

"I love coming to the US. I don't want to be banned..." Martha began.

"Or worse, not be able to leave," Jennifer said.

Martha chuckled.

The room went silent. Jennifer's eyes fell on the coffee table. "I don't know if I'm ready to give up yet. We've worked so hard to get here," she explained. "I can't believe I'm saying this, but maybe we have all the skills we need. Maybe we only need to plan a little bit more."

Martha hesitated. "Essentrix Labs has hurt countless women in the Congo, and they've harmed me too. The company takes from people and expects them to never fight back. Well, that's not going to be me this time. We are strong enough to pull this off. I'm not ready to go back yet. Plus, I don't want the girlfriend time to end."

"Oh, it's on!" Nari cried. "Together, we will rock this mission!"

The women cheered, except for Lorinda, who was silent.

"I've been wanting to ruin Essentrix Labs for years." Lorinda exhaled slowly. "And I respect you ladies so much for moving forward, but I don't know if I can be involved anymore. There's so much at risk for me with my immigration status. I could get kicked out of the country. This is my home. I think I'm going to have to step out."

Jennifer's jaw dropped. "But we need you! We can't run the heist without you!"

"She's right," Hana added. "You're an essential member of the team. Without your support, this could fall apart. We'll give you a bigger cut to stay on."

Lorinda looked at the floor. "I'm happy to introduce you to the team on the inside. I'll be there in spirit. I really don't want to walk away, but I have to."

A solemn expression took over Jennifer's face.

Nari swallowed hard. She reached over and hugged Lorinda. "We're going to miss you."

CHAPTER 24

ROBERTA

Thirteen days until heist day

Roberta came into work early. She had barely slept the night before and couldn't wait to get started.

The day before, the department had received an anonymous tip about a corporate theft, and the chief had assigned her to work on the case with Freddy. She had no idea how she had gotten so lucky.

She had gotten into policing to know and protect her community. With this case, she could finally earn the clout to develop her dream program, one where residents and the force would work together to make Omaha better. She was ready to put in as many hours as she needed to find the perpetrators.

An employee of Essentrix Labs was allegedly stealing Sorbelate from their employer and selling it to a group of four women. The women would then resell the product for a profit on the black market. It seemed like a pretty lucrative scam for everyone involved.

Roberta was researching the history of Essentrix Labs when Freddy approached her desk.

"Good morning, Roberta," Freddy started.

She bristled. She wasn't ready to be addressed by her first name so early in the morning. She caught herself frowning and forced a smile. He was more senior than her, and she hoped he wouldn't try to take over her parts of the investigation.

"Good morning, Officer Anderson," she responded. "I'm excited to work on this case. I haven't been able to find any high-value corporate thefts like this one in the Omaha area over the last thirty years. And this is the first time on record that a theft has been attempted against Essentrix Labs."

He raised an eyebrow. "You're right. There's no playbook for this. It's new to the whole department. We've got our work cut out for us. This morning, we can do a site tour and start to interview employees. If we can find the internal seller, that will be great."

She brought her hand to her chin. She liked the way he was thinking. "I'd love to uncover a motive. I'm looking forward to cross-checking our interviews with the employee attendance logs and security records."

His face was stiff and unreadable. "Who knew we'd get a case like this in sleepy Omaha? I know the chief put you on the case because he's really impressed with your investigative ability. Looking forward to cracking this one together."

Roberta beamed. The chief had noticed her and was impressed with her work. She couldn't wait to call her mom when she got home.

That morning, Roberta and Freddy loaded up the patrol car and headed to Essentrix Labs to interview employees and look for evidence.

When they arrived, their coworker Emily was already there, set up in an empty office with a line of employees stretching down a long hallway.

"Any leads yet?" Freddy asked as he and Roberta entered the office. Emily closed the door behind them.

"Not so far. Maybe it's the skeptic in me, but some people seem like they're hiding something." Emily had been typing her notes in an old but solid-looking gray laptop.

Maybe it was the inexperience or the drive to make a name for herself. But while Freddy nodded in a detached way, Roberta promised herself immediately that she would identify the people behind this robbery. She felt a sense of steely resolve that didn't come around often in the Omaha State Police Department.

"I'll be happy to take over the interviews," Freddy said, his expression blank. Roberta felt herself deflate.

"Sounds good," Emily responded. "I really could use a break and a good bagel."

Freddy grinned. "Roberta, would you be able to search the perimeter for clues? It's worth a try."

"I'm on it, Freddy." This was not Roberta's ideal afternoon, but she was here to put in the time and build her reputation. She would put her all into the search.

The day had gotten hot, and she was already sweating in her uniform as she stepped out to examine the property exterior. She loved that the building bordered a large, verdant park, with plenty of blooming flowers.

As she started her walk around the outer fence, a woman in uniform waved to her. Roberta recognized the uniform immediately as belonging to Essentrix Labs.

"Hello, Officer," the woman said.

"Hello there," Roberta replied. "Nice weather we're having."

"Love the sunshine," the woman agreed. She paused, a concerned look on her face. "Look, I don't know if I'm not supposed to talk to you, but I know something about this heist."

Roberta perked up. "Thanks for coming to me. What do you know?"

The woman came closer. "I need to stay anonymous. I'm not going to tell you my name."

"That's fine. I will keep your identity hidden from the team," Roberta said.

"Thank you," the woman remarked, her voice low. "I overheard this guy in logistics talking about the heist. Apparently, the criminals are going to rob a different Essentrix Labs facility in Omaha, the one on Mill Creek Lane. They've seen the cops here and don't want to get caught."

"Thank you," Roberta said emphatically. "That's very helpful. Do you have any other—"

"Sorry, that's all I can share," the woman said as she turned and walked away.

Roberta wrote down the details of their conversation in her pocket notebook. She felt excited and grateful that she had a lead in this case. And the lead had come to *her*.

Maybe she should keep this lead and her insight a secret until she could determine whether it was credible. Besides, if she told Freddy and Emily, they might take over the investigation.

She continued her walk around the perimeter of the fence, watching as people came and went for their lunch breaks. As she rounded a corner, she reached the side of the compound that was more abandoned. It jutted against the park. She scanned the park and noticed a pile of cloth on the ground, closer to the street. She vaguely remembered spotting it a few weeks ago on patrol with Freddy.

She walked over to the sage-green cloth and could tell it was a bathrobe as she got closer. It looked like it had been outside for a while. She picked it up. Nice fabric. It had a heft to it. She looked at the tag. *La Veille*. Seemed like a French name. She had never heard of the brand before.

Turning the robe over, she noticed it had pockets. She reached inside the left pocket and pulled out a business card.

Here we go. Her pulse quickened as she looked it over. There was a name at the top of the business card. *"Amir Haddad."*

She quickly folded up the bathrobe and slid the business card in her pocket.

Maybe this meant nothing. Maybe a drunken college student had stopped by the park and lost their bathrobe. Or maybe, this Amir was connected to the case somehow. Maybe she was getting closer to cracking the case.

A huge smile overtook Roberta's face.

CHAPTER 25

JENNIFER

Thirteen days until heist day

Nari had been driving by Essentrix Labs in Papillon in different cars and disguises throughout the day. It was easy to detect the police presence, and the team agreed they were ready to train their informant.

Martha had identified an employee in compliance that was isolated at work. After three years at Essentrix Labs, she'd never gotten a raise. She logged everything, but her team ignored her ideas. She seemed ready to rebel.

All four women gathered at Nari and Jennifer's apartment to debrief. It was an exciting moment.

"Our informant did a great job," Nari said. "I've confirmed that she's spoken to an Omaha State Police cop about our fake heist. And she thinks the cop bought it."

"Yes!" Martha raised her fist in the air.

"Now, we've got to feed the same information to Johannes," Nari added. "Jennifer, you've got a special bond with Johannes already. Your pureness of spirit would be enough to convince him that you're telling the truth."

Jennifer shook her head. "I can't do it."

"*Sí, se puede.* This is easy for you now," Martha told Jennifer, patting her shoulder. "I think you've already earned your negotiator Girl Scout badge."

Jennifer shivered. She was a terrible liar. She lied to her mom in middle school, when she and her best friend were headed to the mall instead of to study group. Her unsteady voice gave her away. When she was confronted by her mom, she crumbled under the pressure and cried. She hadn't been able to maintain the lie for five minutes.

The fate of the team could be resting on her shoulders. She knew Nari was right. She wouldn't make Johannes suspicious. She tried to channel the voice of her grandma. "Jenny, I'm proud of you. I know you can lie when you need to." Imagination Grandma sure was an enabler.

"Remember," Nari said, looking her in the eye. "We're here to support you. If you need help, mute the phone, and we'll tell you how to respond. You are going to do great."

Jennifer gulped. She decided she would channel the spirit of Amina Keita, her favorite comic book character, who traveled through the ancient African kingdoms of Mali, Sudan, and Eritrea. Fictional, sure, but she always knew what to say to the most commanding people.

There we go. Jennifer now had a power to inhabit.

She looked at her script and ran through it in her mind again. *Sound natural, Jenny,* she said to herself in her grandma's voice.

One by one, Jennifer dialed the digits to call Johannes. After two rings, he picked up.

"I'm calling about something important." Jennifer tried to sound genuine while edging up the fear in her voice. "I think the cops are onto us. We're thinking of switching our heist to a new location."

She looked up and saw the team giving her a thumbs-up. She smiled.

Johannes paused. "That sounds wise," he said. "What are you planning to do instead?" There was a surprising warmth to his tone.

Jennifer took a shaky, deep breath and covered the mouthpiece. Nari gave her a knowing, supportive look.

"There's another Essentrix Labs facility in South Omaha on Mill Creek Lane. We've got contacts there. It seems the cops haven't been looking into that facility. It's looking like a good opportunity for us," Jennifer finished, feeling a nervous sense of accomplishment.

"Alright," Johannes said. "This change is probably for the best. Can you still move the same amount of product there?"

"Yes," Jennifer replied. "We're training to get ready for it." At least the training part was true, and she was able to say it fluidly.

"Excellent," Johannes remarked.

She talked to Johannes for a little while longer, saying the minimum needed to move the conversation toward its close. They talked about his new dog Fritzi (peppy, friendly to strangers), and the Viennese summer (beautiful and appreciated). She shared an anecdote—totally true—about nearly tripping over a dog leash on her run that morning.

"I know the team is going to do great," he said. "I think it's a good idea to change locations."

Yup, Jennifer thought triumphantly. *Can't wait for you to send cops to the wrong location.*

"Great talking to you, Johannes. Give Fritzi a hug for me," she said as kindly as she could.

She hung up and felt her body go slack. All of her muscles were engaged to withstand the force of the conversation.

"Okay, roomie, you are officially unstoppable!" Nari said, patting Jennifer's back. Martha and Hana each took one of Jennifer's hands to squeeze.

The tension drained from Jennifer's face. She felt like a hero, conquering kingdoms and making millions under the ancient Songhai Empire of Mali. That money would be worth at least a billion today, adjusted for inflation and exchange rates.

She had successfully convinced a possible enemy that the plans were changing. She felt like she could convince anyone of anything.

"Alright, back to business, ladies." Nari held her body steady. "I have an idea. I think we should tip the cops off about Johannes's gemstone heist."

Jennifer drew in a sharp breath.

"I don't think that's a good idea." Martha folded her arms across her chest.

"Hear me out," Nari replied. "We retaliate. We take some of the heat off of us. We'll call in an anonymous tip. If Johannes is the mole, his plans all blow over on him."

"But he knows who we are," Jennifer added, her face growing warm.

"Jennifer's right," Hana said. "Johannes still doesn't know

that we suspect anything. If we were to tip off the cops, he'd give our identities to them immediately. We lose all of our leverage that way."

Nari looked deflated. "Right, Mom." She sighed. Jennifer wanted to pull Nari aside and tell her she was still amazing.

"Moving on." Hana inhaled deeply. "Lorinda put me in touch with the team on the inside. I've been working to build their trust. A few of them aren't cooperating. They want more money. The two people in charge of inventory told me they can't meet the extra demand."

Jennifer's eyes widened.

"In the meantime, I've fed different decoy heist intel to each member on the inside. Things like shipment times, inventory codes, and the gear we're using. That way, if any of that info makes its way to the cops, we'll know who leaked it," Hana explained.

"Perfect," Nari said. "Also, Martha, can you hack into their phones and see if there's any suspicious chatter going on?"

"You've got it, *patrona*." Martha tipped her head forward.

"Without the inside team, this mission falls apart," Hana continued. "Martha, I'm going to need your help persuading them.

"I'm happy to help," Martha replied. "Let's talk to them tomorrow."

Jennifer's pulse quickened. "We're still going to work with them, even though we're not sure who we can trust?"

Nari nodded. "We'll have to tread carefully. We still need their help and don't want the mole to know we're on to them."

"We've got to keep them comfortable. We'll only share small pieces of info with each person. No one will know the big picture." Hana pulled out their hand-drawn maps of the heist and escape routes. "In the meantime, let's treat this mission like nothing has changed. Let's go over our plans in detail."

Nari poured a glass of ice water for each member of the team, and they settled in for an evening of strategy.

As Hana spoke, Jennifer's thoughts wandered to Amir. She longed to win him back ever since he heard about the second heist and immediately left the milkshake shop. She wasn't a criminal. She was just a regular woman from the Midwest who liked to write comic books and occasionally build alliances with crooked cops.

She pulled out her phone and texted Amir. Maybe she'd leave out any heist references for now. *"Hey, Amir, I had so much fun playing laser tag. I'd love to see you again."* She added a heart eyes emoji then erased it.

Later that night, while Jennifer was brushing her teeth, Amir called her back. "Hey, I'm sorry I left so abruptly. I was so surprised. I really like you and don't want you to go to jail," he said in a hushed tone.

She drew in a breath and nodded before realizing that he couldn't see her. "You're right."

Amir continued, "Imagine everything that you would lose if you got arrested. Your runs on the Missouri River, the opportunity to start your surfing business, and karaoke nights. I mean, I guess you could still sing in jail, but the acoustics are so bad."

She let out a giggle as a tear trickled down her cheek. She didn't want to give up any of those things. And she didn't want to build a relationship with Amir at a visitation table in front of a guard.

"It could be all gone in a moment. Be careful. Make sure you know what you're getting yourself into," he said softly. "And trust yourself. You're new to this but can still contribute."

She closed her eyes and felt her chest swell. "Thank you. I've learned so much already. I almost feel like I can do anything."

CHAPTER 26

NARI

Twelve days until heist day

J ennifer, Nari, and Freddy gathered at a small corner booth at Silver Spoon. It was 7 AM, and Freddy was dressed in jean shorts and a faded concert tee with a long curly brown wig.

There was one other table with diners, but the rest of the restaurant was empty.

"Can I have an autograph, rock star?" Nari said, stifling a giggle. "Thanks for meeting us here."

Freddy tapped some ketchup onto his fried egg bagel sandwich. "Of course. I'm living the glamorous life with this extra avocado." He covered his mouth as he took a bite. "I've got some intel for you. We've got a young officer on your case. Roberta Fonseca."

"Roberta..." Jennifer inhaled sharply and turned to Nari. "Oh my *gosh,* we know her! From Lorinda's party!"

Nari's chest tightened. She remembered the dark-haired woman wearing an *Ankara* print blouse.

"Glad you're acquainted. I'm not sure how much she knows, but I can't shake her. She is putting in extra hours and asking the team all sorts of questions about your case," Freddy continued between bites.

"I *knew* she couldn't be trusted!" Jennifer cried.

"She's got the day off, and she's going to visit the horse racing track and casino tonight for Twilight Night. Here's the good news. When she left last night, she was in a rush. I noticed she had her notebook on her when she got into her car. She's in her twenties, but she's old school. She writes everything in that notebook and guards it closely." Freddy pulled out his cell phone and showed them a picture of a gold American hatchback. It looked about ten years old. "Here's the license plate."

Nari scribbled the number onto a paper napkin. "This is great intel. Thanks, Freddy."

"Pleasure doing business with you. Tell Martha thanks for getting me the evidence I needed to close out the home burglary case." Freddy tipped his hat. He wrapped the rest of his bagel sandwich in a napkin. "This was too good to leave behind. I'll be billing you for it later." He grinned, placing a ten-dollar bill on the table as he left the restaurant.

"What are we going to do?" Jennifer's voice trembled.

Nari raised an eyebrow. "You've gotten great at talking to cops..."

Jennifer's face fell. "Seriously? Again?"

"My mom and Martha are busy this evening talking to the inside team. I know you can do it. You'll distract Roberta while I break into her car. You can talk to her about literally *anything*. Martha will get some intel on her for you, and she'll make you up so Roberta will never recognize you. I'll need to photograph her notebook and put it back. Then I'll lock the doors when I'm done like nothing ever happened. Piece of cake," Nari explained.

Jennifer paused. "I want to fight you on this, but I'm getting better at these things, aren't I?" she whispered, as a smile started to form on her face.

"That you are, roomie. That you are," Nari responded.

CHAPTER 27

JENNIFER

"I can't wait to see the master in action," Jennifer said in awe as she watched Nari drive a nineties tan sedan up a gravel path to the casino's horse racing wing. "It's too bad I'm going to miss most of your performance." Her heart was pounding, but she hoped she was projecting confidence to her roommate.

"We'll make an incredible team," Nari said as she adjusted Jennifer's curly wig. "You're going to do great as Natalia. I feel like playing some slots with you already."

"Thanks, Nari," Jennifer said, practicing a deeper voice.

As the car slowed, she could hear the crackle of gravel under its tires. Nari turned the car into the next full row, which was fully packed.

"Bingo." Nari pointed as she pulled up to a golden hatchback parked under a tree. She pulled out the crumpled napkin from her pocket and checked it against the license plate number. "There's Roberta's car." She maneuvered back around into a far corner before parking.

"You're on deck." Nari winked, reaching over to adjust Jennifer's earpiece. "You've got this. I'll be listening in on your conversations the whole time."

"I can do it," Jennifer echoed, exhaling heavily with a slight grin on her face. "See you soon, little lady." She waved as she turned and stepped out of the car. When she looked back, she saw Nari slumping down in her seat.

Jennifer smoothed her wig, double-checked that her earpiece was secure, and wiped her sweaty palms on her dress. As she walked up the narrow pathway to the front door of the casino, she passed by happy couples and groups of friends.

For the Twilight Night event, there were going to be ten races instead of the usual five, followed by a live concert featuring a popular local country band, The Rusty Fences. A large group crowded around an outdoor stage, their hands up as they danced to the opener's crooning beat.

Tents lined either side of the stage, selling food and drink from different local restaurants. Concertgoers of all ages were dressed in a mixture of formal and casual wear, with some cowboy boots and hats thrown into the mix.

Jennifer's phone vibrated. There was a small commercial space for rent at Waikiki Beach in Honolulu. She felt a lightness in her chest and bookmarked the listing for later.

Eyes on the prize. She needed to find Roberta and distract her so Nari could get to work. She put her hands up and swayed her hips, studying each person's face as she made her way through the crowd.

She stopped by one tent after another looking for Roberta,

her mouth watering as she glanced at pizza slices, fresh churros, and grilled hot dogs. Finally, she found Roberta standing in line at a taco stand. Jennifer almost didn't recognize her. Her hair was styled into loose curls, and she wore a beautiful form-fitting black cocktail dress with a golden zipper down the back.

Yes! Jennifer thought, her spirit rising. She would happily snag a *carne asada* taco as she approached her target. She got in line behind Roberta.

"I'll take two *al pastor* tacos. Hold the cilantro," Roberta said.

"But the cilantro is the best part!" Jennifer joked in a lower tone. "Right after the pineapple."

Roberta turned to look at Jennifer and beamed, with no look of recognition on her face. "I'll agree with you on the pineapple. But after months of cilantro aversion therapy, I still can't do it! It totally tastes like soap to me!"

Jennifer laughed. "As long as you go for the *salsa roja*, I can respect that. I'm Natalia." She extended a hand.

"Nice to meet you. I'm Roberta." She shook Jennifer's hand. "Have you been to one of these Twilight Nights before?" She pulled out her credit card and paid for her tacos.

"This is my first time. I couldn't miss the opportunity to meet the best and brightest of Omaha, present company included," Jennifer gushed. "How about you?"

Roberta grinned. "You're going to love it. I'd say half of the city is here. I come every chance I can when I get the day off."

"Next," the man working the taco stand said.

"I'll take one *carne asada* taco, extra cilantro," Jennifer chuckled. "And an orange soda. What do you do for a living?" She turned to ask Roberta as she paid.

"Ah, you know, law enforcement. I try to ease into that answer. It can be intimidating. I'm a cop, but I promise I'm friendly." Roberta tilted her head and walked to the end of the table to accept a paper plate of steaming tacos.

Jennifer took her receipt and headed to the end of the table to join Roberta.

"That's great. No disclaimer needed," Jennifer replied. "I'm in finance, so I'm behind a desk all day. I've always wanted a life of adventure. Basically, you're my hero." A woman at the end of the table handed Jennifer a cold orange soda bottle, a glass filled with ice, and a beautiful little *carne asada* taco sprinkled with cilantro. Jennifer felt her mouth water as the steaming smell of grilled beef wafted up to her nostrils.

Roberta spooned *salsa roja* and raw onions onto her tacos. "Hey, I barely passed calculus in college. I'm in awe of you too."

Jennifer smiled, squirting lime onto her taco. She was relieved Roberta wasn't going to ask her any questions related to finance.

"You're doing great, my little disciple," Nari said into Jennifer's earpiece. Jennifer felt her shoulders relax.

"Are you going to bet on these races?" Jennifer asked.

"I bet every time. If there's a horse named Cilantro, it's all yours." Roberta smirked. "I'm heading inside now, if you'd like to join me."

"There's no time like the present. I'd love that," Jennifer replied.

She felt chills go up and down her arms. This evening was going perfectly so far. Roberta seemed to have absolutely no idea that she'd talked to her before. Jennifer felt like a powerful spy who could secretly befriend any foe, slip into a negotiation, and reunify an ancient kingdom. Or something like that.

She followed Roberta through the crowd to the casino's back entrance. The main horse racing room was packed with guests and a loud hum of conversation. A dozen big screen TVs lined the walls playing pre-race coverage. The air was stale and warm.

They walked to the bar, where Jennifer spotted Lorinda's cousin Uchenna sitting alone. She was wearing a glittering red mini-dress with long sleeves. *Of course she's here.*

"This is my friend Uchenna," Roberta said. "Uchenna, meet Natalia."

Uchenna stood and beamed. "It's great to meet you, Natalia," she said in her thick Omaha accent, her handshake firm. She furrowed her brow and cocked her head. "Have we met before?"

Jennifer coughed and leaned on the bar to Uchenna's left. "I get that all the time!" she said, pushing out a friendly tone. "I have one of those faces. Thanks so much for having me, ladies. Which horse are you rooting for?" She poured her orange soda into her glass, took a bite from her taco, and set her plate on the bar.

Uchenna glanced at her with a warm expression. "Clyde's got pretty good odds, and I think he's going to pull it off this time around." She dipped a mozzarella stick in marinara sauce, before passing the plate to Jennifer.

"I usually go with my gut. And I'm feeling like going all in on Porter. Everyone's favorite underdog," Roberta added and took a sip of lemonade. She turned to Jennifer. "Which horse are you going to bet on?"

Uchenna handed Jennifer a horse tip sheet. "In case you're new to this."

Jennifer glanced at the form and chose a horse with moderate odds. "I'm going with Robber." Her face burned, and she immediately regretted her choice. The name hit a little too close to home.

"Sounds like a plan," Uchenna said. "I don't know if you should go with Porter, Roberta. That seems like a risky bet."

Jennifer tucked her hair behind her ears, knocking her earpiece loose with her fingers. *Shoot.* Her secret was exposed. Quickly, she flipped her hair to cover the earpiece and sent it flying into her glass of soda. As she scrambled to catch it, she knocked over her glass and spilled soda all over her smartwatch.

"Oh no!" Roberta motioned to the bartender for help. "Is that an earpiece?"

Jennifer felt her throat get tight. She quickly grabbed the dripping earpiece from the bar and slipped it into her purse. "Oh my gosh, that's uh... That's, yes! I am glued to this thing for work. Maybe this means I need a...vacation." She shook her head.

"Your watch doesn't look so good either." Uchenna examined Jennifer's wrist. "Maybe you should take two weeks off." Jennifer tapped the screen, and it didn't turn on.

Jennifer's heart was pounding. "I'm so clumsy," she said in her normal voice, laughing nervously. She froze and cleared her throat, taking her voice down an octave again. "I'm so sorry for making a mess."

"Please, don't worry about it," Roberta said kindly as she helped the bartender sop up the orange spill with a towel. "It's not a big deal."

"Well, I think this might be your lucky race," Uchenna added. "Orange represents prosperity in some cultures. If you want to bet, the counter's over there." She pointed across the room.

Jennifer was not a gambler and didn't want to spend any actual money on this race. Her eyes wandered to the betting stand, which was a counter divided into three kiosks. A long line of anxious gamblers stretched out in front.

"I think I'll mentally bet this first round," Jennifer said. "Tell me, are either of you good at picking the winners here?"

"Oh, Uchenna always wins something," Roberta observed. "It could be a second career for her."

"I knew I was talking to an expert," Jennifer replied.

The crowd cheered as the horse race began. Uchenna's eyes were fixed on the big screen TV in front of them. "I love when the race starts. It's really anyone's game."

"But maybe Clyde will pull it off," Jennifer wagered.

"I know I'm rooting for him," Uchenna remarked.

"I think I'm going to order some onion rings for us to share. People think I'm crazy, but they actually go well with tacos," Jennifer shared enthusiastically.

"I can't ever get enough onion rings." Roberta shimmied her shoulders for emphasis. She glanced at Jennifer and then back to the horse racing monitors. "But make sure you get some ranch."

Jennifer grinned. "Oh, of course." She waved to the woman working the bar and ordered.

"If you'd excuse me, ladies, I've got to run to my car to get my lip balm. My lips are parched." Roberta pursed her lips together as she stood up and pushed in her stool.

"Wait!" Jennifer cried. Fear rose in her chest as she rushed to stand. "You need to try the onion rings while they're still hot."

Roberta cocked her head at Jennifer and chuckled. "I appreciate your concern, but I think I'll be back in time." She started to walk toward the exit.

Jennifer started to panic. "I'll... I'll come with you!"

Roberta raised an eyebrow and tilted her head. "Sounds like a plan," she said flatly.

Jennifer pulled out her phone and frantically started to type *"emergency"* in an encrypted message to Nari. Halfway through, Roberta glanced at Jennifer's phone screen. Jennifer's breath caught in her throat, and she quickly slipped her phone back into her pocket.

Come on Nari, finish up, Jennifer thought desperately.

CHAPTER 28

NARI

Nari needed to exit the car undetected. As soon as Jennifer left, she glanced in the rearview mirror. A woman in a wide-brimmed hat and a man in a suit were chatting in front of a car a few spaces over.

She flipped through the radio and hummed along quietly to some of her dad's favorite classic jazz music. Within a few minutes, the couple was gone. She grabbed her lace evening tool bag and hopped out of the car. Nari caught her reflection in the car's windows and winked to herself. *Looking good, Nari Park.* She walked casually across the parking lot to the tree-lined zone on the edge where Roberta was parked.

As a group of women approached, she continued walking slowly past Roberta's car, as if she had further to go. She listened in on Jennifer's conversation in her earpiece, grinning as her roommate joked around with Roberta.

One woman glanced over and nodded as she passed. Nari

nodded back and listened to the sounds of gravel crunching underfoot as the distance between them grew. She checked behind her. The women were nearing the casino. She scanned the parking lot. All clear. Nari walked quickly back to Roberta's car, approaching the driver's side door. She looked for the weather stripping. There it was, in the top-left corner.

She bent at the waist and carefully slid the wedge into the window's corner. It went in smoothly, and a small gap opened up.

She heard the sounds of voices and jingling keys approaching. A couple was walking closer, arm in arm. She dove in front of the car and crouched.

Shoot. Nari had left the wedge in the window. She hesitated and then shot up, running around the car to grab it. She squatted back down and prepared to dive in front of the car.

"Having car trouble?" a woman asked.

Nari looked up and saw a woman with long dark hair and a purple ruffled blouse standing within a few feet of her face. She jumped up and quickly shoved the wedge into her waistband.

"You scared me!" Nari forced a laugh. "Yeah, thanks so much for asking. I think I've got a brake issue."

"Oh my gosh, how terrible! You poor thing," the woman replied in a thick Midwestern drawl. She called out to her bearded companion, "Honey, this woman's having brake issues."

The man drew in a breath and looked concerned as he rolled up his red plaid sleeves. "That's terrible. I'm so glad you made it here safely. Now if you'd wait for a few minutes, I can go grab my toolbox out of the truck and check your car out."

Nari looked down and saw the wedge bulging in her waistband. She adjusted her blazer jacket to cover it up. "That's so sweet of you, but you know—"

"Not buts. I insist," the man replied.

"He's so skilled with cars. You really should see what he can do," the woman added.

"You both are so sweet. But please, don't worry. My tow truck is already on its way," Nari said.

"Ah." The man tilted his head forward. "There you go. I'm so glad you're taken care of."

"You are too kind. I hope you enjoy the races," Nari replied. The couple waved at her and continued walking toward the casino.

As soon as they were gone, Nari's earpiece filled with static.

"Jen? Are you there?" she asked, her voice low. There was no response. She took off her earpiece and placed it into her pocket, praying that Jennifer was still working her conversational magic.

"Send an update when you can," Nari texted with her smartwatch.

With no connection to Jennifer, she needed to work quickly. She glanced around the parking lot for the couple and then got back to work, roughly shoving the wedge into the corner of the window.

Nari placed her fingers up against the glass, narrowing her eyes as she peered inside. She scanned the armrest for the unlock button but could see nothing. She fumbled for her flashlight and flickered its beam across the armrest. *Boom.* There it was.

She slid the metal rod through the gap in the window, faced forward, and stretched her body to slide the rod across the armrest. She felt around with the rod until it landed on something hard. Excitement rose in her chest as she lifted the rod slightly and then pushed down. Nothing happened.

The sound of footsteps grew louder. Panicking, she looked to her right. Another group was approaching, but no one seemed to have noticed her yet. Quickly, she lifted the rod again and pressed down. The locks clicked open.

"I haven't seen The Rusty Fences perform in years," a woman said. "I've heard the production value of this tour is incredible."

Nari slid the rod out quickly, grabbed the wedge, and darted to the front of the car as her shoe slipped off. Her heart pounded and sweat dripped down her forehead.

"Ha! Someone lost a shoe," the woman said.

"Is it a nice one?" another female voice replied. "Maybe Steve can find his modern-day Cinderella inside."

Rhythmic footfalls approached. Nari covered her mouth to silence her rapid breathing. "Very funny," the woman replied, her voice feet away from Nari. "She's got decent taste, and she's a size seven. Sound like your princess, Steve?"

"I'll look for a woman with one shoe inside," the man quipped.

It sounded like the woman near her shoe was pausing. Nari closed her eyes and hoped she didn't notice a lingering gap in the window.

"Alright, guys, wait for me." The woman crunched back into the parking lot.

Nari wanted to faint from relief. After about a minute, she peered around the car. The coast was clear.

She jumped up, slid her shoe back on, and dove toward the

door in one fluid motion. As she vaulted inside, the sweet scent of vanilla from the rearview mirror air freshener immediately hit her nose. She opened the center console and rifled through its contents. There were packs of fragrant cinnamon gum, a box of tissues, and some lip balm. No notebook.

She leaned across the car and threw open the glove box, carefully feeling through with her right hand as she shone her flashlight with her left. Her hand hit on cardboard. Could this be it? She pulled out a small red notebook and pumped her first. "Yes!" she whispered.

Each page had a date at the top and notes on different cases. She looked out the rear windshield of the car into the scarcely lit parking lot to see if anyone was coming. She jumped out and ran to the front of the car, closing the door behind her.

Her hands trembled as she placed the notebook on her lap and turned to a date from two weeks ago. She shone the flashlight with her left hand and steadied her right arm against her side to capture centered photos of each page on her cell phone. Her breath steadied as she went.

Suddenly, her flashlight slid into her lap and closed the notebook. She transferred the flashlight to the crook of her neck and tilted her head to one side to hold it in place. Flustered, she flipped to a page around where she left off and continued to photograph each page with shaky hands.

Her smartwatch vibrated, and a notification popped up on the screen. *"Emergency,"* it read.

She froze. Off in the distance, she could swear she heard the disguised voice of Jennifer talking with another woman. Hurriedly, she clicked her last few photos and peered around the side of the car. Two figures approached.

She ran to the driver's side door, throwing it open before diving across the front seats. She fumbled to open the glove box with sweaty fingers and tossed the notebook inside before slamming the door shut. Within seconds, the glove box fell back open, and a few items tumbled onto the floor.

"Seriously?" Nari groaned as she leaned over to clean up the spill and close the glove box more softly this time. She jumped out, closed the door, and rushed back to hide in front of the car.

Her face grew hot as she realized she hadn't locked the door.

"And that's the thing, *Roberta*," Jennifer said, emphasizing Roberta's name. "You've got to put in so many hours of practice to reach that level in basketball. Some kids don't realize that."

Roberta responded, "You can't accomplish your dreams without hard work. I love that you get that. Give me a sec. I'm going to grab my lip balm."

Nari held her breath. She could hear Roberta's car beep.

Thank goodness. Nari felt a wave of relief that Roberta didn't try to unlock the car door by hand first.

Footsteps neared and the car door clicked open. Nari couldn't hear anything. She closed her eyes and desperately hoped she hadn't left anything out.

"That's strange," Roberta said. "I thought I left my lip balm in here. Not seeing it. Oh well." She got out of the car and slammed the door.

"Sorry to hear that, *Roberta,*" Jennifer said. "Well, we don't want to miss the race. *Or* the onion rings. Let's head back inside."

Roberta chuckled. "One second." Nari could hear the car door opening again and the crunching of gravel. Roberta's voice changed. "It seems like my rearview mirror was moved. I never put it in that position."

Nari's breath caught in her throat.

"Oh my gosh, I bet it's loose," Jennifer improvised in a low tone. "You need the right screwdriver to tighten the base. It happens to me *all* the time. Don't let it go too long though. It's dangerous."

"Thanks for the tip." Roberta closed the door again.

The car lock button beeped. Footsteps crunched away. Nari's body went limp with relief.

CHAPTER 29

NARI

Eleven days until heist day

The next morning at 6 AM, Nari knocked sharply on her mom and Martha's hotel room door, with Sumeet and Jennifer beside her. She swore she could hear her mom grumbling.

"I've got it," Martha replied from inside, her voice peppy.

The door flew open. Martha was dressed in black running shorts, a pink fitted tank, and a hoodie. "Hey, ladies! I'm ready to go on our training run. I'm wearing my weightless shoes so I can feel like I'm running on a cloud." She paused. "Oh, and a handsome stranger. Well, hello there."

"Hi, I'm Sumeet," he responded in a friendly tone. "I'm Nari's...right-hand man." Nari could handle that title. Nothing too serious.

"Right-hand man," Martha said. "That sounds promising."

"Always. Head on in, team. I'll wait for you all out here." Sumeet gestured with his hands.

Jennifer and Nari walked into the hotel room as Hana pulled herself out of bed and padded toward the bathroom. She waved to the group.

"Hey," Hana called out from the open bathroom door, "I'm almost ready." Nari could faintly hear the sound of her mom brushing her teeth.

"Tell us about your intel," Martha said. "I'm dying to hear what you found out about Roberta."

"Good news first. Roberta is convinced about the fake heist location," Nari began.

"Yes!" Jennifer cheered.

"Excellent," Martha added. "What's the bad news?"

"Jennifer threw her bathrobe into the industrial park during our first mission. Roberta found it," Nari began.

Jennifer gasped. "Uh-oh." She sat down slowly into a chair behind her.

"But it shouldn't be a big deal, right?" Hana emerged from the bathroom.

"She found Amir's phone number in the pocket. She called him about it, and he pretended not to know anything," Nari continued.

"I think I'm going to need some water," Jennifer said, her voice hoarse.

"Unfortunately, she found a dry cleaning tag inside the robe. She's going over today to investigate. The dry cleaner opens at 9 AM. After our training run, we can plan it out and go together. Martha can destroy any electronic and physical records they have of Jennifer, while the rest of us distract the staff," Nari explained. "It's run by a mother-son team of two."

"I'm on it," Martha said, saluting.

"Perfect," Nari said.

"What else does she know?" Jennifer asked, her face serious.

"She doesn't seem to have any information on us yet. She even ran DNA testing on your robe and didn't find any matches. Luckily, you're not in any databases." Nari tipped her head toward Jennifer, whose shoulders loosened. "But she's investigating buyers. I spoke with Freddy, and he's going to divert her to another fake buyer. Mom, you can play the customer. We're going to throw her off with a fake purchase order and misleading information that will lead her to the decoy heist at Mill Creek Lane. Martha will also leak suspicious inventory logs."

"Great work, *nae jasik.*" Hana beamed. "I'm in. We can use the purchase order to divert Johannes too. Alright, Martha, give us an update on the inside team."

Martha held her hands together tightly. "It's not looking so good. We've got to regroup. After Hana and I visited, I tried to meet with a few members one-on-one. I didn't make it very far. Two key people in inventory said they're not going to be involved unless Lorinda leads them. They don't trust us to keep them safe."

Nari sucked in air through her teeth and began to pace the room. "Without the Sorbelate, we don't have a heist anymore. We'd have to walk away. No payout for us or the women in the mines."

"It's simple," Hana added matter-of-factly. "We need to get

Lorinda back on the team. Jennifer, we're going to need your help here. Martha and I can prep you on what to say."

"We'll get her back." Jennifer exhaled slowly.

"I've also been monitoring the inside team's phones," Martha remarked. "There are a few leads that I'm going to investigate. One member is calling an unregistered number a lot. Another is receiving small money transfers that could be sketchy."

"Great work," Nari said.

"Alright, team, we will prevail." Hana's voice rose. "Let's go for our run!"

Each member put on sunglasses, and they exited into the hallway where Sumeet was waiting for them.

The group took off, and Sumeet punched the elevator button. "Mom, this is Sumeet," Nari said as the elevator descended.

"Hello, dear. Thanks for introducing us to a possible rat," Hana quipped. Sumeet shifted his weight between his feet and looked down. A giggle escaped from Martha's lips, and she covered her mouth with her hand.

"Just kidding." Hana patted Sumeet's shoulder.

"Oh, he probably came straight from the sewer," Sumeet replied. "I totally deserved that. For real though, I'm sorry for setting you up with Johannes."

"Call me Hana, my child," she remarked. "I'm happy you did. I'm confident we can stay one step ahead of the cops. I've got a lot of experience with that, anyway."

Jennifer put her hand into the center. "On the count of three, let's crush it!" Nari and the rest of the group put their hands in the center.

"One, two, three," Jennifer counted off.

"Let's crush it!" the group called out, throwing their hands into the air.

CHAPTER 30

JENNIFER

"Pulling in now," Jennifer said into her earpiece as Sumeet parked the delivery van in front of a small, brown brick building with white lettering on the front that read "Ping's Cleaners."

"Copy," Martha replied.

Jennifer and Sumeet hopped out and opened the back door. The cargo area was filled with brown cardboard boxes that had a blue logo of a delivery truck stamped on the outside. "Nice touch," Jennifer said.

Sumeet grinned. "Thanks. This isn't my first special delivery." He climbed into the back and placed two dollies on the ground as Jennifer quickly and methodically started to load the water-filled boxes into the dollies.

"Sorry these are so heavy." Sumeet started to load boxes alongside her. "At least they don't contain any actual chemicals."

"Hey, no worries. My guns are getting pretty impressive now," Jennifer joked.

"I can tell, bodybuilder," Sumeet responded.

Within a few minutes, they were ready. Jennifer glanced at her watch. 9:03 AM.

"Shall we?" She looked down at her and Sumeet's delivery uniforms and giggled to herself. She wore a low baseball cap that covered her eyes and large sunglasses. Together, they wheeled the dollies into the store.

"Hello!" Jennifer said cheerfully as they entered. "I have a delivery for Ping Li."

A middle-aged woman with black slacks and a white floral cardigan sweater emerged from behind a row of suits and blouses. "Hiya! I'm Ping. So many boxes..." She eyed the delivery. "I didn't realize we were so short. Thanks for coming."

"My pleasure," Jennifer replied. "We've got extra safety protocols for solvents, so I'm going to need to confirm what I have and get your signature on each item."

"Of course. We don't normally get customers at this time, so this is perfect. Bao, get out here!" Ping shouted toward the back of the store.

A man of about twenty years emerged from the back holding a lint roller. He grinned sheepishly. "Hello." A faint chemical smell wafted toward Jennifer's nostrils. Sumeet waved.

Jennifer produced a list on a clipboard. "I'm going to need your help matching up each box to this list." A small sticker with a long string of numbers and letters was attached to each package. She wanted to chuckle to herself. Sumeet had done a brilliant job setting this up.

Ping and Bao each grabbed a box. "A3WJL..." Ping began.

"Wait," Jennifer said. "Start over. Let me find the As. Okay, great. Here we go. If you can read out slowly to me, Ping. Bao, you read to my colleague here."

The mother and son duo each focused on the string of digits on their box. Jennifer could hear movement in the back of the store but kept her gaze fixed on the elder Li. "That seems right. Could you reread the last three letters for me?"

Out of the corner of her eye, she could see Martha slipping between rows of clothes and garment bags into the office.

Ping began to get flustered. "Can't you two go over these numbers together?" She pointed at Jennifer and Sumeet. "I'm sorry, but we run a very busy business here. My son and I have work to do."

"I totally understand, Ms. Li," Jennifer responded. "I promise we'll be done soon. I just need your signature on each item for safety reasons. Thanks so much for your patience. If the four of us do this together, the process will go by so much faster."

Ping gritted her teeth. "Alright, ma'am, but I'm giving you five more minutes. Then the two of you need to finish and I'll sign afterward."

"Of course, Ms. Li. We're here to serve, and your happiness is our top priority," Jennifer said. Ping's face softened. Jennifer didn't know where she was pulling these quotes from, but she was growing more and more confident in the role of a bumbling delivery driver with a heart of gold.

Jennifer and Ping continued to confirm different boxes against the list, one by one. Within a couple of minutes, Bao sighed loudly. "Mom, I was in the middle of a rush order. I need to get back to work."

"Oh, *now* you want to work," Ping chuckled, glancing at her son.

"It'll be a few more minutes, I promise," Sumeet interjected.

"Thanks, but I really think my mom can handle this," Bao said to Sumeet.

"Wait—" Jennifer chimed in.

The front door opened, and Hana and Nari entered. Nari was wearing a belted, sleeveless coral jumpsuit with giant circular sunglasses and a tightly slicked back ponytail. She looked like an heiress. She clutched a white floral cocktail dress with a series of stains on the front. "Excuse me," she said to Jennifer as she pushed past. "My dress is ruined! It's an emergency, and I need your help!"

Hana strode up alongside her, and Sumeet edged his dolly to the side to make room for her. She placed a stack of sweaters on the counter next to her daughter. "I've heard your team can work wonders on cashmere. Name your price, and I'll pay it. But we're going to need you to be *meticulous.*"

"Not a problem at all," Ping said. "Thank you so much for trusting Ping's Cleaners. Bao, can you check the customer's sweaters for stains while I help out this young woman?"

Bao nodded and started to unfold the top sweater. "Could you show me where the stains are on this one?"

"If you'll give us a minute," Ping said to Jennifer.

"No problem." Jennifer grinned. She turned to look at Sumeet, who was stifling a smile.

Nari huffed. "There are so many stains on here. First, my friend had too much to drink and spilled red wine all over me."

Ping studied the garment. "I'm sorry to hear that. Don't

you worry. We should be able to get red wine out of this fabric."

"Thank you," Nari sighed loudly. "Then I tried to get away and knocked over a bowl of salad dressing into my lap. There is oil *everywhere*, Ping. Everywhere. Before I hand this dress over, I'm going to need to know what treatments you'll be using. I was wearing this when my husband proposed, and I can't risk losing it. This material is delicate, you know."

Sumeet was holding his fist to his mouth. He started to laugh but covered it up with a cough.

"Of course. I know how important this dress is to you. We will treat it like our very own. First, we will use a mild solvent to break down the oil. Then we will blot the stain rather than scrub," Ping started.

Jennifer glanced behind the counter to see Martha's dark-brown curls flitting behind a row of clothing covered in garment bags. That seemed promising.

There was a faint shuffling noise as Martha made her way to the back door. Bao glanced over his shoulder.

"Hey!" Hana said to Bao. "That's only one of the stains. Look at these ones on the other side."

Bao exhaled as if he was trying to hide his annoyance. He did a pretty good job. "Please, show them to me."

"All good," Martha said into Jennifer's earpiece. "Crisis averted."

"Oh my gosh," Jennifer gasped as she glanced down at her paperwork. "I am so sorry, Ms. Li. This delivery is actually for another dry cleaner down the street. My colleague and I here must have swapped invoices with another team. We are so sorry to disrupt your day."

Bao threw up his hands. "Seriously? Sheesh," he muttered under his breath.

Ping raised an eyebrow. "I knew we didn't need that much inventory," she chuckled. "Oh well. What can you do?"

Jennifer and Sumeet reloaded some of the boxes onto their dollies and made their way to the door.

"Thanks to you both for your understanding. Now you have a beautiful day," Jennifer said in a peppy voice.

As she steered her dolly out the door, Jennifer could feel herself wheeling over someone's foot. "Whoops!" She moved her dolly to one side and looked up. It was Roberta, in full police uniform.

"I'm so sorry," Jennifer said, flustered. She averted her gaze, worried Roberta would recognize her.

"No problem, ma'am. I'm sure I came from nowhere. Have a good day." Roberta looked up at Jennifer's face, and a brief moment of recognition flickered in her eyes.

Jennifer pushed her dolly past Roberta and to the van, holding her breath as her shoulders tensed. Sumeet was close behind her.

CHAPTER 31

JENNIFER

"Another successful mission in the bank!" Hana announced when they arrived back at the apartment.

"Nari, you were hilarious," Jennifer gushed.

"Thanks, Jen," Nari laughed. "My mom and I play the high-maintenance duo well. But the real hero here..." She motioned to Martha. "Ms. Ramírez!"

Martha grinned and spun around. "Thank you, thank you. I deleted all records of Jennifer—and you too, Nari. And I don't think Ms. Li will be needing these anymore." She pulled a garment tag and receipt from her pocket. "Jennifer, would you like to do the honors?"

Jennifer danced over to Martha. "Don't mind if I do!" She excitedly tore each piece of paper and ran to the kitchen trash to throw them away. "Whoop whoop! Evidence gone!"

"Some more good news, ladies," Hana announced. "I spoke with Roberta on the phone yesterday as Janet Hobbes from

Golden Crumb. I told her I bought Sorbelate and gave her evidence that will lead her to the fake mission." She bowed triumphantly.

"Amazing!" Jennifer replied. "Roberta's never going to find us now."

"Everything is falling into place," Nari said.

"Our inside team is looking clean so far." Martha put her hands on her hips. "One member's been calling her aunt every day on her burner phone to talk about her inheritance. The woman with the small daily deposits is taking out crypto to avoid paying taxes. Not good choices, but nothing for us to worry about."

"We'll wait to see if any of the fake heist plans we've fed them make it to Freddy," Hana noted. "In the meantime, we need to seal off all potential sources of the leak. Nari, have you looked into Sumeet? I'm starting to wonder if we can trust him."

Nari froze, and her face twisted in confusion. "Sumeet?"

"He has a lot going on. He could be loyal to someone else. Like Johannes," Hana explained.

"It's not Sumeet, Mom," Nari snapped. "I've worked with him on so many deals. He's had my back in tons of sketchy situations. We can rely on him."

Jennifer's breath caught in her chest and her eyes flitted between Nari and her mom.

"You can't let your feelings get in the way, *nae jasik.*" Hana folded her arms across her chest. "You're being naive. We don't know who we can believe."

Nari clenched her teeth. "Mom, I am extremely capable—" She paused abruptly and began to pace the room. Slowly, her expression neutralized, and she looked at the floor. "Maybe I've let myself get too close to Sumeet. I know better than to get attached."

"Hopefully it's not him," Martha said apologetically as she touched Nari's arm. "But I'm going to have to dig into his background. I'm sorry."

"I'll keep my distance for now." Nari inhaled deeply.

Jennifer walked over and gave Nari a hug. "I don't think it's Sumeet," she squeaked. A brief glimmer of gratitude flickered in Nari's eyes.

"Moving on," Hana said sharply.

"Yes. We've got to get Lorinda back," Nari began. "Jennifer, we'll need you to pitch her. Invite her out for something fun. What's something she's been wanting to do with you?"

Jennifer paused. "Karaoke!" Now that she was friends with Lorinda, she absolutely owed her a night of singing.

"Perfect," Hana said. "Invite her out in a group so she doesn't have her guard up. Then, when you can get her alone, let her know how much we need her. The mission can't go on without her. That means no pain to Essentrix Labs and no freedom for the women in the mines. Together, we'll make a difference. We will continue to protect her by keeping her on the outskirts of planning."

"See who you can assemble for a karaoke night by this evening." Martha brushed her hair behind her ears.

Jennifer pulled out her cell phone and saluted the team. "I'll text Lorinda and everyone else we both know."

"What's the backup plan if we can't win Lorinda back?" Nari asked.

"We're going to have to come up with a way to get the product ourselves," Hana replied. "Not ideal."

Jennifer felt a chill go up her arms. She imagined getting into a round of hand-to-hand combat with the night guard on duty at Essentrix Labs in order to gain access to Sorbelate. The team would set off a bomb to gain entry into the building. She'd go to jail for life. She shuddered.

. . .

It was a warm evening. Jennifer was wearing her silver sequined dress, normally set aside for special occasions only. But singing her way into saving the heist was a pretty special occasion. She felt like an ancient spy. Maybe she'd be as powerful as her comic book hero Amina Keita tonight, negotiating deals with evil marauders and securing treasure chests full of gold for her people. She might have to battle them a little bit, but she was trained in these things.

Except Lorinda wasn't evil. Thank goodness. She just had to convince Lorinda to steal the gold with her. Totally different conversation.

Jennifer surveyed the bar. Lorinda had chosen the place. It was more formal than she was expecting, filled with well-dressed people ready to croon into the microphone. She looked down at her dress and grinned. She would fit right in.

There was a giant, elevated stage with three microphones and a teleprompter, surrounded by windows on all sides. A suited DJ stood in the corner. "Welcome to the jungle," he started off. "I'm your host, DJ Andrew. You can also call me Andy Beats." Jennifer bounced her head as a cool, relaxed beat took over the room.

"Hey, partner!" Lorinda called out from the bar, running

over and throwing her arms around Jennifer. She wore dramatic dark makeup and a red A-line dress with a flouncy taffeta skirt. She looked incredible. "This was such a good idea. I can't wait to sing with you."

Lorinda guided Jennifer to a round table in the center of the room in perfect view of the stage. Her cousin Uchenna was seated there, wearing a high-waisted black skirt and green and white polka-dotted blouse with puffy sleeves.

Jennifer imagined herself saying, "Hi, Uchenna! Remember me? Natalia?" That would probably end in handcuffs.

She tried to remember what she would know from her first time meeting Uchenna. It felt like ages ago, back when she was Jennifer 1.0. She took a deep breath. "Hey, Uchenna, it's great to see you again! How's basketball going?"

Uchenna hugged Jennifer. "Oh, you know. Winning every game, as always."

"Karlie and Mandy are here too," Lorinda said, pointing.

Mandy, as in...Jennifer's boss? New territory everyday. Jennifer wanted to laugh and cry at the same time. She had no idea what to say to Mandy outside of work. But at least having her boss there would keep her on alert. She wouldn't accidentally let her guard down and start blabbering about the heist.

Karlie approached the table and waved, while Mandy danced over next to her. Karlie's blue floral dress looked great against her bright-blue eyes.

"Jennifer!" Karlie hugged her. The two of them danced together to the smooth beats and soulful singing that were pumping through the speakers.

"Who's ready for power ballads?" Mandy bounced her arms in excitement.

Karlie threw her arms in the air. "I will *lip sync* anything."

"I hope you don't mind, but I've already added us to the list," Lorinda announced. "I chose a song I think we'll all know and love."

"You tricky, tricky woman." Mandy shook her head. "I thought I'd have at least an hour to warm up first."

"As long as we all sing together, you won't even feel a thing!" Jennifer quipped.

Their server, a tall and pale woman with her brown hair swept back into a tight ponytail, approached to take the group's orders. Jennifer wanted to order orange soda but hesitated, in case that would jog Uchenna's memory from the casino. Instead, she went for grape with extra ice.

Jennifer glanced across the table, where Uchenna seemed to be looking at someone behind her. "I'm so glad you could make it!" Uchenna exclaimed, standing.

Jennifer grinned and turned behind her. Roberta was approaching the table wearing a lacy purple dress.

Oh my gosh, Jennifer thought. Her chest started to tighten immediately. *Does this woman ever stay home?*

"Hello, everyone." Roberta waved.

Jennifer panicked, realizing she wasn't wearing a disguise. Maybe Roberta hadn't seen her and she could casually dive under a neighboring table.

She would have to sit in front of Roberta—maybe even next to her—and simply be Jennifer. Not Ava or Natalia. Jennifer, a wanted woman in a million-dollar heist against her employer. For good measure, three of her coworkers were here too. She grabbed her ice water and started to gulp it down. Lorinda looked at her apologetically and shrugged.

Uchenna stood up. "This is my best childhood friend, Roberta. She can sing with the best of them. She's got a great shot too—if she's playing dodgeball. *Just kidding*, Roberta! Amazing basketball player." She patted Roberta on the shoulder.

Roberta laughed. "Touché, Uchenna. I'll get you back soon." She shook each person's hand around the table, hugged Lorinda, and then reached Jennifer.

"I think we've met before!" she said to Jennifer and then paused. "At the New Yam Festival party. Do you remember that?"

"How could I forget!" Jennifer said with forced enthusiasm. She stood and hugged Roberta. Was that taking it a little too far? She wasn't sure. "We chatted over cups of Zobo. Great to see you again." She strained to keep a smile glued to her face, conscious that her eyes would start to bulge if she pushed it too far.

Luckily, Roberta didn't seem to notice. She grabbed an empty chair from a neighboring table and sat next to Jennifer.

Roberta turned to Jennifer. "You've got to tell me what's good here."

Freedom, Jennifer thought. *Sweet, sweet freedom.*

"We're getting pizza," Mandy piped in. "But I want to try the fries, if those sound good to you."

Nope. She wants the onion rings.

"I love fries," Roberta started. "But what I'm always craving are onion rings."

"Especially if they're dipped in ranch!" Jennifer added. *Oh my gosh. Where did that come from?* She tightened her shoulders and balled her hands into fists in her lap.

Roberta paused. "Yes! Dipped in ranch! I can't believe you do that too!"

Jennifer stifled a sigh and nodded back to Roberta. "All day, every day." Lorinda looked at Jennifer and cocked her head to one side.

Jennifer wondered if anything about her connected her to the heist. Maybe hints of smoke bombs underneath her fingernails. Or traces of Sorbelate powder in her hair. Luckily, they'd been practicing with flour, so she could claim she really loved to bake.

"Up next, we've got a performance by Lorinda's Ladies," the DJ announced.

Lorinda clapped her hands. "It's time. Get ready to dance!"

The group of six walked up to the stage, Mandy excitedly climbing the stairs first.

The opener to one of Jennifer's favorite nineties boy band songs started to play. "This song is the *best!*" She jumped up and down.

Lorinda started to dance. "You can't tell me you don't love this one, ladies!"

Karlie and Uchenna danced to the microphone on the far right. Lorinda and Mandy danced to the middle. Everything was happening so fast. Before Jennifer could convince Mandy to trade her spots, Roberta danced up to the last microphone.

"Everybody on the dance floor, gonna make you sway," the group sang. Each woman moved to the beat.

Jennifer approached the microphone and joined Roberta, who seemed to know all the words. *"Lose your mind!"* Roberta belted out, dancing and shimmying her hips. She looked up at Jennifer. "I know you know this one."

Here goes nothing. Jennifer loosened her hips and danced. *"We're gonna make it happen this tiiiime."* She might as well celebrate the fact that so far, Roberta seemed to have absolutely no idea what she had been up to these past few weeks.

"That's right!" the DJ shouted. Jennifer looked out to the audience. People were standing, dancing, and singing along.

"Turn it up, gonna make you mine!" the women belted into the microphone.

The women posed as the song ended, and the crowd cheered.

"Amazing." The DJ applauded. "Let's hear it for Lorinda's Ladies!"

Lorinda got to the stairs first, giving out high-fives to each woman as they descended. She was breathing heavily.

Pizza and onion rings were waiting at the table when they got back. "Celebration time!" Karlie bounced up to the table. "That was such a blast. I even sang for real a couple of times."

"I could hear you. Your voice is actually amazing! You should sing more often," Uchenna commented.

Now seemed as good a time as any to pull Lorinda aside. Maybe sneak off to the bathroom. Jennifer got up and walked to Lorinda on the opposite side of the table. "Hey, Lorinda," she started. "I need to borrow some lipstick. Can you come to the bathroom with me?"

"Of course," Lorinda remarked with a more serious expression than normal. Jennifer wondered if she knew what was coming. Lorinda stood up. "We'll be right back," she said to the table.

The bathroom had three stalls. One of them was occupied. "Hi, Lorinda," Jennifer started.

"Hey, Jen." Lorinda glanced at the feet showing beneath the middle stall. "I know why you brought me in here."

"You do?" Jennifer asked.

Lorinda nodded and waited. The toilet flushed, and a woman with dark curly hair and a silky orange dress emerged from the stall. Lorinda and Jennifer glanced at her.

"Excuse me," she said brightly, washing her hands before heading to the hand dryer. A loud whirring sound took over the room, and the woman exited.

"I can't help in the way you want me to." Lorinda lowered her voice. "It wouldn't be smart for me. I mean, look at how close Roberta is to my cousin."

That was a good point. Roberta probably came over to Lorinda's house all the time.

Jennifer swallowed. "You make a great point. I can't argue with that." She paused and felt her excitement swell. "But remember how you always wanted to take down Essentrix Labs? If we do nothing, we let them destroy lives. We let them exploit people. We stand by and watch them get away with it."

Lorinda winced, her jaw tightening as if she were holding something in.

Jennifer reached out and touched her hand. "We need you. The inside team is falling apart without your leadership. We're having a hard time building their trust. Please consider joining us. I promise we'll keep you protected."

Lorinda exhaled and then looked up at Jennifer. "I really want to," she began. "I support your cause, one hundred percent. But I can't. It's too risky. I'm trying to make my life here. I have to choose my missions carefully. This one isn't for me."

Jennifer's heart sunk. She turned on a faucet and splashed

cold water on her face. "I know there's a lot at stake for you." She patted her face dry with a paper towel. "But imagine how you would feel if you let Essentrix Labs get away with this."

"I'm so sorry," Lorinda said softly, patting her shoulder. "But I can't. I'll meet you back outside."

Lorinda left the room, and Jennifer looked at herself in the mirror. Her head was spinning. She had failed her team. She had no idea what they were going to do now.

She could hear the bathroom door creaking open. In walked Roberta.

"Hey," Roberta said warmly. "Uchenna tells me that you and some of these other women work for Essentrix Labs along with Lorinda."

Jennifer froze and balled up her paper towel. "Yes," she squeaked.

"I'm off the clock now, but I'd love to talk to you all further about an investigation I'm leading with the Omaha State Police," Roberta said.

Jennifer steeled herself up to seem concerned. She gasped. Maybe Roberta wouldn't notice the delay. "Is everything okay?"

"It's confidential right now," Roberta added. "But your co-operation is greatly appreciated."

Jennifer's gaze dropped solemnly. "Any way that we can help, I'm there."

CHAPTER 32

JENNIFER

"Now this dance party, ladies, is our office," Hana exclaimed, radiating glamour in her long, curly black wig. "There's no reason we can't celebrate our wins while we get some work done."

Caribbean Fire was packed with men and women dressed in bright colors and neutral linens, swaying freely to the vibrant sounds of tropical music. Jennifer breathed in the sweet smell of citrus and felt at home immediately. Golden market lights hung overhead, and vivid beach paintings covered the exposed brick walls.

Maybe the island oasis vibe would distract the team from Jennifer's failed attempt to save the heist.

Nari approached the host stand confidently, blending into the crowd with her curly black bob, wide-brimmed straw hat, and coral sundress. "Hello there! Can we have a private VIP table?" she asked before trotting over to the DJ booth.

Jennifer grinned widely. She had never sat at a VIP table before. Maybe it would be made out of marble, with white leather couches that no one was allowed to spill on.

The host guided the women around the throng of joyful revelers to a secluded corner. She passed out menus as the women took their seats.

Nari joined the group, filled with a bubbly energy. "Tonight, we're transporting the team to Turks and Caicos! The DJ's going to play my favorite ripsaw band, and I've ordered the best island treats for the table."

Jennifer bounced in her seat and clapped excitedly. "You've outdone yourself again, roomie! Does this place remind you of your childhood?"

"It feels just like Providenciales, the main island in Turks and Caicos where I grew up." Nari's face glowed as she looked around the room. "I'll admit, we were a little secluded at first because we were living in a safe house and running from the cops. But as time went on, we became locals. We settled into the warm, chill vibe. Our neighbors gave us food and treated us like family. We kayaked and danced together."

"And most importantly, we learned to dance for no reason." Hana grinned.

The server arrived and passed out plates of food that smelled of rich, buttery cheese and fried cornmeal. Jennifer's mouth watered.

"I've missed my scotch bonnet hot sauce *so much.*" Hana spooned mac and cheese onto her plate and doused it with a dark-red liquid in a small bottle.

Martha took a bite of a plantain, her eyes glimmering with delight as she chewed. She looked like she was ready to dance all night with her platinum-blond wig and bright-red lipstick. "I've got some good news for you, Nari. Sumeet's clean. His backstory holds up, his communications are solid, and his behavior is normal."

Nari exhaled and blinked before a smile slowly took over her face. "I *knew* we could trust Mr. Vora. I hate to admit that this makes me like him a little bit more."

Jennifer felt a wave of excitement for Nari. "Congrats, roomie." She bounced in her seat and gave Nari a hip bump.

"Sumeet is welcome to heist with us any time." Martha winked. "Alright, let's get to planning."

Uh-oh. Jennifer gulped. The spotlight was on her now. Her mind reeled and words rushed out of her mouth. "I'm sorry I couldn't get Lorinda to join us."

"Hey, don't worry," Hana remarked. "We all tried. And you did a wonderful job, my child. You even came face-to-face with Roberta with no disguise on."

"I'm so proud of you," Nari added, patting Jennifer's arm. "You absolutely killed it, roomie."

Jennifer smiled weakly.

"The mission gets a little bit more complicated now, but I'm confident we can do it," Hana said. "Martha and I can impersonate contractors and gain access to the building. We'll get the lay of the land and figure out how to replicate these plans ourselves. We already know a lot about how inventory and deliveries work at Essentrix, but many systems aren't documented. That's why we need to be there in person."

Nari frowned and wrung her hands. "This is key intel, Mom. I need to be there too."

"Oh," Hana began. "Well, Martha is so good in these situations, dear. We need her to hack into their systems."

"I think all three of us can go," Nari said, an edge to her voice. "I want to see exactly how their team works from the inside so I can plan effectively."

Jennifer froze and watched silently. She had never seen Nari react like this during a strategy session. It seemed like Martha's attention was fixed on Nari too.

"That's great, *nae jasik,* but this is really more of a two-person job. And Martha and I are the most experienced," Hana replied. "You might need to go off script, and that can be hard to do. Besides, Martha and I can help guide the mission."

"I can't gain experience if you don't let me join," Nari snapped. "You'll never know how much I can do if you keep pushing me out." She stood up and stormed away from the table, pulling her straw hat down over her eyes as she made her way around the dance floor and out the front door.

Hana sighed and looked up at Martha and Jennifer. "Did I do something wrong? I was just being honest with her."

"I understand where you're coming from," Martha replied. "And we do need experienced people on the job. But I don't see any harm in having three of us on-site."

"I don't see why she needs to be there. We can get all the intel we need with two people." Hana folded her arms across her chest. "And it's more secure with fewer people."

"I think she might feel like she's in your shadow." Jennifer tilted her head to the side. "I know she's been so happy to have you join, but sometimes you plan everything." She thought back to Nari's commanding presence on the first mission. "Maybe she wants to be in the driver's seat sometimes too."

Hana nodded and glanced down at the table. A moment passed in silence. "I think you're both right. I'll go talk to her." She stood up and followed Nari's path out of the nightclub.

Jennifer excused herself to the bathroom. She wanted the same freedom that Nari had built for herself. As she stood in front of the mirror, she felt her body fill with an electric energy. She looked at her reflection and recited to herself, *You are strong. You are powerful. Go, Jenny.* She pulled out her cell phone and searched for marketing research firms in Hawaii. She clicked on the first result for a company called Island Research, filled out the form, and hit send.

When she returned, Hana and Nari were back at the table. "I'm excited to join the team as we infiltrate Essentrix Labs tomorrow," Nari announced.

"I know you'll get great intel, roomie," Jennifer said.

Hana cleared her throat. "And we'd love to have you on-board too, Jennifer."

"How can I help?" Jennifer asked in a serious tone.

"I know you don't work in operations like Lorinda," Nari began, "but it would be great if you could help Martha with mapping out the facility and getting intel on security protocols. You can gain access to insider information that wouldn't be recorded anywhere."

Jennifer felt her throat go dry. She hadn't done anything yet while actually at work that could connect her to the heist. "I guess I could get a tour of the facility for my work."

"That's a great idea. You'd be amazed what you can learn from casual conversations too," Martha shared.

Jennifer inhaled sharply through her nose. Martha seemed so calm. Doing something for the heist team at Essentrix

Labs—with no disguise, in full view of cameras—was a new level of boldness.

Nari put her hand on Jennifer's shoulder. "Think of a good excuse for why you'd need to go there. It'll look like you're doing your job. Stay confident, and no one will suspect you of anything."

Jennifer tried to keep her voice steady. "Thanks, roomie."

Hana folded her hands. "Now, we've also got all four members of the second heist team arriving in Omaha tomorrow. Nari and I will begin training them immediately."

"The leader is my mom's long-time associate, Charlotte." Nari looked at Jennifer. "We've been planning their mission over the last few days while you've been at work."

"Thanks for covering for me, ladies," Jennifer said.

"Hey, our pleasure," Martha responded. "The secondary mission is going to take place at the Essentrix Labs location on Mill Creek Lane in south Omaha. This facility is much bigger than ours, and it has more cameras."

"Luckily, this team is very experienced." Hana tapped her finger on the table. "I've worked with them on multiple jobs in the Americas, Europe, and beyond. They do not make mistakes."

Jennifer could feel her face brighten as she cut into a slice of pineapple.

"Without the inside team, we'll have to do some additional leg work to get hundreds of empty boxes loaded into the decoy getaway delivery truck." Martha took a sip of her ginger beer. "The other team won't have to carry the boxes from one location to another, like us."

"Plus, their truck will match ours exactly," Hana explained.

"At any point, if we need to evade the cops, they'll be there to help us."

"The whole point of this fake-out heist is to draw police attention away from our mission," Martha said. "That's why we're paying them so well. We're not only expecting them to get pursued by the police—we're also depending on it."

Jennifer's eyes widened as she snacked on fried cornmeal flatbread. "These women are heroes. And this bread is incredible."

"Those are Johnny cakes. I like them with ketchup." Nari nudged the bottle over. "We're going to help the back up team plan things perfectly, down to the last second."

Nari's phone started to vibrate. "It's Freddy," she said. The group hushed and huddled in closer together.

She put her phone on speaker. "Hey Freddy, what's new?"

"The anonymous tip about the heist came from Toronto, but the number was spoofed. The telecom company traced the call to its first major cell phone tower ping in Vienna, Austria. I hope that can help you find your mole." Freddy hung up.

"Oh my gosh! It's Johannes!" Jennifer's stomach dropped. A small part of her had hoped the mole would be someone else.

Hana shook her head. "He was the rat all along."

"And we're already ten steps ahead of him," Nari chimed in.

"We've got this mission in the bag. Heist girlfriends for life!" Martha whooped.

An upbeat, tropical instrumentation floated through the speakers. The crowd murmured and moved to the beat.

"This is the Ripsaw Roses!" Nari clapped her hands. "My favorite band from Turks and Caicos!"

"We've got the rhythm to make you sway," a woman

sang in a melodic, soulful voice. A light metallic scraping beat took over the track.

"Oh my *gosh*." Jennifer leaned in. "What is that sound?"

"That's the lead singer!" Nari exclaimed. "She's scraping a screwdriver against the teeth of the ripsaw!"

Hana bobbed her head to the beat of the music. "Well, my team, it's time to celebrate and *mash up di place*! Let's get this party started!" She jumped up to the dance floor and waved for the group to join her.

An infectious energy took over as the heist crew danced their way into the crowd. Jennifer stomped her feet and couldn't stop beaming.

•   •   •

Ten days until heist day

Jennifer's palms were sweaty. Mandy looked up at her expectantly as Jennifer approached her desk.

"Hey, Mandy. I'd like to tour our warehouse facility in Papillon," Jennifer began confidently. "Our chunky peanut butter retailers are reporting how important a safe, efficient warehouse is to them. I'd love to get some insights into our logistics processes. This could really be a differentiator for us."

"I like your initiative, Jennifer. Let me connect you with Lorinda. Maybe you can join one of her facility walk-throughs today," Mandy replied.

Jennifer cleared her throat to cover up her urge to laugh. At least this was Mandy's idea. She could defend herself to Lorinda later. "That sounds great," she said brightly.

Mandy typed onto her keyboard. "I'm glad you stopped by, because I want to get your take on the Greenleaf Feed packaging redesign." She glanced over at Jennifer. "You had such great insights last time on our poultry line."

Ah, great. Mandy's face was serene. There was no way she knew the animal feed was made from cobalt mined by women suffering in the Congo. Months ago, Jennifer had no idea either. She had performed market research to help sell the feed to farms all across the country. She had delivered her report, neatly printed and bound to Mandy's desk, feeling accomplished while completely oblivious to the devastation occurring on the other side of the world.

She felt sick and swallowed hard. "I would love to, Mandy." Her voice quivered.

Suddenly, Lorinda appeared in the doorway. Jennifer exhaled as tension drained from her body.

Lorinda's expression was strange and hard to read. "Hey, team," she began, her voice taut. "Jen, I'd love to have you join my facility tour today. Let's head over now."

"Looking forward to it," Jennifer said with forced cheerfulness.

"Wonderful," Mandy replied. "Thanks for being so accommodating, Lorinda. I can't wait to see what you two are able to accomplish together."

Jennifer nodded to Mandy and followed Lorinda down the hallway as her loose ballet flats flapped underfoot. Lorinda turned to face her, her face strained. "If you wouldn't mind, I'd love to stop by the break room for tea before we head over to tour the facility."

This didn't seem like it was going to go well. Maybe

Lorinda was going to confront her and ask her to never talk to her at work again. Fair enough.

The two of them made their way into the empty break room, past the high tables. Jennifer followed Lorinda to the tea kettle.

Lorinda whispered, "I can't be connected to this. I'll assign someone else to take you on the tour. And as a friend, I've got to tell you that this is really bold. Be careful, okay?"

"I get it," Jennifer said, her voice low but urgent. "And I will be. I don't blame you for not wanting to be involved. But I've got to ask. How many years have you worked here now?"

Lorinda paused and her face stirred. "At least six."

"You've had to sit by and watch for six years while Essentrix Labs profits from suffering. More than anyone, you know how bad they are." Jennifer leaned in closer.

Lorinda turned and grabbed a tea bag before turning on the electric tea kettle. She exhaled slowly. "I do know."

"You are an incredibly influential person. You take dirty money from politicians' pockets and use it to transform women's lives." Jennifer felt warmth rise to her cheeks. "But imagine what we can do together, fighting against an evil that has exploited us *directly*. One that has forced us to promote suffering so they can get rich. You don't have to keep waiting until the moment is right. By taking a stand, you take back your own power."

Lorinda was silent. She looked thoughtful as she poured hot water into a ceramic floral teacup, ripped her paper tea packet open, and dipped her bag into the water.

Jennifer watched as Lorinda mixed sweetener into her tea cup with a wooden stirrer. "Think of the impact you could make with *millions* of dollars."

Lorinda blew on her tea and looked up at Jennifer. "I'll take you on the tour. I'll get you the information you need. I'm a team player, and I want to help out the marketing group."

"Yes!" Jennifer cheered before silencing herself and looking back at the counter casually.

CHAPTER 33

NARI

Hana pulled the black getaway van in front of a small blue house a few blocks from the Essentrix Labs facility in Papillon.

Martha adjusted her uniform. She was on deck as an IT maintenance contractor again, while Nari and Hana would play delivery drivers.

"Most of the inventory team will be on their lunch break for the next fifteen minutes. But move quickly, because some of them will start to come back earlier. Security is tight after the police presence, so you'll have to be careful." Martha pulled up a small map on her cell phone and pointed. "According to Jennifer's intel, there are camera blind spots along this middle row. From what I can tell, the Sorbelate is stored over here in a locked room on the far end of the warehouse."

Hana pulled a rubber stopper from her pants pocket. "Perfect. I'll use this to keep the door open—discreetly—while I can take note of how the inventory is arranged. Nari, you'll run the delivery while I'm gone. I'll meet you back when I'm all done."

"Perfect. See you soon." Martha hopped out of the vehicle and walked toward the building.

Hana wheeled the van around and approached the facility. The building was starting to become so familiar to Nari. It seemed so strange that she had never been inside.

"You can lead the way once we get inside, *nae jasik,*" Hana said. "I trust you."

Nari grinned. "Thanks, Mom. There's no one I'd rather be on this mission with."

Hana wheeled the van toward the vehicle entrance. A man in uniform was working in the small guard building. "Welcome to Essentrix Labs," he said as he stepped out.

"Thank you," Hana replied brightly. "I've got a delivery here for the receiving department. Where should I drop it off?"

"Mind if I take a quick look at that paperwork?" the man said. Hana passed it to him. "Come on in, straight ahead. When you reach the second building, make a right. You can't miss it." He opened the gate and waved them through.

Nari felt a rush already. Her mom maneuvered the van into the loading dock for the receiving department under a large gray overhead door. A thin, tall woman wearing a hat and glasses waved them up a concrete ramp to the entrance. She had curly light-brown hair and blue eyes. Hana parked the van, and Nari jumped out.

"I've got a delivery for the receiving department." Nari glanced at her watch.

"Perfect," the woman replied. "Once you've got the boxes loaded, follow me inside. I'll take you to the warehouse."

"Sounds good." Nari flitted her gaze off to the side like she was busy and detached. She turned and walked to the back of the van where her mom was already unloading boxes into dollies.

The packages were larger and heavier than their Sorbelate boxes, and Nari and Hana needed to lift a few of them together. Martha had hacked into the Essentrix Labs inventory system and labeled each box perfectly to impersonate a delivery scheduled for later that day.

Nari and Hana wheeled their dollies to the loading dock and up a metal ramp. Nari clutched a clipboard under her arm.

"Can I see your delivery manifest?" the woman asked.

Looking off into the distance so she'd seem distracted, Nari unclipped the top piece of paper from her clipboard. "Here you go."

The woman glanced it over. "Follow me."

"They don't pay us enough for what we do," Hana muttered for effect.

"Ain't that the truth, sister," the woman replied, laughing. "Sometimes, they don't even pay us at all."

Nari raised an eyebrow.

As they walked up the ramp and through the entrance, they passed two security guards on either side. One of them nodded to Nari in acknowledgement. She tipped her hat.

Dozens of inventory workers milled about the noisy concrete floor. The sounds of whirring machinery filled the air. A man drove by on a yellow forklift stacked high with pallets of bulging white paper bags.

The warehouse was packed with giant shelves that seemed to be about forty feet high. Pallets of rectangular food boxes sat aside stacks of crates, large burlap sacks, and giant cardboard delivery boxes.

"Which section are you delivering for?" The woman folded her arms across her chest.

"Dry goods," Nari responded confidently. She glanced at her mom, who was subtly surveying the warehouse for the secure Sorbelate inventory room.

"Follow me," the woman said. "I apologize. We haven't upgraded our system yet so we don't have inventory scanners. I know, get with the times, right? I have some paper forms I'll share with you."

The outdated inventory system could work to their advantage. Nari suppressed a grin. Instead, she wheeled her dolly ahead and rolled her eyes. "Hey, it's much worse for you than it is for me. I'm sorry you have to deal with that every day."

"Don't I know it. They're going to force me into early retirement," the woman responded dryly.

As Martha had predicted, there were no warehouse workers in the dry goods area, but four security guards flanked the perimeter. No big deal. Nari and her mom would be in and out of there in no time. There would be no reason to raise suspicion.

The woman walked them down a middle aisle past rows of high shelves on either side. She made a left about halfway through, Nari and Hana pushing their dollies behind her.

"This is where we take deliveries." The woman pointed to a lower shelf and handed some paperwork to Nari. "When you're all done, come back to me and I'll help you get squared away. Let me know if you have any questions." She walked away.

Hana turned to Nari, her voice low. *"Nae jasik,* you unload. I've located the secure room. It's straight ahead and then off to the right on the far right end of the warehouse. I'll go check it out."

Nari nodded. Her mom walked down the aisle between the shelves. Nari lifted the first box and scanned her delivery manifest to check it off.

A security guard peered around the aisle and approached Nari. "Excuse me, what are you here to deliver?" he asked, an edge to his voice. His ID card hung from his belt loop. *"Luis,"* it read.

Nari stiffened and forced a smile. "Oh, big variety. We've got cornstarch, packaging supplies, maltodextrin…" She swept her hand toward the boxes.

"You mind showing me your delivery manifest?" Luis asked. "Standard procedure."

"Of course." She unclipped the top sheet of paper from the clipboard and handed it over. "Hot summer we're having, huh? I love doing these deliveries so I can enjoy the air-conditioning in the warehouse."

Luis's expression softened. "For sure. I used to do security at outdoor concerts. It was the *worst* in the summer. Here, I actually get cold sometimes." He glanced over the document for a couple of seconds and raised an eyebrow. "You're with Bellingham Foods. I talked to the team today. They said they were sending an extra ten units of saffron to make up for the spoiled delivery last week. Why don't you have that listed here?"

"Oh, that must have been a mistake." Nari's hands trembled. Her mom didn't think she could improvise. She had to prove her wrong. "We've been having...issues with our system all morning. I'm so sorry about that. As soon as I get back to my van, I'll call the warehouse and get that straightened out for you."

"That's strange." He narrowed his eyes. "Ralph confirmed it was entered into the system. Would you mind if I call your dispatch team and figure out what's going on?"

"Oh, that's not a good idea!" she exclaimed. "You'd be on hold for an hour. I'd love to handle it for you on my end."

He shook his head and looked at her. "Something doesn't seem right."

She shifted her weight from one foot to the other. "I know. Things have..." She exhaled and tried to block out her mom's words. *Focus, Nari Park. You've done this dozens of times.* "Things have been slipping through the cracks lately. I will be sure to get that saffron delivered to you soon."

Luis raised an eyebrow. "I'm here to help if you have any questions."

As he walked away, Nari felt her shoulders go slack. She scanned the delivery manifest again. There were at least twenty boxes to get through. She studied the first label, extending each package out for as long as she could.

Suddenly, her smartwatch buzzed. *"Code red,"* the screen flashed. *"I'm locked inside."* Her chest tightened.

She glanced to either side. The security guards were at their posts. She grabbed her dolly and wheeled it through the center aisle toward the far side of the room.

Nari could see the secured room from afar, past the shelves. Two security guards stood on either side at a distance of about ten feet. There was a keypad next to the door with a card scanner below. She backed up her dolly into the aisle and held up her clipboard like she was orienting herself.

"Don't worry, Mom. I'll get you out," she texted back, her heart racing. She glanced at the time. The inventory team would be back in a few minutes and their cover would be blown.

She could ask Martha to hack into the keypad, but that might take too long.

Quickly, Nari walked down the aisle and searched for Luis. Sure enough, he was still there, inspecting a fire extinguisher with his ID card clipped to his waist.

She wheeled her dolly back to the inventory shelf, picked up a box, and pretended to let it slip. But the box fell faster and harder than she'd expected. Before she knew it, it fell forcefully onto her ankle, then landed on the floor below with a thud.

"Ouch!" she shouted, louder than intended.

A beat passed. Then another. Nari's breath was shallow, and a cold sweat went down her back. They didn't have any time to spare. "Oh my *gosh*." She pretended to stumble and knocked another box off her dolly.

Luis appeared. "Everything okay?"

"Thanks for checking on me." Nari grimaced. "I'm so clumsy. This box slid out of my hands, and then I lost my balance and clipped another one."

"Here, let me help you with that." Luis bent over to help her pick up the first box. She leaned in and slipped the security badge off of his belt loop before quickly sliding it into her pocket. Then, she picked up the other side of the box.

"Thanks so much. You know, I forgot my gloves, and boxes have been slipping out of my hands all day." She shook her head.

He looked at her apologetically as he leaned down for the second box. "I know the feeling! I hope you get to go home soon."

"So sorry to ask for your help. I really appreciate it," Nari sighed.

"Of course. I mean, these jobs are hard," Luis said breathlessly. "I hope you have worker's compensation. I have been injured multiple times—"

"Absolutely," Nari replied quickly. "Well, I should really get back to loading this inventory. I've got so many deliveries to get done today. Thanks again."

Luis grinned and tilted his head forward. "Have a good one." He turned and walked back to his post.

Once he was out of sight, she quickly wheeled her dolly down the aisle between the shelves and toward the secured room. Two security guards still flanked the door. Nari glanced at her watch. She had approximately three minutes before someone would catch her mom.

Nari confidently wheeled her dolly across the far wall. She swiped her arm over a row of light switches, turning off lights on the entire left section of the facility. She continued walking ahead.

The two guards by the secure room shook their heads. "Power outage in inventory," one of them reported into his walkie-talkie. They began to walk toward the wing that Nari had left. Steadily, she strode toward the secure room, her expression blank.

She scanned Luis's card against the key scanner and heard a beep. She knocked on the door two times, turned the doorknob, and walked forward. She could hear the door opening slowly behind her as she continued back to the dry goods inventory area. The tension melted from her shoulders. They were safe. For now.

·   ·   ·

Nari sat in the driver's seat of the getaway van next to Hana, where they waited on a side street for Martha.

Hana turned to face Nari. "I am extremely proud of you, *nae jasik*. I made a huge mistake today with the door stopper, and I didn't plan for contingencies correctly. You saved the mission. I can't believe I wanted to do this without you. You are an incredibly strong leader, and you can pull off any job."

Nari's face grew warm, and she could feel tears forming in her eyes. "Thank you, Mom. I'm a great leader because I've learned from you."

Hana reached over and brushed a few strands of hair from Nari's forehead. Nari could see tears in her eyes as well. "I've just given you a little guidance over the years. You're a great leader because you're smart and dedicated. I'm so sorry for underestimating you. I'll never do it again. I'm so grateful to be on this mission with you and to be able to experience this together. I'm lucky to have you as a partner and as a daughter. I love you."

"I'll remember this forever," Nari replied. "I love you too."

Nari and her mom embraced.

·   ·   ·

The air was cool, and a light breeze blew through the cornfields. The team stood on a large patch of flattened grass underneath the dark twilight sky. Nari's eyes had adjusted to the darkness, and she could see a large green tractor flanking the field.

Nari had sold the farm to a good friend during her wholesaling days. It had a corn maze that operated as a tourist attraction during the fall months. She grinned as she looked at the team assembled there.

"Now that we're all together, what did you find at Essentrix Labs this afternoon?" Nari asked Martha.

"The good news is we'll be able to easily manipulate their inventory. The bad news is that it'll be really hard to infiltrate the facility and move the Sorbelate based on their current scheduling," Martha said. "I think we've got to go with plan B. I can get us badges to pose as new employees. We'll replicate the same process as the inside team. We'll have to do some pretty elaborate planning to pull it off, but I believe in us."

Nari glanced around the group and gulped. "The inside team is hesitant to trust us without Lorinda. And they already know about the heist. Wouldn't they catch onto us pretty quickly?"

"You do make a good point, *nae jasik*," Hana agreed. "We'd have to move the inventory right under the noses of the team at Essentrix Labs. And those people would know what to look for. We might have to see if we can manipulate the scheduling a bit."

Martha nodded.

"We can still operate the mission, right?" Jennifer asked.

"Of course." Hana dipped her chin. "We've still got over a week to figure this out. Let's continue with our training run and then Martha can guide us through scheduling afterward.

There's no time like the present. Let's get ready to rumble!" She blew her whistle.

Nari's cheeks stung with embarrassment, but no one on the team seemed to mind that the phrase was at least thirty years old. Jennifer waved her hands above her head, and Martha grunted. Each woman exchanged high-fives and picked up four five-kilo boxes filled with practice flour before running to the corn maze entryway. Martha went first, sliding sideways as fast as she could to simulate the beginning portion of the heist, where they would hug the brick wall to avoid the cameras. Nari followed shortly after with Jennifer and then her mom behind her.

Suddenly, Nari heard rustling among the corn. "Who's there?" She slowed her run to a halt. A figure stepped into the maze.

It was Lorinda. "Hey team," she said, her face glowing.

Nari's eyes widened in shock. "Hi, Lorinda." One-by-one, each member of the group placed their boxes on the ground.

"Jennifer, what you said really resonated with me. I haven't been able to sleep since we spoke," Lorinda began.

Nari glanced at Jennifer, whose eyes seemed to sparkle.

"I've been sitting by and watching Essentrix Labs exploit people for far too long. I want to support this mission. I know you can't do it without me," Lorinda said. "I'm in."

The group cheered. Nari threw her arms around Lorinda. "Welcome back."

CHAPTER 34

JENNIFER

As Jennifer got ready for bed, her encrypted app buzzed three times. It was Johannes. *"How's everything going with Mill Creek Lane?"*

"It's going great. We've already found a new buyer," she typed, adding a winking emoji. She uploaded a copy of the fake invoice Nari had created.

Within a minute, Jennifer's phone buzzed. *"Excellent,"* Johannes wrote. *"I see you quoted them on a higher price per kilo too."* He seemed completely convinced of the new location. Jennifer danced for a few seconds in the mirror as she brushed her teeth.

Nari wasn't here to tell her what to say. No harm in going off script for a little bit. *"Nari's the best seller. What are you up to this week?"* Jennifer messaged. *"Any boat trips to Bratislava planned?"*

"Funny you mention that. I haven't taken that trip in years,

since Mercy was with me. She made everything come alive. It's not the same exploring without her," he said.

She felt a lump rise in her throat. She splashed her face with water. "I'm so sorry to hear that," she typed. "It sounds like Mercy was such a lovely person."

"She was. Every part of Vienna still reminds me of her. I wouldn't be able to go for walks around the city if I didn't have my dog Fritzi," he wrote. Within a second, another message came through with a picture of Johannes and Fritzi at a cafe. "I got him in her honor. She always wanted a dog, and we could never make it work."

She reminded herself that Johannes was the bad guy, turning them in to help himself out. But he seemed so down to earth, and so in need. She figured she could be honest with him about other parts of her life, as long as she didn't accidentally reveal anything about the heist.

"Dogs can really help with grief," she typed. "They give you so much unconditional love. After my dad died, I missed my grandma's dogs so much." She attached a photo of her dad with her grandma's Pomeranians and hit send before continuing to write. "Luckily, Nari was really there for me. She helped me research his military service in Germany, and she took me dancing to distract me. We became so much closer after that."

"Wow, I had no idea," he replied. "I'm so sorry for your loss. No wonder your bond with Nari is so special."

Jennifer's breath grew tight in her chest, and she felt like crying. She started to pin up her twists then took a break to type. "Thank you. For me, losing my dad has never gotten easier. So much reminds me of him too. But Mercy is with you when you live out her values. And that can help you feel better."

Eight days until heist day

Nari was waiting for Jennifer when she got home that evening. Jennifer relished her time alone with Nari. After bringing in so many new heist members, it felt like she and Nari were always passing each other in the apartment.

Jennifer's phone vibrated. "Johannes is texting me about the heist." She handed Nari the phone. "Check it out."

Nari looked at the cell phone screen and read aloud. "Jenny, can you send updates?" She looked up at Jennifer, a mock look of shock on her face. "You don't let *anyone* call you Jenny, except your grandma! Are you bonding with this man?"

Jennifer hit Nari lightly with a pillow. "He's been through a lot these past few years! Plus, he's a really interesting person."

She hoped Nari wouldn't scroll up in her chat history.

"I'll give you that," Nari admitted. "Hey, the more you're bonding with him, the better off we are. That's what I love about you. You're so genuine that you can convince anyone of anything." She paused. "But don't ever accidentally start confiding our mission details to Johannes."

"I've got that part down. How should we respond this time?"

Nari thought for a moment. "Talk to him about the fake mission but continue to be vague. No identifying info." She paused. "We've been doing a great job getting him on our side lately. Let's kick it up a notch. Bring up a reference to his wife to get him emotional."

"Got it, boss," Jennifer joked. Nari passed the phone back to her.

"Everything is coming along well," Jennifer said as she

typed. "We're mapping out the facility and learning the security schedule."

"That's the perfect level of detail," Nari said.

Jennifer hit send. She stopped to think about how to weave Johannes's wife into the next message. "Nari and I stopped by the African handicraft shop today and looked at crafts from Kenya," she read aloud, as Nari nodded in agreement. "I think Mercy would have been a great member of the team. We've decided to dedicate the heist to her."

This message accomplished two goals. It fit what Nari wanted, and it matched up perfectly with what Jennifer had been secretly discussing with Johannes lately. This double life thing was starting to become easier for her.

"Bingo!" Nari said. "You're amazing."

Jennifer beamed.

One minute later, a text from Johannes came in. Jennifer's phone vibrated.

Johannes sent two heart emojis.

Later that night, Jennifer was alone in bed. She was winding down and getting ready to read her latest historical romance novel set in Ancient Greece. At least she could read something good until they got arrested.

She pulled out her phone and looked at her encrypted texting app, scrolling through her past messages with Johannes. He was clearly a lonely man overcome by grief. What good was all his money if he didn't have people to enjoy it with?

"I'm so sorry for what you're going through," she messaged into the app. *"You're like an honorary member of our Mercy Heist team. Thanks for introducing us to this opportunity. I'm excited to give back. Once the heist is over, we want to send money to the women*

who work in the mines. Could you help me get in touch with them? I hope you're doing something fun today."

The next morning, she stretched and lazily picked up her phone from its charging location on her nightstand.

"Thank you so much," Johannes wrote. "Mercy would have loved you. I'd be so happy to connect you with the mine workers and their families. Here's my contact, Kazi. She speaks Katanga Swahili and can't wait to hear from you."

Kazi. What a beautiful name. Jennifer couldn't believe the time had finally come to meet a woman who worked in the mines.

She opened up her translation app and started typing. "Hi Kazi. My name's Jennifer. It's so nice to finally meet you. I'm sure you know about our mission. You inspire us so much. We're fighting back to get you the money you deserve." She felt her face grow warm in anticipation as she sent her message.

She tried to stay calm as she got up and padded to the kitchen. As she measured out her electrolyte mix, her phone vibrated. She translated Kazi's response and grinned. "Jennifer, what a blessing to hear from you. We will never forget your team's support. May you be protected in all that you do. Know that we're also fighting back as much as we can."

"Thank you for your kindness. I love that you're doing that," Jennifer wrote.

"We're documenting every abuse we can on our phones," Kazi responded. "We're also planning a work slowdown. It's dangerous, but we're doing as much as we can."

"Oh my gosh," Jennifer typed. "You're so brave. Please stay safe. You deserve every freedom, health, and joy in the world." She paused, feeling her emotions swell. "What will you do once you get the money?"

"I'm going to start a school for girls. I want to build opportunities for the next generation. One woman on my team is going to open a health clinic. Another is opening a trucking company, and a few women want to come together to buy a farm. That's just the beginning," Kazi replied.

Jennifer leaned against the counter and reread the message from Kazi. She felt lighter with each pass. *"That is incredible. Other people have gotten rich from your sacrifices. It's time for you to get your cut and transform your community. It's time for you to quit and never look back,"* she wrote.

"Your kindness means so much to me," Kazi responded. *"Let's fight our employer together."*

CHAPTER 35

ROBERTA

Seven days until heist day

"Off the record, I've been looking into past employees with grudges," Roberta explained to Uchenna as they walked by rows of plump zucchinis and perfectly fuzzy peaches at Central Farmers Market. "People who might want to take revenge. There are a few who seem promising."

"Don't worry. You don't have to tell me anything," Uchenna replied. "But if you need help with some amateur internet research, I'm your woman. That's my specialty."

Roberta smiled and studied a carton of raspberries. "I'll let you know, Agent Archives. Something about this case sets me on fire. These criminals think they can outsmart the cops."

"But they'll never outsmart you." Uchenna swiped a braid over her shoulder. "You're putting in way more hours on this case than anyone else. I know you're going to catch them. Every day you're getting closer."

"Thank you." Roberta stood taller, imagining the honors she'd receive. "Roberta Fonseca is receiving our award tonight for bravery and cunning displayed over the last year," the chief would say.

"I also got my hands on a leaked copy of the inventory logs at Mill Creek Lane. There's extra Sorbelate being received from Papillon that isn't attached to any delivery. And the inventory audit's been postponed," Roberta explained.

They passed by an apple stand, and Uchenna's eyes lit up. She grabbed a two-pound bag. "It sounds like you're still... going out on your own with some of these leads?"

"You could say that," Roberta replied.

Uchenna shook her head as she walked to the clerk and paid for her apples. They kept walking through the market, the sun shining through the trees. "You know you've got to tell the team eventually."

Roberta nodded. "I know. Earlier today, when the rest of the team was at lunch, I considered telling them. I started to type out an email in the empty bullpen. I made it seem like the leads were recent." She glanced at Uchenna, whose eyes were wide. "But I couldn't do it. I never hit send and erased the email. This is the only way I'm going to be able to investigate things myself. I'll tell them when the time is right."

She knew she sounded ridiculous. If she got caught, she could easily lose her badge or even get criminal charges. But for now, she didn't care. She'd figure out how to cover her tracks later.

•   •   •

The next morning, as Roberta entered the bullpen, a forensics tech approached her. "Your security footage from Essentrix Labs came in." She adjusted her large, round glasses.

"Thank you," Roberta replied, buzzing with energy. She couldn't wait to begin studying the video. She poured herself a cup of decaf coffee and made her way to the digital evidence room. She sat down and carefully entered her case number into the system.

There it was. Roberta tapped her fingers on the table in anticipation as the file loaded. Halfway through, the loading bar stopped, and a black screen appeared. A message popped up. *"Corrupt file. Playback unavailable."*

Roberta furrowed her brow. She restarted the computer and tried opening the file again. The same message appeared.

The file wasn't flagged or listed as corrupted, which meant that it must have broken after it was uploaded. That was strange. She bit her lip and checked to see if anyone had opened the file successfully. Sure enough, someone accessed the file about half an hour after it was uploaded. The system displayed their IP address, a string of indecipherable numbers.

Her throat tightened as she approached the tech. Maybe it was only her machine. "I'm not able to open the security footage for Essentrix Labs. Can you try it on your computer?"

The tech raised an eyebrow and clicked a few times on her machine. "The file's corrupted. That's strange. It was fine when I uploaded it this morning."

Roberta's throat went dry. *Tech glitches happen all the time. Not everything is a lead.* She steadied her body. "Thanks. Did anyone else ask you for the file?"

"Not that I know of. I'll look into this further for you," the tech replied.

Roberta made her way downstairs, where Freddy was waiting outside his patrol car with two cups of coffee and muffins. *Not bad.*

"I hope you like cinnamon pecan. That flavor was on sale," Freddy shared.

The two got into the car and sat down, and Freddy pulled the car out of the lot. "Thanks," Roberta said. "How did the internal email audit at Essentrix Labs go?"

"Inconclusive, unfortunately," he replied. "Nothing stands out. It's routine chatter about scheduling and vendors."

"Would you mind if I looked into the data?" she asked. "I'd love to double-check the emails."

"I appreciate the offer, but you're better off looking into more promising leads," he said.

Perfect. Freddy didn't want her involved in this part of the investigation. She swallowed hard.

"By the way, I have some good news," he continued. "I got an anonymous tip that the heist team is considering a new location."

Roberta hardened and sat still in her chair. She felt her face getting warmer. *Great.* Now Freddy was going to be the hero, leaking her tip before she could. Well, at least she wouldn't get caught for withholding information.

"Really?" She tried to sound natural as she fiddled with the lid on her coffee cup. "That's surprising. They're smarter than I thought."

"Yeah," he replied. "I hear they want to go after another business entirely. My anonymous source says they know we're onto them. Now they're looking at Omaha Central Bank."

She nodded, her jaw tightening. So now there was another heist location? Freddy knew more than her. She doubled down on her resolve to keep the other location a secret.

Roberta neutralized her expression as she took a bite of her muffin. "Interesting. Now they're turning into classic bank robbers."

"It's not what I expected either. The chief is sending us to the bank today to interview employees and try to find out more." Freddy blew on his coffee.

"Sounds great." She forced herself to respond, stewing silently over Freddy's discovery. She would need to work extra hard now to uncover something major at the bank. "Onward and upward."

CHAPTER 36

NARI

Six days until heist day

Nari's phone buzzed. Sumeet was at their apartment to pick her up. She felt a wave of excitement course through her body. It was so good to be able to trust him again.

In fact, the emotions were maddening. She was starting to crave their one-on-one time. When they were apart, her mind would wander to him. She would replay memories and ache to see him again.

Nari felt buoyant walking to Sumeet's black SUV in her gray skinny jeans and turquoise fitted tee. She wore a red wig and sunglasses.

"What do you have for me, Vora?" she asked as she stepped inside.

"Your favorite. Burgers and fries." He held up a greasy white paper bag filled with takeout.

Nari extended a hand for a high-five as she felt a warmth rise in her chest.

Sumeet started the engine and began to drive. "I checked on the Papillon location last night for a security presence. There were two guards on-site at around 1 AM."

She gasped. "That's never happened before."

"I know," he replied, his right hand at the bottom of the steering wheel. "I talked to Keisha in security. She called in sick and didn't save the schedule changes before she left. It won't happen again, she says."

"Thanks. I'll give her a call and make sure we have backup plans in case anything happens on heist night," she said.

"You look amazing today, by the way." He reached over and touched her thigh.

Nari felt her face grow warm. She took in Sumeet's navy-blue slim-fit tee. "You don't look so bad, yourself."

Soon, he pulled up to an empty suburban parking lot of Play-Time Factory, an abandoned toy store that had gone out of business. The lot was located next to the edge of a closed-down highway entrance. The asphalt was cracking, and weeds were pushing through.

She and Sumeet had parked a small white delivery truck on the edge of the lot the night before after filling it with hundreds of boxes, each packed with five kilos of practice flour.

"Ready to go?" Nari asked eagerly, looking out onto the orange traffic cone obstacle course Sumeet had built.

"Not so fast, Park. I have a fried chicken sando to enjoy first." Sumeet grinned. He ran his fingers through Nari's hair and kissed her. She felt shivers go down her spine.

He pulled out two sandwiches wrapped in paper and

handed the green-wrapped burger to Nari. "I have a confession to make. I got you the jalapeño melt because I wanted to try it." He laughed mischievously. The paper bag crinkled, and the smell of salty oil wafted up to Nari's nose as he pulled out a large order of fries in a paper tray and ketchup packets.

She took a bite of her burger and luxuriated in its juicy and savory flavor. "I'm totally okay with your burger choice. This is incredible. I think it might change my life." She sipped from a giant cup of icy orange soda to calm the jalapeño burn in her mouth.

"I think you said that a couple days ago with the bean and cheese burrito," he quipped. "Now open up."

Nari turned her head toward him and opened her mouth. He tossed a fry inside. "Score!" he whooped. She cheered and chewed the fry.

Sumeet was looking at her, a small smirk taking hold on his face. She leaned over and started to kiss him. He put his arms around her and brushed a few strands of hair from her forehead. She put her hand on his bicep. He felt so warm and welcoming. Soon, they were making out.

She pulled away before her emotions got too hard to control. "Ready to lose?"

"Oh, it's on!" he exclaimed. "You'd better watch yourself!"

Nari put on her earpiece and ran to the delivery truck, swishing her hips exaggeratedly as she looked back at Sumeet. She could swear she saw him winking at her. She climbed into the driver's side of the truck cabin.

"Let's go!" he said through the earpiece.

Nari fired up the engine and immediately sped ahead through the opening in the traffic cones. Sumeet waited five seconds and began to follow her. She glanced at his SUV in her rear camera and put her foot on the gas.

She reached a sharp turn and slammed on the brakes before whipping the truck around a set of orange cones. The tires squealed and she tapped a cone. She could hear the boxes shifting in the back.

"This is like trying to drive a refrigerator!" she said.

"If you're that good at racing a fridge, I'm scared to see what you can do with a sports car," he joked. "Watch out. I'm on your tail."

She straightened the truck out and saw Sumeet speeding toward her. She stepped on the gas again. The engine growled and the vehicle lurched forward. She whipped the truck around a row of cones, barely slowing this time.

"Nice turn!" Sumeet added.

Up ahead, Nari could see the finish line. Her adrenaline spiked. She pressed hard on the accelerator and sped through, Sumeet just a second behind her.

"Not bad for a delivery truck!" he exclaimed. "You gave me a run for my money."

"I'm glad you liked that," she replied. "That was a little too close for comfort. We're going to need to come here to practice every day until the heist."

"I thought you'd never ask," he said.

Nari wheeled the truck around and parked it back on the edge of the lot. Sumeet pulled up next to her, and she got into his SUV. She looked over at him as he ran his fingers through his hair. She felt defenseless and had the urge to stay in his passenger's seat for hours.

"That was amazing. Ready for round two?" he said.

CHAPTER 37

ROBERTA

Five days until heist day

"It's gone. We have no record of who opened the Essentrix Labs footage before it broke." The forensics tech motioned to the blank access log on her screen.

Roberta's eyes widened, and she looked around the empty room. "Gone as in... There was a system error?"

The forensics tech shook her head and her jaw tightened. "It's too clean. I think someone did it manually."

Roberta could feel her anger rising. "Whoever broke the video knew the log would give them away." She leaned in closer and lowered her voice. "Can you create a fake backup file of the footage? If they try to mess with the video again, we can catch them in the act."

"I'm on it." The tech tilted her head forward. "I've got some footage of a corporate park I can use. I'll create a silent alert that'll show us who opened the file and where."

Roberta had an ally now. "Perfect. Thank you."

Her stride quick and purposeful, Roberta walked back to the bullpen. Fuming with anger, she sat down and opened up her laptop. She glanced around the room, unsure who she could trust. A couple of colleagues looked back absentmindedly, but most seemed busy.

She pulled up the bank investigation case notes and began to read furiously. The evidence looked strong. The anonymous caller leaked heist plans, like timing and entrance points, and a blueprint of the bank's security systems. Emily's incident report included interview transcripts with three bank employees who had seen a middle-aged female suspect casing the perimeter on different days. She scanned through the report until she reached the bottom, which was signed the day before by the shift supervisor, Sargent Shannon Vail, at 3:36 PM.

Hmm...Sargent Vail. Roberta's throat tightened. That couldn't be right. Sargent Vail was pulled off her normal schedule to work on a special case yesterday. She pulled up the shift schedule and scanned through it. There it was. Sargent Vail had worked on an override assignment for a convenience store robbery at that time. She wouldn't have been at the station to sign off on the report.

That could only mean one thing. The signature was forged. Roberta brought her shaking hands to her forehead. Maybe Emily was trying to bypass scrutiny in her investigation. Maybe she wanted to speed up the process, or she made a paperwork error and didn't want anyone else to catch her.

But something about the bank heist didn't seem right. A corporate heist would be more low-key. It was clean. Roberta bet the perps chose it because they wanted easy money. So why would they switch to a bank heist? They'd suddenly have to learn how to use weapons, evade the cops, and operate with a surgical precision that was probably completely foreign to them. It didn't make sense.

She froze. What if the bank robbery was a setup? Maybe Freddy and Emily knew about the secret heist on Mill Creek Lane and were covering it up. Maybe the tampered footage revealed how the Papillon facility was diverting inventory to Mill Creek Lane. They didn't want Roberta or anyone else showing up to the secret location. They were protecting the perps.

Roberta inhaled sharply and balled her hands into fists. She had no choice. She had to call in sick on heist night and go to Mill Creek Lane, undercover. Without anyone's permission. It was the only way she could make sure the criminals got the justice they deserved.

She pulled out her wallet and glanced at two worn photos of her grandparents. Her grandfather on her dad's side was an awarded cop in Brazil in the 1950s. At a time when women were not allowed to be police officers, her mom's mother served as an informant to the cops in small-town Sicily. She was doing this for them. She would carry on their legacy for justice.

That night, on her drive home, Roberta knew she would need to have someone she could lean on for support, even if that person was a civilian. She called her most trusted friend for help, Uchenna.

•   •   •

"This investigation is being run terribly, and now someone is tampering with evidence." Roberta dribbled a basketball at the vacant court near Uchenna's house. "I can't trust the team. I'm going to break out and go to the secret heist location on my own." She tightened her grip on the ball, jumped up stiffly, and made her shot. The ball hit the side of the hoop and bounced back down. Uchenna caught it.

"I love you Roberta, but that is crazy." Uchenna spun the ball on her fingertip. "You could lose your job or, worse, get seriously hurt. What if you're up against a group of criminals?"

"I probably will be," Roberta said evenly. "From early intel, it looks like a team of four women. But they're amateurs. I can take them on."

Uchenna jumped up and shot the ball through the hoop. The net made a whooshing sound. "Four against one. Amateurs could be even worse if they're unpredictable. You shouldn't try to take them on by yourself. Why don't you tell the rest of the team about it so you can have some backup?"

"You're right, but if I tell the force about this they would take over and derail the investigation." Roberta trotted after the ball as it bounced across the court. She grabbed it and spun it in her hands. It fell onto the ground below and landed on her foot. "Someone on the team is hiding something because they don't want me to catch the perps. I can't trust anyone except you. I need your support on heist night to talk things through. You don't have to do anything—just be on call."

Roberta lined up her shot and fired. Too hard. The ball smacked against the backboard and back at her. She passed it back forcefully to Uchenna, who caught it with a thud.

Uchenna dribbled the ball between her hands. "Look, this case is important to you, and I know you have the skills to solve it, but I'm not qualified. I get all of my experience from cop shows. The last undercover thing I did was sneak a box of chocolate-covered raisins into the movie theater.

"You need people on your side who know what they're doing. Plus, imagine your liability if you're not on the clock."

Roberta swallowed. This was the most dangerous thing she'd ever done. If the perps were armed and she wasn't prepared, this could be her last mission. "The risks don't matter to me anymore. I'm done being pushed aside while I try to get justice served. I can stop these criminals."

"You're not bulletproof. I don't want to get a call that you didn't make it." Uchenna sighed. "But I know you're going to do this no matter what. You've been stubborn since junior high. I'll be there for you." She passed the ball to Roberta.

Feeling energized, Roberta shot the ball and made it this time.

That evening, Roberta bought a pair of walkie-talkies from an electronics store to talk to Uchenna on heist night. They weren't secure or sophisticated. But the cops would be less likely to monitor civilian frequencies. They would be off the grid.

She breathed in slowly. This was so real. If she wasn't careful, her career could be over. And then there would be no one to stop the corruption from destroying her department. Her stomach turned.

She wasn't religious, but she prayed the perps would be as inexperienced—and nonviolent—as possible. With a little focus, maybe she'd be able to cuff a couple of them, foil the con, and bring justice to the criminals.

CHAPTER 38

JENNIFER

One day before the heist

J ennifer stumbled out of bed at 6 AM for her morning run. She was ready for the mission to be over. The late nights weren't thrilling anymore. Instead, she was struggling to run in the morning and get to work on time.

Groggy and bleary-eyed, she grabbed her ear buds and downed a cup of coffee, followed by ice water.

She glanced at her phone and spotted a message from the owner of the marketing research firm in Hawaii that she'd been talking to. *"I think your idea has a lot of potential. Let's talk soon."* Even though she was half asleep, Jennifer couldn't fight the smile that was forming on her face.

As her feet hit the pavement and her breath quickened, she could feel her body start to come alive.

In the cool morning air, she felt a sense of fulfillment with

22222222222222

how well the teams were prepared. They'd been working closely with Freddy to keep the cops off their trail. He gave the team regular updates each day, sometimes meeting Jennifer at coffee shops throughout town to share intel. Lorinda was working closely with Keisha in security to ensure heist night would be staffed by insiders who stayed off the grounds during the mission.

Jennifer knew the plans so well now she could practically do them in her sleep. The team moved like a slick, well-oiled machine. And their running and strength training routine was keeping everyone agile.

The core heist team had even started to split up for the past week during daytime, trying to avoid being seen together so close to heist day. All heist events were happening after dark.

Jennifer started to limit her participation in heist social events so she could get enough sleep. She gave the missions a hard cutoff at 12 AM so she could be up and out the door at 8:30 AM for work and still be relatively coherent.

But even that was cutting it close. She was starting to nod off at work. She even fell asleep at her standing desk. She tried her hardest to stay awake in meetings by drinking cup after cup of ice water. The bathroom visits were nonstop, but it would be *the worst* to get fired if the big payoff never came through.

It would only be a matter of time before she could make off with a huge windfall of cash, quit her job, and begin her surfing enterprise. Business would boom, and she'd need a vacation. Jennifer would casually show up in Amir's corner of Dearborn in a luxury rental convertible. They'd have an hour of fast-paced banter before spontaneously taking off on a last-minute trip to the beautiful beaches of the Seychelles in East Africa.

They'd go snorkeling and look at coral reefs and turtles. Perfectly low key and average.

She couldn't wait for the spark between her and Amir to grow into something more.

That morning, as she finished her run, Jennifer decided she had earned a nap before heist night. Hana and Nari would be staying awake the whole time, but Martha was on Team Naps too.

During her walk break, she pulled out her phone and translated a message to Kazi. *"We're going to make you proud tomorrow. You and the team will get what you deserve. Plus interest."*

Her phone buzzed. *"Thank you so much for fighting for us. Your team has shown true humanity. We're sending you many blessings for a safe mission."*

She bit her lip to keep the tears from falling.

When she arrived back home, Amir was sitting on the couch with a bag of golden chocolate coins.

"Amir!" she gasped in surprise.

"I wanted to get you yellow jelly beans, but I remembered how much you prefer the gold coins." Amir grinned.

Jennifer laughed and threw her arms around him as she sat on the couch beside him. "I can't believe you're here."

"I wanted to make sure you made it through this mission okay," he said. "And I realized there was only one way to do that. I'm going to work as backup security with Sumeet at the Papillon facility."

Her eyes widened. "Oh my gosh, that's amazing. Thank you so much. But I don't want you to be in danger either."

"I'm being selfish. I want to keep you out of jail," Amir

insisted as he squeezed her butt. Electricity coursed through her. "Besides, I know you're on the right side of justice, even if the cops don't know that yet."

He slowly smoothed his hands through Jennifer's hair and began to kiss her gently. A rush of heat rose to her cheeks as she brought her hands to his shoulders.

"I'm yours," he said, inhaling softly.

CHAPTER 39

ALL

Heist day

Nari pulled her car up to the edge of the park bordering the Essentrix Labs building in Papillon. Martha, Hana, and Jennifer sat silently inside.

"Go time," Nari said as the car came to a stop.

Each woman put on her ski mask, exited the car, and quietly closed her door.

This time, the Essentrix team had packed most of the Sorbelate into an unlocked shipping container on the opposite side of the field. Nari looked around for the small white delivery truck inside the facility where the rest of the boxes should be packed.

The night was dark, and the street lamps shone a dim white light onto the field. Martha, Nari, and Jennifer took off running across the field to the shipping container, while Hana sprinted to the fence opening. Hana flashed the peace sign at the group as they separated.

When they reached the shipping container, Nari and Jennifer braced their bodies and pushed hard upward to slide the door open. Every woman grabbed two boxes in each arm as they'd practiced, holding them tightly to their chests and running toward the fence opening.

Jennifer's breath was quick and shallow. Her sweaty palms slid as she tried to steady her grip on the boxes. *Stay cool, Jennifer.* Her vision darted toward the vehicle entrance, where she could barely see Sumeet and Amir's SUV parked in the shadows. She relaxed a little.

Meanwhile, Hana had made it inside and swiftly climbed up to her lookout point on the roof. Her hands were wet from the metal ladder's nighttime dew, and she wiped them onto her jeans.

Hana pulled out her tablet and activated the live spyware feed. No communication from the cops so far. "All clear," she said.

Nari reached the fence next after Hana, fluidly sliding each of her boxes through the fence opening. She turned her body sideways to slip through herself.

Instead of waiting for Nari to finish, Martha and Jennifer dropped off their packages and ran back to the shipping container to grab another load.

Nari carefully held the boxes close to her chest and slammed her back against the brick wall, misjudging the distance. She coughed, gasped, and struggled to tighten her grip. She was still panting as she inched past the surveillance zone, and she ran jaggedly toward the white delivery truck as dark shadows covered her path.

As she sprinted across the field, Jennifer remained focused on two things. Not dropping boxes and not tripping. She couldn't see her feet if she looked straight down, so she glanced to the side every few strides to check for hazards. She looked over at Martha, who seemed calm and focused. Jennifer sped ahead, her heart pounding in her ears. She reached the gap with her load intact, relieved, and began to slide her boxes through.

Inside the grounds, Nari had arrived at the white delivery truck and dropped her boxes. She was breathing steadily now.

She pushed up with both hands on the two back door handles that secured the right side door of the truck. The door swung open, and a white box of Sorbelate fell out, swiping Nari's bare arm. The boxes must have shifted after the Essentrix team moved the truck into place.

A stale smell wafted out from the lightly lit cargo area. It tickled her throat. Nari coughed again. She lifted her boxes up to chest level and onto the truck floor as Jennifer ran up behind her.

As the team's tallest member and resident Tetris player, it was Jennifer's time to shine. She easily placed her boxes on the truck floor, vaulted onto the ladder, and leapt inside. "I've got this," she whispered. Nari gave her the thumbs-up and ran back to get more loads of Sorbelate.

The truck was about twenty-percent full after being loaded by the inside team, but the boxes had shifted and were strewn across the cargo bed floor. Jennifer would have to be on top of her game to fit all the packages into one truck.

She squatted down to grab four scattered boxes then sprung up to run them to the back wall. She tripped on a bungee cord and fell forward, the boxes of Sorbelate flying up and crashing on the floor in front of her.

She barely broke her fall with her arms, falling squarely onto her chin and nose.

"Ow!" Jennifer cried out loudly.

Her ski mask was ripped and damp to the touch. She pulled it off, blood dripping from her nose. She touched her chin and winced in pain. It was bleeding too. Shakily, Jennifer wiped the blood from her face with the ski mask.

Jennifer wanted to cry. She rested for a moment and steadied herself on the wall. Her head was spinning. *What would Amina do?* she thought, exhaling deeply. She tossed her ski mask into the front seat, leaned down to grab some boxes, and started to pack.

Nari was running back toward the brick wall and passed Martha on her way. Martha saluted goofily. Nari glanced at her watch. They were making great time.

Up on the roof, Hana picked up on a radio frequency in her earpiece. The cops were reporting on activity at the bank. Perfect. She surveyed the parking lot with her night vision binoculars, and there was no sign of anyone else on-site. "Cops are at the bank. All clear." She pumped her fist.

CHAPTER 40

ROBERTA

Roberta pulled up to the Essentrix Labs facility at Mill Creek Lane.

Street lamps cast a muted light onto a few vehicles that were parked on either side of the road. She found a spot in the shadows and parked, turning off the ignition. She squinted and scanned the facility's entry and exit gates. There was no sign of movement.

She shuddered, remembering she had no idea what she was up against. The criminals could be armed. And if they didn't know how to use their weapons, they'd be even more reckless and erratic.

This would all be worth it, Roberta reminded herself. She had trained for this moment. She could be the undercover hero her city needed.

Quietly and fluidly, she got out of her car and moved closer to the entry gate. Shadows played across her face. She narrowed her eyes and saw a figure darting forward. *There we go.*

She ran toward the south-side vehicle entrance. She shone her flashlight directly onto a masked woman who was crouching behind the gate access pedestal.

"Freeze!" Roberta shouted, placing her right hand on the gun holster on her hip.

The perp stood up and ran back into the complex as plumes of smoke billowed out around her. Within seconds, Roberta couldn't see anything.

The sound of explosions filled the air. Roberta's chest tightened, and she dropped to the ground for cover.

"Active heist, possible weapons," she shouted hoarsely into her walkie-talkie. She could hear a faint noise coming from the speaker in response.

Visibility was better on the ground, but she could still only see a couple of feet above the concrete. She had completely lost all sense of direction. The perpetrator—and the rest of the team—could be anywhere. Her breath was shallow. This team was more advanced and more dangerous than she had thought. She had no idea what she could be up against.

Roberta bit her lip in resolve. She began to crawl and coughed as she tried to wave the thick curls of smoke away.

She paused. Was that the faint sound of a vehicle speeding toward her? She clicked on her flashlight but could only see smoke.

The vehicle's sound got louder. Roberta stood quickly and gritted her teeth. She reached out her arms and felt around aimlessly for the gate access pedestal so she could intercept the team as they tried to escape. It reminded her of a kindergarten game of pin the tail on the donkey.

Maybe the car would get close enough for her to see it.

Then she'd have to shoot the tires to halt the robbery. She wouldn't have to hurt anyone, and she could still be the city's defender.

A truck engine rumbled toward her as its tires squealed.

"Omaha State PD! Stop the vehicle!" she shouted over the explosions, drawing her gun.

A vehicle slammed into Roberta. She flew backward and landed forcefully on her back. Her gun went flying out of her hands. She gasped and coughed as a truck backed away from her.

She sprawled on the ground, reeling and dizzy. Her ears were ringing. A jolt of pain shot through her arms, and her legs wouldn't move.

For a split-second, she wasn't sure if she was paralyzed. She wiggled her toes inside of her shoes. Good sign. She felt herself filling with a hot, fiery anger.

The truck's tires screeched as it maneuvered around her. She flinched. "Please don't run me over," she breathed.

A fresh cloud of smoke came swirling down on her. She felt around for her gun on the ground, but it was gone.

Roberta tried to yell, but all she could do was cough. She had no idea how close she was to the entryway and couldn't hear anything over what she could now tell were noise machines. The sound was deafening. She had a pounding headache.

But her motivation grew. She wasn't going to let the criminals get away. She pushed herself up on her elbows and gradually lifted herself off the ground as she winced in pain.

She started to crawl on her hands and feet. She reached deep within herself to keep going as her body resisted. Within what seemed like a minute, her head crashed into the fence. Luckily, the fence gave somewhat on impact.

She fell backward and cried out in pain as she landed. Her breath caught in her throat. She was completely in over her head.

Roberta longed to talk to Uchenna, but the noise machines would make that difficult. She pushed herself up again and felt her way along the fence to the one-way pedestrian gate exit. Her wrists were throbbing with pain as she continued crawling. She could barely hear her own thoughts, and the ground felt like it was shifting underneath her. Her stomach churned as she pushed forward blindly and struggled to steady her body.

Finally, she emerged from the smoke. She spotted her car as a wave of relief washed over her. She felt her shoulders loosen and her breath slow down. Her body was shaking as she got into the vehicle. She reclined her seat to ease the pain in her back and started to drive in the most logical direction—toward the city center.

"I've been hit by the heist team's getaway truck," Roberta spoke raggedly into her civilian walkie-talkie as she struggled to grip the steering wheel.

"Oh my goodness, are you safe?" Uchenna responded, her voice rising.

"Never better," Roberta said through gritted teeth. "Now I'm going to catch them."

Uchenna's concern gave Roberta the boost she needed. She turned on her Omaha State Police walkie-talkie and listened in. If these perps thought they could get away, they were dead wrong.

CHAPTER 41

ALL

Jennifer, Nari, and Martha moved the packages quickly from the shipping container to the facility. They were slipping through the fence like clockwork.

Jennifer could pinch her nose between box loads to slow down the bleeding. She ably arranged the boxes inside the truck, with blood dripping occasionally from her nose onto the boxes below.

The group was jittery after hearing about the decoy heist team's run-in and accident with a cop. Nari kept glancing at the vehicle entrances. Martha fumbled with boxes. Jennifer was breathing faster than normal.

"Don't worry," Nari said, as they ran to the shipping container. "The cops aren't coming here. They've forgotten about this location."

"You're right," Martha replied. "No way they'll watch three buildings."

Nari was hauling her second-to-last round through the fence when Hana spoke into their earpieces, "There's a cop on the way! Get moving, now!"

Nari felt a knot in her stomach.

The team moved quickly to enter through the fence and load up the truck. Jennifer's skin prickled, and her palms were sweaty. She felt the urge to vomit.

"Let's go," Martha hissed. "We'll leave the rest of the boxes behind. Come on, Hana!"

"I'll stay back and play defense," Hana replied. "You all go now!"

"Alright, let's move!" Nari breathed. The three women squeezed into the front seat bench, and Nari threw the truck into reverse.

Hana tossed her supplies into her backpack, slid down the damp ladder, and ran after the truck.

Nari sped to the gate with her lights off. She spotted a police car under a streetlamp on the other side. "The cop's over here, Mom!"

"I'm on it." Hana ran through the pedestrian one-way exit and toward the police car, where an officer was stepping out. She pulled the tab on her smoke bomb and threw it at the woman's feet, sprinting away to avoid the smoke as it exploded.

"Hey, get back here!" the cop shouted. "Omaha State PD!"

"Cop on foot," Hana breathed into her smartwatch as she ran.

Smoke filled the air. Nari cautiously pulled the truck out of the facility. They hadn't thought through this whole visibility thing. Luckily though, they'd traced the exit route enough times that she knew where to go.

As she pulled out into the street, sirens erupted around them. *Uh-oh.* The officer must have called for backup.

"*Ándale, amiga!*" Martha cried from the passenger's seat. "Go, Nari!"

Smoke still covered much of the street, and Nari couldn't tell where the sirens were coming from.

She accelerated and crashed into the front end of a police car. "Step out of the vehicle *now*," the cop bellowed through his radio.

Nari threw the truck into reverse and drove as fast as she could back into the dense, white smoke. She could hear the sound machine going off and recognized the explosion track immediately.

She spun the truck up over the curb and onto the field. The sirens were close behind them. She still felt like she had an advantage, even in their lumbering, boxy vehicle.

Nari drove clear across the field and could finally see on the other side. The truck bounced violently along the way. She needed to lose this cop before she could make her way to the parking garage.

The cop had taken the long route around the field, rather than through it. Nari pushed the pedal to the floor and flew over the curb. The truck landed with a crash, fishtailing back and forth a few times before straightening out.

"We're behind the cop," Sumeet said into his smartwatch. He sped after the police car and slammed into its bumper. Sumeet and Amir's bodies flung forward on impact. Sumeet drove around the patrol vehicle and shouted, "Smoke!" Amir activated and threw a smoke bomb at the cop's windshield as Sumeet drove ahead toward the team's truck.

"You guys rock!" Jennifer exclaimed.

Sumeet and Amir cheered back.

Martha brought her watch to her face. "Decoy team, cop chase in progress. Backup requested."

"Copy," Charlotte, the head of the other team, responded. "We're headed over now. We've got your GPS tracker loaded up."

The cop car had made it through the smoke and was gaining on them. Nari could see a set of lights trailing the cops in her rearview camera. That had to be Sumeet. She needed to think fast.

She accelerated the truck around a corner and onto the main roadway. There were no other cars nearby. She surged into the parking lot of a Shop N Save and took a hard left down the narrow alleyway behind the neighboring shops. Jennifer and Martha flung to the left, and Jennifer knocked against Nari.

"My bad!" Nari said.

The tires squealed, and the smell of burnt rubber wafted up. A few seconds after making their turn, the police car drove behind them, its sirens whirring. Nari checked the rearview camera and saw the cops gaining on her, Sumeet close behind.

She gritted her teeth and stepped on the gas. Up ahead, a night shift worker was unloading a truck of produce boxes. Nari swiped away in time but knocked over a flurry of banana boxes that flew into the cop car behind her.

"Sorry, buddy," Nari muttered to the worker.

"That should slow them down!" Martha yelled enthusiastically.

Nari turned sharply onto a side street. She sped over a hill, and the truck flew into the air before it came crashing back down.

"I'll get some smoke bombs ready." Jennifer pulled the devices from her backpack.

"Great call," Nari responded. "Can someone check on my mom?"

Martha spoke into her watch, "Hana, where are you? Are you okay?"

Hana did not respond.

Nari navigated onto another main street and pushed the accelerator down hard. They were going nearly ninety miles per hour, and the truck was shaking. The cops weren't visible behind them anymore, but the team could still hear sirens.

"Shoot!" Nari yelled as they entered a construction site. The road had narrowed to one lane on each side. A crew wearing orange vests was jackhammering and repairing the road.

"Don't hurt them, please!" Jennifer pleaded.

"I won't," Nari cried back.

Nari accelerated through a narrow passageway that now included the middle turn lane. Construction workers scattered as she raced through. The cops were gaining on them again, their sirens whirring as they entered the site.

"You ready?" Jennifer asked Martha.

"All good!" Martha replied. Jennifer handed the first smoke bomb to her. Martha extended her body out the window, pulled the tab, and hurled the bomb toward the cop car behind them.

The cop car skidded and lost control as smoke came spilling out of the bomb, slamming into a dump truck behind them.

"Yes!" Martha cheered, watching the scene in the rearview

camera. "We've got them! Keep going Nari!" She squeezed Jennifer's arm.

Nari exited the construction site. "Finally free!"

"Hey, warn us the next time you set off a smoke bomb," Amir yelled into the team's earpieces, the sound machine spewing out the sounds of explosions behind him. "We've crashed into the cop car and are trying to halt them."

"So sorry, thanks team!" Martha exclaimed.

Another cop car came hurtling toward them. "Get the bomb ready!" Martha yelled. Jennifer activated another smoke bomb. The cop car hit their bumper, and the women lurched forward.

"Pull over your vehicle, now!" the cop cried.

Jennifer passed the bomb to Martha. "Bomb's going out," Martha announced as she leaned out and hurtled the smoke bomb at the police.

Nari sharply rounded a corner, and the decoy team's truck pulled up behind them. "We'll take it from here," Charlotte exclaimed through the earpiece.

"You're amazing," Martha responded.

"So glad to hear everything's going well," Hana panted into the earpiece.

"Mom!" Nari exclaimed. "Are you okay?"

"All good. I ran from the cop but I escaped onto a bus," Hana replied under her breath. "I think I lost her."

"I'm so happy you're safe!" Nari yelled back.

"Get us to the parking garage so we can switch trucks!" Jennifer shouted.

"Yes, chief!" Nari said, turning the truck down a side street to go back in the direction they came from. The decoy truck continued driving straight ahead.

"Don't worry, team," Charlotte said. "We've got this!"

"We're almost there!" Martha announced, glancing at her tablet.

Nari tore ahead into the night air. They were in a peaceful residential area, free from people and noise. The street was mostly dark. She swiped a trash can, and it flew into the air, spewing trash across the peaceful street.

"Oops," Nari said. "Sorry, neighbors."

"Alright, get ready to move," Jennifer said.

"As fast as we can, ladies!" Martha agreed.

Within a minute, Nari pulled the truck into the empty parking garage, tires squealing as she flung it around each level. Nari maneuvered the truck to the roof. The getaway truck was parked on the far side of the garage. Someone was standing next to it.

"Oh no..." Martha said.

"Get the smoke bombs and noise machine ready," Nari added, slowing the car down.

As they inched toward the truck, the figure took shape. It was Hana.

"Oh, thank God. Mom!" Nari gasped, hesitating for a moment. She came to her senses. "Let's go, team!"

Martha hopped out of the vehicle while it was still moving and high-fived Hana. Nari threw the truck into park, and she and Jennifer jumped out. Hana had already shimmied under the getaway truck to grab the keys and unlock the vehicle. The second truck was slightly larger and it was black, instead of white.

The reunited crew hustled to move the boxes from the active truck to the getaway vehicle. Jennifer's hands were shaking, and she looked over her shoulder as they packed. With a few feet between the trucks, the transfer was complete within a few minutes. The team left the original truck behind and drove away quickly in the new one. Hana sat on Martha's lap so they could all fit in the cabin.

"I'm so happy you're safe, Mom!" Nari breathed, looking over at Hana. Her posture softened, and relief flickered across her face.

Hana sighed. "That chase was insane. Jen's the only reason I made it out of there!"

"Hey, you're a natural," Jennifer replied, gripping her nose.

"Decoy team, how are you?" Martha spoke into her smart-watch.

"We're in the clear," Charlotte responded. "After five smoke bombs, we made it to our getaway vehicle. All is good."

"Great job, team!" Nari cheered.

There was one final step left, unloading the boxes of Sorbelate into Nari and Jennifer's apartment. In the weeks leading up to the mission, the team couldn't find a better storage location. Jennifer and Nari were okay with the risk.

This time, they were more prepared. When they arrived at the apartment, Jennifer and Nari ran inside to grab dollies to transport the boxes.

The team quickly filled the dollies with packages, wheeled them into the apartment, and unloaded them into each woman's bedroom. The boxes took up almost every available inch in the rooms, but they fit somehow.

"Aww sweetie," Martha said to Jennifer as they walked into the living room, reaching out to pat her head. "You aren't looking so good."

Hana gave Jennifer a hug and motioned toward the couch.

"Have a seat." Jennifer sat down, her head throbbing. Her nose was swelling, her chin was scraped up, and she was starting to bruise under her right eye. Hana brought her a bag of frozen peas, which Jennifer accepted gratefully.

"Let's check in on the cops." Martha pulled out her tablet. The group gathered around her. The police were patrolling the opposite side of town, a few miles from each facility. "No cars in our vicinity."

"Perfect," Hana said. "Now let's listen to them."

Martha opened the spyware app. "I'm on Belham Lane headed south," a woman's voice said.

"Wait, we should call for help for that cop that the other team hit, right?" Jennifer asked.

"Good idea," Hana said. "I'll make an untraceable call from my burner phone and leave an anonymous tip." She stood up and went into Jennifer's room.

"No sign of either vehicle," the woman on the spyware app continued. "How about you, Freddy?"

Nari perked up. "Freddy!"

"None on my end. I think we should check the area by the bank again," Freddy responded. "They may be getting ready to commit a third robbery."

"That's right, Freddy. Throw them off!" Jennifer exclaimed.

"10-4," the female cop responded.

"Success," Martha announced, putting away the tablet.

Jennifer bit her lip. "Do you think we made it out okay? At least for today?"

Nari grinned and flopped down on the couch. "So far, so good."

"We did it, team. We're about to have an amazing payout," Martha said, her face glowing.

Jennifer's eyes glistened. "We're going to change these women's lives in the mines. Then I'm going to travel the world. You're all welcome to join me, of course."

Hana emerged from the bedroom. "I made the call. That sounds like a pretty great idea, but the first trip is on me."

"Not so fast, Hana. What if I want to cover the first one?" Martha shot back.

"First, you've all got to come visit the Caribbean. We'll explore Turks and Caicos and swim in some crystal-clear warm waters," Nari said.

Jennifer's eyes widened.

"I can't wait to show you where I grew up, Jen." Nari beamed.

"Alright. Hana, we need to get out of here." Martha motioned toward the front door. "I've booked us two new hotel rooms in separate places. Let's go."

"Thanks, Martha. We've all earned ten hours of straight sleep," Hana quipped.

"Maybe twelve for Jennifer." Martha smirked. The group gathered and exchanged hugs.

CHAPTER 42

ROBERTA

"Any news, Roberta?" Uchenna asked.

"I'm hurt. I think I need to pull over." Roberta grimaced as she clutched her walkie-talkie. She felt completely deflated and exhausted to her core. This case had consumed her life, and now she had to step away and let the rest of the team have all the glory.

"I'm so sorry," Uchenna responded softly. "Can I come help you?"

"All good, Uchenna. Thanks. I'll call you back later."

As soon as she hung up, Roberta drove to the hospital and checked herself in for a couple of hours. Her nurse said she had a mild concussion and minor wrist fractures. She was lucky to have made it out like she did.

She couldn't stop thinking about the case. She kept replaying the crash in her mind. The shock as the truck hit her and the struggle to get back up. The burn in her lungs from the thick smoke that encircled her. It had been over-powering.

At least her career was still intact. No one knew she had gone to secretly patrol on an off day. She could come up with a story for how she injured her wrists. Maybe she could claim a rollerblading accident. You know, on a day she claimed to be sick. *Nothing suspicious there.*

Once she got home, Roberta propped herself up on a mountain of pillows and listened in on the police radio chatter until dawn. After chasing the heist crew across town, the rest of the police team had either gotten into accidents or had been diverted by smoke bombs.

Her head pounded, and she was filled with a gnawing anger. She had felt certain that her team was completely dropping the ball on the investigation—on purpose. But they had found and pursued one group of perpetrators while she went after another. She should have felt relieved that her team was performing, but instead she felt a sense of injustice that she couldn't quite explain. At least no one else could catch the criminals. It wasn't only her who had missed out.

The next morning, Roberta's phone buzzed. Her wrists throbbed in pain as she picked it up.

"I'm at your door," Uchenna texted. *"Come get me."*

Roberta reached over to her bedside table and swallowed a painkiller. She winced as she made her way out of bed and limped to the door in her fuzzy slippers. Uchenna stood on the porch holding a vase of yellow tulips.

"Hey." Uchenna's voice filled with concern as she threw her arms around Roberta. "How are you feeling?"

"It's so good to see you." Roberta's jaw loosened at the

sight of her friend. "My head's killing me. But the worst part is that the criminals got away."

Uchenna walked toward the kitchen table, set the vase down, and relaxed into a blue armchair. "If you're the same Roberta I've always known, this isn't over yet." She leaned forward, her eyes glimmering.

Heat rose to Roberta's face, and she balled her hands into fists. "You're right. The perps are still out there. I will keep searching until I find them."

CHAPTER 43

JENNIFER

Three days after the heist

Jennifer stood next to Nari in the kitchen. She picked up the Omaha Free Press newspaper from the countertop and glanced at the headline, two-thirds of the way down the front page. "Omaha in Shock: Massive Theft of Key Sweetener Ingredient." She could feel Nari reading over her shoulder.

Jennifer's skin prickled with goosebumps. She glanced at the hallway closet door where much of the Sorbelate was packed. The Flatland Industries deal had already gone through, but they still had two hundred boxes in their apartment, sitting and waiting to be found each day.

She shuddered as she imagined a follow-up newspaper article featuring their photographs as two thieves on the run.

"Don't worry," Nari said confidently as she patted Jennifer on the shoulder. "No one suspects us yet. We've got to wait until the heat dies down. Then we'll be able to sell to any food services company in the Midwest."

"I believe you, roomie. You haven't let me down before." Jennifer sighed as she walked to the couch and flopped down, holding her ballet flats in one hand.

She still had to go into work—at least for now—to avoid suspicion. None of her coworkers seemed to notice that she had changed. Lorinda was flying under the radar too, putting in extra hours and exceeding expectations like her usual self.

Jennifer's phone vibrated three times. It was Martha calling on the encrypted app. "Hey, Marthie," she answered on speaker phone.

"*Hola amiga,*" Martha said cheerfully. "You've got company at work today. Roberta's at Essentrix Labs to question the team."

Jennifer's breath quickened. Nari walked over and put her hand on Jennifer's shoulder before taking a seat next to her on the couch.

"Thanks for letting me know. Let me guess. I should keep my answers simple and stay calm?" Jennifer remarked.

Martha laughed. "That's exactly what I was going to tell you. You don't even need me anymore. Roberta will look for inconsistencies, so say as little as possible. Don't add extra details, and don't get defensive. Stay relaxed, and be yourself. Roberta knows you a little bit already."

Nari nodded. "And don't speculate or guess either. If she asks you for details, say you don't remember or don't know."

Jennifer clasped her hands together. "Sounds like a plan, team. Thanks, Martha. I'll text you both if I have any issues." She slipped on her flats, stood, and saluted, adjusting her belted black silk dress. She was dressed like a confident woman who had absolutely no legal concerns on the horizon. Nari waved as she stepped out the front door.

The walk to work was peaceful, with no signs of police presence. But as soon as Jennifer arrived, she spotted two squad cars parked in the lot. Once inside, the office was empty and eerily quiet. There were no colleagues chattering excitedly about lunch plans. She felt her hands start to sweat.

Mandy approached her, a serious look on her face. "There you are. There was a theft here at Essentrix, and Officer Fonseca—you know, Roberta—is here to investigate. Come join us in the break room."

Jennifer nodded. Her throat was dry, and she had the urge to hide out in the bathroom all day. She'd need at least three glasses of ice water to make it through this meeting.

What would Amina do? She repeated in her head. *No.* She stopped herself. *What would* Jennifer *do?*

The break room was packed with murmuring colleagues seated and standing. Lorinda glanced up at Jennifer briefly, tilted her head subtly, and looked away. Jennifer found a space at the back, near the refrigerator. She stood near a few members of the inside team and hoped that Lorinda had briefed them already.

Roberta stood at the front of the room, next to another female officer with chestnut-brown hair. Her arms were bent, and she held them close to her body, casts peeking out at the bottom of her dark-blue sleeves. Jennifer felt a pang of guilt as she took in Roberta's injuries.

"Hello, everyone. Thank you for coming here today. My name is Officer Roberta Fonseca, and I work with the Omaha

State PD. I want to talk to you all about a theft of Sorbelate that has taken place here at Essentrix Labs," she said, squinting. Her gaze met Jennifer's, and she nodded at her.

Jennifer felt chills run down her body. She tried to remain steady and maintain a serious expression as she tilted her head forward in recognition.

She surveyed the faces of her colleagues around her. They were silent and serious, focused intently on what Roberta was saying.

"We have reason to believe that an inside team is behind the theft. Don't worry—you're not in trouble. All I'm asking for is your cooperation. I'll be conducting interviews today. If you've seen anyone doing anything strange, especially as it relates to the Sorbelate inventory, please let me know. I'll be here all day, and I'll be available by phone afterward." Roberta pulled out a stack of business cards and held them up before placing them on the table in front of her.

The crowd murmured, and looks of discomfort and fear registered on peoples' faces.

Mandy stood and walked to the front of the room. "Thank you, Officer Fonseca. Team, please be supportive with your time today. If Officer Fonseca comes to your desk, I'd ask that you help her as much as you can. You may all return to your work. Thanks for your cooperation."

The team began to slowly filter out of the break room, back to their desks. Jennifer tried to maintain a concerned expression.

"Hey, Jen." Karlie approached her excitedly as they walked out. "Can you believe there was a burglary? Isn't that crazy?" She lowered her voice and leaned in closer. "What if it was someone we know but would never expect?"

Jennifer's throat tightened. "That would be so wild! I hope

the company gets their Sorbelate back!" she said, maybe too emphatically.

"I bet whoever did it is freaking out. It will only be a matter of time until the cops find them." Karlie held eye contact with Jennifer for a little bit too long. "What happened to your face? Are you okay?"

Jennifer chewed on a nail and turned her head. "Oh my gosh, I..." She tried hard to calm the pounding in her head. "I fell off my scooter. It was so crazy, but I'm totally fine! You know what would be great? I would love to go bowling soon to celebrate the end of summer!"

Karlie raised an eyebrow. "I'm glad you're feeling better. But bowling? That's kind of unrelated, even for you. Yeah, let's go soon. Anyway, I'm going to head back to my desk. Want to get lunch with Lorinda?"

"That sounds great," Jennifer said, grateful that her clumsy diversion had worked. When she got back to her desk, Mandy was waiting for her.

"Can't believe what's happening right now. Right in the middle of busy season too." Mandy shook her head.

Jennifer cocked her head and sighed. "I'm at a loss for words."

"I wish they gave us free lunch to compensate us for all our help during the investigation." Mandy snorted and pulled up a chair next to Jennifer's desk. "In other news, I'd love to see your research for the Greenleaf Feed packaging redesign."

Jennifer nodded and began to log on to her computer. She was planning to secretly sabotage the design of the cobalt-based feed with fake intel. She'd take the fall, but it would be months before anyone found out. By then, she would be long gone.

Hopefully, paddling out on a longboard and standing confidently on a deep-blue wave.

As her monitor booted up, Roberta and her colleague approached Jennifer's desk, their police uniforms making it seem like they took up more space than they actually did.

"Hey, Jennifer. Can you come with us?" Roberta motioned for Jennifer to follow.

"Sure thing." Jennifer grabbed her glass of ice water, tapping it nervously with her nail. She was grateful for the walk. Her muscles tensed as she trailed Roberta and the other officer across the room, down a brown-carpeted hallway, and into an empty, windowless conference room. Roberta signaled for Jennifer to sit on the other side of the wood table.

"Thanks for coming to meet with us. I'd love to ask you some questions." Roberta pulled out an Army-green padded chair and sat down. "Have you noticed anything strange lately at work? Anything out of place? Anything unusual going on related to inventory?"

Jennifer paused. This would be a great time to feed perfectly crafted lies to Roberta, if only she had a great story prepared. "I haven't noticed anything. That's why this whole thing is so...shocking." She shivered and squeezed her hands together under the table to stop them from shaking.

Roberta furrowed her brow. "I'm sure you're overwhelmed right now. These types of investigations can be very upsetting. Thanks for bearing with me. Standard question, I've got to ask. Where were you on Tuesday night around 1 or 2 AM?"

"Oh gosh, I would have been fast asleep at that time." Jennifer gulped down some ice water. "I am such a morning person! I was probably dreaming about Ancient Egypt."

Roberta raised an eyebrow and smirked. "Right. Of course."

"Do you ever spend time in the Essentrix Labs warehouse?" the other officer asked, narrowing her eyes as she brought her hand to her chin.

Great. Sure, Jennifer had been in the warehouse. You know, casually, with another heist member, almost a week before the mission. No big deal.

"Not frequently." Jennifer cleared her throat and focused on keeping her voice steady. "But I do head over sometimes for promotion work."

"Good, right answer. According to Mandy, you don't normally spend a lot of time at the warehouse, but you went about ten days before the theft," Roberta said, her voice rising.

"What brought you in this time?"

Jennifer swore she could hear her ears ringing. She wiped her clammy hands on her skirt and tried to inhale slowly without Roberta noticing.

At least she could beat Roberta in hand-to-hand combat if she had to. Roberta would be much less powerful with two broken wrists. Jennifer would masterfully twist Roberta's hands behind her back and hold her in a headlock. "Okay, you win!" Roberta would say helplessly.

Jennifer tilted her head forward and tried to look casual. "Oh, for sure. I might head over a couple of times a year. This time around, I got a tour from Lorinda for a project. It probably took about twenty minutes. Our warehouse facilities are really important to some customers."

"Twenty minutes." Roberta raised an eyebrow. "I've got you recorded on camera for about forty-five. Any reason for that discrepancy?"

Jennifer froze. She couldn't believe she offered up a time-line without being asked for one. "I—I'm sorry. I must have lost track of time." It was the truth.

"I see," Roberta responded, her voice taut. "Did Lorinda take you to the secure Sorbelate warehouse section?"

"No, I don't think so." Jennifer furrowed her brow. "She didn't mention anything about Sorbelate to me."

Roberta's shoulders seemed to loosen. "Did you hear about or see any missing items prior to the theft?"

Jennifer reached her right hand behind her back and crossed her fingers for good luck. "Not at all. To be honest, I really don't work much with inventory. I wouldn't even know what to look for."

"If you had to guess, who would you say did this?" the other officer interjected as she leaned forward.

Jennifer would love to look this woman in the eye and tell her a perfect story that would send the cops in the wrong direction. Maybe, she could implicate the loan sharks who were after Freddy. Come to think of it, she should suggest that to him. Freddy could walk the streets of Omaha without fear, and Jennifer could quit her job and go be rich.

"I wish I could help more." Jennifer shook her head with concern. "I don't even know most of our logistics people."

Roberta nodded. "Thanks for your time, Jennifer. We may have some more questions for you in the coming days."

Jennifer stood and walked to the door of the conference room. She turned back to face Roberta and the second officer. "Thanks for all you're doing to help us out."

• • •

Back at the apartment, Jennifer had quickly changed out of her black silk dress and replaced it with her new matching pink crop-top pajama and robe set. It said, "I'm rich, but I like to be casual about it." Her tension loosened immediately.

Nari followed suit. "It's cozy time!" She emerged dancing from her room, wearing a yellow lace nightgown and silky shorts.

Jennifer's phone buzzed three times on the encrypted app. She picked it up excitedly and placed it on speaker. "Hey, Lorinda!"

Nari's face glowed as she scrambled to sit closer to Jennifer.

"Great news," Lorinda said, her voice hushed. "Martha set me up with a story about a competitor. I told Roberta why I think they did it, and she bought it. The evidence is pretty compelling. Freddy's going to present supporting proof to Roberta later. Gotta go. Talk to you soon."

Nari's eyes lit up, and she threw her arms around Jennifer. "We've got this, Jen!"

Jennifer exhaled deeply. "Yes!" She knew Martha would pull through. That trusty mango seller. Her eyes flickered over to the hallway closet.

Nari followed Jennifer's eyeline and ran her hand over her chin. "Don't worry, this will all blow over soon. We'll sell the rest of the Sorbelate and have millions coming in."

Jennifer nodded. She hoped her roommate was right.

CHAPTER 44

JENNIFER

Ten days after the heist

"Sunshine Foods paid the rest of their bill," Nari said enthusiastically. "My mom's already washed the money through her consulting shell company."

Jennifer beamed. She and Nari had handed off the rest of Sorbelate that morning. After some of the attention had died down, it had been incredibly easy. Nari received a tip from Sumeet that there was a food and beverage company in Kansas City that was in the market for Sorbelate. Even better, Sumeet told Nari, "They're willing to pay more per box. Much more. Pitch them on double."

For five joy-filled minutes, Nari and Jennifer discussed what they'd do with all that extra cash. In the end, it was an easy choice. They'd give the extra money to the Omaha employees of Essentrix Labs whose pay had been withheld. Lorinda would provide them with a list.

After calming themselves down, Nari called Sumeet's contact in Kansas City. The buyer was ecstatic. He agreed to the price immediately and wanted the entire supply.

Nari and Jennifer rented a van, filled it with the rest of the boxes of Sorbelate, and drove it to the facility in Kansas City. Jennifer had even called in sick for the occasion.

The buyer wired the money to Hana's shell company immediately. Nari and Jennifer were rich. They had more than enough to pay off every member of the heist team—including Freddy, Lorinda, and the inside team. They could even keep an extra million dollars each.

"I'll be wiring your cut into different bank accounts with alias names." Nari grinned and handed Jennifer a printed bank statement. "Starting with Amina Keita. Your comic book hero."

Jennifer looked down at the paper and gasped. There were so many zeroes. "I've been waiting for this moment." Her mind was in a million places at once. This was more than enough to move to Hawaii, start her surf business, and order cheesy spinach artichoke dip at restaurants. Every. Single. Time.

She felt herself get teary eyed. "I have something to tell you."

"What's that?" Nari asked expectantly.

"Next month, I'm joining an entrepreneur development program," Jennifer announced. "In Honolulu, Hawaii."

Nari squealed. She jumped up and threw her arms around Jennifer. "I'm so proud of you! Do you need a roommate?" She winked.

•   •   •

That night, they got together for one last meal with the heist crew before everyone would have to head back home. Of course, they had to celebrate where it all began, Seoul Kitchen.

Haeyeon welcomed the crew inside with open arms. "I'm so happy to see you."

The restaurant seemed bigger since they had been there last. One thing was for sure though, Haeyeon was doing great business. The place was packed with people from across Omaha, young and old, and every age in between.

Jennifer looked across the room at her crew. Nari threw her arms around Haeyeon. Hana and Martha chatted happily. Even Freddy was there, joking around with Sumeet and Lorinda. It seemed ill-advised, but it was great to see him again. Jennifer closed her eyes and savored the moment.

Amir put his arm around Jennifer and kissed her. She felt safe and warm in his embrace.

"The famous Amir." Martha leaned in toward Jennifer. "So nice to see you again."

"Great to see you again too," Amir said, his dimples deepening.

"Come sit down," Haeyeon said over the din. "I've made my famous scallion pancakes to get you started. I need to impress the newcomers."

"I've been wanting to try these." Hana sat down immediately and waved for the others to join. "Come on, folks. Get them while they're hot!"

The group started to join her.

Amir took Jennifer's hand in his. "You look beautiful," he said. Jennifer noticed his gaze lowering to her seafoam-green dress, which was clinging to her long and lean frame.

Jennifer smiled. "Thank you." She traced her fingers over the back of his hand, feeling an electricity and excitement coursing through her. She was here, face-to-face with Amir. And she knew that he wanted her.

They joined the group at the table, passing around the scallion pancakes.

The bell on the front door rang. A man walked in, his awkward gait unmistakable. It was Johannes. Jennifer stiffened. Nari was lost in conversation with Martha.

Jennifer tapped Nari's arm. "Nari..." she said.

Nari looked up and saw Johannes. Her eyes widened, and her face lost its color.

Both women looked at Johannes silently.

"Welcome to Seoul Kitchen." Haeyeon handed Johannes a menu. "How many?"

He held up his hand to refuse the menu and walked up to their table.

"Hi, Jennifer. Hi, Nari." He tilted his head forward.

Instinctively, Jennifer grabbed Nari's hand.

"I've come to apologize," Johannes began, "for trying to take the heat off myself and sabotage your mission." He pulled out an empty chair at the end of the table and sat down.

Nari and Jennifer exchanged hesitant glances.

"I should never have done something like that. Mercy would be ashamed of me. It was selfish and wrong. Jennifer, you're such a kind and empathetic person." He paused and wiped what seemed like sweat from his brow. "You've made me feel supported. You helped me realize that I needed to redeem myself and make things right. For myself and for Mercy."

Jennifer swallowed. She felt a warmth in her face. She had

no idea where this was going. She half-expected Johannes to say, "Gotcha!" A group of cops would come in and storm the restaurant shortly thereafter and start cuffing the team. Jennifer looked around at the group's faces. Everyone was silently watching Johannes, rapt. Even Amir.

"I called a few companies I know in the Midwest, looking for a buyer for the rest of your haul. I wanted someone who would pay much more. After striking out a few times, I remembered a buyer I know at a food and beverage company in Kansas City. I pitched him on the product at double the price. He was sold immediately. And then I called up Sumeet to share the information with you," Johannes said. He looked over at Sumeet, whose face was glowing.

Jennifer saw Nari shoot a bewildered look at Sumeet.

"I'm sure you never want to work with me again. I don't blame you at all," Johannes said. "But I hope I've at least somewhat made up for what I've done to you."

"Well," Nari started off. She glanced around at the faces of her team. Jennifer nodded at Nari, encouraging her to go on. "That was a pretty amazing deal. Thank you."

"It's the least I could do. I was terrible to you. Of course, I don't want a dime. But if you don't mind, I'll take one of these pancakes." Johannes pointed to the stack of scallion pancakes in front of Hana.

"By all means," Hana said, passing the plate over to him.

"You know," Nari began slowly, "I'm actually glad you tried to sabotage our mission. Otherwise, I wouldn't have gotten to strategize so deeply with all these amazing people." She looked at each member of the group.

Hana glanced at Nari, her face radiant. "We're grateful you

brought us on. This crew is incredible, and it's been way too long since I've worked with you, *nae jasik*. I would love to keep working on deals with you. As equal partners."

"That would mean the world to me, Mom," Nari replied.

"And maybe our group should get back together for a mission or two each year," Martha added.

"Sign me up," Hana said.

Jennifer felt a sense of contentment rising in her chest. It was beautiful, what she and Nari had created.

"And of course, if you're still interested," Johannes said, pulling a notebook from his pocket, "I've got the phone numbers of some other women in the Congo who would love to hear from you too, Jennifer."

Jennifer beamed. "Thank you. I can't wait to get in touch with them." She turned to look at the crew. "I'm sure Lorinda has some ideas about how we can help with entrepreneurship training."

"Absolutely," Lorinda replied. "I've got a team on the ground that can help make it all happen."

"That money and training will be life-changing for their villages," Martha said. "And I've got some good news for you, Lorinda. I talked to my attorney, and I'd like to invite you to join the American subsidiary of my company. I can transfer your green card sponsorship over. Would you like to work for me as a business partner?"

Tears formed in Lorinda's eyes. "Yes, Martha. Thank you so much."

Hana raised a hand. "Well, team, I'd like to formally invite all of you to Turks and Caicos. I've got a couple guest houses there where I'd love to host all of you. You've all earned a solid week of doing absolutely nothing on the beach. Plus, I want you to meet my husband. Martha, I want to fly out your family too." She looked at Johannes. "You're welcome to join us as well."

"I'd love to join," Johannes replied.

"I've been homesick this whole time and really want to go back to Mexico City. But if I can fly out my family..." Martha said, her face glowing.

"I want to see where Nari grew up!" Sumeet rolled a scallion pancake and took a bite out of it before lovingly rubbing Nari's shoulder. She didn't pull away. She accepted his affection. It made Jennifer feel warm inside to see her roommate being loved.

"I want to go too," Freddy said emphatically.

Nari turned to Jennifer. "You're coming, right?"

"I have been wanting to go to a beach for years. I want to go so badly..." Jennifer teared up. "I can't believe this is happening."

"It may not be Hawaii," Nari said. "But we can still go to a surf shop for lessons."

"I've been wanting to learn how to surf for years," Amir remarked. "If you wouldn't mind one extra on the trip, I'd love to join you."

Sumeet cheered, "Amir, brother, we'll take you anytime."

Jennifer looked around the table at all these people who meant so much to her now. After years of dreaming about dipping her toes in the sand and surfing in warm, tropical waters, it was finally going to happen. This was real. Her tears went from sitting in the corners of her eyes to rolling down her cheeks. "It would mean the world to me if you came, Amir," she said.

Amir wiped a tear from Jennifer's cheek. "I wouldn't miss it for anything." He leaned in and kissed her. Surrounded by her crew, Jennifer couldn't think of anywhere else she'd rather be. At least for right now...

CHAPTER 45

ROBERTA

Two weeks after the heist

Each day, Roberta woke up filled with the fiery desire to take down the heist perpetrators. She had gone nearly every day to the Mill Creek Lane location of Essentrix Labs to continue the investigation.

She looked for new evidence on-site that could connect the competitors to the robbery. She searched the grounds for additional clues, finding and collecting smoke bomb casings as she went.

One morning, Roberta went to her favorite coffee shop on the way to Essentrix Labs, Harvest & Hearth. It was 5 AM, and the shop was nearly empty, except for a few early-morning visitors. After placing her order, she strode to the pick up counter and looked at her receipt. A woman tapped her on the shoulder. She looked up in surprise.

The woman was tall and thin, with curly light-brown hair and blue eyes. "Hi, Officer," she said shyly.

"Hello," Roberta replied, turning to face her. "How can I help you?"

The woman motioned for Roberta to step aside into an empty section of the shop. She obliged. "I want to tell you something about Essentrix Labs," the woman said under her breath.

Roberta nodded. "Please, tell me more."

"I've seen you at my work. I know you're investigating a theft right now at Essentrix Labs," the woman whispered. "But I want to tell you about a theft that my employer has been committing."

Roberta paused and looked at the woman. "I'm listening. You've got my attention."

"Essentrix Labs is forcing workers to put in unpaid time off the clock. They're not paying overtime. And they take money out of our paychecks when the equipment breaks." The woman's eyes darted around her. "Please don't tell anyone I told you. I don't want to lose my job."

Roberta's jaw dropped "Thank you for telling me," she said softly. "If you don't mind, I'd love to ask you a few questions. You don't have to reveal your identity to me. This will be off the record."

"I'm happy to help," the woman replied.

Roberta got into policing because she wanted to change lives for the better. She wanted to build systems that would protect and advocate for the people of Omaha.

Essentrix Labs employed hundreds of people. If this case turned out to be credible, Roberta could impact many more lives than in the heist investigation. *This* was a theft she could really get behind. She could investigate it all on her own and blow it wide open. She felt her motivation shifting.

The Sweetest Getaway

SASHA PRESTON

Exclusive Bonus
Book Club Discussion Questions
About the Author

CAPER CHAT

Tell the world what you think—and unlock a bonus!

Had a good time with the loveable heist crew?
Please take a moment to leave a review on

Amazon (especially helpful): https://bit.ly/AmazonTSG

or
Goodreads: bit.ly/GoodreadsTSG

Your words help other readers find the story—and
mean the world to an indie author like me. 🩶

As a thank-you, grab your **exclusive bonus chapter** here
and find out what happens after the book ends:

https://www.sashapreston.com/bonus-chapter

Let's keep the adventure going.

BOOK CLUB DISCUSSION QUESTIONS

1. If you had to run your own heist on short notice like Nari, who would you turn to for help, and why?

2. What would you do if you were Jennifer, and you got asked to join a heist in the middle of the night? Would you have gone along with the plan?

3. The heist crew is made up of strong, unique personalities. Which character did you relate to most—and why? Did your opinion of anyone change as the story unfolded?

4. Throughout the story, Nari fights to gain Hana's respect. Do you think Hana's tough love was good for Nari? Why or why not?

5. Who's the cuter couple: Amir and Jennifer, or Sumeet and Nari?

6. If you could visit one scene from the book, which one would you choose and why?

7. Which character would you most want to be friends with, and why? Which character would you least want to be friends with, and why?

8. If The Sweetest Getaway were adapted into a movie, who would you choose for the main characters?

9. What moment shocked or delighted you the most?

10. Which character's role would you want in the heist—and which would you absolutely avoid?

11. What was your favorite "uh-oh" moment, and how do you think you would've reacted if you were part of the team?

SASHA PRESTON writes women's fiction crime capers full of excitement, humor, and heart—stories where close friendships and adventure come together to inspire your next big escape (or at least make you *think* about planning one).

When she's not writing, she loves exploring, exercising, and spending time with her husband, daughter, and girlfriends.